The
Educated Evans
Stories

The
Educated Evans
Stories

'Educated Evans,' 'More Educated Evans,'
'Good Evans,' and 'A Present for Evans'

Edgar Wallace

LEONAUR

The Educated Evans Stories
'Educated Evans,' 'More Educated Evans,' 'Good Evans,' and 'A Present for Evans'
by Edgar Wallace

FIRST EDITION

First published under the titles
'Educated Evans,' 'More Educated Evans,' 'Good Evans,' and 'A Present for Evans'

Leonaur is an imprint
of Oakpast Ltd

ISBN: 978-1-78282-483-1 (hardcover)
ISBN: 978-1-78282-484-8 (softcover)

http://www.leonaur.com

Contents

Educated Evans

1.—THE BROTHERHOOD

Inspector Pine was something more than an Inspector of Police. He was what is known in certain circles as a Christian man. He was a lay preacher, a temperance orator, a social reformer. And if any man had worked hard to bring Educated Evans to a sense of his errors, that man was Inspector Pine. He had wrestled with the devil in Mr. Evans' spiritual make-up, he had prayed for Mr. Evans, and once, when things were going very badly, he had induced Mr. Evans to attend what was described as "a meeting of song and praise."

Educated Evans respected the sincerity of one whom he regarded as his natural enemy, but discovering, as he did, that a "meeting of praise and song" brought him no financial advancement, he declined any further invitations and devoted his energies and excursions to picking up information about a certain horse that was running in a steeplechase at Kempton Park on Boxing Day.

Nevertheless, Inspector Pine did not despair. He believed in re-storing a man's self-respect and in re-establishing his confidence; but here he might have saved himself a lot of trouble, for the self-respect of Educated Evans was enormous, and he was never so confident as when, after joining in a hymn, two lines of which ran:

The powers of darkness put to flight,
The day's dawn triumphs over night,

. . . . .he accepted the omen and sent out to all his punters "Day-dawn—inspired information—help yourself." For, amongst other oc-cupations, Educated Evans was a tipster, and had a *clientèle* that in-cluded many publicans and the personnel of the Midland Railway Goods Yard.

One day in April, Educated Evans leant moodily over the broad parapet and examined the river with a vague interest. His melancholy face wore an expression of pain and disappointment, his under-lip was out-thrust in a pout, his round eyes stared with a certain urgent agony, as though he had given them the last chance of seeing what he wanted to see, and if they failed him now they would never again serve him.

So intent was he that one who, although a worker in another and, to Evans, a hateful sphere, bore many affectionate nicknames, was able to come alongside of him and share his contemplation without the sad man observing the fact.

Fussing little tugs, lethargic strings of barges, a police-boat slick and fast—all these came under the purview of Educated Evans, but apparently he saw nothing of what he wanted to see, and drew back with an impatient sigh.

Then it was that he saw his companion and realised that here, on the drab Embankment, was one whom he had imagined to be many miles away.

The newcomer was a tall man of thirty, broad-shouldered, power in every line of him. He was dressed in black, and a broad-rimmed felt hat was pulled over his eyes. He was chewing a straw, and even if Mr. Evans had failed to identify him by another means, he would have known "The Miller"—whose other name was William Arbuthnot Challoner —by this sign.

"Why, Miller, I thought you was dead! And here was I speculatin' upon the one hundred and ninety million cubic yards of water that passes under that bridge every day, and meditatin' upon the remarkable changes that have happened since dear old Christopher Columbus sailed from that very pier, him and the Pilgrim Fathers that discovered America in Fifteen Seven Nine—"

The Miller listened and yet did not listen. The straw twirled between his strong teeth; his long, saturnine face was turned to the river; his thoughts were far away.

"A lovely scene," said Mr. Evans ecstatically, indicating the smoky skyline; "the same as dear old Turner used to paint, and Fluter—"

"Whistler," said his companion absently

"Whistler, of course—dear me, where's my education!" Mr. Evans rolled his head in self-impatience. "Whistler. What a artist. Miller—if you'll excuse the familiarity. I'll call you Challoner if you're in any way offended. What—a—artist! There is a bit of painting of his in the National Gall'ry. And another one in the—the Praydo in Madrid. Art's a perfect weakness with me—always has been since a boy. Do you know

8

Sergeant? Great American painter. One of the greatest artists in the world. An' do you know the celebrated French artist, Carrot?

"Do you know," began The Miller, speaking deliberately, and looking at the river all the time, "do you know where you were between 7.30 p.m. and 9.15 p.m. on the night of the eighth of this month?"

"I do," said Educated Evans promptly.

"Does anybody else know—anybody whose word would be accepted by a police magistrate gifted with imagination and a profound distrust of the criminal classes?"

"My friend, Mr. Harry Sefferal," began Evans, and The Miller laughed hollowly and with an appearance of pain.

"You have only to put your friend in the witness-box," he said, "you have only to let the magistrate see his sinister countenance to be instantly remitted to Dartmoor for the remainder of your life. Harry Sefferal could only save you from imprisonment if you happened to be charged with murder. Reading his evidence, the hangman would pack his bag without waiting for the verdict. Harry Sefferal!"

Mr. Evans shrugged.

"On the evening in question it so happened that I was playing a quiet game of solo in the company of a well-known and respected tradesman, Mr. Julius Levy—"

"You're a dead man!" groaned "Miller." "Julius Levy is the man who put the "u" into 'guilty.' Know Karbolt Manor?"

Mr. Evans considered.

"I can't say that I do," he said at last.

"Near Sevenoaks—the big house that Binny Lester burgled five years ago and got away with it."

Educated Evans nodded.

"Now that you mention the baronial 'all, Miller, it flashes across my mind—like a dream, as it were, or a memory of happier days."

"Is there a ladder in your dream? A ladder put up to Lady Cadrington's bedroom window when the family was at dinner? Dream carefully, Evans."

Mr. Evans wrinkled a forehead usually smooth and unlined.

"No," he said; "I know the place, but I haven't been near there. I can take the most sacred oath—"

"Don't," begged The Miller. "I would rather have your word of honour. It means more."

"On my word of honour as a gentleman," said Evans solemnly, "I have not been to, frequented, been in the vicinity of, or otherwise approached this here manor. And if I am not telling the truth may Heaven smite me to the earth this very minute!"

He struck an attitude, and The Miller waited, looking up at the skies.

"Heaven didn't hear you," he said, and took the arm of Evans. "Pine wants to see you."

Educated Evans shrugged his resignation.

"You are taking an innocent man," he said with dignity. The Miller bore the blow bravely.

The Miller was always The Miller to a certain class. He was taxed in the style and title of Detective-Sergeant W. Arbuthnot Challoner, Criminal Investigation Department. He was an authority upon ladder larceny, safe-blowing, murder, gangery, artfulness and horses. Round Camden Town, where many of his most ardent admirers had their dwelling-places, he was called The Miller because of this queer straw-nibbling practice of his.

He was respected; he was not liked, not even by Educated Evans, that large-minded and tolerant man. Evans was both liked and re-spected. In North London, as distinct from South London, erudition has a value. Men less favoured look up to those proficient in the gentle art of learning. Educated Evans was one of whom the most violent and the least amiable spoke with respect.

Apart from his erudition (he had written more speeches for the defence than any other amateur lawyer), he was undoubtedly in the confidence of owners, trainers, jockeys and head lads. He admitted it. He was the man who gave Braxted for the Steward's Cup and Eton Boy for the Royal Hunt Cup. There are men holding affluent posi-tions in Camden Town who might trace their prosperity to the advice of Educated Evans. It was said, by the jealous and the evil-minded, that St. Pancras Workhouse has never been so full as it was after that educated man had had a bad season.

"It was a matter for regret to me," said Evans as he shuffled along by his captor's side, "that the law, invented by Moses and Lord What's-his-name, should be employed to crush, so to speak, the weak. And on the eve, as it were, of the Newbury Spring Handicap, when I *did* hope to pack a parcel over Solway."

The Miller stopped and surveyed his prisoner with curiosity and disapproval.

"Solway," he said deliberately, "is not on the map. St. Albyn could give Solway two stone and lose him"

The lip of Educated Evans curled in a sneer

"Solway could fall dead and get up and *then* win," he said extravagantly. "St Albyn ain't a horse, he's a hair trunk. The man who backs St. Albyn—"

"I've backed St. Albyn," said The Miller coldly. "I've had it from the owner's cousin, who is Lord Herprest, that, barring accidents, St. Albyn is a stone certainty."

Educated Evans laughed; it was the laugh of a man who watches his enemy perish.

"And they *hung* poor old Crippen," he said.

There was this bond of sympathy between The Miller and his lawful prey—that they were passionate devotees of the sport of kings. When The Miller was not engaged in the pursuit of social pests (among whom he awarded Educated Evans very nearly top weight) he was as earnestly pursuing his studies into the vagarious running of the thoroughbred racehorse.

"What about Blue Chuck?" he asked. "There's been a sort of tip about for him."

Evans pulled at his long nose.

"That's one that might do it," he admitted. "Canfyn's told his pals that it won't be ready till Goodwood, but that feller would shop his own doctor. I wouldn't believe Canfyn if he was standin' on the scaffold and took an oath on Foxe's *Book of Martyrs*."

Passers-by, seeing them, the shabby man in the long and untidy coat and the tall man in black, would never have dreamt that they were overlooking a respected officer of Scotland Yard and his proper prey.

"What makes you think that St. Albyn hasn't a chance, Evans?" asked The Miller anxiously.

"Because he ain't trying," said Evans with emphasis. "I've got it straight from the boy who does him. He's not having a go till Ascot, an' they think they can get him in the Hunt Cup with seven-five."

The Miller blew heavily. That very morning Teddie Isaacheim, a street bookmaker who possessed great wealth and singular immunity from police interference, had laid him fifty pounds to five and a half (ready) about this same St. Albyn. And five and a half pounds was a lot of money to lose.

"If you'd asked me I'd have told you," said Educated Evans gently. "If you'd come to me as man to man an' as a sportsman to a sportsman, instead of all this ridiculous an' childish nonsense about me actin' in a thievous and illegal manner, I'd have give you the strength of St. Albyn. *And* I'd have put you on to the winner of the one o'clock race tomorrow—saved specially. . . not a yard at Kempton. . . . . not busy at Birmingham—havin' a look on at Manchester, but *loose* tomorrer!"

"What's that, Evans?"

"The Miller's" voice was mild, seductive, but Evans shook his head, and they marched on.

"Never," said the educated man with great bitterness, "never since old Cardinald Wolseley was pinched for giving lip to King Charles has a man been more disgustin'ly arrested than me. If I don't get ten thousand out of the police for false imprisonment. . . if I don't show up old Pine for this—"

"Is it Clarok Lass, old man?" asked "Miller," as they came in sight of the police station.

"No, it ain't Clarok Lass," said Evans savagely. "And if you think you're going to get my five pound special for a ha'porth of soft soap, you've got another guess coming. I'm finished with you, 'Miller,' I am. Didn't I give you King Solomon an' Flake at Ascot last year? Didn't I run all over the town to put you on to that good thing of Jordan's?"

"You've certainly done your best, Evans," agreed his captor soothingly, "and if I can put in a word for you—what did you say was going to win that one o'clock race?"

Educated Evans pressed his lips tightly, and a few seconds later The Miller was his business-like self.

"Here is Evans, sir; he says he knows nothing of the Sevenoaks job, and he can produce two witnesses to swear that he was in town at the time of the robbery. Maybe he can produce forty-two—"

Inspector Pine came in whilst Evans was being searched by the gaoler, and shook his head grievously.

"Oh, Evans, Evans! "he sighed. "And you promised me faithfully that you'd never come again!"

Educated Evans sniffed.

"If you think I came here on my own, sir, you're wrong."

Again the white-haired inspector shook his head.

"There's good in every human heart," he said. "I will not lose hope in you, Evans. What is the charge?"

"No charge, sir, detention. We want him in connection with the Sevenoaks affair, but there are a few alibis to be tested," said The Miller.

So they put Educated Evans into No. 7, which was his favourite cell, and Evans wondered what horse in the Newbury Cup was numbered 7 on the card.

That night certain heated words passed between the Honourable George Canfyn and the usually amiable attendants at the Hippoleum Theatre. George, who had dined, retaliated violently.

George Canfyn was a man of property and substance, an owner of racehorses and a gentleman by law. His father was Lord Llanwattock. His other name was Snook, and he made candles in a very large way. And in addition to candles he made margarine, money and political friends. They in turn made him a Baron of the United Kingdom. The law made him a gentleman. God was not even consulted.

George was the type of man who liked money for money's sake. Most people tell you that money means nothing to them, only the things you can buy with it. George liked money plain. He wanted all the money there was, and it hurt him to see the extraordinary amount that had failed to come his way. He lived cheaply, he ate meanly, and he changed his trainer every year.

If a horse of his failed to win when he had his packet down, he did everything except complain to the Stewards. He never had the same jockey more than three times, because he believed that jockeys cut up races and arranged the winner to suit their own pockets. He believed all trainers were incompetent, and all the jockeys who weren't riding his horse to be engaged in a conspiracy to "take care" of it.

When he won (as he did very often) he told his friends before the race that his horse just had a chance, and advised them not to bet heavily. George hated to see the price come down, because he invariably had his bets with the S.P. offices. And when it won, he appeared surprised, and told everybody how he nearly had a fiver on, but thinking the matter over in a quiet place, he decided that, with the income tax what it was, it was criminal to waste money. And some people believed him.

George was in a fairly happy state of mind when he went out to the Hippoleum, for that morning he had come up from Wiltshire after witnessing the trial of Blue Chuck, his Newbury Cup horse. Blue Chuck had slammed the horses in the trial and had won on a tight rein by many lengths. And not a single writing person had tipped Blue Chuck. It was certain to start amongst the "100-6 others," and George was already practising the appearance of amazement which he would display when he faced his acquaintances.

In the cheerful contemplation of Wednesday Mr. Canfyn sallied forth, his complacency fortified by three old brandies, which had cost him nothing, a sample bottle having been sent to him by a misguided wine merchant. And then came the disaster.

Three policemen brought him into Hallam Street Station, and here the matter might have been satisfactorily arranged if the third of the three old brandies had not started to put in some fine work.

"I'll have your coats off your backs for this, you scoundrels!" he screamed, as they searched him scientifically. "I'm the Honourable George Canfyn, the son of Lord Llanwattock—"

"What's the charge?" asked the weary station-sergeant, who was not unused to such scenes of agitation.

"Drunk and disorderly and assault," said the policeman who had brought in this scion of nobility.

"I'm not drunk!" roared George.

"Don't take those things away from me, they're my private papers! And count that money—if there's a penny missing, have you kicked out of the police force—"

"Number 8," said the man on the desk, and they led George below.

"Oh, that a man should put an enemy into his mouth to steal away his brains," murmured the inspector, standing in the open doorway of his room. "Drink is a terrible thing, sergeant!"

"Yes, sir," said the sergeant, and looked up at the clock. It was perilously near ten.

The inspector went back to his room with a sigh. The big table was covered with cards and addressed envelopes, and the inspector was an elderly man and very tired. He looked for a long time at the accumulation of work that had to be finished before the midnight post went out.

Inspector Pine was, amongst other things, Secretary of the Racecourse Elevation Brotherhood for the Suppression of Gambling. And the cards were to announce a special meeting of the Brotherhood to consider next year's programme. And, as yet, not one of the thousand cards had been stamped with the announcement that, owing to a regrettable prior engagement, the Bishop of Chelsea would not be able to attend.

He was so contemplating the unfinished work when there was a tap at his door and "The Miller came in.

"A miracle has happened, sir," he said. "I've found three decent people who can swear that Evans was practically under their eyes

14

when the larceny was committed. Mr. Isaacheim, the well-known and highly-respected commission agent——"

"A bookmaker," murmured Inspector Pine, reproachfully.

"Still, he's a taxpayer and a ratepayer," said The Miller loyally. "And though to me gambling is a form of criminal lunacy, we must take his word. And Mr. Corgan, of the 'Blue Hart'——"

"A publican," said old man Pine in distress.

"And a sinner. But he's a well-known town councillor. Can I tell the gaoler to let Evans go?"

Inspector Pine nodded, and his eyes returned to the unfinished work.

"You don't know anybody who could help me to put these cards into envelopes, I suppose, sergeant?"

It was an S.O.S.: an appeal directed to The Miller himself.

"No, sir," replied Miller promptly; and then, as a thought occurred to him: "Why don't you ask Evans? He's a man of education, and he'd be glad to stop for a few hours."

Educated Evans had spent a sleepless five hours in a large and sanitary cell, meditating alternately upon man's injustice to man and the depleted state of his exchequer. For his possessions consisted of twelve-and-sixpence put by for a railway ticket to Newbury, and the price of admission. For purposes of investment he had not so much as a tosser. It was the beginning of the season, and his *clientèle* had been dissipated by the mistaken efforts on his part to carry on business through the winter. It would take him to the Jubilee meeting before he could re-establish their confidence.

He heard the sound of an angry voice, and, peering through the ventilator of the cell, saw and recognised the Honourable George Canfyn being led to confinement. When the gaoler had gone:

"Excuse me, Mr. Canfyn," said Educated Evans, in a hoarse whisper, his mouth to the ventilator. He was all a-twitter with excitement.

"What do you want?" growled the voice of the Honourable George from the next cell.

"I'm Johnny Evans, sir, better known as Educated Evans, the well-known Turf Adviser. What about your horse, Blue Chuck, for tomorrow?"

"Go to hell!" boomed the voice of his fellow-prisoner.

"I can do you a bit of good," urged Evans. "I've got a stone pinch——"

"Go to blazes, you——"

15

In his annoyance he described Educated Evans libellously.

Educated Evans was meditating upon the strangeness of fate that had brought the son of a millionaire into No. 8, when the lock of his cell snapped back.

"You can go, Evans," said The Miller genially. "I've gone to no end of trouble to get you out—as I said I would. What's that horse in the one o'clock?"

"Clarok Lass," said Evans and The Miller swore softly.

"If I'd known that, I'd have left you to die," he said. "You said it wasn't Clarok Lass—here, come on, the inspector's got a job for you."

Wonderingly, Educated Evans followed the detective to the inspector's room, and in a few gentle words the nature of the job was explained.

"I will give you five shillings out of my own pocket, Evans," said Inspector Pine, "and at the same time I feel that I am perhaps an instrument to bring you to the light."

Educated Evans surveyed the table with a professional eye. He was not unused to the task of filling envelopes, for there was a time when he had a thousand clients on his books.

"Miller," glad to escape, left them as soon as he could find an excuse, and the inspector proceeded to enlighten his helper in the use of the stamp.

"When the stencil is worn out you can write another. Fix it over the inking pad so, and go ahead."

It was a curious stamp, one unlike any that Evans had ever used. It consisted of an oblong stencil paper, fixed in a stiff paper frame and a metal ink-holder. The inspector showed him how the stencil was written with a sharp-pointed stylus on a stiff board, how it had to be damped before and blotted after, and Evans, who had never stopped learning, watched.

"It will be something for you to reflect upon that every one of these dear people is an opponent to the pernicious sport of horse-racing. For once in your life, Evans, you are doing something to crush the hydra-headed monster of gambling."

"Where's that five shillings, sir?" said Evans, and the officer parted.

He was on the point of leaving Evans to his task when the station-sergeant came in.

"Here's the money and papers of that drunk, sir," he said, and deposited a small package on the desk. "Perhaps you'd better put them in the safe. He's sent for his solicitor, so he'll probably be bailed out. But he made such a fuss about his being robbed that it might be better to keep them until he comes before the magistrate in a sober mind."

Mr. Pine nodded and opened the big safe that stood in one corner of the room as the sergeant went out. First he put the money, watch and chain and gold cigarette case in a drawer. Then he took up the little pocket-book and turned the leaves with professional deftness.

"Another gambler," he said sadly.

"Who's that, sir?"

"A man—a gentleman who is unfortunately with us tonight," said Inspector Pine, and paused. "What is a trial, Evans?"

"A trial, sir?"

"It is evidently something to do with horse-racing," said the inspector, and read, half to himself:

Blue Chuck 8-7; Golders Green 7-7; Makin 7-0. Won four lengths. Time 1.39.

. . . . That has to do with racing, Evans?"

Educated Evans nodded, not trusting himself to speak.

"You have your five shillings, Evans. I will leave you now. Give the letters to the sergeant; he will post them. Goodnight."

From time to time that night the sergeant glanced through the open door of the inspector's room, and apparently Educated Evans was a busy man. At midnight, just as the Hon. George Canfyn's solicitor arrived, he carried his work to the station-sergeant's desk, and after the sergeant had made a quick scrutiny of the private office to see that nothing was missing, Evans was allowed to depart.

At ten o'clock next morning Inspector Pine was shaving when his crony and fellow-labourer in the social field (Mr. Stott, the retired grocer) arrived in great haste. And there was on Mr. Stott's face a look of bewilderment and annoyance.

"Good-morning, Brother Stott," said the inspector. "I got all those cards out last night—at least, I hope I did."

Mr. Stott breathed heavily.

"I got my card, Brother Pine," he said, "and I'd like to know the meaning of it."

He thrust a piece of cardboard into the lathered face of the inspector. There was nothing extraordinary in the card. It was an invitation to a meeting of the Brotherhood for Suppressing Gambling.

"Well?"

"Look on the other side," hissed Mr. Stott.

The inspector turned the card and read the stencilled inscription:

If any Brother wants the winner of the Newbury Handicap, send T.M.O. for 20s. to the old reliable Educated Evans, 92 Bingham Mews. This is the biggest pinch of the year! Defeat ignored! Roll up, Brothers! Help yourself, and make T.M.O. payable to E. Evans"

******

"Of course, nobody will reply to the foolish and evil man," said the inspector, as he was giving instructions to The Miller. "Every member of the Brotherhood will treat it with contempt; still, you had better see Evans."

When The Miller arrived at 92 Bingham Mews (it was the upper part of a stable) he found that melancholy man opening telegrams at the rate of twenty a minute.

"And more's coming," said Educated Evans. "There's no punter like a Brother."

"What's the name of the horse?" asked The Miller in a fever.

"Blue Chuck—help yourself," said Educated Evans. "And don't forget you owe me a pound."

The Miller hurried off to interview Mr. Isaacheim, the eminent and respectable Turf accountant.

2.—MR. HOMASTER'S DAUGHTER

Mr. Homaster's daughter was undoubtedly the belle of Camden Town, and when she retired from public life, there is less doubt that Mr. Homaster's trade suffered in consequence.

But as Mr. Homaster very rightly said that even the saloon bar was no place for a young lady, and although, as a result of her withdrawal, many clients who had with difficulty sustained themselves at saloon prices returned in a body to the public portion of the "Rose and Hart," where beer is the stable of commerce, Mr. Homaster (he was Hoch-meister until the war came along) bore his loss with philosophy, and his reputation, both as a gentleman and a father, stood higher than ever.

Miss Belle Homaster was the most beautiful woman that Educated Evans had ever seen. She was tall, with golden hair and blue eyes, and a fine figure. Across her black, tightly-fitting and well-occupied blouse she invariably wore the word "Baby" in diamonds, that being her pet name to her father and her closer relatives.

18

Evans used to go into the saloon bar every night for the happiness of seeing her smile, as she raised her delicately pencilled eyebrows at him. She never asked unnecessary questions. A lift of those arched brows, a gracious nod from Evans, the up-ending of a bottle, a gurgle of soda water, and Evans laid a half-crown on the counter and received the change with a genteel "Thenks."

Sometimes she said it was a very nice day for this time of year. Sometimes, when it wasn't a very nice day, she asked, with a note of gentle despair: "What else can you expect?"

It was generally understood that Evans was her favourite. Certainly he alone of all customers was the recipient of her confidences. It was to Evans that she confessed her partiality for asparagus, and it was Evans who heard from her own lips that she had once, as a small girl, travelled in the same 'bus as Crippen.

A friend of his, at his earnest request, spoke about him glowingly, told her of his education and his ability to settle bets on the most obtuse questions without reference to a book. The way thus prepared by his friendly barker, Evans seized the first opportunity of producing samples of his deep knowledge and learning.

"It's curious, miss, me and you standing here, with the world re-volving on its own axle once in twenty-four hours, thereby causing day and night. Few of us realise, so to speak, the myst'ries of nature, such as the moon and the stars, which are other worlds like ours. They say there's life on Mars owing to the canals which have been observed by telescopic observation. Which brings us to the question: Is Mars inhabited?"

She listened, dazed.

"The evolution of humanity," Evans went on enjoyably, "was in-vented by Darwin, which brings us to the question of prehistoric days."

"What a lot you know!" said the young lady. "Would you like a little more soda? The weather's very seasonable, isn't it?"

"The seasons are created or caused by the revolutions of the world—" began Evans.

But she was called away to tend the needs of an uneducated man who needed a chaser.

Everybody knew Miss Homaster. Even The Miller. When that light and ornament of the criminal investigation department desired an interview with any of his criminal acquaintances, he was certain of finding them hovering like obese moths about the flame of her charm and beauty.

At eight, or thereabouts, Sergeant William Arbuthnot Challoner would push open the swing doors of the saloon bar and glance carelessly round, nod to such of his old friends as he saw, raise his hat to Miss Homaster and retire.

The news of her engagement was announced two days before she left the bar for good. It was to the unhappy Evans that she made the revelation.

"I'm being married to a gentleman friend of mine," she said, what time Educated Evans clutched the edge of the counter for support. "I believe in marrying young and being true. A wife should be a friend to her husband and help him. She ought to be interested in his business. Don't you agree, Mr. Evans?"

"Yes, miss," said Evans with an effort. "For richer and poorer, in sickness and in woe, ashes to ashes."

The Miller learnt of the engagement from Educated Evans.

"I believe in marriage," he said. "It keeps the divorce court busy."

A heartless, cynical man, in whom the wells of human kindness had run dry.

There is a legend that once upon a time The Miller had a fortune in his hand, or within reach of that member. The Miller never discussed the matter, even with his intimates. Even Educated Evans, who counted himself something more than an ordinary acquaintance, with rare delicacy never referred to that tremendous lost opportunity.

Yet there it was: Fortune, with a row of houses under each arm, had kicked at the door, and The Miller had hesitated with his hand on the latch.

Rows of houses, a motorcar, Tatts every day of his life if he so desired, and his ambition moved to such a lofty end—and lost because The Miller refused to credit the evidence of his own ears or to accept the dictum of the ancients, *in vino veritas.*

Mr. Sandy Leman was certainly *in vino* when The Miller pinched him for (1) drunk, (2) creating a disturbance, (3) conduct calculated to bring about a breach of the peace, (4) insulting behaviour. ("He was," to quote the expressive language of Educated Evans, "so soused that he tried to play a coffee stall under the impression it was a grand pianner.") As to the "*veritas,*" was The Miller justified in believing that there was only one trier in the Clumberfield Nursery, and that trier Curly Eyes? Mr. Sandy Leman proclaimed the fact to the world on the way to the station, insisted on seeing the divisional surgeon to tell him, and made pathetic inquiries for Mr. Lloyd George's telephone number in order to pass the good news along to one about whom (in moments of extreme intoxication) he was wont to shed bitter tears.

The Miller had the market to himself, so to speak, and after much hesitation had five shillings each way. And that, after having decided overnight to take a risk and have fifty to win! Curly Eyes won at 100-6. The Miller read the news, cast the paper to the earth and jumped on it. That is the story.

Along the platform of Paddington Station came Educated Evans at a slow and not unstately pace. His head was held proudly, his eyes half-closed, as though the sight of so many common racing people en route for Newbury was more than he dared see, and in his mouth a ragged cigar. Race glasses, massive and imposing, were suspended from one shoulder, an evening newspaper protruded from each of the pockets of his overcoat.

Educated Evans halted before the locked door of an empty first-class carriage and surveyed the approaching guard soberly.

"Member," he said simply.

"Member of Parliament or Member of Tattersall's?" asked the sardonic guard.

"Press," said Evans, even more gravely. "I'm the editor of *The Times.*"

The guard made a gesture.

"Where's your ticket?" he asked, and with a sigh Educated Evans produced the brief.

"Third class—*and* yesterday's," said the guard bitterly. "Love a duck, some of you fellows *never* lose hope, do you?"

"I shall take your number, my friend," said Evans, stung to speech. "The Railway Act of 1874 specifically specifies that tickets issued under the Act are transferable and interchangeable—"

The guard passed on. Evans saw the door of a corridor car open and the guard's back turned. He stepped in, and, sinking into a corner seat, blotted out his identity with an evening newspaper.

"I always say, sir," said Evans, as the train began to move and it was safe to appear in public, "that to start cheap is to start well. Not that I'm not in a position to pay my way like a gentleman and a sportsman."

His solitary companion was also hidden behind an extended newspaper.

"It stands to reason," Mr. Evans went on, "that a man like my-

21

self, who is, so to speak, in the confidence of most of the Berkshire and Wiltshire stables, and have my own co-respondents at Lambourn, Manton, Stockbridge, and *cetera*, it only stands to reason that, owning my own horses as I do—hum!"

The Miller regarded him coldly over the edge of his newspaper.

"Don't let me interrupt you, Evans," he said, politely. "Let me hear about these horses of yours, I beg! Tell-a-Tale, by Swank out of Gullibility, own brother to Jailbird, and a winner of races; Tipster, by Ananias out of Writer's Cramp, by What-Did-I-Give-Yer."

"Don't let us have any unpleasantness, Mr. Miller," said Evans, mildly. "I'm naturally an affable and talkative person, like the famous Cardinal Rishloo, who, bein' took to task by Napoleon for his garolisty, replied 'There's many a good tune played on an old fiddle.' "

"Not satisfied," continued The Miller, "with defrauding the Great Western Railway by travelling first on a dud third-class ticket, you must endeavour, by misrepresentation of a degrading character, to obtain money by false pretences."

The Miller shook his head, and the straw between his teeth twirled ominously.

"What are you backing in the two-thirty?" asked Evans pleasantly. "I've got something that could lay down and go to sleep and then get up and win so far that the judge'd have to paint a new distance board. This thing can't be beat, Mr. Miller. If the jockey was to fall off this here horse would stop, pick him up, and win with him in his mouth! He's that intelligent. I've had it from the boy that does him."

"If he does him as well as you've done me," said The Miller, "he ought to glitter! I'm doing nothing but your unbeatable gem in the Handicap. Isaacheim wouldn't lay me the money I wanted, so I thought I'd come down. Not that the horse will win."

The melancholy face of Educated Evans twisted in a sneer.

"It will win," he said with calm confidence. "If this horse was left at the post and started running the wrong way he could turn round and *then* win! I know what I'm talking about. I can't give you the strength of it without, in a manner of speakin', betrayin' a sacred confidence. But this horse will WIN! I've sent it out to three thousand clients—"

"That's a lie," said The Miller, resuming his perusal of the *Sporting Life*.

"Well, three hundred—an' not far short."

Mr. Evans fingered the crisp notes in his pocket, and the crackle of them made music beside which the lute of Orpheus would have sounded as cheerful as a church bell on a foggy morning. He had certainly received inspired information. If Blue Chuck was not a certainty for the Newbury Handicap, then there were no such things as certainties. He had seen the owner's description of the trial in the owner's pocket-book.

All that morning Mr. Evans had been engaged in despatching to his clients—for he was a tipster not without fame in Camden Town—the glorious and profitable news. For an hour he had carried the tidings of great joy to an old and tried *clientèle*. Some had been so well and truly tried that they publicly insulted him. Others to whom, leaning across the zinc-covered counter of the public bar, he had whispered the hectic intelligence, had drawn a pint, mechanically, and said "Is this another one of your so-and-so dreams?"

Educated Evans had time to catch the 12.38. Mr. Evans could have afforded a first-class ticket, but he held firmly to the faith that there were three states that it was the duty of every citizen to "best." First came the government; then, in order of merit, came railway companies; thirdly, and at times even firstly, appeared the bookmaking class.

He had secured his ticket from a fellow sojourner at the Rose and Hart. Its owner valued it at two hog. Evans beat him down to eightpence.

"Making money out of Blue Chuck is easier than drawing the dole," said Evans, as I know. Mr. Miller, you understand these things. What would you put eighteen hundred pounds into if you was me?"

"Eh?" said the startled Miller. "You have got eighteen hundred pounds?"

"Not at the moment," admitted Evans modestly. "But that is the amount I'll have when I come back. It's a lot of money to carry about. House property is not what it was," he added, "nor War Loan, after what this Capital Levy is trying to do to us. Who *is* this feller Levy, Mr. Miller? It's Jewish; but I don't seem to remember the Christian name."

As the train was passing through Reading, Educated Evans delivered himself of a piece of philosophy.

"Bookmakers get fat on what I might term the indecision of the racin' public," he said. "The punter who follows the advice of his Turf adviser blindly and fearlessly is the feller who packs the parcel. But does he follow the advice of his Turf adviser blindly and fearlessly, Mr. Miller? No, he doesn't."

"And he's wise," said The Miller, without looking up from his paper, "if you happen to be the Turf adviser."

"That may be or may not be," said Educated Evans firmly. "I'm merely telling you what I've learnt from years an' years of experience—and mind you, my recollection goes back to the old Croydon racecourse. It's hearin' things, it's bein' put off, it's bein' told this, that, and the other by nosy busybodies that enables Sir Douglas Stuart—ain't he? well, he ought to be—to spend his declining days on the Rivyera."

"The trouble with you, Evans," said The Miller, folding his paper as the train slowed for Newbury, "is that you talk too much."

"The trouble with me," said Educated Evans, with dignity, "is that I *think* too much!"

He parted from the detective on the platform, and was making his way toward the entrance of the Silver Ring when he stopped dead. A lady was crossing the roadway to the pay gate, and the heart of Educated Evans leapt within him. He knew that black fox fur, that expensive velour hat, those high-buttoned boots. For a second the economist and the lover struggled one with the other, and the lover won. Educated Evans followed hot on her trail, wincing with pain as he paid 2s. 6d. and followed the lady to the paddock.

She turned at the sound of her name, and it must be said of Miss Homaster that her attitude toward Evans was not only extremely cordial but amazingly condescending.

"Why, Mr. Evans, whoever expected to see you?" she said. "What extraordinary weather it is for this time of the year!"

"It is indeed, Miss Homaster," said Evans. "Is your respected father with you?"

"No, I've come alone," said Miss Homaster, with a saucy toss of her head, "and I'm going to back all the winners."

Here was the chance that Educated Evans had been praying for, the opportunity which he never dreamt would come.

He had pictured himself rescuing her from burning houses, or diving into the seething waters of the canal and bringing her back to safety, perhaps breathing his last in her arms; but he had never imagined that the opportunity would arise of giving her "the goods."

"Miss Homaster," he said in a hoarse whisper, "I'm going to do you a bit of good. I've got the winner of the Handicap. It's Blue Chuck; he's a stone certainty. He could fall down and get up and then win."

"Really?" She was genuinely interested as he told her the strength of it.

He left her soon after (he knew his place) and strolled into the ring. He had been in Tattersall's once before, but the experience was not as thrilling as it might have been. An acquaintance saw him and came boisterously toward him.

"Hallo, Educated!" he said. "I've got something good for you, old cock; I've got the winner of the Handicap up me sleeve. Bing Boy! "

He looked round to see that he was not overheard, and in his interest he failed to see the cold sneer that was growing on the face of Mr. Evans.

"This horse," said his acquaintance, "has been tried good enough to win the Derby even if it was run over hurdles! This horse could fall down—"

"And I should say he would fall down," said Evans, his exasperation getting the better of his politeness. "You couldn't make me back Bing Boy with bad money. You couldn't make me back it with bookmakers who had twilight sleep and forgot all that happened a few minutes before. Bing Boy!" he said, with withering contempt.

Nevertheless, Bing Boy was favourite, and the horse that Educated Evans had come to back was at any price. Evans was disconcerted, alarmed. He went into the paddock and saw the scowling owner of his great certainty. He did not look happy. Perhaps it was because he had spent the greater part of the previous evening in an uncomfortable police-station cell.

Evans went in search of the man who gave him Bing Boy to get a little further information.

And they were backing Smocker. He was a strong second favourite, and it was difficult to get 7 to 2 about him. A man Evans knew drew him aside to a place where he could not be overheard by the common crowd and told him all about Smocker.

"This horse," he said impressively, as he poked his finger in Evans' waistcoat to emphasise the seriousness of the communication, "has been tried twenty-one pounds better than Glasshouse. He won the trial on a tight rein, and if what I hear is true—and the man that told me is the boy that does him—Smocker could fall down—"

"There'll be a few falls in this race," said Educated Evans hollowly.

The first few events were cleared from the card, and betting started in earnest over the Handicap, and yet Educated Evans delayed his commission. To nearly three hundred clients he had wired, "Blue Chuck. Help yourself. Can't be beaten." And here was Blue Chuck sliding down the market like a pat of butter on the Cresta Run! Tens, a hundred to eight, a hundred to seven in places.

"Phew!" said Educated Evans.

The notes in his pocket were damp from handling. He made another frantic dive into the paddock in the hope of finding somebody who would give him the least word of encouragement about Blue Chuck.

Again he saw the owner of Blue Chuck, scowling like a fiend.

And then somebody spoke to him, and he turned quickly, hat in hand.

"Why, I've been looking everywhere for you, Mr. Evans," said Miss Homaster.

"I've got such a wonderful tip for you. Your horse—Blue Chuck, wasn't it?—isn't fancied in the least bit. The owner told a friend of mine that he didn't expect he'd finish in the first three."

The heart of Educated Evans sank, but it was not with sorrow for his deluded clients.

"Smocker will win." She lowered her voice. "It is a certainty. I've just been offered five to one, and I've backed it."

"Five to one?" said Educated Evans, his trading instincts aroused. "You can't get more than four to one."

"*I* can," said the girl in triumph. "I'll show you."

Proud to be seen in such delightful company, Educated Evans followed her, through the press of Tattersall's, down the rails, until near the end he saw a tall, florid young man—no less a person than Barney Gibbet!

"Mr. Gibbet, this is a friend of mine who wants to back Smocker. You'll give him five to one?"

Gibbet looked sorrowfully at Educated Evans.

"Five to one, Miss Homaster?" he said, shaking his head. "No, it's above the market price."

"But you promised me," she said reproachfully.

"Very well. How much do you want on it, sir?"

The lips of Educated Evans opened, but he could not pronounce the words. Presently they came.

"Three hundred," he said in broken tones.

"Ready?" asked Mr. Gibbet, with pardonable suspicion.

"Ready," said Educated Evans.

It proved, on examination, that he only had £240. He had conjured up the other £60, for he was ever an optimist. In the end he was laid £1,100 to £220.

"You won't mind if I give you a cheque for your winnings?" asked Mr. Gibbet. "I don't carry a large sum of money round with me; it's not quite safe amongst these disreputable characters you meet upon racecourses."

"I quite agree," said Educated Evans heartily, and went up to the stand to see the race.

It was a race that can easily be described, calling for none of those complicated and intricate calculations which form a feature of every race description. Blue Chuck jumped off in front, made the whole of the running, and won hard held by five lengths. Two horses of whose existence Educated Evans was profoundly ignorant were second and third. Smocker was pulled up half-way down the straight.

Educated Evans staggered down from the stand and into the paddock. His only chance, and it seemed a feeble one, was that the twelve horses that finished in front of Smocker would be disqualified. But the flag went up, and a stentorian voice sang musically, "Weighed in!"

Educated Evans dragged his weary feet to the train.

"It doesn't leave for an hour yet," said an official.

"I can wait," said Educated Evans gently.

Just after the last race The Miller came along the platform looking immensely pleased with himself. He saw Evans and turned into the carriage.

"Had a good race, my boy?" he asked. "I did, and thank you for the tip."

"Not at all," murmured Evans in the tone of one greatly suffering.

"They tried to lumber me on to Smocker, but no bookmakers' horses for me!"

"Is he a bookmaker's horse?" asked Evans with a flicker of mild interest.

"Yes, he belongs to that fellow Gibbet—the man who's engaged to Miss Homaster.

Educated Evans tried to smile.

"If you feel ill," said the alarmed Miller, "you'd better open the window."

3.—THE COOP

Sometimes they referred to Mr. Yardley in the newspapers as "the Wizard of Stotford," sometimes his credit was diffused as the "Yardley

Confederation"; occasionally he was spoken of as plain "Bert Yardley," but invariably his entries for any important handicaps were described as "The Stotford Mystery." For nobody quite knew what Mr. Yardley's intentions were until the day of the race. Usually after the race, for it is a distressing fact that the favourite from his stable was usually unplaced, and the winner (also from his stable) started amongst the "100 to 7 others."

After the event was all over and the "weighed in" had been called, people used to gather in the paddock in little groups and ask one another what this horse was doing at Nottingham, and where were the stewards, and why Mr. Yardley was not jolly well warned off. And they didn't say "jolly" either.

For it is an understood thing in racing that, if an outsider wins, its trainer ought to be warned off. Yet neither Bert Yardley, nor Colonel Rogersman, nor Mr. Lewis Feltham (the two principal owners for whom he trained) were so much as asked by the stewards to explain the running of their horses. Thus proving that the Turf needed reform, and that the stipendiary steward was an absolute necessity.

Mr. Bert Yardley was a youngish looking man of thirty-five, who spoke very little and did his betting by telegraph. He had a suite at the Midland Hotel, and was a member of a sedate and respectable club in Pall Mall. He read extensively, mostly such classics as *Races to Come,* and the umpteenth volume of the Stud Book, and he leavened his studies with such lighter reading as the training reports from the daily sporting newspapers—he liked a good laugh.

His worst enemy could not complain to him that he refused information to anybody.

"I think mine have some sort of chance, and I am backing them both. Tinpot? Well, of course, he may win; miracles happen, and I shouldn't be surprised if he made a good show. But I've had to ease him in his work, and when I galloped him on Monday he simply wouldn't have it—couldn't get him to take hold of his bit. Possibly he runs better when he's a little above himself, but he's a horse of moods. If he would only give his running, he'd trot in! Lampholder, on the other hand, is as game a horse as ever looked through a bridle. A battler! He'll be there or thereabouts."

What would you back on that perfectly candid, perfectly honest information, straight, as it were, from the horse's mouth?

Lampholder, of course; and Tinpot would win. Even stipendiary stewards couldn't make Lampholder win, not if they got behind and shoved him. And that, of course, is no part of a stipendiary steward's duties.

Mr. Bert Yardley was dressing for dinner one March evening, and, opening his case, he discovered that a gold dress watch had disappeared. He called his valet, who could offer no other information than that it had been there when they left Stotford for Sandown Park.

"Send for the police," said Mr. Yardley, and there came to him Detective-Sergeant Challoner.

Mr. Challoner listened, made a few notes, asked a few, a very few, questions of the valet, and closed his book.

"I think I know the person," he said, and to the valet: "A big nose—you're sure of the big nose?"

The valet was emphatic.

"Very good," said The Miller, "I'll do my best, Mr. Yardley. I hope I shall be as successful as Amboy will be in the Lincoln Handicap."

Mr. Yardley smiled faintly.

"We'll talk about that later," he said.

The Miller made one or two inquiries, and that night pulled in "Nosey" Boldin, whose hobby it was to pose as an inspector of telephones, and in this capacity had made many successful experiments. On the way to the station, "Nosey," so-called because of a certain abnormality in that organ, delivered himself with great force and venom.

"This comes of betting on horse races and follering Educated Evans' perishin' five-pound specials! Let this be a warning to you, 'Miller'!"

"Not so much lip," said "The Miller."

"He gave me one winner in ten shots, and *that* started at 11 to 10 on," ruminated "Nosey." "Men like that drive men to crime. There ought to be a law so's to make the fifth loser a *felony*! And after the eighth loser, he ought to 'ang! That'd stop 'em!"

The Miller saw his friend charged and lodged for the night, and went home to bed. And in the morning, when he left his lodgings to go to breakfast, the first person he saw was Educated Evans, and there was on that learned man's unhappy face a look of pain and anxiety.

"Good-morning, Mr. Challoner. Excuse me if I'm taking a liberty, but I understand that a client of mine is in trouble?"

"If you mean 'Nosey,' he is," agreed The Miller. "And what is more, he attributes his shame and downfall to following your tips. I sympathise with him."

Educated Evans made an impatient clicking sound, raised his eyebrows and spread out his hand.

"Bolsho," he said simply.

"Eh?" The Miller frowned suspiciously. "You didn't give Bolsho?"

"Every guaranteed client received 'Bolsho: fear nothing,'" said Evans even more simply "following Mothegg (ten to one, beaten a neck, hard lines), Toffeetown (third, hundred to eight, very unlucky), Onesided (won, seven to two, what a beauty!), followin' Curds and Whey (won, eleven to ten—can't help the price). Is that fair?"

"The question is," said The Miller deliberately, "Did 'Nosey' subscribe to your guarantee wire, your £5 special, or your Overnight nap?"

"That," said Educated Evans diplomatically, "I can't tell till I've seen me books. The point is this: if 'Nosey' wants bail, am I all right? I don't want any scandal, and you know 'Nosey.' He ought to have been on the advertisin' staff of Shelfridges, or running insurance stunts in the *Daily Flail*."

The advertising propensities of "Nosey" were, indeed, well known to The Miller. He had the knack of introducing some startling feature into the very simplest case, and attracting to himself the amount of newspaper space usually given to scenes in the House and important murders.

It was "Nosey" who, by his startling statement that pickles was a greater incentive to crime than beer, initiated a press correspondence which lasted for months. It was "Nosey" who, when charged with hotel larceny (his favourite aberration), made the pronouncement that motor 'buses were a cause of insanity. Upon the peg of his frequent misfortunes it was his practice to hang a showing up for somebody.

The case of "Nosey" was dealt with summarily. Long before the prosecutor had completed his evidence he realised that his doom was sealed.

"Anything known about this man?" asked the magistrate.

A gaoler stepped briskly into the box and gave a brief sketch of "Nosey's" life, and "Nosey," who knew it all before, looked bored.

"Anything to say?" asked the magistrate.

"Nosey" cleared his throat.

"I can only say, your worship, that I've fell into thieving ways owing to falling in the hands of unscrupulous racing tipsters. I'm ruined by tips, and if the law was just, there's a certain party who ought to be standing here by my side."

Educated Evans, standing at the back of the court, squirmed.

"I've got a wife, as true a woman as ever drew the breath of life," "Nosey" went on. "I've got two dear little children, and I ask your worship to consider me temptation owing to horse-racing and betting and this here tipster."

"Six months' hard labour," said the magistrate, without looking up.

Outside the court Mr. Evans waited patiently for the appearance of The Miller.

"'Nosey' never had more than a shilling on a horse in his life," he said bitterly, "and he *owes*! Here's the bread being took out of my mouth by slander and misrepresentation; do you think they'll put it in the papers, Mr. Challoner?"

"Certain," said The Miller, cheerfully, and Educated Evans groaned.

"That man's worse than Lucreature Burgia, the celebrated poisoner," he said, "that Shakespeare wrote a play about. He's a snake in the grass and viper in the bosom. And to think I gave him Penwiper for the Manchester November, and he never so much as asked me if I was thirsty Mr. Challoner."

Challoner, turning away, stooped.

"Was that Yardley. I mean the trainer?"

The Miller looked at him reproachfully.

"Maybe I'm getting old and my memory is becoming defective," he said, "but I seem to remember that when you gave me Tellmark the other day, you said that you were a personal friend of Mr. Yardley's, and that the way he insisted on your coming down to spend week-ends was getting a public nuisance."

Educated Evans did not bat a lid.

"That was his brother," he said.

"He must have lied when he told me he had no brothers," said The Miller.

"They've quarrelled," replied Educated Evans frankly. "In fact, they never mention one another's names. It's tragic when brothers quarrel, Mr. Challoner. I've done my best to reconcile 'em—but what's the use? He didn't say anything about Amboya, did he?"

"He said nothing that I can tell you," was the unsatisfactory reply, and left Mr. Evans to consider means and methods by which he might bring himself into closer contact with the Wizard of Stotford.

All that he feared in the matter of publicity was realised to the full.

One evening paper said:

Ruined by Tipsters

Once-prosperous merchant goes to prison for theft.

And in the morning press one newspaper may be quoted as typical of the rest:

Tipster to Blame

Pest of the Turf wrecks a home.

Detective-Sergeant Challoner called by appointment at the Midland Hotel, and Mr. Yardley saw him.

"No, thank you, sir." The Miller was firm. He never forgot that he was a public schoolboy (he rowed stroke in his school boat the year they beat Eton in the final), and he was in many ways unique.

Mr. Yardley put back the fiver he had taken from his pocket.

"I will put you a tenner on anything I fancy," he said. "Who is this tipster, by the way?—the man who was referred to by the prisoner."

The Miller smiled.

"Educated Evans," he said, and when he had finished describing him Mr. Yardley nodded.

He was staying overnight in London *en route* for Lincoln, and was inclined to be bored. He had read the *Racing Calendar* from the list of the year's races to the last description of the last selling hurdle race on the back page. He had digested the surprising qualities of stallions that stood at 48 guineas and 1 guinea groom, and he could have almost recited the forfeit list from Aaron to Znosberg. And he was aching for diversion when the bell boy brought a card. It was a large card, tastefully bordered with pink and green roses. Its edge was golden, and in the centre were the words:

J. T. EVANS

(better known as "Educated Evans" !!)

The World's Foremost and leading Turf Adviser

and Racing Critic.

c/o Jockey Club, Newmarket, or direct:

81 Bayham Mews, S.W.1.

"The Man Who Gave Braxted!!

What a beauty!"—*vide* Press.

Mr. Yardley read, lingering over the printer's errors.

"Show this gentleman up, page," he said.

Into his presence came Educated Evans, a solemn, purposeful man.

"I hope the intrusion will be amply excused by the important nature or character of my business," he said. This was the opening he had planned.

"Sit down, Mr. Evans," said Yardley, and Educated Evans put his hat under the chair and sat.

"I've been thinking matters over in the privacy of my den—" began Evans, after a preliminary cough.

"You are a lion-tamer as well?" asked the Wizard of Stotford, interested.

"By 'den' I mean 'study,'" said Evans gravely. "To come to the point without beating about the bush—to use a well-known expression—I've heard of a coop."

"A what?"

"A coop," said Evans.

"A chicken coop?" asked the puzzled Wizard.

"It's a French word, meaning ramp,' said Evans.

"Oh, yes, I see. 'Coup'—it's pronounced 'coo,' Mr. Evans."

Educated Evans frowned.

"It's years since I was in Paris," he said; "and I suppose they've altered it. It used to be 'coop,' but these French people are always messing and mucking about with words."

"And who is working this coop?" asked the trainer politely, adopting the old French version.

"Higgson."

Educated Evans pronounced the word with great emphasis. Higgson was another mystery trainer. His horses also won when least expected. And after they won little knots of men gathered in the paddock and asked one another if the Stewards had eyes, and why wasn't Higgson warned off?

"You interest me," said the trainer of Amboy. "Do you mean that he is winning with St. Kats?"

Evans nodded more gravely still.

"I think it's me duty to tell you," he said. "My information"—he lowered his voice and glanced round to the door to be sure that it was shut—"comes from the boy who does this horse!"

"Dear me!" said Mr. Yardley.

"I've got correspondents everywhere," said Educated Evans mysteriously. "My man at Stockbridge sent me a letter this morning (I dare not show it to you) about a horse in that two-year-old race that will win with his ears pricked."

Mr. Yardley was looking at him through half-closed eyes.

"With his ears pricked?" he repeated, impressed. "Have they trained his ears too? Extraordinary! But why have you come to tell me about Mr. Higgson's horse?"

Educated Evans bent forward confidentially-

"Because you've done me many a turn, sir," he said "and I'd like to do you one. I've got the information. I could shut my mouth an' make millions. I've got nine thousand clients who'd pay me the odds to a pound—but what's money?"

"True," murmured Mr. Yardley, nodding. "Thank you, Mr. Evans. St. Kats, I think you said? Now, in return for your kindness, I'll give you a tip."

Educated Evans held his breath. His amazingly bold plan had succeeded.

"Change your printer," said Mr. Yardley, rising. "He can't spell. Goodnight."

Evans went forth with his heart turned to stone and his soul seared with bitter animosity.

Mr. Yardley came down after him and watched the shabby figure as it turned the corner, and his heart was touched. In two minutes he had overtaken the educated man.

"You're a bluff and a fake," he said, good-humouredly, "but you can have a little, a very little, on Amboy."

Before Educated Evans could prostrate himself at the benefactor's feet Mr. Yardley was gone.

The next day was a busy one for Educated Evans. All day Miss Higgs, the famous typist of Great College Street, turned her Roneo, and every revolution of the cylinder threw forth, with a rustle and a click, the passionate appeal which Educated Evans addressed to all clients, old and new. He was not above borrowing the terminology of other advertisement writers.

> You want the best winners—I've got them.
> Bet in Evans' way! Eventually, why not now?
> I've got the winner of the Lincoln!
> What a beauty!
> What a beauty!
> What a beauty!
> Confidentially! From the trainer!
> This is the coop of the season. Help yourself! Defeat ignored!

To eight hundred and forty clients (the postage alone cost thirty-five shillings) this moving appeal went forth.

On the afternoon of the race Educated Evans strolled with confidence to the end of the Tottenham Court Road to wait for the *Star*. And when it came he opened the paper with a quiet smile. He was still smiling, when he read:

Tenpenny,   1.
St. Kats,   2.
Ella Glass,   3.
All probables ran.

"Tenpenny?—never heard of it," he repeated, dazed, and produced his noon edition. Tenpenny was starred as a doubtful runner.

It was trained by Yardley.

For a moment his emotions almost mastered him.

"That man ought to be warned off," he said, hollowly, and dragged his weary feet back to the stable yard.

In the morning came a letter dated from Lincoln.

Dear Mr. Evans,—What do you think of my coop?—Yours, H. Yardley.

There was a *P.S.* which ran:

I put a fiver on for you. Your enterprise deserved it.

Evans opened the cheque tenderly and shook his head.

"After all," he said subsequently to the quietly jubilant Miller, "clients can't expect to win *every* time—a Turf adviser is entitled to his own coops."

Tenpenny started at 25 to 1.

4.—THE SNOUT

Saturday night in High Street, Camden Town, and the lights were blazing and the tram bells clanging dolefully. About each gas-lit stall a group of melancholy sceptics, for the late shopper is not ready to believe all that loud-voiced stall-holders claim for their wares.

At one corner a dense, hypnotised crowd of men listening to a diminutive spellbinder, wearing a crimson and purple racing jacket over a pair of voluminous tight-gartered breeches.

"... did I tell yer people that Benny Eyes was no good for the City an' Suburban 'Andicap? Did I tell yer *not* to back Sommerband for the Metropolitan? Did I tell yer on this very spot last week, an' I'm willing to pay a thousan' poun' to the Temperance 'Ospital if I didn't, that Proud Alec could fall down an' get up and then win the Great Surrey 'Andicap? Did I . . ."

One of the audience edged himself free from the crowd with a sigh, and, so doing, edged himself into a quiet-looking, broad-shouldered man, who was chewing a straw and listening intently.

"Good-evening, Mr. Challoner," said Educated Evans.

"Evening, Evans," said The Miller. "Picking up a few tips?"

A contemptuous yet pitying smile illuminated the face of the learned Evans.

"From *him*?" he said. "Do you buy detective stories such as is published in the common press in order to learn policery? No, Mr. Challoner—I was a-standing there as an impartial observer an' a student of the lower classes, their cupidity and credulity bringin' tears to my eyes. I won't knock Holley—I know the man; he takes my tips, and goes and sells 'em to the common people. I don't complain, so long as he don't use my name. But the next time he professes to be sellin' Educated Evans' £5 specials for fourpence I shall take action! "

The Miller half turned, and, after a second's hesitation, Educated Evans fell in at his side.

"You don't mind, Mr. Challoner?"

"Not a bit, Evans. If I meet anybody I know, I can tell them afterwards I was taking you to the station." Evans winced.

"Doesn't it do your heart good to see all these people out and about, and every one got his money honestly by working for it?"

Evans sniffed.

"You know your own business best," he said cryptically.

"Perhaps they're not *all* horny-handed sons of toil," admitted The Miller, as a familiar face came into his line of vision.

"If my eyes aren't getting wonky, that was old Solly Risk I saw—how long has he been out?"

Educated Evans did not know.

"The habits of the criminal classes," he said, "are Greek to me, as Socrates said to Julius Caesar, the well-known Italian. They go in and they come out, and no man knoweth. Solly is as wide as that famous African river, the Amazon, discovered by Stanley in the year 1743. But you can be too wide, and snouts being what they are—"

"Snouts?" said The Miller, elaborately puzzled. What is a 'snout'?"

"It's a phrase used by low people, an' I can well understand you've never heard it," said Evans politely.

"If, by that vulgar expression, you mean a man who keeps the police informed on criminal activities," said The Miller, who knew much better than Evans the title and functions of a police informer, "let me tell you that Solly was arrested on clear evidence. That's a bad cold of yours, Evans?"

For Educated Evans had sniffed again.

"As a turf adviser and England's Premier sportin' authority," said Evans, "I've me time fully occupied without pryin' into other people's business. I've nothing to say against Ginger Vennett—"

The Miller stopped and regarded his companion oddly.

"Get it out of your mind that Ginger is a snout," he said. "He's a hard-working young man—more hard-working than his landlord."

"Or his landlady," suggested Evans, and this time his sniff was a terrific one.

"I know nothing about his landlady except that she's good looking, hard-working and too good for Lee," said The Miller, and Educated Evans laughed hollowly.

"So was Cleopatra, whose famous needle we all admire," he said. "So was Lewd-creature Burgia, the celebrated wife of Henry VIII, who tried to poison him by pourin' boilin' lead in his earhole. So was B. Mary, who murdered the innercent little princes in the far-famed Tower of London in—"

"Don't let us rake up the past," pleaded The Miller. "Have you seen anything of Lee lately? They tell me he's gone into the harness business again?"

It was a deadly insult he was offering to Educated Evans, and nobody knew this better than The Miller. He was actually inviting Evans to turn Nose!

"I'm surprised at you, Mr. Challoner," said Evans, genuinely hurt, and The Miller laughed and went on.

Everybody liked "Modder" Lee—so called because in his cups he had a habit of describing the battle of Modder River (in which he took part), illustrating the line of attack by the simple method of dipping his finger in the nearest pot of beer and tracing the course of the Modder on the counter. He was a good friend, a quiet, unassuming citizen, and more than a faithful husband and father to the pretty shrew he had married in a moment of mental aberration.

His one weakness was harness. The sight of a set of harness set his blood on fire and provoked him to unlawful doings. He had taken carts, and had walked away with horses and sold them at the repository under the very noses of their owners, but harness was his speciality.

"It's a hobby," he told his lodger, a tall, good-looking and fiery-headed young man, who did nothing for a living except back a few up and downers and run for a bookmaker. He used to represent a West End firm of commission agents until unprofitable papers appeared in the bunch, and they discovered he was getting quick results over the tape at the Italian Club.

He had been a client of Educated Evans; but, following a dispute as to whether he had or had not received a certain winner (odds to 5s.), Educated Evans had struck his name from the list. And this was a source of great distress to Ginger, for he reposed an unnatural faith in the prescience of the educated man.

"I know more about harness," said Modder Lee, with pride, "than any other man in the business. I can walk down High Street and price every set I meet, and I'll bet that I'm not five shillings out! "

One night the stable of Holloway's Provision Stores was broken into, and a double set of pony harness was missing. Two nights later came an urgent call from Lifton Mews. A set of carriage harness, the property of Lord Lifton himself, had vanished. . . .

The Miller made a few independent inquiries, met (by appointment and in a dark little street) a Certain Man, and made a midnight call at 930 Little Stibbington Street.

The Miller did not call at Little Stibbington Street to inquire after Lee's health, nor was it a friendly call in the strictest sense of the word. Mrs. Lee was in bed, and answered the door in a skirt, a shawl, an apron, and a look of startled wonder. Later, in the language of the psalmist, she clothed herself with curses as with a garment—for she was, ostensibly, a true wife.

"If I never move from this doorstep, Mr. Miller, and I'm a Gawd-fearing woman that's been attendin' the Presbyterian Church in Stibbington Street off an' on for years, if I die this very minute, my old man hasn't been out of this house for three days with rheumatics antrypus. Without the word of a lie, he can't move from his bed, and you know, Mr. Miller, I've never told you a lie—'ave I? Answer me, yes or no?"

"Let me talk to Modder," said the patient "Miller."

"He's that ill he wouldn't know you, Mr. Miller," she urged, agitatedly (if the neighbourhood, listening in to a woman, had not heard the agitation appropriate to the moment, she would have been condemned). "I haven't been able to get his boots on for days. He's delyrius, as Gawd's my judge! He don't know anybody, and, what's more, it's catching—measles or something—and you with a wife and family, too."

"I've caught measles before, but I've never caught a wife or family," said The Miller good-naturedly.

"He won't know you." The reluctant door opened a little wider. "Mind how you go—the pram's in the passage, and the young man lodger upstairs always leaves his bit of washing to dry. . . ."

Wet and semi-dry shirts flapped in the detective's face as he made his way to the back room, illuminated by a small oil lamp.

Entering, he heard a deep groan. And there was Lee in bed, and on his face a wild and vacant look.

"He won't know you," said Mrs. Lee, performing her toilet with the corner of her apron. In support of her statement Modder opened his mouth and spoke faintly.

"Is that dear mother?" he quavered. "Or is it angels?"

"That's how he's been goin' on for days," said Mrs. Lee, with great satisfaction.

"I 'ear such lovely music," said the tremulous Modder. "It sounds like an 'arp!"

"The Welsh Harp," said Miller. "Now come out of your trance, Lee, and step round with me to the station—the inspector wants a talk with you."

Mrs. Lee quivered.

"Are you goin' to take a dyin' man from his bed?" she asked bitterly. "Do you want to see yourself showed up in *John Bull*?"

"God forbid!" said Miller, and with a dexterous twist of his hand pulled the bedclothes from the invalid. He was fully dressed, even to his boots, and packed between his trousered legs was a new set of harness of incalculable value.

"It's a cop," said Lee, and got up without assistance. "There's a snout somewhere in this neighbourhood," he said, without heat. If I ever find him, I'll tear his liver out. And his lights," he added, as he remembered those important organs.

It was his ninth offence, and Lee, as he knew, was booked for that country house in Devonshire near the River Dart and adjacent to the golf links of Tavistock.

Having vindicated her position as a true wife and faithful helpmate, Mrs. Modder Lee returned to her honorary status of Respectable Woman. The Miller saw her coming out of a picture house with the red-haired lodger, and she tripped up to him coyly, a smile upon her undoubtedly attractive features. The Miller always said that if she had had the sense to keep her mouth shut she might have been mistaken for a French lady. He specified the kind of French lady, but the description cannot be given in a book that is read by young people.

"Oh, Mr. Challoner, I *do* owe you an apology for all the unkind things I said," she said, in her genteel voice; "but a wife must stick up for her husband, or where would the world be, in a manner of speaking?"

"That's all right, Mrs. Lee," smiled The Miller, and glanced at her escort. I see Vennett is looking after you."

Mrs. Lee launched forth into a rhapsody of praise.

"He's been so good to me and the children," she said. "He's got a bit of money, and he doesn't mind spending it either—you've no idea how kind he's been to me, Mr. Challoner!"

"I can guess," said The Miller.

The Miller was a philosopher. He accepted, in his professional capacity, a situation which sickened him to think about as a man. One morning he met Educated Evans at the corner of Bayham Street, and that learned man had on his face a look of peace and content which did not accord with his record as the World's Premier Turf Adviser. For Educated Evans had sent out three horses to his clients, of which two had finished fourth and fifth, and the third absolutely last, as The Miller knew.

"It's no good talking to me, Mr. Challoner," said Educated Evans firmly. "My information was that Rhineland could have run backwards and won. He was badly rode, according to the sportin' descriptions, and my own idea is that the jockey wasn't trying a yard."

"If Statesman doesn't win—" began The Miller threateningly, and Evans' face changed.

"You ain't backing Statesman, are you?" he asked.

"I've backed him," said The Miller, and Educated Evans groaned.

"Then you've lost your money "he said with resignation.

The Miller frowned.

"I saw Ginger Vennett and he told me you'd given it to him as the best thing of the century that you had had this from the owner and that you told him to put every farthing he had in the world on it. What's the idea, Evans?"

"The idea is" said Mr. Evans speaking under the stress of great emotion, "that I want to put that snout where he belongs —in the gutter!"

The Miller gasped.

"Do you mean to tell me that you twisted him?"

"I do," said Evans savagely. "He's got all his savings on Statesman, who hasn't done a gallop for a month. If you've been hoisted with his peter, to use a naval expression, I'm sorry, Mr. Challoner; but I've got one for you on Saturday that can't lose unless they put a rope across the course to trip him up."

The Miller hurried away to the nearest telephone and called up Mr. Isaacheim.

"It's Challoner speaking, Isaacheim," he said. "That bet you took about Statesman—I think you'd better call it off."

"All right, Mr. Challoner," said the obliging Isaacheim. "I don't think much of it myself: the horse hasn't done a gallop for a month, and Educated Evans told me

"I know what Educated Evans told you," said "The Miller"; "but it's certainly understood that that bet's off."

In the afternoon The Miller bought an evening newspaper and turned to the stop press, and the first thing he saw was that Statesman had won

When, in the evening, he discovered that the price was 25 to 1, he went in search of Educated Evans, and found that sad man on the verge of tears.

"I did my best. It's no good arguing the point with me, Mr. Challoner," he said. "I've had Ginger round here congratulating me, but telling me that he'd forgotten to have the bet, and that's about as much as I can stand. The only thing I can tell you is *don't back Blazing Heavens* in the two-thirty race tomorrow, because I've give it to Ginger, and I've asked him, as a man and a sportsman, not to tell anybody, and to put his shirt on it. Revenge," he went on, "is repugnant to my nature. But a snout's a snout, and if I don't settle Ginger, then I'm an uneducated man—which, of course, I'm not," he added modestly.

Obedient to his instructions, The Miller refrained from backing Blazing Heavens, and, under any circumstances, would not have invested a red cent on a horse that had 21 lb. the worse of the weights with Lazy Loo. And Blazing Heavens won. Its price was 100 to 6.

Ginger sent a boy with a ten-shilling note to Educated Evans, and asked for his special for the next day.

Educated Evans sat up far into the night examining and analysing the programme for the following day, and at last discovered a certain runner, that not only had 14 lb. the worse of the weights, but enjoyed this distinction, that the training reporters of the sporting Press, who usually have something kind to say about every horse, dismissed him with a line: "Ours has no chance in the Tilbury Selling Handicap."

He saw also a paragraph in the following morning's newspaper that Star of Sachem—such was the elegant nomenclature of this equine hair trunk—was being walked to the meeting because his owner did not think that he was worth the railway fare.

Ginger came round to see Evans at his den; and Ginger was wearing a new gold chain and two classy, nearly-diamond rings, a new hat, and a tie of brilliant colours.

"Morning, Evans," he said briskly as he came in. "Thought I'd come and see you. Me and my young lady are going away to the seaside for our good old annual."

"Ha, ha!" said Evans politely.

"You've done me a bit of good, old boy." The snout laid a large, soft hand on Evans' shoulder. "But I want something better. Give me a stone certainty, and I'll put every bean I've got in the world on it, Evans, and you're on to a fiver. Is that fair?"

That's fair," said Educated Evans, his hopes rising.

"If we win, I'm buying a little public-house in Kensington," said Ginger. "My young lady's going to get a divorce from her husband for cruelty and desertion, and carrying on with the girl at the sweet shop; we'll put the two kids in a home, and there you are. So you see, Evans, it's a bit of a responsibility for you."

"It is," said Evans bravely; "and, speaking as one with a wide and vast experience, I appreciate same, and in the language of Lord Wellington at the battle of Waterloo, I shall only do my duty—Star of Sachem," he said slowly, deliberately, and with proper emphasis, "can't be beat in the Tilbury Handicap this afternoon.

"If that horse were poleaxed he could crawl faster than any of the others can run. I've had it from the boy that does him. They've tried him on the time test to be twenty-one pounds better than Ormonde. He's a little faster than The Tetrarch in the first five furlongs, and he stays. If you don't mind, I'll have the five pounds in advance, because I know a reliable bookmaker, and you mightn't get paid."

Mr. Vennett compromised with three pounds ten; and, miraculous as it may appear, Star of Sachem won by three lengths pulling up, and started at 20 to 1.

Educated Evans had his fiver on the third, which had been given to him by a man who knew the proprietor of a public-house where the owner called for his midday lunch, which was invariably served in a tankard.

It was drawing near to the end of the week when Mrs. Lee called at the police station, and had the good fortune to meet The Miller as he was coming out. Her eyes were red, and she was quivering with natural indignation.

"That fellow, Ginger Vennett," she began without preliminary, "has run away with the girl at the sweet shop, and I want him pinched for taking my wedding ring for the purpose. Of all the dirty, lying, falsifying, perjurious hounds in the world, he's the worst! He's a snout, Miller,' and you know it! Didn't he tell me that he gave away Modder? And to think that I've been nourishing a viper, so to speak, in my bosom—if you'll excuse the language; but this is not the time to be mock-modest.

"To think of all I've done for that man, and how I've turned out of my own room for him, and given him the best of food to eat when he was broke, and my poor, dear husband on the moor worrying his heart out about his poor, dear wife and dear innocent children. . . ."

When The Miller could get a few words in, those few words were of a nature which left Mrs. Lee in a condition bordering upon hysteria. Educated Evans was not in much better case when "The Miller called on him.

"They say he got twenty-two hundred pounds out of Isaacheim," said Educated Evans in a voice that trembled. "Twenty-two hundred—lovaduck! And I give it to him! And all I got was four pounds, and ten bob of that was snide! I had a wire from him from Margate today, and he wants to know what'll win the Brighton Cup.

"And I dare not send it, Mr. Challoner,"

he said earnestly; "I simply dare not send it for fear of the damned thing winning! There's one in the race that will die of heart disease if they go too fast, but if I send it to Ginger it'd walk home alone!"

"Try it," said The Miller urgently. "That woman says he's got such faith in you now that he'll do anything you tell him."

So Evans wrote a wire, which ran:

Little Sambo in Brighton Cup absolutely unbeatable. Take no notice of the market. fear nothing; Go for a fortune, and don't forget your old pal, Educated Evans.

At three o'clock, when the runners came up with the result, "Miller" and Evans stood side by side at the corner of Tottenham Court Road—the extent of "The Miller's" jurisdiction. Two boys came at once, and Evans snatched at the nearest and opened the paper with feverish haste —Little Sambo was unplaced!

"Gotcher!" chortled Evans in triumph.

The Miller was looking at his newspaper. He was reading *The Evening News*, Evans had *The Star*.

"What do you mean—gotcher?" snarled The Miller, and read:

All probables ran except Little Sambo!

5.—MR. KIRZ BUYS A £5 SPECIAL

In An inner waistcoat pocket, buttoned and rebuttoned, Mr. Jan Kirz, kept a five-pound note. Later he grew careless and carried it folded in the top right-hand pocket of that same waistcoat. He would have been wise to have burnt it, as some of the Scottish bookmakers burn their clients' money when the horses they back win at a long price. But he was mean, and the sight of a fiver blazing in the grate would have broken his heart.

Mr. Jan Kirz had, in his time, been American, Dutch, Swiss and Russian. His birthplace was unknown, but it is a fact that during the war he had lived for many months at Alexandra Palace whilst the authorities were disentangling the mystery of his origin. In the end he was released and ordered to report at the nearest police station at regular intervals.

About every other week during that period of strife, it was reported that he had been shot in the Tower. A fishmonger in the High Street, who, by reason of his sporting associations, hobnobbed with swells in the West End, had been shown (by a deputy assistant provost-marshal) a cartridge case with "Kirz" engraved on the outside. So that when Mr. Kirz came back to Camden Town, bearing no signs of having been executed, there was a great deal of disappointment.

Always a wealthy man, the owner of a fine house in Mornington Gardens, he grew in prosperity with the years, and was one of the most consistent, as well as one of the most unsatisfactory, of Educated Evans' clients.

For such was the perversity of fate that he only backed the losers that the learned man sent forth.

"Ah, my poor Effens," said Mr. Kirz sorrowfully, meeting the educated one—Evans had taken up a position at the corner of Mornington Gardens so that he couldn't be missed—"and to t'ink dat you gafe me Golly Eyes und I did not pack it! I t'ought of it fife minutes before der race und den I vergot! Ach! it is terriple hard luck. Und after packing two of your losers!"

Evans was not unnaturally annoyed, for he had an arrangement with Mr. Kirz whereby he drew the odds to a pound on every horse which his patron backed.

"I won't go so far as to say that it's capable negligence—to use a legal expression—on your part, Mr. Kirz," he said, "but I've got a mouth. And my information costs money. I got this horse from the boy that does him, an' *that* costs me a pony. I've got me office to keep up an' advertising, and one thing and another—"

"My poor Effens!" sympathised Mr. Kirz—he was a stout man with close-cropped hair, and was subject to asthma—"dis is derrible! But der nex' time you git me one, dere is der odds to *two* bound!"

So Evans had to be content.

Mr. Kirz was by profession a printer and stationer. His premises were known as "The Old England Cheap Printing Company," and he did a considerable sporting business, though it was rare to find his imprint upon the printing he sent forth. Hamburg and Continental philanthropists, anxious to benefit the British public to an incredible extent, found in Mr. Kirz a willing assistant. He specialised in lottery announcements, snide sweepstakes, and other documents of an illicit nature.

Everybody in Camden Town knew this: the police knew it as well as anybody, and had paid surprise visits to the Old England Printing Works. But by the side of the two machines engaged in this practice was a square opening in the wall, for all the world like a service lift. And at the first hint of trouble, every printed sheet and the forme from which it was struck was cast into the hole and fell to the cellar. And in the cellar was a large furnace which was kept going, winter and summer, to maintain the hot-water supply.

And that is what the police did not know—in fact, nobody knew it except three compositors whose names ended in "ski" (Mr. Kirz printed a Russian newspaper) and three machinemen whose names, curiously enough, concluded with "heim." And so Mr. Kirz grew wealthy, for, in addition to these, he had a valuable side line.

One morning The Miller called on Mr. Kirz at his handsome and palatial residence in Mornington Gardens, and, being a plain man, he came to the point at once.

"Mr. Kirz, you are in touch with all the wrong 'uns in London; who is working all this 'phoney' money?"

He used the American term for "counterfeit" because Mr. Kirz had originally come from the United States.

"Phoney money is derrible." Mr. Kirz shook his head gravely. "Dat is one of der most derrible dings dat a mans can do. It striges at der root of gommercial gonfidence—"

"Don't let us discuss high finance," pleaded The Miller. "Where does it come from? You ought to know; you do more snide printing than any two men, and all the dirt of the town comes through your hands. The Danish Lottery prospectus was your last. Now come across, Kirz. Who is the gentleman who is turning out fivers numbered B/70 92533?"

"Gott knows," said Mr. Kirz. "I haf offen tought dat Education Evans did somet'ing of dat—he has a quiet blace in Bayham Mews, hein? He goes to der racegourse where it is bossible to change—"

"Educated Evans is not that kind of man," said The Miller quietly; "it is one of the West End crowd. Is it Podulski? He named, one after another, certain of Mr. Kirz's acquaintances, and at each mention the stout gentleman shook his head.

"If I know, I tell," he said. "I would not soil my hands wit' such wickedness. *Und* as to *der* Copenhagen lottery, dat is not my business. I ask you to gome and see my plant—any tay, any night. It is a scandoulness dat I am evil spoken of."

"The Miller "had not hoped for any great success in this quarter, though he was certain that Kirz, who knew the foreign-speaking underworld, could have given him a hint. Most discreetly, he did not tell Educated Evans that suspicion had been attached to his fair name.

The Miller was not alone in his distress of mind. His unhappiness was shared by an Assistant-Commissioner of Police, several Superintendents, and the disorder even spread to the sacred precincts of Whitehall. There never were better forgeries than this batch of five-pound notes which had come into circulation, and had it not been for the fact that they all bore the same number detection would have been impossible.

The paper was perfect, the watermark, with its secret gradations, was copied exactly. The notes felt good and looked good, and had been unloaded, not only on the Continent, but in London itself. There was not a bookmaker who did not take two or three in the course of a week. They had been changed at banks, at railway stations, theatres, even at post offices, where five-pound notes are never tendered without involving the man who offers them in an atmosphere of suspicion.

In such moments of crisis, the Home Secretary sends for the Chief Commissioner of Police and says : "This is very serious," and hints that the responsibility rests with the Chief Commissioner. And that worthy passes the kick down until it reaches quite unimportant detective-constables.

The kick came to Sergeant Challoner with direct force, for the forgeries had appeared more frequently in Camden Town than elsewhere.

That evening he went in search of "The World's Premier Turf Adviser."

The western skies were streaked with *eau de nil* and the softest pink, and Educated Evans lounged, with his arms folded on the stone parapet, his chin resting on his elbow, absorbing the glory of the sunset. The Thames or the Albert Embankments drew him as a magnet attracts steel filings. The vague unease which disturbs the soul of genius was soothed to a dreamy languor, the dark and sinister thoughts that assail men of imagination were dissipated by the serenity of the scene.

Day after day, when business was slack or fortune turned a broad back upon his wooings, and the inexplicable failure of his selections had warped and soured his gentle nature, this man of learning turned his steps instinctively to the solace of the steel-grey river and the dun-coloured horizons of London. And here he would stand and dream, and watch with eyes that were comforted, yet did not see the ceaseless traffic that passed to Thames River through the Pool.

When his professional duties allowed, Sergeant Challoner would detach himself from his proper sphere and enjoy a twofold pleasure. For here he could satisfy his aesthetic yearnings and enjoy the society of one who, by reason of his erudition and intimate acquaintance with thoroughbred horses, was respected from Holloway Road to Albany Street. Sometimes the knowledge that he could find Evans in a certain place at a given time was of the greatest value.

Glancing sideways, Educated Evans saw the broad-shouldered figure approaching, but did not move.

"Making up a poem, Evans?" said The Miller," leaning on the parapet by his side.

"No, Mr. Challoner; poetry was never in my line—do you believe in divine guidance, if you'll pardon the expression?"

The Miller was startled.

"Yes, I believe in divine guidance. Why?"

For three nights in succession," said Educated Evans dreamily, "there's been a tip in the sky. Look at it! Pink an' green stripes—Solly Joel's got two in the Jubilee, an' the question is, which? Last month, when I was standing on this very spot, I see a black cloud and a white cloud on top of it, an' Lord Derby won the Liverpool Cup. Another time there was nothing but yeller and pink, and up popped Lord Rosebery's horse at Warwick. If that ain't fate, what is?"

The Miller was more than startled—he was staggered.

"I can't think of anything more unlikely," he protested, "than that Providence arranges the sunset for the benefit of your dirty-necked punters."

Evans shook his head.

"You never know," he said. "There's things undreamt of in your theosophy, as Horatio Bottomley said—I wonder how the old boy's gettin' on? What a lad! Don't it make you feel solemn, Miller, watchin' the river goin' down, so to speak, to the sea? Flowin' straight away to Russia an' Arabia, an' other foreign places until it forms the famous Gulf Stream that causes the seasons, summer an' winter. Carryin' the ships that go here and there—"

"Have you been drinking?" asked The Miller suspiciously.

"If I met a glass of beer in the street I shouldn't reckernise it," said Educated Evans, it's so long since I saw one. No, I'm dealin' with hypothesis an' conjectures. What won the three-thirty, Mr. Challoner?"

"Coleborn," replied The Miller, and Evans heaved a deep and happy sigh. That's the second I've given this week," he said almost cheerfully. "I simply didn't dare to wait for the paper. Any price?"

"Five to two," said The Miller. "I backed it."

A look of peace and calm lay upon the melancholy face of Educated Evans.

"What a beauty! "he murmured. "There'll be sore hearts in the synagogue tomorrer! Five to two. An' sent out on my five pound Job Wire to a hundred and forty-three clients!"

"How many?"

"Forty-three—an' *all* payers! I'm certain of ten, anyway. Nine, not counting Kirz, an' if he twists me again he's off my list for *good*!"

"Do you know anything about Kirz?" asked The Miller, regarding a passing tug with such a fixity of stare that nobody would have guessed that he had any interest in the answer. "What is he?"

Evans sniffed.

"It depends whether he acts honourable," he said cautiously, "as to whether he's an educated American gentleman or a dirty 'Un—if you'll forgive the vulgarity."

"Does a bit of funny printing on the quiet, doesn't he?" asked The Miller, still absorbed in the tug.

"I don't know anybody's business but me own," said Educated Evans, with emphasis. "As Looy the Fifteenth said to the Black Prince, so called because, bein' a lord, he swore he wouldn't wash his neck till Gibraltar was taken, 'Honny swar,' he says, 'key mally pence'—meanin' that if you don't stick your nose where it's not wanted, you won't get it punched. After which, accordin' to statements in the Press, he never smiled again. That's history."

"Sounds like *Comic Cuts* to me," said The Miller. "And it doesn't answer my question. What do you think about him?"

"I'll tell you tonight," said Educated Evans significantly.

In the evening he took his best tie out of the boot-box (wherein were stored his most precious possessions, such as a cigarette end that the Prince of Wales had thrown away and a racing plate worn by the mighty Bart Snowball, Prince of Platers), and hied him to Mornington Gardens. Mr. Kirz was not at home. Nobody knew when he would be home. Nobody knew where he was. Slam! The door closed in his face.

"Common slavery!" said Educated Evans, and proceeded to search the town.

Mr. Kirz was not at the Arts and Graces Club, and he wasn't in the resplendent private saloon of the White Hart, nor yet in the Blue Boar lounge. The dogged searcher turned westward, and by great good fortune overtook Mr. Kirz as he was coming out of the Empire. Mr. Kirz was wearing the garments of festivity. His shirt-front was white and glossy, and on his head was a shining silk hat.

"Ah! My poor Effens!" he began.

"Not so much of that 'poor Evans,'" snarled that exasperated man. "You 'phoned the bet when I was with you, an' unless Isaacheim's dead, you'reon!"

Mr. Kirz was embarrassed; there were with him two other gentlemen, and in the background hovered a lady in crimson chiffon velvet, who flashed and sparkled to such an extent that it appeared that she had been rolling down a diamond heap and most of them had stuck.

"Tomorrow, tomorrow, my Effens," said Mr. Kirz in a whisper. "I cannot dalk pusiness now."

"You owe me five pound," said Evans loudly. "You've kept me messing and mucking about for weeks, an' you're off my list! Pay me what you owe me, you perishin' 'Un, or I won't leave you!"

"My dear goot man —" began Mr. Kirz, holding up his hands in horror at this unsought publicity.

"An' don't start '*camaradin*' me, because it's no good. You're worse than Shylock Holmes, you are. Pay—me—what—chew—owe—me!"

Mr. Kirz, his face purple, his hands trembling, searched his pocket.

"Dake it!" he hissed. "An' neffer led me see your ugly face again! As for your dips, dey are rodden!"

Evans retorted long after his client was out of hearing, and would have continued retorting if it had not been for the arrival of a policeman.

"Hop it," said the man in blue.

Evans hopped it.

He was a happy man, and strode with a free step, his head held high, when he came back to his own land. So proud and haughty was he that he would have passed The Miller without noticing him.

"Come to earth—you!" said The Miller. "What's the matter?"

Evans turned back.

"I've got my dues out of that low alien," he said.

"And what were your dues, Evans?"

"Five of the best." Evans produced a crumpled note. "It's gettin' a bit thick when you've got to go down on your knees to ask for your own! "he said. "An' to think that the likes of me *fought* for the likes of him!"

"I don't remember seeing you on the Somme," said The Miller (who was there), "or hobnobbing with you at Toc H."

"I was a special constable," said Evans with dignity, and the reply brought a little needed laughter into The Miller's life.

"Let me see that fiver," he asked suddenly, and after a second's hesitation Evan passed it to him.

"There's no other policeman in the world that I'd trust with money," he said offensively.

The Miller looked at the note and whistled.

"Dud!" he said, and a cold shiver ran down the spine of Educated Evans.

"You don't mean it?" he quavered.

"I do mean it—look at the number, B/70 92533—it's the number of all the dud notes on the market. Let me keep this—"

"Let you keep it!" snorted Evans. "Am I sufferin' from lack of education and self-respect? I'm going to see this hero Kirz, an' I'm going to tear his pleadin' heart from his pleadin' body!"

"Language, language! "murmured "The Miller."

"I'm goin' to get reparations from Germany," said Evans more calmly, "even if I have to search his pockets, the same as the celebrated Lloyd George said. I'm goin'—"

"You're going to do nothing. Give me that note. You shall have it back."

"I don't *want* it back," wailed Evans. "I want money! "

It took a great deal of persuasion to induce him to part. He went home eventually, his outlook warped and blackened by the misfortune which had come to him.

Educated Evans lived in two rooms over a stable. The apartment was approached by a flight of stairs from the mews below, and the railed landing produced a slight balcony effect and added a touch of the romantic, which was very pleasing to Evans in his more sentimental moods.

He went in, slammed the door, and went to bed without troubling to light the gas. There was no need, for he invariably hung his clothes on the floor. He had fallen into a troubled sleep and dreamt.

It was about an august personage whom it would be improper to mention. He dreamt that he had been sent for to Buckingham Palace, and had travelled there in a coach of state, throwing his cards out of the window to the cheering throng. At the palace he had been arrayed in a long robe of pink and green stripes by a bearded gentleman, who had shaken him by the hand and insisted upon Evans calling him Solly, and then he had been ushered into a crimson and purple chamber with a black ceiling and gold-braided carpet, and the august person had bid him kneel. Evans sank gracefully to one knee, and the august person had said:

"Arise, Sir Educated Evans, England's Premier Turf Adviser and Sporting Awthority! And don't forget that Daydawn is a pinch for the Friary Nursery."

There was a thunder of applause. All the little princes were knocking their heels against the sideboard. So insistent was the noise that Sir Educated awoke and asked medievally:

"Who knocks?"

"Open the toor, Mr. Effens. It is Mr. Kirz—it is of der gr-reatest importance."

Evans rose and put on his trousers and shoes and lit the gas.

"Come in," he said, wide awake. "I suppose you've come to act honourable about that dud fiver?"

"Inteet I haf!" replied Mr. Kirz. He was pale and damp, and in his shaking hand he already held a five-pound note.

Evans took it.

"It was a gread mistake," said Mr. Kirz, holding out his hand expectantly.

"I knew I had dat bad one. And when I missed him I say, 'Oh, my Gott! I give it to Edugated Effens!' Where is it?"

Evans shook his head.

"The police have got it," he said.

Mr. Kirz went yellow and staggered against the wall.

"Mind that washandstand," warned Evans, "it's new. Yes, my friend 'The Miller's' got it—Mr. Challoner, that is to say, and a nicer man never drew the breath of life."

For The Miller was standing in the open doorway, and, following the direction of Evans' gaze, Mr. Kirz turned.

"I want you, Kirz," said The Miller. "Will you step round to the station and have a talk with our inspector?"

"I dit not know dat note was forged," said Mr. Kirz, quivering.

"It wasn't," said The Miller tersely. "It was a good one—the one you've been making plates from—I found the plant in your cellar at Mornington Gardens."

★★★★★

One of the principal witnesses for the Crown stepped into the witness-box and kissed the Book affectionately.

"What is your name and profession?" asked the clerk.

"My name's Educated Evans, and I'm commonly known as England's Premier Turf Adviser and the Wizard of North-West Three. I gave Braxted, Eton Boy (what a beauty!), Irish Elegance, Music Hall, Granely and Sangrail. . . ."

"You nearly got yourself *hung*," said The Miller after the proceedings were adjourned." And, by the way, I'd better give you another fiver for this one we've got—we shall want it as an exhibit. Kirz didn't give you another one, did he?"

"If he did," said the diplomatic Evans, "he owed me another—and more!"

6.—MICKY THE SHOPPER

Educated Evans was sitting in Regent's Park one morning, watching the ducks and waiting for inspiration. It was a day in late May, and the hawthorn bushes were frothy with blossoms, pink and white. There was sunshine on the yellow paths and a tang in the air, for the summer was late in coming, and the world was young and fresh, and smelt clean. And the entries for the Royal Hunt Cup were public knowledge.

Educated Evans was pondering the inexplicable workings of fate that had brought to favouritism for the Derby a horse that he was reserving for his £5 outsider, when he heard the steady pacing of feet, and, looking up, saw a broad-shouldered man with a straw between his teeth.

"Good-morning, Mr. Challoner," he said politely, and Detective-Sergeant Challoner sat down by his side.

"I was wondering whether Amboya can give St. Morden ten pound," said Educated Evans.

"I thought you were turning over some crime," said The Miller. "Amboya is a dog-horse anyway, and if you think you can forestall Yardley, you are booked for a jar."

Educated Evans pursed his lips thoughtfully.

"Mysteries are repugnant to me," he said, "though I've nothing to say against Yardley. The question is: *Is* this Amboya's journey? There's a lot of betting on the event—the foolish public dashes in without advice from experts, and prognosticators, with the result that Amboya is six to one. But will he or she win? I've got news about a Thing that will come home alone if he runs up to his trial—come—home alone."

"In a false start?" suggested "The Miller."

"In a true start," corrected Evans gravely. "This Thing could get left twenty lengths and stop to bite the starter and *then* win. It's the pinch of the century. Some of the widest men who go racing have been backin' this Thing for weeks—before the weights come—before the entries was published."

"I'll buy it," said the interested "Miller."

"That's the only way anybody will get it," stated Evans determinedly. "It's cost me many a sleepless night. I've been toutin' the stable an' watching this Thing at exercise, and the way he goes—with his head on his chest!"

"Forgive my ignorance," said The Miller, "but wouldn't he go as well if his head was at the end of his neck?"

"I'm speakin' metaphor or figure of speech," said Evans, lighting his cigar. It had the appearance of having been picked up after being severely trodden on. "It's Catskin."

The Miller made a scoffing noise.

"You've been listening to the newspaper boys, "he said scathingly. "Catskin has been a street corner tip for weeks. And it doesn't run."

Educated Evans raised his eyebrows.

"Indeed!" he asked politely. "And who might have told you that?"

"The owner," said The Miller. "I'll admit that he shouldn't know as much about it as you, but possibly he's had information about Catskin from the boy who does him. And he's under the impression that Catskin has picked up a nail at exercise and is lame."

"He's wrong," said Evans, with great calmness. "That horse will run and win. He's the kind of horse that a nail or two wouldn't worry."

"The trainer told Mr. Oliver," said The Miller, "that Catskin wouldn't run again this year; and the boy that does him says so, too," he added ingeniously.

This was indeed convincing. The owner might not know, the trainer could be honestly mistaken; but the boy who did Catskin was evidence beyond question.

"That Mulcay is *hot!*" said Evans, harking back to the trainer. And here he spoke so incontrovertible a truth that The Miller "could not contradict him.

Micky Mulcay came from Ireland, a country which has given us so many fine, sporting, open-hearted and honest trainers.

By this description Micky would not have been known to his intimate friends. If he had trained for the "clever division," or for dubious owners, he would not have lasted on the Turf for ten minutes. But he had the intelligence to accept in his little stable of Parlhampton only the horses of men of the greatest integrity, men whose names were synonymous with honour and straight dealing.

They made an excellent frieze about the wall of the Steward's room when he was called to explain the running of Cabbage Rose one hectic day at Kempton.

The Stewards accepted his explanation—("They ought to have given him somethin' from the poor box," said Educated Evans sardonically)—and thereafter none questioned his doings. Micky was a philosopher, who realised that life was short and money hard to come by. Over his desk was hung the motto, "*Make hay while the sun shines.*" And he made it—even when it was raining.

Owners who do not bet heavily like to see their horses win whenever they can. Micky liked to see them win when his wife, his brothers-in-law and a couple of trusted friends had slipped in as many wires to S.P. merchants as the Post Office could deal with. No wise man ever backed a horse from Micky's stable if Micky, his wife, his brothers-in-law and his trusty friends were on the course, however sanguine he was.

Micky was the man who invented the phrase : "Horses are not machines." It was Educated Evans who furnished the historic reply : "It's a good job for all concerned that they're not talking machines."

"That Mulcay is that hot," said Evans again, "he'd keep a room warm. Catskin could doddle it! But is Micky's money down?"

The Miller shook his head.

"I saw Lord Claverley at the Midland—I went down on duty, though why I give you intimate information I don't know," he said. "And Micky wouldn't shop his lordship."

The lips of Educated Evans curled in a sneer.

"Micky would shop his own young lady Sunday-school teacher," he said. "Every time he passes the Zoo the snakes stand up and touch their hats to him. That feller's so underhanded that he can steal with his toes. There's only one man he wouldn't shop, an' that's Micky Mulcay, bless him!"

Educated Evans did not say "bless him."

"I don't like your expressions of hate," said The Miller, rising to go. "Anyway, Evans, you can count out Catskin."

"If the boy that does him says so, I suppose it's right," said Evans, and, left alone to his own reflections, gave his mind up to the problem of the Derby Stakes.

A few days after the Derby was won, Catskin ran at a Midland meeting and was beaten by a moderate horse. He started at 6 to 4 on. His Hunt Cup price had been 100-6. It drifted to 25-1.

Evans observed the change with no great interest, until one afternoon, when he was strolling down Regent Street in order to be near the Piccadilly Tube when a Lingfield result came up, he saw Mr. Micky Mulcay and his brother-in-law. They were walking at a slow pace past the Piccadilly Hotel, and Evans, who never lost an opportunity of acquiring information, crossed the road and came very slowly past them, his eyes fixed on the ground, his mind apparently occupied with weighty matters.

And as he passed, he heard Micky say in his inimitable brogue

"Sure; try Hereford, but be certain, Dennis, that the post office is open on Wednesday. Some of these country offices—"

That is all Evans heard, and his heart beat thumpingly. Hereford. . . . . . post office. . . Wednesday!

Instinctively he filled in the gaps. They were backing Catskin S.P.! His soul grew jubilant at the thought of all that this knowledge meant to him.

And then Evans was seized with a sudden resolve to do something he had never done before in his life. That evening he left for Steyne-bridge, five miles from which historic market town was situated the training quarters of Mr. Mick Mulcay.

It is sad to relate that Educated Evans had never before seen a training ground, if we except Newmarket and Epsom. And the ways of stables were as much of a mystery to him as the breakfast tastes of Tut-ankh-Amen. Fortunately, he secured a bed at the inn which was nearest the stable more fortunately still, Catskin was the one horse in all the wide world that Educated Evans could have recognised without colours and number-cloth.

It was a bay with three white legs. But for this fact Evans might never have made the journey.

He was up at daybreak, and tramped across the downs to where, if local report be accurate, Mr. Mulcay exercised his string. And sure enough, soon after five, there appeared in the distance a long train of sheeted horses, moving at a hand canter.

When they had gone past him there came, at a terrific pace, three horses, the first of whom was undoubtedly Catskin. The little boy who rode the horse was trying to pull him up, and after he had passed Evans by a hundred yards he succeeded, and turning back to meet Mr. Mulcay himself, very red in the face, and galloping at full speed on his hack.

"What the hell do you mean by galloping the horse when I told you to canter?" he demanded furiously, and his ready whip fell on the small boy's shoulder.

Evans watched, interested, for the boy was the stable apprentice, Lakes, who usually rode Mr. Mulcay's horses when they were not try-ing as hard as they ought. He was still interested when Mulcay turned round and came trotting towards him.

"Who are ye?" he said violently. "And what are ye doing here? Get off my ground."

"If you'll allow me to argue the matter with you," said Educated Evans with dignity. "I—"

Smack.

The whip fell on Educated Evans' shoulders, and for a moment he was paralysed with wrath and astonishment. And then, with a roar, he leapt at his attacker. Mr. Mulcay might be a very dishonest man, but he was an excellent horseman, and the whip fell again, this time on a more tender portion of Mr. Evans' anatomy.

"I'll get you warned off for this!" snorted Evans. "I'll learn you, you—"

It would be unwise to record faithfully all that Educated Evans said on the spur of the moment and in the heat of his annoyance.

"I don't allow anybody to come touting my horses," said Mr. Mulcay with that sublime air of majesty which sits so easily upon an Irish trainer, and is even more appropriate in an Australian. "You get off and stay off!"

Evans very wisely obeyed. All the way back to town he was engaged in the humiliation of Micky Mulcay. In his imagination he saw the tyrant begging his bread on the street, and passed him by without so much as a tip for the next day's seller. But he carried with him another memory than his own embarrassment. He remembered the malignity on the face of Master Lakes, and the wild fury of that small boy struck a sympathetic chord in Educated Evans' nature.

He took the earliest opportunity of seeking out The Miller.

"That horse is going to win, Mr. Challoner," he said, "and it's up to me to spoil the blighter's market! When he saw me he nearly dropped dead! I'm sorry he didn't. He's got that horse all ready, and he's going to shop his pals for the Royal Hunt Cup as sure as my name is Educated Evans, the World's Premier Turf Adviser!"

"You should have kept away from Steynebridge," said The Miller wisely. "None of these trainers like to have their horses touted."

"I'll tout him all right," hissed Educated Evans, and when he was really annoyed, which was seldom, he was very annoyed. He would spend money—what was a pound here or there?—to bring his enemy to his knees.

He had, not so much a friend as a dependent, a man who had seen better days, an elderly, crimson-faced man, who was known as "Old Joe." As he had not been convicted, it never transpired what his other name might be. He smoked shag in a short clay pipe, helped potmen and lived on beer. Nobody had ever seen him eat anything else.

An Old Joe is attached to almost every public-house in Great Britain. They are the pensioners of the publican, a mysterious body of red-faced, greasy-collared guardian angels, who stand with their backs to the wall and brood on the days when carmen drove horses and horse feed was part of the refreshment that every pub supplied.

Educated Evans sent for "Joe, and he came uneasily from his self-imposed task of supporting the walls of the "White Hart."

"Me go down to Hereford "he gasped, shocked. "Why, I've never been out of London in my life, Mr. Evans."

"You'll go out now," said Evans firmly, and you'll do what I tell you."

He explained.

"Send me a wire to the paddock at Ascot the moment you see the number of telegrams put in by that perisher's brother-in-law. They won't be handed in till a quarter of an hour before the race. If you're in the post office then, you can't miss spottin' 'em. All I want you to do is to wire me the number of telegrams this here Mulcay's brother-in-law sends away."

Old Joe took a great deal of convincing, but, on learning that there were several public-houses in Hereford, and that West-country beer was of surprisingly good quality, he left. The journey was going to cost Educated Evans £4, but what was money?

The principal patron of Mulcay's stable was Lord Claverley. He was a man who plunged very occasionally and he plunged only on the advice of his trainer. If there was one thing of which Lord Claverley was certain before the Royal Hunt Cup, it was that Catskin would not win. He not only told his friends, he told his servants, he told his chauffeur; he whispered the words in the ears of illustrious princes and potentates. Catskin gradually drifted out in the preliminary market until it was either 40 to 1 or 33 to 1, according to the temperament and honesty of the layer.

Educated Evans very seldom went to Ascot. When he did, he invariably gave the paddock a miss; but on this occasion he decided that the circumstances warranted an extra outlay, and, with a groan, he paid the terrific sum demanded by the Ascot executive, and gained for himself a small chocolate shield, which, pinned to the lapel of his coat, admitted him either to Tattersall's or the paddock.

The Miller, in a top hat and smart morning coat, saw the unhappy figure leaning against the rails, and approached him.

"You're not in the Royal Enclosure this year, Evans?" he said.

"No, Mr. Challoner," said Evans, without annoyance. "My invitation didn't come. I wouldn't have known you," he added with respectful admiration. "You look like a gentleman."

"If I didn't think that insult was wholly unintentional," said The Miller, good-humouredly, "I should be offended. Well, have you backed your Catskin?"

"For every penny in the wide, wide world," said Evans, emphatically. "I've sent it out to three thousand two hundred and forty clients, and I've been sittin' up two nights doing it. This Catskin is not only a pinch, it's a squinch! It's the greatest certainty there's been since that hurdle race at Hurst Park—three runners and one trying. You know the one I mean."

The Miller shook his head.

"None of the stable are backing him," he said.

"The stable!" sneered Educated Evans. "I could tell you something that'd make your hair stand up. I could make your eyeballs roll! Mr. Miller, I'm going to see Lord Claverley."

The Miller stared at him.

"You'll get yourself pinched," he warned; but this threat had no effect upon Evans.

He knew Lord Claverley by sight, having seen his portrait in the illustrated newspapers, and when the saddling bell was ringing for the Hunt Cup, he saw his lordship walking alone, and seized the opportunity.

"I beg your pardon, m'lord," he said. touching his hat. "You've probably heard of me. I'm Educated Evans, the World's Prime Minister of Tippery."

Lord Claverley looked at him, and his eyes twinkled.

"Oh, you are, are you?" he said. "I'm afraid I can give you no tips, my man."

"I don't want any, me lord." Evan's voice was solemn and convincing. "I want to give you one. Back Catskin!"

For a moment Lord Claverley looked at him as though he were undecided as to whether he should call a policeman and have him thrown on or across the spikes to the course, or whether he should be greatly amused.

"You're wrong, my friend," he said, quietly. "Catskin isn't fancied. That's all I can tell you."

He was turning away, when Evans urgently caught his arm.

"Me lord," he said agitatedly, "don't you take any notice of what they say about Catskin; it'll win Mulcay would double-cross the ghost of his grandmother! I tell you it'll win, and it will win!"

Even Lord Claverley was impressed.

"You're altogether wrong, Mr.—er—Evans," he said. "But I'm afraid I can't discuss the matter with you."

Evans wormed a way through the elegantly dressed ladies at the rails to watch the field parade. Amboya was a hot favourite; Catskin, with the stable apprentice, Lakes, in the saddle, was at any price. The mere presence of an apprentice up, instead of the fashionable jockey who usually rode for the stable, was sufficient to put off 999 out of every thousand punters. But Evans was not put off. That stalwart man invested his last farthing at the longest price he could wring from the perspiring magnates of Tattersall's.

It was from the reserved lawn that he saw the race, and no very detailed description is necessary. Catskin was the first to appear above the crest of the hill; he stayed in front throughout, and he won in a hack canter by six lengths. Amboya was second.

Educated Evans trod on air as he rushed back to the paddock to see the winner led in. Three faces he saw. Mulcay's was green; he walked like a man in a dream. Lord Claverley's face was like thunder. Only on the cherubic countenance of the jockey was there a look of happiness amounting almost to ecstasy.

It was not a popular victory. That it was one of Mulcay's famous "shops" no man on the course doubted. Lord Claverley did not speak to Mulcay, but a look passed between them which made the trainer squirm. And then his lordship caught sight of Evans.

"You're the man I want," he said, and led the shabby figure away from the crowd. "Now tell me all you know about this. Why were you so certain this horse would win?" he asked.

He had to listen, with such patience as he could command, whilst Educated Evans recited his own virtues and the record of his past successes, and then he heard all that that tipster had to tell.

"You say he's backed this horse 'away'—from Hereford? Are you sure?"

"I can tell you in half an hour, me lord," said Evans importantly. "My agent at Hereford—I've got agents all over the shop and touts in every stable—"

"Well, what about him?" asked Lord Claverley impatiently, for he was a very angry man.

Half an hour later a bewildered Evans placed in the hands of his lordship a telegram he had received, and it ran:

Three hundred telegrams handed in, all backing Amboya....

★★★★★★

"Of course, it may be as you say, Mr. Challoner," said Educated Evans philosophically, "and it's very possible that Lakes *did* shop the stable by winning when he oughtn't to have been trying. I won't say it was from Lakes that I had my information if I did, you wouldn't believe me."

"I wouldn't," said The Miller, "because you'd be lying."

"It's very likely," admitted Educated Evans. "Perhaps Lakes was gettin' even with him, the same as I was. And to think that that perishing horse-sweater was backing another one all the time! That's dishonesty if you like. Downright thievery, I call it! But fifty to one! What a beauty! And all out of my own deductions. From information seen with my own eyes."

"Micky Mulcay has lost a lot of money," said The Miller, who also had sources of information, a little more reliable, however, than those which were tapped by his companion.

"I wish he's lost it all," said Educated Evans viciously. "All except eighteenpence—you can get a couple of yards of good rope for eighteenpence anywhere."

7.—THE DREAMER

It is a popular delusion that certain clubs in London have a monopoly of Turf transactions. "There will be a 'call over' at the Omph Club," says a sporting paper; "Tonight the Cambridgeshire card will be called over at the Zimp Club," says another. There is no mention of the Cheese Club in Camden Town, and you might imagine from the character of its membership that if there was any betting there it was so insignificant as to be negligible.

Yet this is hardly the case, for the Cheese was quite an important factor in the sporting world. There were certain big layers in the north whose agents never went south of the Euston Road; other layers of fame who made the Cheese their headquarters and kept their agents at the more pretentious clubs.

For the Cheese had come to be a vital clearing house, and even those great bookmakers, Notting and Elgin, did not disdain the Cheese when they had something particularly hot to lay off. You could get a "monkey" on a horse up to the "off" at the Cheese, and on big race days find men in the club who would take 4,000 to 500 in one bet.

And yet the membership was as mixed as any club in the world. Educated Evans was a member; Billy Labock, who laid £20,000 to £20 the back-end double, was a member: the Hon. Claud Messinger was a member—as hot a member as ever drew the breath of life.

"It seems to me," said Educated Evans despondently, "that such an article as domestic happiness and felicitous connubiality belongs to the Greek Calendar—in other words, *non est*, if you understand the language, Mr. Challoner? And yet Camden Town is full of happy couples."

Detective-Sergeant Challoner nibbled his straw thoughtfully.

"To be happily married, I admit, "continued the educated man, "you've not only got to be as broad-minded as a parson at a raffle, but you've also got to have the patience of Job—an' talking of Jobs, they're workin' one at Gatwick this afternoon—the boy that does the horse says he could fall down an' get up an' *then* win."

"Not Toofick?" The Miller was instantly alert.

"It is Toofick—he's the biggest certainty we've had in racin' since Tishy was beat. Help yourself, an' don't forget that I've got a mouth."

"You were using it to discuss matrimony —who are you thinking about?"

Educated Evans fished the stump of a cigar from his overcoat pocket and lit a match on the leg of his ill-fitting pants.

"Women may have the vote, but they'll never do that," he said. "It's a gift."

"If you know anybody in Camden Town who is happily married," said The Miller deliberately, "I should like to know his or her name."

"I could name hundreds," said Evans, and his melancholy face grew more dismal at the thought, "thousands even. I'm not talking about lovey-dovey happiness. When I see a couple goin' on as if they're not married, they usually ain't. I'm talking from the depths of my experience and education about people that the poets write about. Two minds with but a single horse, two hearts that bet as one—Tennyson or Kiplin', I'm not sure which. I haven't much time for poetry, what with interviewin' owners an' jockeys—"

"Let us keep to facts," interrupted The Miller. "Who is happily married amongst your extensive circle of victims, past and present?"

Educated Evans uttered a note of impatience.

"Would you say Mr. Joe Bean is happily married?" he challenged.

The Miller considered.

"His wife never strikes me as being hilariously pleased with life," he said.

"I don't know whether she drinks or whether she doesn't," said Educated Evans, "and it's not my business whether she gets hilarious—which every educated man knows means 'soused.' But she's happy. She told me the other day, when Joe was ill, that if he popped off she'd never lift her head again."

"Because she'd forgotten to pay Joe's insurance money," said the practical "Miller," chewing thoughtfully at the straw in his mouth. "She told *me* that! Said she'd never forgive herself, and that she hadn't been so careless since her first. Who else?"

"Mr. and Mrs. Hallam Corbin." Educated Evans pronounced the name with self-conscious emphasis. "You wouldn't know 'em, Mr. Challoner; they're out of our class—got a house in Ampthill Square. I know 'em because they're reliable clients of mine. Keep their own servant an' thinkin' of buying a motorcar. Class."

The Miller looked at his companion with a speculative eye.

"I know them too," he said shortly.

"Happily married, are they? Well, well."

Mr. and Mrs. Hallam Corbin had swum into the ken of Educated Evans as a result of a publicity campaign undertaken by him. This consisted of a four-line foot-of-column announcement in all the leading sporting dailies:

Well-Known Commissioner,
in touch with leading stables, would like to hear from
a few reliable sportsmen of unimpeachable integrity.
Only educated people need apply.

In consequence he had heard from very unexpected persons, amongst whom was Mr. Hallam Corbin. Miraculously enough, the horse which that well-known commissioner, Educated Evans, despatched to such reliable sportsmen of unimpeachable integrity won in a trot at 6 to 1, and as the odds were promised to 10s. by some two hundred "unimpeachables," he made a profit of £60. He ought to have made £600, but punters aren't honest—not even as honest as tipsters.

Amongst those who acted honourable (Mr. Evans' own expression) were the Hallam Corbins. They sent him a fiver, which was more than his due, and asked him to lunch at 375 Ampthill Square, which was a distinction to Evans beyond his wildest dreams. For Ampthill Square is more than respectable—it is class. People who live in Ampthill Square are Rich, have Areas, and have as much as two quarts of milk by the first delivery. Some—indeed many—have motor-cars, wear evening dress, even when they are in their own houses and are not expecting visitors.

Educated Evans had known Ampthill Square from his childhood. He had walked through it on summer Sunday evenings with and without a young lady—little did he think that he'd ever be asked in by the front door—and to dinner! Even though the dinner was called lunch.

Mr. Corbin was of stout build and had livid pouches under his eyes. Mrs. Hallam Corbin was stoutish and girlish. She was the sort of lady who was all good spirits and go. You would never imagine she was more than fifty-four; at the same time— and here Mrs. Corbin would have been profoundly annoyed had she known—you would not have thought she was any less.

Educated Evans dressed himself with unusual care. For this occasion he removed the sheaf of newspapers which permanently occupied his overcoat pocket; he wore his pink and grey tie, and a stand-up collar which cut his throat every time he turned his head.

A trim and good-looking maid opened the door to him, and he was ushered into a drawing-room of surprising splendour. A mirror which must have been worth several pounds, a carpet of surpassing luxury, gilt armchairs and settees, large and valuable palms standing on pedestals that could not have been bought out of a five-pun note, rich velvet curtains, and on the mantelpiece a confusing gold clock, the hands of which pointed to half-past six (morning or evening, Evans did not know), and surmounted by two ladies, who had evidently just come straight from the bath and had mislaid their camisoles, reclining back to back. All these things Educated Evans took in with a glance.

Then Mr. Corbin came in, both hands outstretched.

"My dear Evans," he said, "I'm glad you have come. My dear wife will be glad."

"It's very kind of you," said Evans, coughing, self-conscious of the pink and grey tie on which the dazed eyes of Mr. Corbin were resting. "I must say I'm not much of a society man, though naturally, mixin', as I do, with high-class trainers an' jockeys an' owners an' what not, I've seen a bit of life. I always say," said the learned man, "that class is all right in its way, but give me education an' understandin'. A lot of people that go about wearin' high collars and top hats haven't got the slightest idea about physical geography, etymology, syntax, or prosody, whilst if you get 'em on the subject of history their mind's a blank, if you'll pardon the expression."

"Yes, yes," said Mr. Corbin, who evidently took no interest in the precious gift of education. "Here is my dear wife."

His "dear wife "floated in at that moment and fell upon Educated Evans to an alarming extent.

Contrary to the statements that had been made about the fabulous wealth of the Corbins, the lunch was not served on gold plates, nor were there twelve courses. Mr. Corbin ate a chop; Mrs. Corbin toyed with a cutlet; Evans, who did not feel that it was polite to eat in public, nibbled an occasional pea.

When lunch was over the mystery of the invitation was solved.

"We've been discussing you," said Mr. Corbin soberly, as he pushed back his plate and handed his cigar-case to Evans. As you probably know, Mr. Evans, my dear wife is clairvoyant."

Evans nodded politely.

"Though I'm not a family man," he said, "I'm glad. I think everybody ought to have one or two children—"

"By 'clairvoyant,'" explained Mr. Corbin hastily, "I mean she is gifted with second sight—she has visions of the unseen world."

"Goodness gracious!" said Evans, impressed.

"She has the power," said Mr. Hallam Corbin gravely, "of projecting her spirit to the infinite and of roaming at will upon the planes of ethereal nothingness

"Good Gawd!" said Evans, and shifted his chair a little farther away from this alarming lady.

She is in daily communication with Napoleon, Julius Caesar, Alexander the Great—you have heard of these famous people?"

A faint smile lighted the gloom of Educated Evans.

"History is my weakness," he admitted. "Give me a history book an' I'll read for hours. Solly Joel had a horse called Napoleon, but naturally I'm too educated to make any mistake about your meaning. You're referrin' to the celebrated French King that said '*Up, guards, and at 'em!*' in the days of the far-famed French revolution

"Exactly," replied Mr. Corbin, a little dazed. "Exactly. Now, my love"—he turned to his wife—"perhaps you will tell our friend?"

He excused himself and went out of the room. Mrs. Hallam Corbin's smile was sweet, her manner most gracious.

"I'm sure you'll think we're very mercenary, dear Mr. Evans," she said, and before Educated Evans could decide in his mind what was the correct thing to say, she went on, "but my dear husband thinks that he ought to make money out of my dreams."

"Your dreams, ma'am?"

She nodded.

"I dream winners," she said simply. Twice, often three times a week, I dream winners. I see numbers hoisted in the frame: I see colours flash majestically past the post I hear voices saying 'So-and-so has won.'"

"Dear, dear! said Evans, wondering why, in these circumstances, Mr. Corbin subscribed to his five-pound special. As though she read his thoughts, she continued:

"I suppose you are asking yourself why we seek your clever advice? Mr. Evans, it is because we could not believe our good fortune, and we simply *had* to have our dreams confirmed by the cleverest Turf adviser of the day!"

Evans coughed.

At this point Mr. Corbin returned to take up the narrative, and became severely practical and friendly.

"Now, Evans, my boy, what is the best way of exploiting my dear wife's gift? She had an extraordinary dream last night—saw a horse win at Gatwick. A horse called Too Thick. We've searched the programme, but no such horse is entered."

"Toofick!" said Educated Evans, trembling with excitement. "And he's a certainty! That horse could fall down and get up and *then* win!"

"Indeed!" said Mr. Corbin. "How stupid of me! And she dreamt that Lazy Loo was second and Mugpoint was third. That is the amazing thing about her dreams. Now the point is, Mr. Evans, my dear wife doesn't wish to go into the tipping business at all. In a woman it would be unseemly."

"Exactly," said Evans. "I quite understan'."

In truth he understood nothing.

"What I have been considering is whether one could not *back* the horses that my dear wife dreams about—back for large and—er—generous sums. The question is, where?"

"The Cheese," said Evans promptly.

Mr. Corbin knit his brows, puzzled.

"The Cheese—you don't mean the Cheshire Cheese?" he asked.

"Never heard of the Cheese?" demanded Evans, almost shocked.

"Why, you can see it from your back winder!"

Whereupon Mr. Corbin insisted upon taking him to a classy room at the back of the house, and here, through a gap between two other houses, the decorously red-curtained "library" of the Cheese was plainly visible. It was called "the Library" because it contained four tape machines, a bulletin board and a nearly complete set of Ruff's *Guide to the Turf*.

"Well, well!" said the astonished Hallam Corbin. "I had no idea that that was a betting club. Well, well! Is your eyesight good, Mr. Evans?"

For a moment Evans was taken aback.

"My eyes," he said emphatically, "could see two jockeys winkin' at one another at the seven-furlong post, I'm that keen-sighted."

"Splendid," murmured the other, and led the way back to the dining-room. Mrs. Hallam Corbin had disappeared.

"My wife always lies down after lunch. It is then that her best dreams occur. Which is very awkward, Mr. Evans, because she seldom dreams a winner until within a few minutes of the race. It must be the transmission of thought—a psychic phenomenon which has puzzled the greatest experts of the day. Now if I only had a friend at the—what did you call the club?"

"The Cheese," said Evans.

"If I only had a friend there to whom I could *signal* the horse of her dream Why, we could make a fortune "

Evans thought.

"It could be done," he said; "but how?"

"Let me consider," said Mr. Corbin; and Evans remained silent whilst the mighty brain of Mr. Hallam Corbin revoluted. "I have it," he said at last. "I will have a number of large cards painted in numbers. I will give you every morning a programme, and against each horse I will place a number. If we can see the club, the club can see us—though, of course, my dear Mr. Evans, nobody but you must know the secret of my dear wife's clairvoyance. When you have seen the number you will back the horse and you shall have ten *per cent.* of the winnings."

Educated Evans left Ampthill Square with a thick roll of twenty pound notes and a feeling that he also was walking on those ethereal planes which were as familiar to Mrs. Corbin as High Street, Camden Town.

His first act was to get a newspaper, and, reading the result of the "job" race, he gasped. Too Thick won, Lazy Loo was second, Mug-point third! Exactly as the smiling lady had dreamt! And she couldn't have known, because she had been with him all the time.

Even bookmakers who knew Educated Evans and respected him as a source of profit, hesitated to lay him £200 to £80 Lamma a couple of days later until Evans produced the money. The bet was hardly laid before the tape clicked the "off." And Lamma won. The next day he had £300 to £90 Kinky. It won.

On the following Tuesday, after making a few insignificant losses ("You'd better not back winners every day," said the practical Mr. Corbin, "or they won't lay you."), he took £200 to £50 Kellerman in a seller at Hurst, and there was time for the layer to 'phone away part of his bet before the "off" was signalled.

"They tell me you're backing them for yourself, Evans," said The Miller, meeting him that afternoon after racing, "and that you're making a lot of money."

"Not a lot," said Evans complacently. Just enough to keep the celebrated wolf from the fold. Money means nothing to me," he said. I never forgot the famous King Morpheous. Everything he laid his mitts on turned into gold and silver, owin' to which he got filled teeth, and everybody thought he was American."

Detective-Sergeant Challoner pulled meditatively at his pipe.

"Where are you getting your information, Evans?" he asked softly. "From the angels?"

"From the boy that does 'em," said Evans soberly.

He had an interview with Mr. Hallam Corbin that evening to pay over some money, and Mr. Corbin's manner was short, and not especially sweet. Nor was his manner towards Mrs. Corbin exactly in accordance with Evans' idea of domestic serenity.

"I told you to put fifty pounds on the horse Mrs. Corbin dreamt," he said, "and you say you only put a pound on. And I've got information that you took two hundred to fifty from Bill Oxford—don't you start twisting *me*, Evans! "

"Twist you?" said the outraged Evans. "However can you think of such a thing! Why, if I went misbehavin' towards Mrs. Corbin's dreams I should expect to be struck by one of them Clara's Voyages—"

"It's like this, Mr. Evans," began Mrs. Corbin sharply; "our expenses are very heavy—"

"You shut up!" snarled her husband; and it began to dawn on Educated Evans that they were not as happily married as they might be.

"Don't do that again, Evans," said Mr. Corbin, paying over the ten pounds which represented the agent's commission.

The next day when Evans offered to take £150 to £30 Hazam Pasha in the three o'clock race, his bet was refused.

"I don't know how you beat the tape, Evans," said the principal layer not unkindly, "but you do. And I can't afford to lay you."

Evans left the club soon after and found The Miller waiting on the doorstep.

"What is Number Six on your list?" asked The Miller.

Evans professed astonishment.

"Now take the advice of an old soldier," said The Miller. "Leave the Corbins to stew in their own juice. I've been watching the back of their house, and I saw the number put up at the window—six. And you saw it too. It isn't the tape, because they beat the tape."

He shaded his eyes and looked up at the roof, and saw what he had not seen before—a strand of wire between two chimney-pots. Behind the Corbins' house (which they rented furnished) was a mews, and in Mr. Corbin's coach-house stood a large and antiquated motorcar, the blinds of which were invariably drawn when it passed through the gates of any racecourse that was honoured by its presence. And on the top was something that looked like a wire hanger.

Sergeant Challoner inspected the car that night with the aid of a key that opened the garage. The interior was still warm from the heat which valve lamps create. The seat had been removed and certain instruments and batteries completely filled the interior.

Mr. Corbin had finished dinner when The Miller called.

"I'm summoning you for being in possession of a wireless transmission set without a licence from the G.P.O.," said The Miller. "I could pinch you for conspiracy to defraud, but I won't. You and your gang have been sending wireless results from the course, and you've made a fortune."

Mr. Corbin glared at the officer.

"I'd have made a fortune if that rat-faced-tipster hadn't twisted me!" he snapped.

"There's no honesty in this world," sighed Evans when he heard the news, "Fancy him a-making me a party to a low-down swindle! It's disgusting!"

"You can ease your conscience by sending your ill-gotten gains to the Temperance Hospital," suggested "The Miller."

"I wouldn't be such a hypocrite," said Educated Evans.

8.—The Gift Horse

Men may acquire fame in a night, but reputation is a thing of slower growth. Mr. Evans did not earn the coveted prefix of "Educated" in a day, or a week, or yet a year. The sum of his learning totalled through the years, and behind his title lay a whole mine of information delved by him and distributed gratis to the world.

Once there had appeared on the stage of a London music-hall a human encyclopaedia who answered instantly and accurately any question that was flung at him by members of the audience. Thus, if you had any doubt as to the exact date of the Great Fire of London or the name of the horse that won the Derby in 1875, you secured admission to the music-hall at which this oracle appeared and squeaked or roared your question, to have whatever doubts you might possess immediately dissipated.

Educated Evans had never appeared in the glare of the footlights, but standing in a graceful attitude at the bar of the White Hart, his legs crossed easily, one elbow resting on the zinc-covered counter, he had from time to time settled bets, delivered historical orations and corrected misapprehensions.

Furthermore, he had framed letters to obdurate creditors, indited warning epistles to offensive neighbours (not his neighbours but the neighbours of those who had sought his services) and had prepared defences to be read from the dock. These latter invariably began: "My lord and gentlemen of the jury, I stand before you a poor and hardworking man who has been led astray by evil companions."

These defences often brought tears to Evans' eyes as he wrote them, a sob to the throat of the unfortunate prisoner who read them, though the effect upon judge and jury was, alas! of a negligible character.

It was the day after such a defence had been read in the dock of the Old Bailey by one "Simmy" Joiner that Evans, wandering disconsolately along the Hampstead Road, his mind entirely occupied by the contemplation of his affluence, came face to face with Inspector Pine.

"Good-morning, Evans," said the old inspector gently, and Mr. Evans woke from his reverie with a start.

"Good-morning, sir," he said rapidly. "I was just thinking whether I would come down to the Brotherhood meeting tonight. I'm beginnin' to feel the need, if I might use that expression, of a little religion."

Inspector Pine shook his head sadly. He was, as has already been explained, a Christian man, and took a leading part in certain social movements assigned to bring spirituality into the lives and souls of small punters.

"I fear we shall not see you, Evans," he said "tomorrow is our gift meeting."

The predatory instincts of Evans were awakened.

"I'll come, sir," he said respectfully, "though it won't be for the gift. I'm willin' to take anything you give me, because it's in a good cause—"

"You are mistaken, Evans," said the inspector gently. "At tomorrow's meeting we will *receive* gifts. Money or articles that can be sold for the good of our great racecourse mission. We will accept even a portion of your ill-gotten gains."

The light of interest died out of the learned man's eyes.

"I'll have a look round, sir," he said; "bein' hard up, I can't subscribe as I'd like to."

The inspector frowned.

"A liar is worse than a thief!" he said sternly. "I happen to know that you have made a great deal of money from your disgusting tipping business!"

Educated Evans hastened to explain.

"It's like this, Mr. Pine—" he began, but the old man interrupted him.

"Evans," he said sombrely, "there are two things that will bring a man to ruin—bad company and horses! The time will come, Evans, when you'll hate the sight of a horse."

"Personally, I prefer motorcars, Mr. Pine," said Evans, anxious to propitiate.

"The sight of a horse will drive you to despair. You'll shudder when you see one. Today you wallow in your ill-gotten gains, but the pinch will come!"

"It's come, Mr. Pine," said Educated Evans eagerly; "Light Bella for the two o'clock race tomorrow—help yourself! It's been kept for this—not a yard at Birmingham! Get your winter's keep, Mr. Pine!"

But he spoke to the winds. Inspector Pine had stalked majestically on his way.

Sergeant Challoner, C.I.D., heard from his superior's own lips and with every evidence of sympathy the story of Evans' obduracy.

"Disgusting, sir," he agreed, shaking his head. "What did you say was the name of the horse that was winning tomorrow?"

"I didn't trouble to remember," said the inspector suspiciously.

"Why do you ask, sergeant?"

"Curiosity, sir," said the sergeant.

Mr. Pine scratched his chin reflectively.

"What a splendid thing it would be," he mused, "if one could fight this gambling curse with money wrung from the very people who encourage and thrive upon it, eh, sergeant?"

The Miller thought so too.

"What a—er—*tour de force*—I'm not quite sure whether or not that is the phrase—it would be if one could act upon the information of this rascal and—er—"

"Exactly, sir." The Miller's face was blank. It was exceedingly difficult not to laugh.

Just as soon as he could get away he went in search of Educated Evans, and ran him to earth on the doorstep of the "White Hart's" saloon bar."

"Not only have you demoralised the proletariat of Camden Town," complained The Miller, "but you have corrupted the police service— the inspector wants your next £5 special."

Educated Evans beamed.

"But I think it is only fair to warn you that if your snip doesn't come off he'll get you ten years," said The Miller, and Mr. Evans was not unnaturally annoyed.

"That's against the lore," he said testily; "it is laid down in Magnum Charta that you cannot lose if you can't win. There's historical instances, such as Oliver Cromwell—"

"Never mind about Oliver Cromwell," said The Miller; "what is this snip of yours for tomorrow?"

"Light Bella," answered Evans promptly: "this is the squinch of the season. Don't back it till the last minute, or you'll spoil the price. This is the biggest racin' certainty since Eager beat Royal Flash. This horse could fall on his back an' wag himself home with his tail! He's been tried twenty-one pound better than Captain Cuttle—help yourself!"

"Is it a he or a she?" asked the puzzled Miller.

"I'm indifferent," said Evans.

Racing was at Hurst Park on the following day, and Educated Evans was a passenger by a comparatively early train. He invariably travelled first class, for Mr. Evans was partial to "toney" society. And, anyway, nobody worries about examining tickets on busy race-days, though of late the inspectors have shown a marked aversion to allowing passengers through the barriers on the strength of an ante-dated platform ticket.

The carriage filled up quickly, and Evans, ensconced in a corner seat (as usual) with an early evening paper widely opened to hide him from the view of passing officials, found himself in goodly company. There was Lecti, the jockey, and Gorf, the trainer, and a couple of men whom he took to be Stewards of the Jockey Club; they spoke so definitely and so authoritatively. (They were, in fact, racing journalists, but Evans could not be expected to know this.)

Seated opposite Evans was a stout, military-looking gentleman, who fixed the tipster with a cold and unfriendly stare.

"Nice morning, sir," said Evans briskly. He had a happy knack of making people feel at home.

"Is it?" said the other icily.

"Very interesting race that two o'clock selling," said Evans, "and to anybody without information an inscrutable problem. 'Appily, I know the boy that does a certain candidate—"

"If you talk to me I shall hand you over to the police!" said the cold, military-looking man in his chilliest military manner.

Educated Evans shrugged his shoulders. Even education is no protection against vulgar abuse.

The day was in many ways a memorable one. He had brought with him forty-eight pun ten, and it was his intention to take five hundred to forty about Light Bella. Two sets of circumstances prevented his carrying his plan into execution. The first was the fact that Light Bella opened at 7 to 4 the second was his tardy arrival in Tattersall's owing to a heavy shower of rain that drove him into cover. Light Bella was 5 to 4 when he plunged into the human whirlpool that surrounded the only bookmaker who was willing to lay that price, and he had taken 50 to 40 when the bell signalled the start.

He climbed to the stand and had the mortification of seeing Light Bella beaten a head for third place.

"Not a yard!" hissed Evans, and all within range of his voice agreed with him—except a few who had backed the winner.

There was one miserable satisfaction, and that, in his own inimitable language, was that he had not "blued the parcel."

He strolled, oblivious to the falling rain, towards the paddock and came to the sale ring just as the steaming winner was knocked down to its owner.

"I will now sell Fairy Feet, by Gnome, out of Pedometer," said the big auctioneer in the rostrum, and Evans recognised the voice. It was the military-looking gentleman who had treated him with such discourtesy. Evans edged into the crowd with a sneer upon his expressive face.

"Who'll start me at a hundred?" demanded the auctioneer. "Fifty? Well, ten—?"

"Ten," said a voice, and the bidding for the weedy-looking animal that had entered the ring rose slowly to 25 guineas.

"Twenty-five?" said the auctioneer, looking straight at Evans; and then to the surprise of that learned man he nodded.

Evans, who was nothing if he was not a gentleman, nodded back.

"Thirty," said the auctioneer. Somebody bid thirty-five, and the man in the rostrum nodded to Evans.

"I saw you the first time," said Evans, and nodded back.

"Forty," said the auctioneer, and a few seconds later the hammer fell. "What's your name, sir?"

Evans nearly dropped. The auctioneer was speaking to him.

"Educated Evans," he answered, and heard like a man in a dream.

"Sold to Mr. Ted K. Evans."

Evans often debated to himself at a later date what he should have done. He might have run away. He might have disclaimed any responsibility; he might have done so many of the things that were afterwards suggested to him.

Instead, numbly, like a man under the influence of an anaesthetic, he paid £42.

And the worst was to come. He had scarcely paid when his elbow was nudged by a small boy. Attached to the small boy by a leading rein was Fairy Feet.

"Who's your trainer, sir?"

Evan's jaw dropped. Only for an instant did he lose his self-possession, and then he took the rein.

"Don't ask questions," he said, and led the leggy animal away.

The paddock was emptying, for the rain was pelting down.

Evans looked round wildly and then moved towards the gate.

"Excuse me, sir," said the new owner to the gateman, "do you happen to know where I can leave this horse?"

The staggered gateman shook his head.

"Where do you train?" he asked.

Camden Town," said Evans vaguely.

"Why don't you take him home?" suggested the gatekeeper; and it seemed a very good idea.

The glow of ownership descended upon Evans as he trudged up the muddy road toward Hampton Court Station. It wasn't such a bad idea after all. In his mind's eye he cast new advertisements.

Educated Evans!
Racehorse Owner and the World's Premier Sporting Prophet.
Owner of Fairy Feet, Winner of the Steward's Cup.

He stopped dead in the middle of the road, and, turning, surveyed his purchase. There was a look of infinite sadness in the eyes of Fairy Feet. It almost seemed as if the intelligent animal realised the amazing absurdity of Evans supposing that it could win anything.

"Come on," said Evans, and the docile creature followed him to the railway station. There was no need for the lead rein. Fairy Feet would have followed Evans anywhere except to a racecourse, for Fairy Feet hated racecourses and was as firm an opponent to the practice of horse-racing as Inspector Pine.

"I want to get this horse to Camden Town," said Evans. The station-master looked dubious.

"We haven't a spare horse box, but we'll get one down tomorrow," he said. "Why don't you walk him home?"

The idea had occurred to Evans, and, as if to encourage him, the rain had ceased to fall. He was passing over Kingston Bridge when the rain began again. He was footsore, weary, sick at heart. Searching the examples of human suffering which his education presented, he could recall no more horrible experience.

At eight o'clock that night a bent and weary figure shuffled into Bayham Mews, followed in a sprightly fashion by a light-hearted thoroughbred racehorse.

Fortunately, young Harry Tilder, who does the horses of Jones and Bonner, the cash butchers, was on duty, and Evans fell upon his neck.

"Got a racehorse, Harry," he gasped. "Paid a thousan' pounds for him! Can you put him up an' give him a bit of meat or something till the morning?"

Young Harry looked at Fairy Feet in the waning light, then he looked at Evans.

"Can't do it, Mr. Evans," he said. "I don't want to be mixed up in this."

"But he's mine!" wailed Evans. "I bought him for a thou—for forty guineas."

"You said a thousand just now," said Young Harry. "It can't be done.

75

Take him round to Bellamy's."

But Mr. Bellamy, the horse-dealer, would have none of it.

"I've kept honest all my life," he said, "and I'm not going to change my plans. I don't want to say anything against you, Evans, but I know that you've been in trouble before."

★★★★★

Inspector Pine had often attempted to persuade The Miller to attend the meetings of the Brotherhood, but hitherto his efforts had failed. Sergeant Challoner had a sense of humour, and a sense of humour is an effective bar to hypocrisy. But he had evaded his obligations so often that he decided on this occasion to keep a promise— often made and as often broken.

The Brotherhood held their meeting in a little tin hall in a turning off Great College Street. Here were planned the programmes for the various great race meetings. Here, pale and long-haired young men laboriously painted banners with holy words and bore them forth amidst the unnoticing throng, and very proud were the bearers of banners that they were not as other men.

Inspector Pine was in the chair, and, after the meeting had been solemnly opened, he presented the accounts of the year.

"There is, my dear friends," he said, "a heavy deficit. Perhaps some friends who are outside our fold will come to contribute their mite"—he looked down at The Miller, and that uncomfortable man went red and felt in his pocket—"but in the main we must depend upon our own efforts. It may not be gold or silver nor precious stones that our brethren will care to offer. But whatever you contribute will be welcome."

The gifts in cash were few; in kind, many. A red-faced brother brought to the platform a steel fender amidst loud applause. Another member of the Brotherhood carried up a sack of potatoes. One fell at The Miller's feet, and he picked it up. It was not of the finest quality.

Yet another member of the audience brought a pot of jam—almost every one brought something.

The Miller, remembering a spasmodic gramophone that he had and which only went when it felt so inclined, regretted that he had not brought it with him. At last the final gift had been brought up, and Inspector Pine rose and beamed upon the congregation.

"I am glad to say" he began, when the door at the end of the hall was flung open violently and a man staggered in.

He was drenched from head to foot, and one lock of hair fell saucily over his long nose. Behind him, wet and shining and surveying the hall and its occupants with interested and intelligent eyes, was a lank quadruped.

"Ladies and gents," said the bedraggled stranger, "I'm well known to most of you, bein' Educated Evans, the famous and celebrated Turf adviser, an' I've brought a little gift."

A profound silence met this remarkable announcement.

"There's them that say you can get tired of horses," said Educated Evans pushing back his lock, "and they're right This here horse is the celebrated and far-famed Fairy Feet, sired by the Tetrarch and dam'd by everybody that's ever had anything to do with him—he's yours!"

So saying, he dropped the leading rein and slipped from the room, slamming the door behind him.

Fairy Feet looked round, and then with a neigh of anguish as she realised the base desertion, lifted her hind legs and kicked the frail door into splinters.

Running out into the street The Miller saw Educated Evans flying down the street with a dark horse hot in pursuit. Probably Fairy Feet had never run quite so fast as she did that night.

9.—STRAIGHT FROM THE HORSE'S MOUTH

It Is generally believed in Somers Town that a policeman would "shop" his own aunt for the sake of getting his name before the magistrate, but this is not the case. A policeman. being intensely human. has what the Portuguese call a "*repugnancio*" to certain jobs.

Sergeant Challoner, C.I.D., was called into the office of his superior and entrusted with a piece of work which revolted his soul— namely the raiding of Issy Bodd's flourishing ready-money starting-price business, which he carried on at his house off Ossulton Street.

Complaints had been made by a virtuous neighbour.

"Tibby Cole," said The Miller. "He's annoyed because Issy caught him trying to work a ramp on him, and one of Issy's minders gave him a thick ear."

"My dear Sergeant!" said the shocked Inspector Pine. "There is really no reason why you should employ the language of Somers Town."

The Miller went forth to his work in no great heart. He was too good a servant of the law to send a warning, and he came upon the defenceless Issy at a most compromising moment.

"I'm very sorry, Bodd," he said, as he effected the arrest. "I'll take all the slips you've got—you can get bail, I suppose "

"You couldn't have come on a better day," said the philosophical Mr. Bodd. "All Camden Town's gone mad over Sanaband, and as I never lay off a penny, it looked as if I was going through it."

Sanaband, as all the world knows, started a hot favourite for the Northumberland Plate and finished last but one, and everybody said: "Where are the Stewards?"

Thousands of people who had had sums varying from a shilling to a hundred pounds on the favourite, gnashed their teeth and tore their hair, and said things about Mr. Yardley, the owner and trainer of Sanaband, which were both libellous and uncharitable.

Bill Yardley himself saw the finish with a whimsical smile, and, going down to meet the disgraced animal, patted his neck and called him gentle names, and people who saw this exhibition of humanity nodded significantly.

"Not a yard," they said, and wondered why he was not warned off.

Yardley in truth had backed Sanaband to win a fortune, but he had spent his life amongst horses and backing them. He knew that if Sanaband had been human, that intelligent animal would have said:

"I'm extremely sorry, Mr. Yardley, but I've not been feeling up to the mark this past day or two—you probably noticed that I did not eat up as well as usual this morning. I've a bit of a headache and a little pain in my tummy, but I shall be all right in a day or two."

And knowing this, Yardley neither kicked the horse in the stomach nor did he tell his friends that Sanaband was an incorrigible rogue. He casually mentioned that he had fifteen hundred pounds on the horse, and nobody believed him. Nobody ever believes trainers.

"What's the matter with you, you old devil?" asked Mr. Yardley, as he rubbed the horse's nose, and that was the beginning and end of his recriminations.

In far-off Camden Town the news of Sanaband's downfall brought sorrow and wrath to the heart of the World's Premier Turf Adviser and prophet, and the situation was in no sense eased by the gentle irony of Detective-Sergeant Challoner, whose other name was The Miller.

"I do not expect miracles," said The Miller, "and I admit that it was an act of lunacy on my part to imagine that you could give two winners in a month."

"Rub it in, Mr. Challoner," said Educated Evans bitterly. "How was I to know that the trainer was thievin'? Am I like the celebrated

Mejusa, got eyes all over my head?"

"Medusa is the lady you are groping after," said The Miller, "and she had snakes."

"Ain't snakes got eyes?" demanded Educated Evans. "No, Mr. Challoner, I got this information about Sanaband from the boy that does him. This horse was tried to give two stone an' ten lengths to Elbow Grease. My information was, that he could fall down—"

"*And* get up, *and* win," finished the patient Mr. Challoner. "Well, he *didn't* fall down! The only thing that fell down was your reputation as a tipster."

Educated Evans closed his eyes with an expression of pain.

"Turf Adviser," he murmured.

The whole subject was painful to Evans. Just as he had re-established confidence in the minds and hearts of his *clientèle*, at the very moment when the sceptics of the Midland Goods Yard at Somers Town were again on friendly terms with him, this setback had come. And it had come at a moment when the finances of Educated Evans were not at their best.

"It's a long worm that's got no turning," said Educated Evans despondently, "an' there's no doubt whatever that my amazing and remarkable run of electrifyin' successes is for the moment eclipsed."

The Miller sniffed.

"They never electrified me," he said.

"Two winners in ten shots—"

"*And* five seconds that would have won if they'd had jockeys up," reproached Evans. "No, Mr. Challoner, my education has taught me not to start kicking against the bricks, as the saying goes. I'm due now for a long batch of losers. If Sanaband had won—but it didn't. And I ought to have known it. That there thieving Yardley's keepin' the horse for Gatwick."

The sneers that come the way of an unsuccessful Turf adviser are many. There is an ingratitude about the racing public which both sickened and annoyed him. Men who had fawned on him now addressed him with bitterness. Hackett, the greengrocer, who only a short week ago had acclaimed him great amongst the prophets, reviled him as he passed.

"You put me off the winner," he said, sourly. "I'd have backed Oil Cake—made up my mind to back it, and you lumbered me on to a rotten five to four chance that finished down the course! It's people like you that ruin racing. The Stewards ought to warn you off."

"I'm sorry to hear you say that, Mr. Hackett," said Educated Evans mildly. "I've got a beauty for you on Saturday—"

Mr. Hackett's cynical laughter followed him.

A few yards farther on he met Bill Gold, an occasional client and a 'bus conductor.

"I wouldn't mind, Evans," he said, sadly, "only I've got a wife and eight children, and this was my biggest bet of the year. How I'm going to pay the rent this week Gawd knows! You ought to be more careful, you really ought!

It was a curious circumstance, frequently observed by Educated Evans, that his clients invariably had their maximum wager on his failures, and either forgot to back his winners or had ventured the merest trifle on them. In this they unconsciously imitated their betters, for it is one of the phenomena of racing that few ever confess to their winnings, but wail their losses to the high heavens.

Misfortune, however, has its compensations, and as he was passing through Stebbington Street he met a fellow sufferer.

"Good-morning, Mr. Bodd," said Evans respectfully—he was invariably respectful to the bookmaking class. "I suppose you had a good race yesterday—that Sanabad wasn't trying."

Mr. Issy Bodd curled up his lip.

"Oh, yes, I had a good day," he said sardonically. "Three hours at the station before my bail come, and a fine of fifty and costs—and six hundred slips destroyed and every one of 'em backing Sanaband.

I've had a crowd round the house all the morning getting their money back on the grounds that if you can't win you can't lose. The public knows too much about the rules to suit me. It's this popular education, Evans, and novel reading that does it. If I hadn't paid out, I'd have lost my trade, though how I'm going on now, heaven only knows."

He looked at Evans with a speculative eye, listening in silence as the educated man recited his own tale of woe.

"That's right," he said, as Educated Evans paused to take breath. "You've struck a streak of bad luck. I don't suppose you'll give another winner for years, and I don't suppose I'll have another winning week for months."

They stared at one another, two men weighted with the misery of the world.

"It would be different if I was in funds," said Evans. "If I could afford to send out a classy circular to all clients, old an' new, I'd get 'em back. It's printing and advertising that does it, Mr. Bodd. My educated way of writing gets 'em eating out of my hand, to use a Shakespearean expression. I'm what you might term the Napoleon Bonaparte of Turf Advisers. It's brains that does it. I'm sort of second-sighted, always have been. I had to wear spectacles for it when I was a boy."

Mr. Bodd bit his lip thoughtfully. He was a business man and a quick thinker.

"A few pounds one way or the other doesn't make any difference to me," he said slowly. "You've got to put it down before you pick it up. What about a share in my book, Evans?"

Educated Evans could scarcely believe his ears.

"Not a big share—say three shillings in the pound," said Bodd, still speaking deliberately. "Your luck's out, you won't be giving winners for a long time—I've studied luck and I know. Most of your Somers Town mugs bet with me. That last big winner you sent out gave me a jolt. And it doesn't matter much whether you give winners or losers—you can't hurt yourself. A little punter is born every minute. *And* I'd put up the money for all the advertising."

The sinister meaning of Mr. Issy Bodd was clear, and Educated Evans felt himself go pale.

"Get out a real classy circular," Issy went on, "with pictures. There's nothing like pictures to pull in the punter. Get a picture of a horse talking. It's an idea I had a long time ago. Have the words 'Straight from the Horse's Mouth!' Silly? Don't you believe it! Half the people who back horses haven't seen one—especially since motor-cars came in. Me and Harry Jolbing have got most of the street business in Camden Town, and Harry's had a bad time, too."

"Do you mean that I'm to send out losers?" asked Evans, in a hollow voice.

"One or two," said the other calmly. "Anyway, you'll send losers. It's worth money to you. If you do the thing well, and with your education you ought—we ought to get a big win."

Evans shook his head.

"I tried to give losers to a fellow once," he said, "and they all won."

"You couldn't give a winner if you tried," said Mr. Bodd decidedly. "I know what luck is."

That evening Educated Evans sat in his library, preparing the circular. He was the tenant of one room over a garage. When he slept, it was a bedroom; when he ate, it was a dining-hall; but when he wrote, it was library and study.

And thus he wrote:

STRAIGHT FROM THE HORSE'S MOUTH
That sounds ridiculous to anybody who doesn't know
EDUCATED EVANS
(The World's Premier Turf Prophet).
But with Educated Evans that phrase has a meaning of the
highest importance and intelligence!
It means that he's got the goods!
It means that he's in touch with secret information!
It means that his touts and army of investigators
have unravelled a great Turf Mystery!
What a beauty!
What a beauty!
What a beauty!
THE BIGGEST JOB OF THE YEAR!
Get back all your losses! Double your winnings!
Put down your maximum!

There was more in similar strain.

Mr. Issy Bodd helped. He got a friend of his to draw a horse's head. It was a noble head. The mouth of the fiery steed was opened, and from its interior came the words:

I shall win at 10 to 1!

The misgivings of Educated Evans were allayed at the sight of this masterpiece.

To some two thousand five hundred people this circular was despatched. Most of the names were supplied by Messrs. Bodd and Jolbing, and the words "*Put down your maximum*" were heavily underlined.

Despite the exceptionally low price at which the peerless information was offered, the response was not encouraging.

"It doesn't matter," said Mr. Bodd. You can send them the horse, whether they pay or not."

The race chosen was the Stockwell Selling Plate at Sandown, and the selection of the horse occupied the greater part of the day before the race. A committee of three, consisting of Educated Evans, Mr. Bodd, and Mr. Jolbing, a prosperous young man who wore diamond rings everywhere except on his thumbs.

"Polecat?" suggested Evans. "That horse couldn't win a race if all the others died."

Mr. Bodd shook his head.

"He was a job at Pontefract last month," he said. "I wouldn't be surprised if he popped up. What about Coal Tar?"

"Not *him*!" said Mr. Jolbing firmly. "He's just the kind of horse that might do it. He's being kept for something. What about Daffodil? He finished last at Windsor."

Educated Evans dissented.

"He got left," he said. "Daffodil's in a clever stable, and Mahon rides, and they like winning at Sandown."

"What about Harebell?" suggested Mr. Jolbing. "She's never finished in the first three."

"She's been leading Mopo in his work, and Mopo won at Newcastle," said Mr. Bodd. "That horse could win if they'd let her. No, I think the best one for you, Evans, is Grizzle. He's been coughing."

Evans smiled cynically.

"The boy that does him told me that Grizzle is fit and fancied. In fact, Grizzle is the very horse I should have tipped for the race."

The entry was not a large one, and there remained only five possibles, and two of those were certain to start first or second favourites.

"What about Beady Eye?" asked Mr. Bodd.

"It doesn't run," said Evans, "and there's no sense in sending a non-runner."

"Gardener?" suggested Mr. Jolbing, laying a glittering finger on the entry. That's your horse, Evans."

But both Educated Evans and Mr. Bodd protested simultaneously.

"Gardener belongs to Yardley, and you know what he is," said Evans reproachfully. "I wouldn't be surprised to see Gardener win. The only horse that I can give is Henroost. He *couldn't* win!"

Here they were in complete agreement, and the committee broke up, leaving Evans

to do the dirty.

That evening, with all the envelopes stamped and addressed and ready for despatch, Educated Evans strolled out for a little fresh air and exercise. At the corner of Bayham Street he met Mr. Hackett, the eminent greengrocer. Mr. Hackett was in wine, for it was early-closing day and he had spent the afternoon playing an unprofitable game of nap at his club.

"Oh! there you are, you perishing robber!" he sneered, planting himself in Evan's path. "You ruiner of businesses! Educated! Why, you haven't got the education of a rabbit!"

Had his insults taken any other form, Educated Evans might have passed him by in contempt. But this slur upon his erudition roused all that was most violent in his usually amiable character.

"You're a nice one to talk about education!" he sneered, in return. "I could talk you blind on any subject—history, geography, or mathematical arithmetic!"

"A man who sells lies—" began Mr. Hacket insolently.

"It's better than selling caterpillars disguised as cabbages and rotten apples," said Evans heatedly. "It's better than selling short-weight potatoes to the poor and suffering—"

And then, before he could realise what was happening, Mr. Hackett, all his professional sentiments outraged, hit him violently on the nose.

In three minutes the most interesting fight that had been seen in Camden Town for many years was in progress. And then a strong hand gripped Evans by the collar, and through his damaged optic he saw the silver buttons of London's constabulary.

The Miller was in the station when Evans and Mr. Hackett were charged with disorderly conduct, to which, in Mr. Hackett's case, was added the stigma of intoxication; and, in his friendly way, the detective went forth in search of bail. It was impossible, however, to discover the necessary guarantee for Evan's good behaviour. He could neither approach Jolbing nor Bodd; and when The Miller returned with the information Evans was frantic.

"I've got some work to do tonight, Mr. Challoner," he wailed. "Three thousand tips to send out!"

The Miller hesitated. He was going off duty, and he had a genuine affection for the little tipster.

"What are you sending out, Evans?"

"Henroost, for that seller tomorrow. It ought to go before eleven o'clock," moaned Evans. "Couldn't you find anybody? Couldn't you stand bail for me, Mr. Challoner? I'd never let you down."

The Miller shook his head.

"An official is not allowed to go bail," he said. "But I'll see what I can do for you, Evans. I suppose they've not taken the key of your expensive flat from you?"

"The key's under the mat, just outside the door," said Evans eagerly. "Henroost—don't forget, Mr. Challoner. If you get somebody to do it for me, I'll never be grateful enough."

At half-past eleven the following morning Educated Evans addressed a special plea from the dock with such good effect that the magistrate instantly discharged him. He did not see The Miller who was engaged in investigating a petty larceny; but, hurrying home, he was overjoyed to discover that the table, which he had left littered with envelopes, was now tidy.

He had spent a very restless night, for the occupant of the adjoining cell was an elderly Italian with a passion for opera, who had sung the score of *La Boheme* from the opening chorus to finale throughout the night.

Educated Evans lay down on his bed and was asleep instantly. The sun was setting when he rose, and after a hasty toilet, realising his responsibility, he went out to discover the result of the great race.

A glance at the result column in the *Star* filled him with satisfaction and pride, though he had at the back of his mind an uneasy feeling of disloyalty to his *clientèle*. The race had been won by Coal Tar, which had started at ten to one, and Henroost was unplaced. Thus fortified, he strolled forth to meet Mr. Bodd, and came upon him in Great College Street and the face of Mr. Bodd was darkened with passion.

"You dirty little twister!" he hissed. "Didn't you say you'd send out Henroost? You cheap little blighter! Didn't I put up the money for your something so-and-so circulars? Didn't I pay for the unprintable stamps that you put upon the unmentionable envelopes that I bought with my own money?"

"Here, what's the idea?" began Evans.

"What's the idea!" roared Mr. Bodd, growing purple in the face. "You sent them out Coal Tar! It won at ten to one, and every one of your so-and-so clients had his so-and-so maximum—don't let Jolbing see you, he'll murder you!"

Dazed and confounded, Evans bent his steps to the police station, and met The Miller as he descended the steps.

"Excuse me, Mr. Challoner," he faltered. "Didn't you send Henroost?"

The Miller shook his head.

"No, I sent Coal Tar. Just after I left the station I met one of our inspectors from Scotland Yard, who had had the tip from the owner. Evans, your luck's turned!"

"As a tipster—yes," said Evans, and weeks passed before The Miller quite understood what he meant.

10.—The Goods

It is an axiom that the best-laid plan of mice and man frequently falls to the earth with a dull sickening thud. So far as man is concerned, the truism holds, though as to the disappointments and setbacks of mice we lack exact information.

Mr. Charles Wagon was not a great trainer in the sense that he filled the eye of the racing public. He was master of a small stable in Wiltshire, and had, as his principal patron, a Kentish Town publican (who was also a sinner).

He won few races, but when he did win, the horse was the goods. It had twenty-one pounds in hand and nitro-glycerine in its stomach, for nitro is a great stimulant of sluggish racehorses, and under its influence a high-spirited thoroughbred does almost everything except explode.

Mr. Wagon came up to town to lunch with his principal patron, and they sat together in the gilded hall of an Oxford Street restaurant, and the patron, a gentleman who had not seen his feet for years, except in photographs, was inclined to be fulsome.

"I'll say this of you, Wagon, that you're a perfect wonder! Your stable costs me twelve hundred pun' a year, but it's worth it. Now, what about this Little Buttercup?"

"He's as fit as hands can make him, and you can put your money down fearlessly," said. Mr. Wagon.

He was justified in his optimism. Little Buttercup had run six times and had never finished nearer than fourth, because Mr. Wagon was taking no risks. When a horse of his won, there were no "ifs" or "buts" about it. There was never an uneasy moment when it looked as though something was coming up on the inside to beat it. He preferred wet days or hot days, when a perspiring flank did not show or was excusable, and, above all, he preferred a six-furlong seller.

"Nobody knows anything about it," he said. "My head lad's safe, and I've got such a fat-headed lot of boys that if they saw a winner they wouldn't know it."

The patron fingered his empurpled cheek. The thing is," he said, "that this horse mustn't be amongst the arrivals or the probables. If my pals see that he's arrived they'll want to know all about it. If he's not in the list I can always say I didn't know it was running—see what I mean?"

Mr. Wagon nodded.

"I'll borrow a motor-box and send it over in the morning," he said.

"Don't worry about that."

"And there mustn't be a penny for him on the course," said the publican (and sinner). "I can get everything on away. He'll win all right?"

Again Mr. Wagon nodded.

"Don't fret yourself about that," he said "give him a livener just before the race, and he'll dance home."

"There's another thing," said the publican (whose name was, most inappropriately, Holyman), "keep them tipsters and touts off your ground. There's a fellow called Educated Evans round our way who's always nosing round for tips. It's people like that who ruin horse racing. The Jockey Club ought to do something."

"Trust me," said Mr. Wagon.

In the next few days the training establishment which housed that equine giant, Little Buttercup, was the home of mystery. Little Buttercup was ridden by his trainer, and the horse was galloped at unlikely hours.

Mr. Holyman need not have feared Educated Evans. That worthy man was beyond asking for tips. His luck was out, and it was all the more annoying, even maddening, that, passing the fish shop of Jiggs and Hackett, he had been moved to enter and to offer the sceptical Mr. Jiggs certain advice which had materialised. Evans had sent a loser to his dwindling list of clients, and by word of mouth had given a winner to a notorious twister—and this at a moment when he was reduced to choosing horses by the process of adding up all the motor-car numbers he saw and selecting a horse that came to that particular number in the published list.

"7341," muttered Evans, as a 'bus whizzed past. Seven and three's eleven, and four's fifteen, and one is sixteen. Sixteen is one and six, and one and six is seven."

Then he would look down a handicap and choose the most likely seven.

He despised himself, but something had to be done. The fickle goddess of fortune must be lured into the right way. Men whose luck is dead out do things that they would not care to confess even to their intimates. Educated Evans spent whole days adding up the numbers of cabs and cars and buses, and on a certain morning was obsessed by the numeral 9.

Nine was the very last number he saw at night—the first that greeted his eyes when he came out to breakfast one sunny morning.

Indeed, it was the 19th of May, and Educated Evans, realising this remarkable coincidence, chose the ninth horse in the Braxted Selling Welter at Birmingham.

That morning Detective-Sergeant Challoner, C.I.D., strolled into Mr. Stubbins' coffee-shop off Ossulton Street, and a dozen people nodded politely as he sat down and ordered a cup of tea and a tea-cake.

"Good-morning," said The Miller, genially, to his *vis-à-vis*. "Nice morning, Mr. Clew."

"Very nice, Mr. Challoner," said his *vis-à-vis*. "It's a treat to be alive."

"It is indeed," agreed The Miller. "I saw you last night in the High Street, didn't I?"

"Very likely," said Mr. Clew, who was a large man in the greengrocery. "I usually go out with the missus for a breather."

"Thought I saw Young Harry with you?" suggested the detective, as he sipped his tea. "How is he getting on?"

"I haven't seen him for months," replied Mr. Clew emphatically.

"Where is he living now?" asked The Miller, in a careless, conversational tone. Now everybody, or nearly everybody, in the shop knew that Young Harry was "in trouble." He had also been in the coffee shop half an hour before the detective's arrival, but, yielding to the earnest advice of friends, had gone elsewhere.

"Don't know what he's doing now," said Mr. Clew. "Living in the south of London, I understand. He's got a job."

"I want to get him another," said The Miller truthfully, for Young Harry had broken and entered enclosed premises, to wit the stables of Grudger Bros., the eminent bakers, and had feloniously removed therefrom six horse blankets, a set of harness, two motor lamps, an inner tube, and a tin of petrol, the property of the aforesaid Grudger Bros. And he was wanted. And, what was more important, would be caught, for Young Harry was

like hundreds of other Young Harrys, he "hid" himself by going to stay with his brother-in-law, whose address the police knew.

The little thief is the best friend of the police. He catches himself.

The Miller did not come to the coffee shop for information. He came for Young Harry. He knew very well that every friend of Young Harry would be suffering from myopia and loss of memory, and that if he had stood before them that morning they would not have seen him, and if he had told them just where he would be at a certain time they would have forgotten the fact.

The Miller was sipping his second cup of tea when Educated Evans drifted in. and on his sour face was a mask of gloom.

"Young Harry—no, Mr. Challoner, I haven't seen him since the day the young princess married the highly-respected Viscount Lazzles."

(Educated Evans had a few minutes before passed Young Harry at the corner of Stebbington Street.)

He took the place vacated by Mr. Clew and ordered one hard-boiled egg and a cup of coffee.

"How is the trade, Evans?" asked The Miller.

Educated Evans raised his eyes from the business of egg chipping.

"It would be good if people acted honourable," he said bitterly: "but acting honourable is a lost art. When the celebrated owner of Franklin an'Vilna and other four-legged quadrupeds—which is a foreign expression, meaning horse—dug up Come-and-Have-One, the highly renowned Egyptian, he was delving, so to speak, into the past, as it were, when sportsmen *was* sportsmen and acted honourable, paying the odds to five shillings or ten shillings, accordin' to the class of information."

"I doubt if the tipsters flourished in the days of the Pharaohs," said The Miller, biting off the end of a cigar.

"I bet they did," said Evans confidently. "There's always been fellows that told what was going to happen. What about Moses? Him that his mother found in the bulrushes and kidded it belonged to her aunt? What about Aaron, who went and predicted that his sons should cover Tattersall's like the grass on the field? What about—"

"Who amongst your ragged-seated *clientèle* hasn't been acting honourably?" asked The Miller.

"Jiggs, the fishmonger, for one. I went specially in to see him yesterday, just as he was takin' the appendix out of a sturgeon, and I said: 'Mr. Jiggs, you've got to have your maximum on Flying Sam,' I said. 'This horse has been tried to beat Harritown at ten pounds.'"

"And did he stick his knife into you? asked The Miller.

Evans shrugged his shoulders rapidly.

"Flying Sam won at 'eights,'" he said simply. "Information *v.* Guesswork. Knowledge *v.* Picking 'em out with a pin. And what did I get for it? A cod's head—it cost me eightpence to disinfect my room afterwards. It shatters your confidence. And I've got a Fortune in my pocket! I've got a horse for a race tomorrow that can only lose if the race is abandoned. This horse is 'The Goods.' I've been waiting for him all the season. They tried him last Saturday after all the touts had gone home, and they brought Golden Myth from Newmarket, and the horse *slammed* him. Won his trial with his head on his chest, pulling up."

"Not Golden Myth," murmured The Miller, gently. "He's at stud."

"They brought him out of stud," said Evans. "It was either Golden Myth or some other horse. The boy that does him is the nephew of my landlord's cook, so I *ought* to know."

"What is it?" asked The Miller, his curiosity fired.

"Little Buttercup," said Evans, in a confidential whisper—"The Goods! And don't forget I've got a mouth, Mr. Challoner."

He strolled along toward Euston Road with The Miller, and it was at the juncture of that thoroughfare that the detective said :

"Evans, I'll introduce you to the king pippin of your illicit profession—Mr. Marky!"

The man he addressed was walking briskly toward King's Cross Station. He was a tall man, expensively attired, and at the mention of his name Evans gasped.

"Not *the* Marky, Mr. Challoner?" he said, in an awe-stricken whisper, and found himself shaking hands like a man in a dream.

"Glad to meet you, Mr. Evans," said the newcomer. "In the same line of business as me, are you? Well, I hope you have better luck than I've had lately."

In the presence of such majesty Evans was dumb. For Wally Marky was the greatest of all the sporting prophets. He was the man whose advertisements covered whole pages of the sporting press—Wally Marky, the Seer of Sittingbourne—Wally Marky, England's Supreme Turf Adviser—Wally Marky, who never charged less than the odds to two pounds, though he didn't always get as much.

"Evans has got a beauty today," said The Miller. "The Goods! Had it from the owner, didn't you, Evans?"

Evans nodded, and wished he was a million miles away. To deceive his *clientèle* was one thing; to ring a wrong 'un on the great Marky, with his thousands and tens of thousands of paying clients, was another. At the thought of the awful responsibility the tongue of Educated Evans clave to the roof of his mouth.

"What is it?" asked the interested Marky.

"Little Buttercup," said Evans hollowly. "Trained by Wagon, who dopes his horses. I've been on the look-out for that one. It hadn't arrived this morning. I wonder—"

Mr. Marky frowned.

"You've had it from a good source? I've a good mind to try my luck with it—excuse me."

He turned away to the nearest telephone booth, and Evans began to breathe freely. In five minutes his shattered confidence had returned.

Educated Evans became more and more enamoured of the child of his fancy. Until that morning he had hardly known of the existence of Little Buttercup, and had certainly never heard of Mr. Greenly, under which name the bashful publican raced. Even The Miller, who was not usually impressed, went away with a sense of opportunity.

It was the last despairing effort of Educated Evans. He hurried from shop to shop; he flitted through the Midland Goods Yard until he was summarily ejected by a policeman; he called on every client, possible and impossible: and the burden of his tale was the passing swiftness and the inevitable victory of Little Buttercup. And, in course of time, he came to the Flamborough Head, that magnificent palace of glass and mirrors, whereof the reigning monarch was the apoplectic Mr. Holyman.

Mr. Holyman was in the bar, counting out little stacks of change for his barmaids to use; for he was one of those men who trusted neither his right hand nor his left.

"Good-morning, Mr. Holyman."

Mr. Holyman turned his bovine glance upon Evans.

"Morning, Evans," he said, almost cheerfully. "I haven't seen you around here for a week. You'll have something with me?" he asked.

"You'll have something with me, Mr. Holyman," said Evans, with quiet triumph. "I've got a horse for you."

Mr. Holyman shook his head.

"No, you haven't got any horses for me, Evans," he said good-naturedly. "Tips are out of my line, as you well know."

"This isn't a tip," said Evans, lowering his voice to an agitated quaver, "this is a gift from heaven! It is a thing I have been waiting for all the year! This horse has been tried to give twenty-eight pounds to Town Guard, and the money's down."

"What's the race?" asked Mr. Holyman, his interest mildly aroused.

"The Braxted Selling Plate, at Birmingham." Evans looked up at the clock. "You've got ten minutes to get on and share the good fortune that I've brought to the mansion and the hut, to the highest and the lowest.

"I'll tell you something else, Mr. Holyman," he said. "It's never happened to me before. Who do you think I met this morning?" Here Evans was telling nothing but the truth. "Marky!"

He stepped back to observe the effect of his words. The name of Marky is known throughout the sporting world.

"I met Marky—introduced to him," said Evans, with the satisfaction that the average man might display were he relating a chance meeting with the Prince of Wales. "He shook hands with me, quite affable and gentlemanly. His luck's out, too. Us tipsters are having a bad time. So I gave him Little Buttercup—"

"What!"

Mr. Holyman's face turned a dark, rather vivid, shade of blue.

"You gave him what?" he howled.

"Little Buttercup. It's a pinch. The owner's a friend of mine—"

Mr. Holyman glared helplessly round, and the first thing he saw was a pewter pot. It missed the head of Educated Evans by inches.

There were only two runners for the Braxted Selling plate. Mr. Wagon's jockey had weighed out before the appalling fact became known that Little Buttercup was Marky's Fear-Nothing £5 Special. And Little Buttercup won by the length of a street. It took two mounted policemen and a stable lad to get him back to the paddock, and then they had to bring a knacker's cart to frighten him. The price was 8 to 1 on.

"What a beauty!" sneered "The Miller "when he met Evans the next morning, and Educated Evans shrugged his shoulders more rapidly than ever.

11.—THE PERFECT LADY

"If," said Inspector Pine, emphasising his argument in his best platform manner by hammering his palm with his clenched fist, "if horseracing isn't—er—pernicious and brutalising, if it isn't low, sergeant, how is it that it attracts the criminal and the law-breaker?"

It was a favourite argument of his. This he had expounded on a dozen platforms.

"If racing isn't the sport of rascals,"—his grey head wagged in an ecstasy of righteousness—"why don't you see God-fearing men and women on the racecourse?"

Sergeant Challoner, C.I.D., had heard all this before, but had not troubled to supply the obvious answer.

"The trouble with a good many people, sir, is that they think that if they do not like a thing, or if some form of amusement or recreation doesn't appeal to them, it must be bad. There are people I know who would shut up all the fried-fish shops because they don't like fried fish. I can give you a hundred names of God-fearing people who follow racing."

He reeled off a dozen, and there were an illustrious few even the inspector could not deny.

"It isn't because it's racing, it's because racing has many followers that the thieves follow it. If a million people follow the game, it is certain, by the laws of average, a few thousand of them will be thieves—just as it is certain that sixteen thousand will have appendicitis and thirty-five thousand bronchitis. The few thousands look a lot because they are the only fellows you and I hear about."

The inspector shook his head.

"I'm not convinced," he said. "Look at that rascal Educated Evans."

"Evans is honest. He hasn't always been lucky, and he got two months for a larceny that he knew nothing about. I am certain that if he could afford to pay for the proceedings, he could get the conviction quashed."

"I am not convinced," declared the inspector.

"Because you don't want to be," said The Miller—but said it to himself.

It was perfectly true that Evans knew thieves, and that association with lawless men was an everyday experience. He knew them because he lived poorly in a poor neighbourhood, and the majority of thieves are poor men. They do not thieve because they are poor—they are poor because they thieve.

Racing appealed to most of them because it held the illusion of easy money.

Hundreds of dishonest women go to church for the same reason. A dismal face and a whining tongue produce coal tickets and blankets and small gifts of cash. If the annual conference of the Royal Society were the occasion of distributing largesse the hall would be thronged by cadgers displaying the same interest in Einstein's Theory of Relativity as old Mrs. Jones takes in the Lent services and the vicar's Sunday Afternoon Talks to Mothers.

Why, even at Rosie Ropes' wedding there were beaming ladies

who had no interest in matrimony whatever, but had come because at the cost of half an hour's sitting in an uncomfortable pew they were assured a good dinner and an afternoon's amusement, with wine and fruit thrown in. And maybe a gramophone.

It was not often that Educated Evans went to parties, for society and social functions of all kinds he did not hold with. But the marriage of Mr. Charles Ropes' daughter Rosie to young Arthur Walters was an event of such importance that he could not very well refuse the invitation, extended from both sides, to pop in for a glass of sherry wine and a bit of cake.

Not that Evans was a winebibber. He did not hold with such effeminate drinks, his favourite potion being a foaming beaker of bitter. The nuptials of the Ropes and Walters family were something more than an ordinary union. To Educated Evans it was the wedding of a Five-Pound Special to an occasional Job Wire, for both parties represented consistent supporters of his.

The Ropes' house, where the do was to be, was in Bayham Street, Mr. Ropes being in the government and entitled to wear brass buttons every day of the week, and the wedding breakfast (which to the mind of Evans was more like lunch) was as classy an affair as he had ever seen.

To Educated Evans fell the task of proposing the bride and bridegroom, which he did in sporting terms, as was appropriate to his renowned position.

"May they run neck-and-neck from the gate of youth and dead-heat on the post of felicity!"

Several other people proposed the bride and bridegroom, and most of them hoped that their troubles would be little ones.

After the bride and bridegroom had departed by car for Westcliff-on-Sea, the harmony ran smoothly until, under the influence of port wine and an unaccustomed cigar, young Tom Ropes started snacking about education and horse-racing.

"It's my own fault," said Educated Evans when he was relating the events to The Miller the following day. "You can't touch pitch without being reviled, as Shakespeare says. It was the Flora Cabago that got into his head—boys ought to stick to Gold Flakes. If it hadn't been for her I'd have chastised him."

"Her?" repeated the puzzled Miller. "Which 'her'?"

"Miss Daisy Mawker," said Educated Evans awkwardly. "A friend of mine, and as nice a young woman as you've ever dropped your eyes on."

"Pretty?" asked the interested Miller.

"As lovely as a picture," said Evans enthusiastically, "and educated! We had a long talk about history and geography. What she don't know about foreign parts ain't worth knowing. She's got two lady friends, Miss Flora and Miss Fauna, that's been everywhere; she mentioned 'em all the time—"

"Flora and Fauna are terms meaning flowers and animals," corrected The Miller gently.

"She's very fond of flowers," said Evans, "and she keeps rabbits, so practically it's the same thing. She's got the heart of a lion, and she's heard about me. The first thing she says to me was Are you *the* Mr. Evans?"

"And you admitted it?"

"There was nothing else to do," said Evans modestly. "She ups and asks me if I was the celebrated Turf adviser that everybody was talking about—what could I do? Like the far-famed Sir What's-his-Name Washington, when asked if he let the cakes burn, I couldn't tell a lie."

The Miller nodded.

"There must be times when even you get like that. I suggest that you were under the influence of drink."

Educated Evans cast upon him the look of a wounded fawn.

"The wine was good—they got it from a grocer's in Hampstead Road that's selling off—but wine means nothing to me. I could drink a bucket without telling the story of my life. What wasn't wine was lemonade—which she drank, being a lady. And when young Tom started snacking and sneering she got up and said, If you lay a hand upon my gentleman friend I'll push your face off.'"

"She wasn't a titled lady by any chance?" asked the sardonic Miller. "There's a touch of Mayfair about that observation. You'll miss not seeing her again."

"I'm seeing her tonight," said Educated Evans with a secret smile. "We're going to the pictures to see Mary Pickford—she's often been mistaken for Mary Pickford herself."

"I hate you when you're coy," said The Miller. "Evans, this is going to interfere with business. I never knew that you were a lady's man, either."

"I've had me lapses," admitted Evans, and smiled reminiscently.

The Miller rubbed his chin thoughtfully, and his grave eyes surveyed the World's Premier Turf Prophet thoughtfully.

"I'm sorry I missed that wedding," he said. "Young Tom well dressed?"

"Like a gentleman," said Evans reluctantly. "I didn't know him—long-tailed coat, classy straw hat, patent leather boots, beautiful gold ch—"

He stopped suddenly.

"Yes," suggested The Miller. "Beautiful gold chain, you were going to say. Any rings?

"I didn't notice," said Evans hastily. "Now I think of it I don't think he had a chain on at all."

Mr. Ropes, senior, was employed in a government office. His son had also been in government service—twice. The Miller had got him the job. Ropes, senior, was wont to confess that children are a trouble, and he had excellent reason, for young Tom was by nature and instinct a "tea-leaf," which, in the argot of his kind, meant that he got his living by finding things that had not been lost. His downfall was ascribed by his lenient parent to "bad company." In truth, there was no company that Tom did not make a little worse by his presence.

"Besides," said Evans, "Tom's going straight now—he's got a job."

The Miller smiled.

"They always have jobs, Evans. But Miss Daisy Mawker—where did she spring from? Is she a friend of the bride's or the bridegroom's or the best man's?"

"She's a friend of mine," said Educated Evans stoutly. "She may be acquainted with young Tom; I'm not saying that she isn't. But if she knew the kind of feller young Tom was she would, in a manner of speaking, recoil with horror!"

There was a very good reason why the straw-chewing Miller should be interested in the adornment of young Tom Ropes. There had been a burglary at Finsbury. A jeweller's shop had been entered and trinkets to the value of a few pounds had been abstracted. It was fairly well known that it was the work of a gang that young Tom ran with. The haul, however, had been disappointing, most of the jeweller's stock being in the safe.

The question of this simple burglary did not exercise the knowledgable authorities so much as the information which had come to them that there had been a joining of forces between young Tom's crowd and "Gaffer" Smith's confederation. "Gaffer" was notoriously versatile, and there was nothing, from pitch and toss to manslaughter, outside the range of his operations.

Educated Evans met his Daisy that afternoon in Regent's Park, a favourite rendezvous of his. For the occasion Educated Evans had dressed himself with unusual care, even going to the extent of paying threepence that his scanty locks might be dressed to the greatest advantage.

Miss Daisy Mawker was pretty in a bold way. She was a straight-backed, athletic girl, with a rosy face and a pair of hard blue eyes; and if her ankles were a little thicker than they should have been, and her hands slightly on the coarse side, she was to Evans' enraptured eye what Venus might have been with a little bit of luck.

She refused Evans' gallant offer to row her about the lake for an hour, and he was relieved.

"Never did like the water," said Miss Daisy Mawker. Every time I go to Paris I get seasick."

"You're a bit of a traveller, Miss Daisy," said Evans respectfully. "I must say I like travelling myself. I've often been to Brighton just for the day. Travelling broadens your mind," he went on, "it's education and enlightenment. Look at Christopher Columbus. Where would he have been if he hadn't travelled? And where would America have been? Even the Americans wouldn't have heard about America if it hadn't been for him."

She nodded her head graciously.

"I suppose you're single, Mr. Evans?" she said, and Evans protested his bachelorhood with great heat.

"I only asked because so many fellows pretend they're single when they're not," she said demurely, tracing figures on the gravel with the end of her umbrella. "And when you find them out they say their wife's in a lunatic asylum, so they're as good as single. What a wonderful life you must live, Mr. Evans, going round to all these racecourses and seeing horse races. It must be beautiful! And then, I suppose, the jockeys tell you what is going to win and you send it round to all your friends."

Evans coughed.

"Not exactly. The jockeys very seldom know what's going to win," he said. "I used to rely on jockeys once, but after I had been let down—never again! They mean well, mind you," he said. "Look at Donoghue. He told me the other day—well, perhaps it's not gentlemanly to repeat his words. No, I never take any notice of jockeys. And as for trainers"—he shrugged his shoulders many times—you can't believe trainers. They're like the celebrated Ananias who turned round to have another look and was turned into a salt-cellar."

"What a lot you know!" she sighed.

"Do you ever get excited when the horses are racing? I should simply be thrilled to death."

"Haven't you ever seen a race?" asked Educated Evans. "Not," he said, disparagingly, that it's much to see. I simply don't take any notice of 'em. My man comes and tells me how much I've won or how much I've lost—a thousand one way or the other doesn't make any difference to me. When I'm going well," he added hastily. "Of course, I'm not always going well."

It occurred to him at that moment that he might be conveying a wrong impression if he gave her to understand that he was exceedingly well off.

"I wonder you have time for racing at all, Mr. Evans," she sighed. She had a habit of sighing. "What with picking up the bits of knowledge that you've got, and your education, and your clients"—she was still tracing designs on the gravel. And then: "I should so like to see a real horse race, though, of course, I shouldn't like to go alone. I should be so frightened. What I want to do is to go to a race meeting with somebody who is experienced, somebody who knows everything about it."

Educated Evans realised she was referring to him.

"I should be glad to take you, Miss Daisy," he said eagerly. "The expense is, comparatively speaking, nothing at all. I don't suppose you'd mind going in the Silver ring?"

"What's that?" she asked in surprise. "Is it a ring made of silver?"

Evans explained that the Silver Ring was the real aristocracy of the Turf. In the Silver Ring men bet more fearlessly, and prices were higher than in any other ring. Tattersall's, so far from being a desirable place, was an enclosure in which the price pincher flourished. She hesitated.

"I think I would rather go into Tattersall's, if that's the name," she said. "But, of course, dear Mr. Evans, I wouldn't think of allowing you to pay my expenses. I'm a very independent girl."

Evans murmured his half-hearted protest.

"I am, indeed! And I heard Tom say he was going down to Sandown on Eclipse Day. What is Eclipse Day?"

Evans explained again.

"Friend of yours, Miss Daisy?"

"Who—Tom? Well, he's not exactly a friend, he's an acquaintance.

He's not the kind of man I would have any dealings or associations with," she said.

"That's exactly what I said to Mr. Challoner," said Educated Evans triumphantly, and the smile faded from the girl's face.

"Mr. Challoner?" she said, a little sharply. "Do you mean that detective? Surely you don't have anything to do with him? You're the last person in the world I should think was a snout—nose, I mean, Aren't I being unladylike?"

"In a way he's a friend of mine," said Evans, a little taken aback. "He has my selections, so, in a manner of speaking, he's a client."

Her face cleared.

"Oh, if that's all," she said. "I know these birds do bet on the sly, and then they go round pinching the poor little street bookmakers, don't they? I've read about that in the newspapers," she added quickly.

It was arranged before they parted that they should meet on the following Wednesday at Waterloo Station under the clock; and Evans, having despatched innumerable messages, both by hand and telegram, dealing with the outstanding possibilities of Glue Pot winning the mile seller, hurried forth to meet his lady.

The sight of her took his breath away. Never a more ladylike person had he seen in her simple blue costume and little black hat. Nothing flash, nothing ikey, just plain and ladylike. He was proud to be seen with her.

They travelled to Esher first class. For once in his life Educated Evans travelled on a first-class ticket. And all the way down he spoke on a subject agreeable to himself, namely—Educated Evans.

They were walking across the park when he broached the subject which was in his mind.

"If I was you, Miss Daisy, I don't think I should have any truck with young Tom Ropes," he said, but she raised her eyebrows.

"Why ever not?" she asked. "Isn't that him in front?"

"Yes, with some of his leery pals," said Educated Evans, "so don't walk fast."

"But why shouldn't I, Mr. Evans?" asked Daisy. "You are making me so terribly frightened. Isn't he honest?"

"He never robbed me of anything," said Evans diplomatically.

"I should hate to think he wasn't honest," said Daisy Mawker, shaking her head. "I can't abide people who aren't perfectly straightforward, can you, Mr. Evans? What I mean to say is that if they're on the hook they're so unreliable. You never know where they are, do you? There's a friend of mine, she's got a *fiancé*, and she never knows his address. Sometimes he's at Wormwood Scrubs, sometimes he's at Wandsworth—it's just wasting stamps to write to him."

"Yes, yes," said Evans, a little dazed. Be had no fault to find with her ladylike behaviour throughout the day. She stood on the top of the stone steps of the stand, and Evans went down to do her betting for her, and every time she won he brought the money back, and every time she lost she said:

"You must remind me to pay you that five shillings on our way home, Mr. Evans."

The crowd was a tremendous one, as it always is on Eclipse Day, and just before the last race the sensible girl suggested that they should make a move to the station. When they reached the other side of the course, however, she changed her mind and insisted on seeing the last race. And then, and only then, did they make their way to the railway arch under which the passengers must pass *en route* to the station platform.

"Don't let's go any farther. I saw some friends of mine," she said. "We'll wait here until they come."

"You won't get a seat in the train," he warned her.

"Oh, yes, I shall," she said, with a saucy toss of her head. "You wait here beside me. Now don't you leave me, Mr. Evans."

"Do you think I would?" breathed Educated Evans tenderly, and he thrilled as she caught his hand and squeezed his little finger.

The stream of home-goers that crossed the park was now multiplied in size, and presently Evans saw young Tom Ropes, though apparently that youthful brigand did not see Evans, for he showed no sign of recognition.

The press was now tremendous, and he and the girl had to flatten themselves against the wall, and it was with difficulty that the crowd squeezed past. Every now and again someone would bump against Evans. Twice it was young Tom Ropes, who also seemed to be waiting for a friend.

And then of a sudden there was a stir in the crowd. Somebody struck out, and Evans looked with open mouth at the strange spectacle of young Tom Ropes in the hands of The Miller. Where The Miller had come from, unless he had dropped through a crack in the arch, Evans could not guess.

In an instant the archway was alive with plain-clothes police. "Let us get out of this," said Miss Mawker hurriedly.

She had not taken two steps when somebody gripped her arm. Evans was on the point of asserting himself when, looking up, he recognised The Miller.

"Want you, Daisy," said The Miller pleasantly. "We've got the rest of the gang, I think."

"Look here, Mr, Challoner," began Educated Evans, struggling to follow the sergeant and his captive.

In a quiet and secluded station on the other side of the line six bedraggled men were in the process of being ushered into a waiting police van when Evans, following The Miller and Miss Daisy Mawker, came upon the scene.

"We've got the men, and we haven't got the loot," said an officer who was evidently in charge, and added, "Hullo, Daisy, had a good day?"

Daisy made a reply which shocked Educated Evans beyond words.

"I suppose this somethinged 'can' was snouting for you?" she said. "Well, he's in it with the rest of us."

"I know all about that," said The Miller. "Turn out your overcoat pockets, Evans!"

"Me?" said the horrified Evans.

"You," said The Miller. "I'll give you a clean bill because I know just how they brought you into it."

In Evans' pockets were eight watches, seven note-cases, five purses, two scarf-pins, and a lady's diamond brooch. Evans could only watch like a man in a dream as the property came to light.

"You were the carrier," said The Miller on the way back to town. "They always get a mug for that job. She planted you against the railway arch so that the gang should have someone to take the plunder as they found it. By the way, she's young Tom's sweetheart."

"She ain't mine," said Educated Evans savagely. "I'm done with wimmin!"

12.—THE PROUD HORSE

Educated Evans left the Italian Club, having lost £4 18s. at a game which was known locally as "Prop and Cop." He had propped so misguidedly, and copped with such bad lack of brilliance, that the wonder was—as The Miller, to whom he confided his woes, told him—that he had any trousers left.

Yet Educated Evans was not an unhappy man; for that day had

seen the success of his £5 Special. And on the previous Sunday "Tat-tenham" had said nasty things about a trainer who was reputedly an enemy to all touts and tipsters, and had expressed his views on the same in the public Press.

Sergeant Challoner walked with Evans to the end of the mews wherein the educated man had his habitation. As they stood talking, the keen-eyed Miller saw a light shining at one of the windows above a stable.

"The Turners are up late," he said.

"The kid's ill," said Educated Evans shortly, and, taking leave of the detective, he made his way rapidly along the uneven roadway. He did not go direct to his own room, but, climbing the opposite stairs, came to a pause on a landing very similar to his own, and knocked at the door which led to the lighted room. He knocked gently, but the door was instantly opened by a haggard-looking woman.

"How is he?" asked Educated Evans, quietly; and she made way for him to enter.

The room was a little better furnished than Evans' room, but it was less airy. On a stuffy bed lay a small boy, very wan and hollow-eyed. The perspiration glistened on his white forehead, but he grinned at the sight of Evans.

"Hullo, Mr. Evans!" he piped.

"Hullo, Ernie!" said Evans, sitting down on a chair by the side of the bed.

"Been to the races, Mr. Evans?"

"No, I can't say that I have," admitted Evans.

"And I'll bet your horse didn't win," said the child, speaking with difficulty, and fixing his solemn eyes upon the bare-headed tipster.

"If you bet that you'd bet wrong, Ernie. It did win! I thought you was better or I'd have come home earlier."

Ernie was an old pal of Educated Evans. They were in the habit of holding speech together across the intervening space which separated one balcony from the other. Mrs. Turner was a widow; her husband had been killed in an accident when working for the firm that owned the stables above which she lived. They had given her a small pension, and, more important at that time, had given her the two rooms rent free for life.

The woman herself did not come into the purview of Educated Evans, for she was not interested in the thoroughbred racehorse, nor very greatly interested in Mr. Evans. But Ernie and he went walking together, surveyed the spring glories of the park, and sailed boats upon the lake.

He went to the door with the woman.

"What did the doctor say?" he asked in a low voice.

"He says he ought to go away into the country, and it's his only chance," said the woman, with a catch in her breath. "He'll die if he stays here. The doctor's tried to get him into a convalescent home, but there's no vacancies; and I can't afford to keep him away for any time."

"Mr. Evans!"

He turned to the bed.

The child had struggled up on to his elbow and was watching him with his odd, pitiful face.

"What about that prahd 'orse?"

"That what?" said Evans, puzzled.

"You told me you'd let me see a prahd 'orse."

"Oh, a proud horse," said Evans correctly, and remembered his promise. "What do you mean by a proud horse, Ernie?" he asked.

"You know, Mr. Evans—the 'orses that 'old their 'eads up in the air, they're so prahd. There used to be two down 'ere—the undertaker's 'orses; but he took 'em away. I'd like to see a prahd 'orse. I could sit all day and look at a prahd 'orse," said the child, with queer earnestness.

"Ain't there any proud horses in the mews?" asked Evans. "What about Haggitt's?"

The child's pale lip lifted contemptuously.

"'E isn't a prahd 'orse," he said scornfully. "Why, 'e 'olds 'is 'ead down like a cow. I'd like to see a prahd 'orse, Mr. Evans—them that champs their feet on the ground."

Evans scratched his nose.

"Now you come to mention it, Ernie, I'll confess I haven't seen a proud horse for years. I think the motorcars must have knocked all the pride out of 'em."

"There are lots. The undertaker's 'orses was prahd," said the small boy.

Evans crossed over to his room, feeling uneasy in his mind. Financially, things were not going too well with him, or he would have offered, without hesitation, to send the child away into the country.

His was the kind of nature that goes out to children, and it hurt him to even think of that queer little morsel of humanity in the stuffy bed in that hot and airless room. Once he got out in the night and looked out of the window. The light was still burning. When he did go to sleep it was to dream of proud horses, black as night, with high, arched necks and frothing mouths and hoofs that pawed incessantly. And in his dream they were pulling a shabby little coach. And under the driving seat was a little white coffin.

He woke up sweating and pushed open the window. The dawn was in the sky and the air smelt sweet and good. The windows opposite were closed, hermetically sealed; the door was jammed tight and locked.

Evans lit the gas and sat down to study the day's programme published in the overnight paper, but he could not keep his mind to the possibilities of profit. Every entry was a proud horse with an arched neck that "champed" the ground.

At the particular moment when the kindly heart of Educated Evans was lacerated by the thought of suffering childhood, a proud horse was being pulled up on the Wiltshire Downs. His name was Veriti. He had cost, as a yearling at the Doncaster sales, 13,500 guineas, and he was, so Mr. Yardley, the eminent trainer, told the owner in dispassionate tones, worth exactly 13,500 marks at the present rate of exchange.

"He looks good enough," said Lord Teller, a shivering man who had been dragged out of bed to witness the wholly unsatisfactory trial in the cold hours of the morning.

"Unfortunately, my lord," said Mr. Yardley politely, "the London Cup is not a beauty show. If it was, I think Veriti would get very nearly first prize."

Being the great Yardley he could talk to one of the newest of the peerage frankly and in plain words.

"He can do it if he would do it," he said bitterly, watching the beautiful Veriti as he stepped daintily round and round the waiting circle; "and it isn't lack of courage. It's just wilfulness—super-intelligence, perhaps."

"What will you do? said his lordship. "I shall run him," said Yardley. "He will start a hot favourite, and when he finishes down the course knowledgable people will look at one another meaningly, and the *hoi polloi* will talk about another one of Yardley's mysteries, and yet another nail will be driven into my reputation."

He walked over to the horse, smoothed its arched neck and patted it.

"You're a dirty dog, Jim," he said.

(His lordship learnt for the first time that the name under which a horse is registered is not the name by which it is known in a stable.)

"You're a mouldy old thief! What's the matter with you?"

Veriti did not wink, but Yardley, who understood the very souls of horses, thought he saw a look of amusement in his eyes.

"You'll have one chance, my lad, and that's at Alexandra Park. A cab-horse can win at Alexandra Park. And if you don't behave yourself on Saturday, you'll go to the stud at nine guineas, and you know what that means!"

Veriti did not raise his eyebrows, but he raised his ears as though he understood. And really the question of his fee was less important to Veriti than his popularity. For the moment he was exceedingly unpopular, but that did not worry him.

Mr. Yardley was a painstaking and thorough trainer, and it was all to his advantage that veiled Press comments and innuendoes passed him by without making the slightest impression. He was that gentleman whose practice it was to run two horses in a race and win with the outsider. It was the popular idea that these results were cleverly planned. To such a suggestion Mr. Yardley merely offered a cryptic smile and the remark that horses were not machines.

He brought Veriti out two mornings after, and gave him a gallop with the two best horses in his stable. And he was not overwhelmingly surprised when Veriti won the gallop pulling up, because he was, as Mr. Lyndall would say, "a horse of moods."

"I suppose that means that you'll finish down that infernal course on Saturday," mused Mr. Yardley, looking into Veriti's eyes—and it may have been a coincidence, but Veriti nodded.

Educated Evans had made up his mind to have a great day on the Saturday, for his punters were, in the main, people who speculated their maximum on that day. He had planned a grand circularising of every name on his books with the winner of the London Cup. That he should have chosen Veriti is not remarkable, for Veriti had run second in the Chesterfield Plate at Goodwood. But somehow the zip had gone out of Evans' life that week. Morning and night, and sometimes in the middle of the day, he was to be found in the widow's room, sitting by the child, who seemed to fade before his very eyes.

Evans saw the doctor, a busy man with very little time to fuss.

"The child would be saved if you could get him away to the country and keep him there," he said to Evans, when the educated man met him at the bottom of the stairs. "I am giving this advice, well knowing that this poor woman cannot afford to send the child away. I've done my utmost to find a free convalescent home for him, but without success."

"What would it cost, doctor?"

"Three or four pounds a week," said the doctor brusquely, and Evans' heart sank, for he was very near the end of his own resources, and his livelihood was a precarious one.

"Do you know what I think, Mr. Evans?" said the mother, coming outside the door on to the landing and talking in a hushed voice. "I think that boy's life would be saved if he could see that kind of horse he's always talking about. It's funny how things run in your mind when you're ill. That's all Ernie wants."

Evans went into the room. The child was lying with his wasted hands beneath his cheeks, his eyes fixed on vacancy.

"Hullo, Ernie, old boy! "

Evans patted his shoulder gently. The dark eyes turned up to meet the tipster's face.

"What about that prahd 'orse?" he said weakly.

"I'm going to see what I can do about it," said Evans. "I'll be bringing one down the mews, and then I'll carry you to the window, and you can see it for yourself. Mrs. Turner, don't you think you might have your windows open a bit?"

She was shocked at the suggestion.

"That's what the doctor's always saying," she complained. "That means that Ernie will lie in a draught and catch a cold."

To Evans's discerning eye the boy was slowly sinking; and he spent the Friday afternoon, when he should have been attending to his business, in a vain search of the neighbouring mews for any horse that bore the slightest resemblance to Ernie's description. Not even the funeral horses were available, for it was a bad summer and the horses were working overtime. Evans could not help thinking—

He had to go to Alexandra Park; there was nothing else to do. The child was getting on his mind; and everlastingly that thin, whining voice intoning, "Want to see a prahd 'orse," rang in Evans' ears.

He himself saw one. In a half-hearted way he had sent Veriti to some fifty clients, and he saw Veriti finish a bad ninth.

And then a great idea was born in his mind, and he hurried out of the cheap ring along the road and into the paddock. That he got into the paddock at all without the necessary ticket was a tribute to his courage and resourcefulness.

He arrived as Veriti was being sheeted under the disapproving eye of the great Yardley; and surely Veriti was a picture of a horse. Unfortunately, they will not pay out on pictures, as Mr. Yardley had truly said.

"Excuse me, sir."

Yardley turned and saw a face which for the moment eluded him.

"I know you. Who are you?" he asked, not being in the mood for polite conversation.

"You remember me, sir, I'm Educated Evans."

For a moment Yardley glared, and then a twinkle came into his eyes.

"Oh, you are! I remember you, you rascal. What do you want? I've no tips for you, and I'm broke."

"I don't want any money, sir," said Evans huskily, and oppressed by the fearful liberty he was taking. "But is there any chance of this horse coming to Bayham Mews?" he blurted.

"To where?" asked the startled Yardley.

"To Bayham Mews, sir—Camden Town."

"There's a chance of his going into a cab, if that's what you mean. There's also a chance of him going into the cats'-meat shop," said Yardley. "What do you mean, my friend?"

Brokenly, incoherently, Educated Evans told his story, gulping out the plaint of little Ernie.

"A proud horse? What is a proud horse? Oh, I think I know what you mean," said Yardley slowly, and turned his eyes upon Veriti. "He's proud enough, though God knows why," he said, and chuckled in spite of himself. "Yes, I think he'd fill the bill. But you really don't imagine I should send his lordship's horse to amuse a small slum child, do you?"

"No, sir," said Evans miserably.

"Then you're a damned fool," said Yardley. "What is your address?"

Educated Evans, scarcely believing his ears, gave ample directions. At a quarter past six that evening, when he was sitting with Ernie, not daring to believe that the trainer would carry out his promise, there came a clatter of hoofs in the yard, and Evans dashed to the window.

Coming back without a word, he lifted the child in his arms, and, in spite of Mrs. Turner's protests, carried him on to the landing. And there Ernie saw the proudest horse he had ever seen—a horse so proud that it refused to run with other horses, but invariably and sedately trailed in the rear.

"O-oh!" said Ernie, and his round eyes grew rounder.

Veriti never looked better. He had been stripped of his sheet, and his coat glistened in the afternoon sun.

"O-oh!" said Ernie. "Ain't 'e prahd?"

And proud he was, with his head held high and his delicate feet picking a way across the cobbled stones.

For a moment the horse held the eye of Educated Evans then, looking past him, he saw Yardley. The great trainer came slowly towards him and mounted the stairs.

"Is this the child?" he said.

"Yes, sir," said Educated Evans.

"Looks as if a little fresh air would do him a world of good," said Yardley. "What do you think of my proud horse, laddie?

"He *is* prahd! "said Ernie.

"I should say he was," said the grim Yardley. "Nothing infectious about this child, is there?"

"No, sir," said the woman, to whom he spoke.

"I'll send my car for him the first thing in the morning. The wife of my head lad will look after him, if he's well enough to travel."

And so Ernie Turner went down into Wiltshire, and there was an amazing sequel. As though conscious of the compliment that had been paid to him, Veriti won the next time out, and won pulling up. He started at 100 to 7. The favourite, which finished down the course and started at 6 to 4, was also one of Yardley's. And in the paddock after the race, wherever men congregated, it was agreed unanimously that Yardley ought to be warned off.

13.—THROUGH THE CARD

"I have often wondered," said The Miller reflectively, "why a man of your education and ability doesn't find another way of earning a living, Evans. I admit that it is better than thieving, and more desirable than a good many other methods of earning a livelihood that are followed by mutual friends. But it's a little precarious, isn't it, or do you make so much money that you expect to retire?"

Educated Evans scratched his chin and looked up at his visitor. Detective-Inspector Challoner, C.I.D., was a frequent caller at the little room over the stable which was Evans' dwelling-place, and he had come that morning at a very unpropitious and depressing moment, for Evans had set out twelve consecutive losers, and it almost seemed as if he would never touch a winner again.

So depressed was he that he was engaged in his favourite course of study, which was the sixth volume of Chambers's *Encyclopaedia*, which began at the Humber and finished at Malta.

On these and on all matters in between, except perhaps such subjects as the habits of the Lecythidacæ, which was a little above him, he was an authority. He knew all about Robert Lee and Pope Joan, Japan, and Iron, and International Law, and Ink and India-rubber, and Incantations, the Lick Observatory and the Liturgy, because these were dealt with in the volume. And he had no other volume.

He was half-way through a learned article on "The Use of Lights in Public Worship" when The Miller's big frame loomed up in the doorway.

"I owe three weeks' rent," said Educated Evans despondently. "The washerwoman's got me shirts, and won't let me have 'em back until I pay her up all the back. I owe twenty-three and twopence for gas, and I've got four and sixpence that I borrowed from Li Jacobs. That's the money I've saved! "

"What do you do with all your money?" asked The Miller in quiet wonder. "You must make a lot sometimes, Evans."

"Some people," said Educated Evans, "like the celebrated Henry the Eighth, who married twenty-five wives, do in their stuff on horses and women. You have to be a king to do it in that way. I've done all mine in on horses without the assistance of any young lady."

He got up and went to the mantel-piece and filled a clay pipe, and the fact that he was reserving the end of a cigar that lay by its side was sufficient evidence that his position was a parlous one.

"I've done with horses from now onwards," said Educated Evans. "It's phantom gold," he said recklessly. "Find me a job: I'll take it."

"Higgs wants a man," suggested The Miller.

"Higgs!" said the scornful Evans. "Do you think I'd work for a man like that? He's a twister. A ten-pun' note wouldn't pay what that man owes me for information supplied at great cost—you've no idea of my expenses, what with travellin', giving money to stable boys and head lads—"

"You're amongst friends," said The Miller soothingly. "Don't let's tell the tale. What about Mr. Walters? He'd give you a job."

Evans shrugged his shoulders.

"Am I the kind of man who'd work for a fellow like Walters?" he asked haughtily. A man, so to speak, who makes a mock of education?

No, Mr. Challoner, I'll see what Saturday brings in. And if Roving Betty doesn't win the Duke of York Stakes, then I'll have to look around. I'm not grousing"—he was very serious now—"but somehow I've never been able to touch big money, Mr. Challoner. Facts been against me."

"You mean Fate," said The Miller.

"I'm talking about bookmakers more particularly," said Educated Evans. "I've never been able to bring off a coup. Not a real coup. Of course, I've bragged a lot in printin'—I wish I had the money that I've spent with Dickens the printer but between friends, if I may presume, I've never touched the money that I've always dreamt about. I'm a bit of a dreamer, Mr. Challoner."

"So I've noticed," said the other, not unkindly.

"I can sit here," said Evans, tapping the book in front of him, "and dream as only educated people can dream. I've ridden Derby winners, I've owned the biggest sprinter of the age, I've taken a hundred thousand pounds a day out of the ring—in my dreams. And, mind you, I wouldn't be without 'em for anything. Of course, I never shall take a hundred thousand out of the ring, and I'll never get that cottage and field."

The interested Miller sat down.

"Let us hear about your cottage and field, Evans. That's a new one on me."

"I've got an idea of a beautiful little cottage in the country. I saw one advertised for sale the other day on the back page of *The Times*. Two thousand pounds! Me doing the kitchen gardening and making a bit by selling flowers and teas for cyclists—if they drank beer they'd fall off—and a horse in the field. Get an old selling plater and breed from her. That's my idea of happiness."

The Miller puffed slowly at his long cigar.

"And it's not a bad idea either," he said.

"But if you had the money you'd do it in, Evans."

"Not me!" said Evans decisively. If I ever touch for a bit—and God knows I never shall—I'd give up buying *The Sportsman* and take in *The Christian Herald*—it's more exciting, anyway. I took a 'bus down to Bromley the other day for a bit of fresh air, and it's a nice ride. There's a place with about two acres—a little cottage, an old well, just like in the pictures. Why, I'd be a king there—"

"What would it cost?"

"Eight hundred and fifty pounds. I saw the owner. Kidded him I might be buying it one of these days," said Evans dismally. "Me buy a house! Why, I couldn't buy a rabbit-hutch!"

Friday afternoon saw Evans, with his dwindling stock of envelopes, folding what he knew was his last appeal to an incredulous public. Most of the circulars were delivered locally. Saturday brought him a solitary five-shilling postal order. Evans went without breakfast that morning and carried his overcoat to a repository near at hand, and received in exchange 4s. and a ticket.

He stood on the kerb, his hands in his pockets, the picture of dejection, staring blankly at the White Hart, the landlord of which had once welcomed him as a friend, and the shadow of ruin was upon him.

Evans was not a great drinker. His magnificence in his cups had led to so many awkward and embarrassing moments that he had abandoned the practice with no great regret, for drinking to Evans was one of the most expensive forms of recreation.

In his pocket he had 11s., and if he carried out the mad idea which possessed him that morning and went to Kempton Park he might starve on the morrow.

So brooding, The Miller passed him on his motor-bicycle, and, seeing the melancholy figure, stopped his machine and got off.

"How did they come in, Evans?"

"They came in one by one," said Evans bitterly. "The first has arrived; the second may come at any time between now and Christmas. I've got a dollar, and it cost me more than that for envelopes."

"Can I lend you a pound?" asked The Miller, but Evans shook his head.

"You'll never get it back," he said miserably.

"Take it," said The Miller, and, thrusting the note into his hands, moved off.

"Don't forget Bactive Lad," called Evans after him, the ruling passion strong in death. He stood with the note in his hand, and then a sudden resolve came to him, and he crossed the road and walked into the saloon bar. The proprietor was not visible, but the chief officer eyed him suspiciously. It seemed that the news of Evans' poverty had spread throughout the land.

"A double Scotch and soda," said Evans firmly.

He had never drunk whisky before in the morning, but he felt that he must do something or die of sheer inanition. He threw the pound note on the counter and tossed down the drink at a gulp.

"I'll have another," he said, and when he had had the other and had leant against the bar, frowning thoughtfully for fully five minutes without saying a word, he came to a sudden decision.

"Going to Kempton, Evans?" asked the senior barman.

Educated Evans turned his stony eyes upon his interrogator.

"'Mister Evans,' if you don't mind," he said haughtily. "'The Honourable Mr. Evans,' my good feller."

"I'm sorry," said the barman, aghast.

"You took a liberty," said Evans, "that no common man should take with an educated gentleman."

He brushed some invisible dust from his sleeve, and with a shrug of his shoulders walked out.

Providentially a taxicab was passing, and Evans hailed it.

"Waterloo, my man," he said, "Get there in ten minutes and I'll give you a fiver."

Happily the cabman recognised him.

"What's the hurry, Evans? There are plenty of trains."

"I have a special train," said Evans gravely, and fell into the taxicab. He intended to step in, but he fell in, for his foot slipped on the running-board.

Mr. Evans alighted at Waterloo with greater *éclat*. He stepped out of his cab on to the foot of Henry B. Norman, an American millionaire and an excellent sportsman.

"Say, haven't you any feet of your own to walk on?" said the plutocrat.

"Pardon," said Evans in his stateliest manner, and threw five shillings at the taxi-driver. "As a gentleman I apologise. As a gentleman you accept. God bless you!" And he seized the hand of the astonished millionaire and wrung it. "Come and have a drink," said Evans.

Mr. Norman's eyes narrowed.

"I guess you've had almost as much as you can take, my friend," he said. "You're all lit up like the Hotel Dooda"

"Come and have a drink," insisted Evans, closing his eyes. He always closed his eyes in these circumstances; it lent him a certain dignity which was impressive.

Now, Mr. Norman was waiting for a friend who had not turned up. He was going to Kempton Park because, as the owner of an American stud, he was keenly interested in English racing. But that morning, when he had left his valet's hands, he had not the slightest idea that at eleven-thirty he would be standing in the public bar drinking whisky with a disreputable gentleman who hinted mysteriously at his noble birth.

"It's not generally known," said Evans, leaning affectionately on the counter, "that my father was the fourteenth Earl of Pogmore. I'm not sure if it's Pogmore or Frogmore, but what does it matter?"

"Precisely."

"You're an American. I knew in ten minutes," said Educated Evans, nodding his head wisely. "That's wunner things I learnt at Eton."

"At Eton?" said the staggered American.

"I was brought up at Eton and Harrow," said Evans, "but it's not generally known."

"Who the dickens are you, then?" asked the American, thinking that he had by chance happened upon a member of the shabby nobility.

"Lord Evans, of Bayham House—of Bayham Castle, I mean," said Evans.

"Going to Kempton?"

"I'll go through the card. There isn't a horse running today, my dear American fellow, that I don't know everything about. Owners, trainers, jockeys—" he waggled his head expressively—"I get everything!"

It was at that moment that the millionaire's friend found him.

"Goodbye, Mr. Evans, or Lord Evans, as the case may be," said Norman good-humouredly.

He shook hands with his host, and was halfway to the door when he stopped.

"I'll give this poor soak the surprise of his life," he said, and taking out five clean, crisp notes from his pocket-book. "A present from the United States," he said, and slipped them into Evans' hand.

Things were going remarkably well with Evans.

He arrived at Kempton by a very ordinary train. The Miller, who had cycled down, watched him, open-mouthed, as he strolled into Tattersall's, slamming down a five-pound note.

"Here, what's wrong with you, Evans?" The Miller tackled him as he entered Tattersall's ring.

"Ha, Miller, I owe you a pound, I think? Take it, my good fellow."

He waved the note in the air, and The Miller, anxious to avoid a scene, took it.

"Miller, old boy"—he gripped the detective's arm—"I've got summun to tell you. I'm not what you think I am, dear old boy." He forced back the tears that had come into his eyes with an effort, blew his nose, and repeated: "I am not what you think I am."

"You're soused," said The Miller, reproachfully.

"No, no, old boy, I'm not soused. I'm an unfortunate man, dear Miller."

His attentions were becoming more than embarrassing, for he had his arm affectionately round The Miller's shoulder—as far as it would reach."

"Dear old boy, I'm the nat'ral son of the Earl of Evans! Now you know!"

He stepped back dramatically, and came into collision with a bookmaker who was taking a light *al fresco* lunch.

"I'm not that either," said Evans, in reply to the bookmaker's observation. "I'm—"

He looked round for The Miller, but the latter had seized the opportunity and vanished.

The horses were at the post when Evans, sitting on the steps of the stand, his head between his hands, suddenly woke with a start. Fumbling with his card, and walking to the nearest bookmaker, he demanded so loudly that it could be heard almost all over the ring:

"What price Midget's Pride?"

"Eight to one to you," said the bookmaker.

Evans dropped a roll of money in his hand, and with some difficulty the bookmaker counted it.

"Twenty-three pounds seventeen and sixpence. Do you want it to this?" he asked, incredulously.

"To that," said the grave Evans

"Take back the silver. I'm not betting that way." He thrust the coins into Evans' hand. "A hundred and ninety-four to twenty-three Midget's Pride. You needn't take a ticket. I'll know that dial anywhere."

Midget's Pride won cleverly. Evans was unaware of the fact until the bookmaker hailed him.

"Hi, you! Come and get this money you've robbed me of!"

Evans thrust the notes into his pocket and went into the bar. When he emerged he was another man. His eyes were bright, his head was high. He had lost his hat.

The second race was a two-year-old seller. A horse started a hot favourite at 13 to 8. Evans took 6 to 4 to all the money he could find in his pocket.

Just before the last race The Miller was standing by the rails discussing with a brother professional the appearance of several well-known faces in the ring when he saw Educated Evans strutting along the alleyway that led from the paddock.

"Good-morning, 'Miller.' Good-morning, my man," he said, with a lordly wave of his hand. "Been through the card?"

"Right through the card. Look at this." He put both hands in his pockets and drew forth notes in such profusion that dozens fell to the ground.

"Let 'em be," said Evans loftily. "Leave 'em there for the common people. I've just seen the Stewards about that dead-heat in the last race. Disgustin'!"

"There wasn't a dead-heat in the last race, you damned fool!" growled The Miller. "The winner was a clear length in front of everything else."

"It looked like a dead-heat to me," said Evans. "I distinctly saw two horses."

As the field was going to the post Evans staggered to the leading bookmaker of Tattersall's.

"Good-morning, Mr. Slumber," he said.

(In other times and circumstances he would have trembled to approach the great man.)

"What price Standoff?"

The great Harry Slumber surveyed his customer with a calm and critical eye.

"Seven to one."

"Lay me fifty-nine thousand to seven thousand and the money is yours," said Evans gravely.

It was then that The Miller thought he ought to interfere.

★★★★★★

Evans woke the next morning with a feeling that by some tragic accident his head had been caught between steam rollers and slightly flattened. When his hand went up, however, he found no difference in the shape. He was aching in every limb, and, staring round, he found he was in a room of familiar appearance.

There was a steel door and a grating, a bell-push, a hard, leather-covered pillow and a blanket. The bed itself was a wooden bench. A large jug of water slaked his burning thirst, and then, just as he was going to ring the bell and ask for information, a lock snapped and the door of the cell opened. The Miller looked at him and shook his head.

"What a nice man you are, Evans "he said bitterly. "After I'd taken the trouble to bring you home and put you to bed!"

"What did I do?" asked Evans.

"What did you do?" said The Miller. "You came and kissed Inspector Pine, that's what you did! I thought he'd have killed you."

Evans groaned.

"I've had such a wonderful dream. I dreamt I had been to Kempton and won thousands."

"Three thousand two hundred pounds," said The Miller, calmly, "and you're a lucky man to have it."

Evans jumped up as if he had been shot.

"Did I go through the card?" he asked hollowly.

"You went through the card, and the boys would have gone through you if I hadn't been there," said The Miller. "Evans, you're a disgusting fellow. And here comes Inspector Pine," he said, "to ask if your intentions were serious."

More Educated Evans

1.—The Return of the Native

It is an axiom of life that the course of true love never ran smoothly. There were certainly snags in the current of Mr. Cris Holborn's affair, but the largest and most considerable of these was Florrie Beaches' mamma, who was stout and snacky. She snacked Mr. Holborn about his profession (she herself being a lady of property and owning the house in Mornington Crescent); she snacked him about his gentlemanliness; she snacked him on the question of stable odours (she invariably held a handkerchief to her bulbous nose when he came into her drawing-room) and she snacked him about his education.

Sometimes, in desperation, Mr. Holborn snacked back. He told her that he was one of the best known trainers of racehorses in England, but he was "Cris" to scores of the gentry and nobility, and that if a farmer's son was not good enough for the daughter of a retired publican, well, he'd like to know who was?

It may be said in passing that Mr. Beaches had not only retired from The Trade, but he had also retired from earth, and at the moment was resting at Kensal Rise under a huge slab of Aberdeen granite, on which was carved a tissue of falsehoods concerning his virtues as a father and husband and his great loss to the world.

And in a sense Cris Holborn's retort was justifiable. He was one of the best known trainers in England and one of the cleverest. In the language of the crude men who support the art and practice of horse-racing, he was "hot," and when his horses won, he won alone: sometimes not even the owner of the horse was aware of the forthcoming jubilations.

On a night in February, Mrs. Beaches snacked to such purpose, and was supported so effectively by her charming daughter, that things happened in Mornington Crescent. Neighbours heard the sound of shrill and angry voices, a door slammed violently, and there was the sound of breaking glass. . . .

★★★★★★

Peace reigned in Selbany Street Police Station. The station sergeant nodded over his book, the policeman on duty at the door yawned frequently and wondered if the clock over Disreili's, the High Class Jewellers, had stopped.

The hour was 1 a.m., and it was raining greasily as it can only rain in Somers Town. It had been a dull night, being Thursday, when men go soberly to their homes and play draughts with their children and win—if the children have any discretion. A night when the picture houses are half empty, and the bung at the Rose and Cabbage leant his bloated hands on the zinc counter and severely condemned socialism to an empty saloon.

There were only three men and one perfect lady in the cells at the back of the station: crime for the moment was unpopular.

Sergeant Arbuthnot Challoner, whom men called The Miller because he chewed straws, came in hastily out of the darkness, put his reeking umbrella in one corner of the hall and hung his shining mackintosh on a peg.

"Yes," he said sardonically, in reply to the grey-haired station sergeant, "it *is* a nice night!"

The clock ticked solemnly and noisily.

"Nothing doing?"

"Nothing," said The Miller shortly. He had been standing for two hours in the rain waiting for a motor-car thief who was expected to retrieve the car he had garaged.

At that moment, when the night seemed as barren of promise as the pages of Dr. Stott's sermons, a car drew up opposite the station entrance and there sailed into the charge room Miss Florrie Beaches and her ma. Miss Beaches was golden-haired and blue-eyed. She wore an evening dress of gold and crimson and a theatre wrap of blue and white. She had orchids at her waist and about her neck a choker of imitation pearls the size of pigeons' eggs. Her ma was more soberly arrayed in black with glittering jet ornaments.

"Is this the police court?" asked Miss Beaches with a certain ferocity.

118

"It is the police station," said The Miller. Florrie closed her eyes and nodded.

"That will do," she said quietly. "I wish to have a summons against Mr. Cris Holborn for insulting my dear mother and breach of promise, though I wouldn't marry the dirty dog not if he went down on his bare knees to me! He's a low type and if my poor dear father had been alive he'd have bashed his face in!"

"He would indeed," murmured Mrs. Beaches.

The Miller would have explained, but—

"When a lady lowers herself to be seen out with a common horse trainer," Miss Beaches went on rapidly, "when she does everything for a man as I've done, introducing him into society so to speak, and when he didn't know what a fish knife was till me dear mother taught him, it's hard to hear your dear mother called an interfering hag."

"*Old* hag," murmured Mrs. Beaches. "Don't forget the winder glass, Flo."

"I'm coming to that, ma. Also I wish to charge him with breaking two panes of glass in our front door by his violent temper. I'm going to show this man up! Him and his lords that he knows!"

"Which we don't believe," prompted Mrs. Beaches.

"And the words he said about publicans is a disgrace," Florrie went on, "him and his horse that's going to win at Lincoln—"

"With twenty-one pound in hand," added the other under her breath.

"With twenty-one pounds in hand?" repeated The Miller thoughtfully.

"That's what he says," said Miss Florrie, "though I know nothing about horse-racing, my dear papa having brought me up very strict. Now I want to know if I can't have a summons—"

"Excuse me, miss," said The Miller gently, almost benevolently, what was the name of this horse?

"I can't think of it for the moment," said Miss Florrie, to whom the identity of the animal was much less important than the exposition of her grievances "but if I did know I should tell that common man that always used to be hanging about Camden Town—Elevated Evans."

"Educated Evans," corrected The Miller.

"He is not living here just now, but if I can do anything in the way of spreading the good news—"

"That's neither here nor there," said Miss Florrie tartly. "Can I have a summons?"

And The Miller explained that summonses were never granted at a police station, and certainly never granted at one o'clock in the morning. He also expressed his doubt as to whether the offence of Mr. Holborn had been as heinous as she imagined. To the best of his ability he gave her the law on the subject. It is not unlawful to refer to a future mother-in-law in terms of *opprobrium*, and he also explained that the word "hag," whilst it might mean a vicious old lady, might also describe one who could bewitch.

"At the same time," he said sympathetically, "I feel that I would like to help you get your own back, Miss Beaches, and if you would mention the name of this horse I'd see—"

At this point the silent mother became voluble.

"It's no good your wasting your time here, my dear. They can't do anything, and if they could they wouldn't. All these men stick together. The best thing to do is to see your dear father's solicitors in the morning. If I don't have the law on Cris Holborn. . ."

They made a noisy exeunt.

It was rather strange, as they say in Somers Town when they mean to imply coincidence, that this reference to Educated Evans should have been followed up that very morning by the appearance in court of a local larcenist who in the old days invariably traced his downfall to the fact that he was a subscriber to Educated Evans' £5 specials; for Mr. Evans had been the World's Champion Prophet and Turf Adviser.

Miss Beaches had gone home with her mother, some of her ardour for vengeance a little cooled. She awoke at nine o'clock to find her mother with a letter in her hand. It had come by hand from her outrageous lover—she recognised his novel spelling.

"Ah, well, ma!" she said. "Perhaps I was hard on him: I knew he'd send me an humble apology first thing in the morning."

"It"s got to be humble," said her ma ominously. "'Ag I may be, but old I'm not!"

"You've got to allow something for youth," said Florrie romantically as she tore open the envelope. "The poor boy wasn't himself—"

She read the letter: it was very short.

I'm done with you and that old nagger your ma. I'm lowering myself to associate with a lot of bung's relations. Farewell. Never cross my parth again. Cris.

P.S.—Send back the ring I gave you, I may want it.

Florrie didn't scream, she did not faint. She jerked her hair savagely into a ball and jabbed a hairpin into the confusion.

"That settles him!" she hissed.

Her ma was making savage noises. Florrie ran to the door and pulled it open. "Em-ma!" she screamed.

Her maid, who was also housemaid, parlourmaid and errand girl, flew up the stairs.

"Go and find that tipping man you was—were talking about yesterday—go and bring him here at once!"

She returned, rolling up the sleeves of her *kimono* pugilistically.

"Nagger. . . !" moaned her ma.

"Goin' to make thousands of pounds, is he!" said Florrie fiendishly. "I mustn't tell anybody, mustn't I? I'll show him. . . .Digger Boy! That's the name of the horse, ma! Digger Boy—I'll Digger Boy him."

She said other things—such as may be pardonable in a lady under the sad circumstances.

In the meantime Emma was searching Camden Town for a local prophet who was not without honour in his own district.

A day or two later Camden Town was startled by the most stupendous item of intelligence that had been dropped in years. Educated Evans was back!

The news ran like a prairie fire from the Midland Goods Yard to the Holloway Road—from Great College Street to the Nag's head. Men heard and halted their pewter pots between counter and lip and said "Go *on!*" Some confessed that they thought he was dead; others corrected this impression regretfully. Down at the "White Hart" an old man stirred and glanced uneasily at the door. Miss Pluter, the new barmaid at the "Stag and Crown" (she who wore "Gertrude" in diamonds across her blouse) expressed a desire to see the man about whom she had heard so much, and a dozen knights and squires of the saloon bar offered eagerly to fetch Evans the very next night.

Mr. Evans had returned to the scenes of his vicissitudes and triumphs! He had once gone through the card at Kempton one remarkable day and had made two, three, five, ten thousand pounds according to the source of report. He had retired; he was an owner of houses; he had an estate in the country and occasionally wrote to former clients on note-paper headed "Haddon Hall, Pilberry Road, Bromley," and that in printed characters.

It was believed that he had a servant of his own and was so rich that he wore a clean collar every day of his life. Further, it was alleged by one who had visited him that he had his dinner at the hour when most respectable people have finished their tea and are having a sluice in the kitchen preparatory to a visit to the pictures. This story, however, was not credited.

Nor did the news of his return find general acceptance. Camden Town had been an uneducated place since Mr. Evans drove away in a taxi-cab smoking a Masa cigar ("all the fragrance of Havana for 6d."), waving his hand graciously from the window. Many a man who could not afford a mouthpiece regretted his going, for Evans was as good as a lawyer, and many an address, calculated to move the stoniest-hearted magistrate, had he composed. It was Evans who got Bill Barrett off a lagging by a defence (read by Bill in the dock) showing that he had suffered from loss of memory and sleep-walking since a child. Bill certainly boggled some of the words (his pronunciation of "somnambulism" was wonderful to hear), but there were tears in his eyes as he read things about himself that he had never known till that moment.

In the days of his activities Educated Evans had had one faithful servant. His name was Samuel Toggs, he having been so christened in the dim and glorious ages when hansom cabs were a novelty and malefactors were publicly executed before Horsemonger Lane Gaol. He was called "Old Sam," partly because Sam was his name and partly because of his many years. His occupation in life, in those days, was the support of the "White Hart," a noble hostelry. He supported this palace of sin by keeping his back against it from 10 a.m. to chucking-out time. In olden days he drew water for thirsty cab-horses and received a penny for each draw, but horses belonged to the past and he knew not petrol. A strange, burly old gentleman, with tender feet and an opalescent beard that might have been white with care, he wore, summer and winter, two overcoats and a pair of black woollen mittens, a woollen scarf and a bowler hat that he had found in the roadway after a fight on Christmas Day, 1891.

Mr. Evans had been a force in Camden Town, being an educated man and one learned in the ways of thoroughbred racehorses. So, if you believed him, no horse won unless he had received Mr. Evans' express permission to do so, and that in writing. Sometimes he gave them permission and they didn't win, but, as he said, horses are not machines. He asked his clients (for he supplied information for a trifle to all who acted honourable) to remember that he gave Braxted (What a beauty! What a beauty!) at 20-1. He made a lot of money and retired to the country: what was more natural than that, when he lost a lot of money, he should come back to town?

It is strange that, as Educated Evans had journeyed towards the metropolis, he should think kindly, almost tenderly, of Old Sam. That beer-soddened ancient was in a sense a *protégé* of Evans'. Though from morning until night he propped up the walls of the "White Hart," standing with his back firmly fixed to the wall, and refusing to be enticed away by any save the potman, he had made an exception in the case of Mr. Evans, for whom he ran errands, hobbled about with messages to clients, and sometimes collected money on behalf of his patron. Old Sam had touched his cap to the educated man and had once called him "sir," but this was on the night that Sam had paid for his own drink twice.

It was not until two mornings after his return that stress of business permitted the educated man to look up his old acquaintances, and it was by a pure accident that the first of these should be The Miller—a lover of racing and no bad friend to Evans.

Mr. Challoner was standing opposite the Cobden statue, doing nothing, when his absent gaze rested on a man who was walking up Bayham Street. He was not tall, he was not broad. He was to an extent well-dressed. In one corner of his mouth was a large cigar; he swung a nearly-gold-headed cane as he strutted towards High Street, and if his bowler hat and brown boots did not accord with his morning coat, he had the air of a nobleman.

The Miller's jaw dropped as the man came nearer, for he recognised instantly the World's Premier Prophet and Turf Adviser.

"Well, well!" said The Miller, when the first greetings were over. "So you're back, and Camden Town has one more mug."

"It's all very well for you to go passing personal remarks," said Educated Evans, with a touch of asperity in his voice, "but what's the good of locking the stable door after the horse has ate his wild oats, I ask you, Mr. Challoner?"

Sergeant Challoner did not take offence at the brusqueness, even rudeness, of the reply, but continued to nibble his straw reflectively, his grave eyes fixed upon the Prophet.

"You had a fortune," he said slowly. "You won it by being clever enough not to back your own tips, and by reducing yourself to a condition of beastly intoxication before you went racing. When you handed up your money and told the bookmakers what horse was going to win, you happened to speak the truth—*in vino veritas.*"

"I know Veritas—he's a two-year-old in Persse's stable—but Vino

123

is an animal I don't remember."

"Having accumulated this wealth, you took your ill-gotten gains, purchased a farm, and not only committed the unspeakable folly of owning racehorses, but added the general lunacy of attempting to train them."

Educated Evans shook his head sorrowfully.

"It was the feeding that done it," he said. "Was I to know that horses didn't eat bones and birdseed? Is there a book published on the subject? Did Mr. Gilpings when he wrote his highly clarsical articles in the weekly newspapers, mention anything about feeding animals? Anyway," he added hopefully, "I'll get it all back over the Lincoln. There's a horse in that race that hasn't been tryin' for four years. There's a big stable commission, and he's *loose*! This horse could hop home on his fetlocks. I'm sending it out on my Five-Pound Owner's Special Wire, so don't put it about, Miller."

The detective sighed.

"Camden Town has been a dull and truthful place without you," he said. "What's the name of this horse?"

"Otono," said Educated Evans. "I've got a thousand pounds to twenty about it from Izzy Isaacsheim."

The Miller rubbed his nose thoughtfully.

"He was scratched this morning," he said gently, and Mr. Evans made a clucking noise with his mouth.

"Thank Gawd I didn't back him!" he said, and did not even attempt to excuse his perjury. "With that animal out of the way, it's a stone certainty for Cold Meat. That horse has been specially kep' for this race. I've had it from the boy who does him."

"When you get anything good, you might come and see me," said The Miller, preparing to mount his bicycle. Cold Meat's been sold to go to Belgium. I thought you might have seen it in the papers yesterday—the way they send these worn-out old horses to Belgium is a scandal."

He waited, and then:

"How's Old Sam?" asked Evans.

The Miller got down from the pedal of his bicycle.

"Haven't you heard?" he asked, in a hushed whisper.

"Not dead?" asked Evans, preparing to be shocked.

"No," said The Miller, and then: "There's no room for you here, Evans—you've lost the art of tipping losers."

Mr. Evans shrugged his shoulders.

"It's a nistoric fac'," he said, "that once you're a bricklayer you're always a bricklayer. It's in your blood. Look at Napoleon Bonaparte, the well-known French officer. When he was took away an' imprisoned on the Isle of Dogs did he sit down an' moan? No, Mr. Challoner, he sees a spider comin' down from the ceilin' an' he says 'Turn again, Napoleon,' an' sure enough he did."

"What?" asked the dazed Miller.

"Turn," said Evans, "an' I've turned. When I read in the so-called sporting press the ad. of this feller an' that feller—actually boastin' about the 7-4 winners they've give, I remember Braxted—20-1. What a beauty! an' Eton Boy, 100-12. What a beauty! an' such like high-class predictions an' prophecies, an' I says to myself, 'Evans,' I says, 'don't let them daylight robbers have all the loot to theirselves 'op in and help yourself.'"

Mr. Evans gave a hitch to his shepherd plaid trousers, lit again his towsled cigar and wiped his moustache on the back of his hand.

"Did Camden Town hang out its flags when you came back?" asked The Miller.

"Sarcasm don't mean nothing to me," said Evans; "it passes me by like Cardinal Richloo, the highly respected clergyman said, like water on a duck's back in one yerhole and out of the other yerhole."

"I seem to have heard that ancient wheeze at the Bedford—in the early nineties," said The Miller. "What are you going to do?"

Mr. Evans studied the busy prospect of High Street before he answered.

"I'm gettin' together my army of touts," he said. "I've appointed me Newmarket an' Lambourn men—an' to all clients new an' old I say 'Fear Nothing!' "

"And what do they say?" asked the interested Miller.

Evans coughed.

"They ain't had time to reply yet," he said. "I only sent out yesterday to a few clients—about three thousand."

"Liar," said The Miller softly, and Mr. Evans smiled as though he knew better.

"Seen anything of young Harry Leafer—he used to be a client of yours?"

The question was carelessly put but Mr. Evans shot a suspicious glance at him. For the whisper had gone round and it had reached him, that young Harry had disappeared suddenly and urgently only that morning. It was even said that he had gone to Brighton or some

125

other foreign part.

"I don't know nothing about young Harry," he said, hurt. "Can't you get it out of your head that I'm a 'nose,' Mr. Challoner?"

"'Nose' is vulgar—say unofficial detective," murmured The Miller, and made preparations to go.

"Look up Old Sam: he'll be tickled to death to see you," he said at parting. Educated Evans sniffed.

"The likes of him look *me* up," he said. "He knows where to find me."

There are few keener pleasures than the happy sense of anticipation which is enjoyed by the wanderer returned to his native home. He pictures the enthusiasm which the news of his return will bring; he sees in his mind's eye men crossing the road to greet him, or the shy children he left behind, now radiant and beautiful young women, advancing timidly to hold his hand, and gazing with awe upon one who had ventured abroad. Educated Evans had not been abroad, but Bromley is a very long way from Camden Town.

He saw no recognisable shy maidens, High Street being notoriously deficient in this quantity. Nor did anybody rush across the road, in imminent peril of being run over, to grasp him warmly by the hand. The landlord of the "Red Lion" gave him a curt nod and did not seem to be aware of the fact that he had been away at all. An acquaintance of other days certainly joined him at the bar at his invitation, but Mr. Evans realised that he would join anybody who uttered the magic password to conviviality, "Wotshors?"

"How's Old Sam?" asked Mr. Evans.

His guest for the moment coughed and looked uneasy.

"Oh, he's all right," he said, and changed the subject.

"I'm opening my new office this week," said Evans carelessly.

His acquaintance coughed again.

"I hope you'll give some winners," he said unpromisingly.

"Braxted," murmured Evans. "People have got a short memory."

"Personally I was at school when Braxted won," said the other with a certain significance.

At the "Old Albany Arms" Evans found two clients of other days, and broke it to them that he was back in business. They seemed uncomfortable. When he asked after Old Sam they were embarrassed.

Was the aged man ill? wondered Evans as he strolled forth into the High Street, and there came upon him the spirit of philanthropy and loving-kindness. Old Sam used to live in a house up a very narrow passage which was called locally "Little Hell," though there were many people who thought that the adjective hardly described the character of the place.

Evans called. Old Sam's landlady was out. Her slatternly granddaughter told him that Old Sam was living in Great College Street. Mr. Evans was shocked. Great College Street is a thoroughfare more or less devoted to the plutocrat.

He sought out the address: a highly respectable and classy one. There was a lawn in front of the house and white curtains at the window, and the bit of a servant girl who answered the door piped that Mr. Toggs was out, and would Mr. Evans come into his sitting-room and wait?

Educated Evans went out into the street, a little dazed. Had Old Sam come into money? He was to learn.

He wended his way to his newly recovered flat in Bayham Mews. He referred to it as a "flat," though in truth it was two rooms over a stable, and he was very lucky to get back his old quarters. Fortune had come to him, as The Miller had said, and he had started forth upon a hectic career as owner and trainer, freely backing his own horses, in consequence of which he had returned to Bayham Mews with ten pounds, one pair of plaid trousers, a gold-plated safety razor and a few inconsiderable articles of property which he had salved from the wreckage of his estate.

Evans had work to do. He had acquired for a song a patent duplicator. A child could work it. There was in fact a picture in the advertisement of a pretty little girl turning out thousands of copies in an hour and smiling the while, as though at the ridiculous ease with which handbills, accounts and announcements of all kinds (to quote the literature which accompanied the picture) might be copied. Evans would like to have met that child. He guessed she was a weight-lifter in her spare moments.

It was easy enough to write your announcement on wax paper. You used a stylo and the point went through. Then you fixed the wax paper on the machine, inked a roller and turned a handle. At first nothing happened. Then a violet oblong, covered with all the available ink, came out.

Evans preferred a rubber stamp, or, alternatively, the services of a young lady in Great College Street, who did that kind of work at a reasonable price and with great rapidity.

Nevertheless, he determined on one more attempt with the patent duplicator. So working, he heard the slow thump of feet on the wooden step that led to his door, and presently the door itself opened, revealing the bulbous face of an aged man. It was Old Sam. But Old Sam in a frock coat—Old Sam in a top hat!

"Hullo, Evans," said Sam huskily, and Mr. Evans nearly dropped.

"Hullo, Evans!" And this from a man who was, so to speak, a slave!

He blinked into the room suspiciously.

"Hullo, Evans," he said again.

The educated man waved his hand haughtily.

"Push off—I've got nothing to give away," he said.

Such a rebuff would have reduced a sensitive man to tears of mortification. Old Sam scratched himself thoughtfully.

"I gotta tip for Digger Boy first day at Lincoln," he said, and Evans gasped at the insolence. Even in his delirium he realised that he'd never heard of such a horse as Digger Boy. But imagine the feelings of Michelangelo in receipt of a letter from a Florentine Correspondence School headed "Let us Show You How to Paint—Send No Money!" or Shakespeare being chided at rehearsal by a small-part lady for splitting his infinitives.

"A what!" asked Mr. Evans, scarcely believing his ears.

"Got it from the young lady who knows the trainer," wheezed Old Sam, stroking his variegated beard. "What a beauty, what a beauty! Help yourself!"

The room spun round. This... this common loafer, this holder-open of taxi doors... this embeered and senile servant to the pot ... actually employing terms which were sacred to Mr. Evans' exclusive profession.

"Wait a minute—a young lady gave you this... horse? Why?"

Old Sam came farther into view. He was resplendent. A cable chain of gold was stretched across his portliness. He wore patent leather boots.

"She sent for me," he said hoarsely, "me havin' a reputation—she sent for me!"

Mr. Evans held on to a chair for support. Had the great revolution arrived? Had the masses destroyed the intelligentsia of the country and assumed control of affairs? Were the lower orders on top and the aristocracy of brains destroyed?

"'Ere, what's the game?" said Mr. Evans, a little breathlessly.

Sam looked uneasy for a moment.

"When you went away I took up this tippin' business an' I've done well," he said. "Can't read myself, but got a boy to look through the papers, and if I liked the name I give it—'aven't you 'eard of Old Sam's Specials?"

Mr. Evans was not dreaming.

"Old Sam's Specials?" he repeated hollowly. "What did you sell 'em for?"

Mr. Toggs shuffled his feet in his embarrassment.

"Tuppence," he said, and Educated Evans nearly swooned.

"Tuppence!"

He looked round for something to throw at the visitor, but there was only the patent duplicator, and even a child could not have thrown that. . . . Sam was halfway down the stairs before Evans could bring his numbed brain to work. He rushed to the landing and looked down into the face of the plagiarist.

". . . Robbin' my brains, you perishin' old swiper. . ." he yelled.

"Digger Boy. . . 'ad 'im from 'eadquarters!" bellowed Sam. "An' don't go pinchin' any of my customers!"

Evans put on his hat and went out to make inquiries. It was true. Almost every little newsagent in Camden Town sold Old Sam's Specials.

"I admit they're different to yours," said one agent, and added: "They win."

It was night time when the real tragedy came home to him. He called at the White Hart, expecting to see Old Sam supporting the wall and to pass him by in disdain. He saw The Miller talking to a policeman near the saloon entrance, but Old Sam was in the private bar. Evans heard him as he opened the door.

"I gotta horse for Lincoln that can't lose. . . this horse could fall down an' get up an' win. Lady sent for me specially to tell me. She says, 'Are you the well-known Educated man?' I says, 'Yes, miss —I'm known as Educated Toggs. . .'"

Evans flung open the door with a savage howl and dashed in.

It was fortunate that The Miller saw and gripped him in time and dragged him out: most unfortunate for Sam that he followed in a valiant mood: a crowning calamity that he should mistake the uniformed policeman with whom The Miller had been talking for his old patron, and should assault him with a pewter pot.

They carried Old Sam to the station on an ambulance, and the next morning an unsympathetic magistrate sent him down for three weeks.

"I hated putting the old man away," said The Miller. "Anyway, Evans, the coast is clear for you now your rival has gone."

"Rival " sneered Evans. "That pie-can! Why, he don't know a horse from a stepladder. I wish he'd been out when I started my season! I'm sendin' out a horse that couldn't lose if he was scratched."

"What is this horse?" asked The Miller.

"Digger Boy—help yourself—and don't forget I've got a mouth!" said Mr. Evans.

2.—A Souvenir

Through his uncurtained window Mr. Evans could see the young lady in grey. She occupied the rooms immediately opposite his own and on the other side of the mews. Her uncle was a musher and drove a taxi which he and his brother George had purchased on the "never never" system. You pay £80 down and more than you can afford for the rest of your life. Her aunt was genteel and wore eyeglasses. They lived in a large suite of rooms which extended over two garages, in one of which the cab was cleaned: it never stayed there for any appreciable time. The uncle drove it by day, and another uncle, whose name was George, by night, or *vice versa*. The taxi-cab never complained about this perpetual motion because it was inarticulate.

Mr. Evans was not interested in the cab, or the uncle, who always seemed to have boils on his neck, or Uncle George, who was a thin, acidulated man who talked to himself all the time. Nor did he look twice at the aunt. But the niece in grey, with her black hair and her saucy way of putting her hand on her hip, and her shining silk stockings—this young woman was, and had been since she first nodded to him brightly and said "Morning," an object of profound speculation and delight. Sometimes she nursed a baby prettily. He discovered in subsequent conversations that it was her sister's.

Mr. Evans was not old. On the other hand, he was not young. And anyway, scholars have no age: they are youthful or ancient according to the measure of their erudition.

"I'll bet she wonders who I am," said Mr. Evans with a quiet, sad smile. Few people know me outside of the profession. I'll bet she says, 'I wonder who that lonely man is: he looks as if he's had a lot of trouble—an' what an interestin' face he's got, mother or auntie, as the case may be!' "

Thus Evans communed with himself before the mirror, not knowing at that time the exact relationship of the lady with the driver of cabs.

One evening he leaned over the balustrade of the landing outside his door. She came out, looked and nodded.

"Evening," she said. "It's a nice evening."

"Not so good as Palermo in the South of France, or dear old India," said Evans. "Give me Egyp' for nice evenin's an' a half-hour's row down the Nile Canal."

She looked at him awe-stricken, red lips parted, violet eyes wide open.

"Have you been there?" she asked.

"Lots of times," said Evans carelessly; "*and* China, which is the most highly populised country in the world. That's where we get china from an' Chinese lanterns."

She leaned over her landing too. There was twelve feet of space between them. Down below a dazed horse-keeper stopped work to listen.

"It must be wonderful going abroad."

Evans shrugged so violently that one of his brace buttons came off and fell with a musical tinkle on the cobble-stones below.

"You get used to it if you're a racehorse owner," he said. " I've won the Calcutta Cup once but gave away the ticket to a footman at my club—couldn't be bothered. The Melbourne Cup—that's a wonderful race! Down in Orstralia."

She drew a long, sighing breath; her eyes were bright. He had, he saw, assumed a new interest in her eyes. The glow of it made his flannel undershirt feel prickly.

"Fancy. . . you own race-horses! Do they ever win?"

Evans smiled tiredly.

"Now and again. I don't like winnin' too often. The other members of the Jockey Club get that jealous there's no holdin' 'em."

"But how mean!"

Mr. Evans started to shrug again but remembered in time. Down below in the mews, the horse-keeper swooned against the wall.

"You can't please everybody," said Educated Evans. "Even Queen Elizabeth couldn't do that—that's why she got her napp—her head cut off by B—Mary the celebrated Queen of Scotch. That led to the Diet of Worms an' the rise an' fall of the far-famed Oliver Cromwell, fourteen hundred and seventy-six," he added.

She was stricken speechless for a moment, and Educated Evans proceeded.

131

"That brings us to the question of Astronomy. Very few people know that the eclipse of the sun is caused by the earth in its revolutions comin' between the moon an' the sun, thus causin' many ignorant people to think that the whole thing's wrong, when as a matter of fact it's an act of nature."

He was now speaking fluently, swinging his hat with the same easy carelessness as a sailor swings the lead. And when he dropped the hat into a puddle immediately below him, he just smiled. He was that much careless.

"Take the law," he said. "There's a good many people don't understand the law. Many a time I've stood up in court and said to the other lawyers—"

"Are you a lawyer too?"

Below the horse-keeper tried to say that Mr. Evans was less of a lawyer than a something liar, but his lips would not frame the words.

"Bit of everything," said Mr. Evans modestly. "Scientific—take sidlitz powders—"

The beautiful girl in grey was spared the need. Her aunt appeared in the open doorway, a mass of undigested knitting in her hands, and called her in.

"Come in, Clara, do!"

"Yes, auntie," said the girl meekly.

"What on earth do you want to talk to that old man for?" demanded the aunt, too audibly: the rest was undistinguishable.

Mr. Evans sneered at her. Old! What a nerve! Still, he had impressed her: he could see that. He went down the wooden steps, retrieved his hat and his button, and returned to the privacy of his "den" to dry the one and sew the other. She knew him now for what he was. An educated man. She was probably talking to her aunt about it at that moment, chiding her parent for her uncharity.

"No, auntie, you are wrong. I won't allow you to say that. He is *not* old—and what is age? One loves a man's mind; his breadth—his education."

That's what he imagined her saying.

What she actually said was:

"Who *is* that funny old geezer, aunt?"

"God knows," said her aunt, a pious woman. "I think he's something to do with dogs."

But Clara Develle was honestly and sincerely interested in Educated Evans and wondered about him. For example, she often wondered if he was right in his head. And she wondered who gave him his plaid trousers, and she wondered if he was a burglar, but decided that he was too tender on his feet for that nippy profession. And as her wonderment grew, there came to her a realisation that there really were possibilities about the educated man.

"Never mind about *him*," said her aunt sharply, when she approached the subject. "Your uncle Alf says things can't go on as they're going. You've got to find something to do. He can't keep you in idleness, because we're poor people, and if we wasn't we wouldn't."

Miss Clara said nothing.

"Your uncle's a man of the world—so is your uncle George," her aunt went on. "There's some things we don't know and don't *want* to know. Certain things have been remarked, but the least said soonest mended. Only it seems *funny*!"

Her niece was evidently in agreement with these cryptic sentiments, hints and innuendos, for she sighed sadly. Mr. Evans did not see her again that night, but he did notice, as he had noticed before, a young man going up the steps after dark.

Dark suspicions gathered in Mr. Evans' mind. Could this young man be a Fellow? Was he a Chap? The thing was preposterous. . . such a child. . . the aunt would never allow it. Not if she was a Good Woman. . .

Occasionally The Miller drifted down Bayham Mews. Generally it was a matter of duty which brought him to this place of silence, but sometimes he mounted the wooden steps that led to the habitation of one who was called, for excellent reason, Educated Evans, in search of social relaxation—for even a detective-sergeant has a human side to his character.

On this chilly night in March The Miller came up the steps and knocked at the door.

"Hullo, Mr. Challoner!" said Educated Evans graciously. "Kindly step inside and take the chair."

"Have you got a meeting, Evans?" asked The Miller good-humouredly.

"No—but I've only got one chair," said Evans.

He wore his overcoat, for the night was cold and the fire that burnt in the grate was so small as to be almost invisible. The Miller glanced at the table, where a paraffin lamp shed its rays upon a litter of paper.

"Just writing to a few of my clients, said Evans, rubbing his long nose. "They don't deserve it, but I've got to do it—Cold Feet for the Hurst Park Hurdle. He's been kept special for it. Not a yard at Lingfield—but this time his head's loose."

"Old Sam says—" began The Miller, but the look of pain, reproach, contempt and acid amusement in Evans' face cancelled his *communiqué*. Old Sam had been a propper of boozers, a holder of horses, an opener of cab doors. As lowly as a slave to Educated Evans, who had given him money and orders. And in the protracted absence of Mr. Evans in the country, Old Sam, traitor, ingrate and saturated beer-hound, had blossomed forth as a tipster.

"I'm sorry I mentioned your rival," said The Miller.

The pain in Mr. Evans' face grew more acute.

If The Miller had any reason for his call he did not state it. Evans was almost glad to see him go. Great was his fortune when later, slipping out to get a quick one, he met the grey girl at the end of the mews. He had an impression that she had just seen somebody off—a brief, blurred glimpse of a figure vanishing in the darkness. Should he speak to her or pass with a stately bow.

"Good-evening, Mr. Evans."

She knew his name.

"Good-evening, Miss—?"

"Miss Develle," she said. "Just been seeing a friend off," she went on. "Not exactly a friend, but a gentleman who is always running after me."

"What a cheek!" said Evans hotly. "I never heard such a thing in my life. It's preposterous!"

They lingered awhile. Her eyes shone hotly out of the dark; the dusk of night was in her hair. Evans grew agitated. It was within five minutes of closing time.

"I'd like to have a chat with you, Mr. Evans," she said earnestly. "You're such a Man of the World, or Gentleman of the World as one might say. I'll be going to the Rialto pictures at eight tomorrow night. Please don't mention it to auntie."

She was gone before he realised; her black hair and violet eyes were swallowed in the void. Educated Evans reeled to the nearest house of refreshment and drank heavily, for him.

They met in the ornate vestibule of the Rialto. Harold Lloyd favoured them with a celluloid smile as they slipped into the dark interior.

". . .Yes, my aunt. My papa married beneath him—he was a Colonel in the army... that little baby's my sister Annie's. . . . Oh, I'm so glad to have a chat with you, Mr. Evans! I'm in such trouble. I must get some kind of work—I really must. It's hateful depending on relations or even relatives. . . ."

She told him of her struggles; of the weary round she went from aunt to aunt—

"There's a cashier wanted at Lammer's. That's my work . . . if only I knew somebody who knew somebody else who knew Mr. Lammer."

Honestly she was not aware that Mr. Lammer was an acquaintance of his. When he explained that he had only to crook his finger for Mr. Lammer to skip like an intoxicated lamb, she thought he was swanking. The most she had expected of her new-found friend was a novel angle which would help her.

When the lights went up he saw (for her hat was removed) that she was a little older than he had thought. This pleased him. He paid for a light fish supper out of his last half-crown and went to bed full of noble resolves.

Mr. Evans, of Sansovino House, Bayham Mews, was not without influence. There were people in Camden Town who never heard his name mentioned without employing the most regrettable expressions to describe The World's Premier Racing Prophet and Turf Adviser; but there were others who through thick and thin were loyalty personified.

Mr. Lammer, the High-Class Draper and Ladies' Outfitter, for example, never ceased to sound the praises of one who, at a critical moment in his history, when every other man who came into his office carried a writ of summons in his inside left-hand pocket, had imparted to Mr. Lammer the exclusive information that Braxted could fall down, have a fit and *then* win the Stewards' Cup.

The distracted Mr. Lammer had in his possession at the time the sum of four hundred pounds, which he had put aside for the rainy day when he would be obliged (in the language of Camden Town) to do a guy. This sum, withheld from his creditors, he invested on Braxted at 25-1. And Braxted won. Twenty-five times £400 is exactly £10,000, and with this sum Mr. Lammer paid his debts, extended his premises and entered upon a newer and brighter life.

He was not a cultured man, being one of those who admitted responsibility for his own success, and he admired the erudition of his humble friend beyond words.

"Certainly, Mr. Evans," he said, as the educated man sat on the edge of a chair in his office and made his request, "I'll do anything I can for you. I've given up backin' 'orses, but if you're ever short of a few pound, step in and ask for what you want. You say that this young lady is All Right?"

Evans drew a long breath.

"She's the daughter of a colonel in the Army," he explained fervently, "and a perfect lady: owin' to a bank failure the family's ruined. She's like the celebrated Dick Whittin'ton an' don't know the way to turn. And she reminds me of the well-known an' highly respected wife of Julius Cesar, the far-famed Italian—she's above the position."

So it was arranged that Clara Develle should go into Lammer's store as junior cashier at a reasonable salary, and Evans purred his way back to Bayham Mews, where the young aristocrat was in residence, and waited for the friendly dark to tell her the good news.

"I must say it's awfully good of you, Mr. Evans," she said rapidly—she was rather a quick talker. "What a bit of luck for me that I met you as I did! I'm sure my poor pa would have died with shame if he knew I was going into business—as a matter of fact he died from eppoplexity during the air-raids, him being a general and naturally brave."

Educated Evans scarcely noticed her parent's promotion.

"Has that feller been worrying you again?" he asked with a sub-tone of ferocity.

On the previous night they had discussed the furtive young man who came and went in the dark. Mr. Evans had recognised him.

"Mr. Erman? Oh, dear, no," she protested. "I'd never dream of looking twice at him. Saucy monkey if ever there was one."

"I saw him talking to you in the mews tonight—" began Evans.

"Merely passing the time of day. One has to be civil in my position. I mean to say, you've got to be polite if you're a lady," she said breathlessly.

Evans, the loyalest of men, felt she should know the worst.

"He's a crook, a hook, and a twister," said Evans. He's done time for burglary and he owes me two pun' ten over Charley's Mount, what I put him on to. Remember, miss, if there's any trouble, I'm around!"

She said she would remember: she said this rather vaguely, as though she were thinking of something else.

"You've been simply marvellous to me," said the general's daughter with a sigh, and when I get working I'm going to give you a little souvenir."

"A bit of ribbon," said Educated Evans sentimentally, "a stay lace—anything to remind me of you—nothing expensive."

Things were not going well with Evans. He might have paraphrased a Mr. Browning and said, "Never the chance and the girl and the money all together."

A week later Educated Evans watched the stream of life passing along Hampstead Road, and mused a little sorrowfully upon the unattainable value of things. Every motor-omnibus that flew by was worth a thousand pounds; not a cyclist plodded across the field of his vision that was not supported by a couple of pounds' worth of old iron and rubber.

The landlord of his suite in Bayham Mews had that morning demanded (with a certain significant reference to the number of people who were begging and praying for the accommodation usurped by Mr. Evans) that the four weeks' arrears of rent should be paid by twelve noon on the following day, failing which—

Detective-Sergeant Challoner stood by his side in as earnest a contemplation of the pageant of life. A keen wind blew down High Street, though the sun shone overhead in a blue and white sky: it was spring. Outside the White Hart the red-nosed Lolly Marks stood behind a big basket banked high with daffodils and narcissi—the placards bore the magic slogan "Lincolnshire Favourite Coughing"—the vernal equinox had swung to Camden Town.

"If people would act honourable," said Mr. Evans, "this would be a grand world to live in. As William Shakespeare, the well-known and highly popular poet, says, 'What a game it is!' and he was right."

"Broke?" asked The Miller, with a certain hard sympathy.

Yet he did not look broke. Mr. Evans for once was dressed up to his position. His moustache was trimmed, his collar was clean, and only an expert could see where he had scissored the frayed edges. A ready-made cravat was embellished by a jewel that might have been a ruby worth a couple of thousand pounds, but probably wasn't.

"To pieces," said Educated Evans, and shrugged his hock- bottle shoulders. "When you re'lise that I sent out the winner of the Newbury Hurdle to three thousan' nine hundred and forty clients, and that all I had back for my trouble was twelve bob and a 'slush' ten-shillin' note that I nearly got penal servitude for passin', you understand why men like the celebrated Sir Francis Columbus went an' lived in America."

"Why don't you see Lammer—he's a pal of yours?"

Evans screwed up his face in contempt.

"I never 'touch' a client," he said, and spoke the amazing truth.

"Why are you waiting here?" asked The Miller after a long silence. "Lookin' for anybody? By the way, you haven't seen Nosey Erman about, have you?"

"No, I haven't," said Evans. "that feller's less than the dust to me, to use a well-known expression."

"I wonder why he's turned up in Camden Town?" The Miller mused. "He's got some game on, I'll bet."

Well Mr. Evans knew the game of the wanderer. He had returned to filch the heart of an innocent girl—the sharp eyes of the educated man had detected the amorous Nosey. His exposure was accomplished.

The Miller pulled at his long nose, and then:

"Come round to my lodgings this afternoon and I'll hand you a pound," he said as he prepared to go. "But don't come if you can tap anybody else."

Between gratitude and sardonic mirth at the prospect of tapping anybody Mr. Evans was slightly incoherent.

Long after The Miller had gone he waited, and presently his vigil was rewarded.

A slim, neatly dressed girl walked quickly up Bayham Street and turned towards the High Street. In an instant Educated Evans was flying across the roadway, and at the sound of his voice the girl turned with a smile.

"Why, Mr. Evans," she said, "I thought you were at Cheltenham!"

"My car broke down," said Mr. Evans mendaciously. "The carburettor keeps on back-firing: for two pins I'd send it back to old Rolls and give him a bit of me mind!"

He fell in by her side, and for two minutes fifty-five seconds and a few fifths he trod on air, and his heart sang comic songs.

Just short of Lammer's Corner she stopped and held out her hand with a sigh.

"You are lucky, Mr. Evans," she said enviously. "It must be wonderful to be your own master: to go where you like and how you like. I wish I had a lot of money.

Evans wished the same thing as fervently, but he did not say so.

She sighed.

"I wish I knew what was going to win that big race at Cheltenham," she said.

"Benny's Hope," replied Evans promptly. "I had it from the owner, who's a personal friend of mine. That horse could fall down, get up,

138

turn round to see what was going to be last, and then win."

"Benny's Hope," she said thoughtfully, and then: "I've got that souvenir for you, Mr. Evans," she said. "You wouldn't think I was fast if I brought it round to your flat one night, would you?"

And before he realised it, she had disappeared through the ornamental portals of Lammer's High-Class Drapers and Ladies' Outfitters.

Evans walked thoughtfully back to his apartment, planning matrimony.

★★★★★★

Educated Evans got out of bed and slipped on his dressing- gown, which was also his overcoat, an extra blanket, and on occasions a mackintosh. The hour was seven; outside in the dark mews rain was falling steadily.

It was not an hour at which one might expect the most enthusiastic of clients would call upon the World's Champion. In truth, of late, Evans had found his erstwhile clientele somewhat sceptical of his information even when he sought them out.

He lit the oil lamp and opened the door. There was nobody in sight, and then he heard a sound, and, stooping, lifted the long basket that stood on the landing and carried it into the room.

"Good Gawd!" said Evans.

He heard the wail before he opened the lid and saw the solemn eyes staring up from the interior of the basket.

"Good Gawd!" said Evans again.

He picked up the baby and laid it on the bed, and with a flutter of eyelids the tiny mortal went instantly into a sound sleep.

Evans examined the basket. It bore the label of a local fishmonger and smelt strongly of the sea. The World's Champion ran his fingers through his hair and strove to recover his composure. And then he heard a heavy step upon the stairs, and the door opened to reveal a figure in a shiny mackintosh.

"Hullo, Mr. Challoner—come in."

The straw between The Miller's teeth was soddened with rain, and as he stood in the room near the door, tiny rivulets of water dripped hurriedly to the floor.

Without any preliminary

"Do you know Mrs. Erman—a pasty-faced girl with goggly eyes?"

I don't—" began Evans.

"You got her a job at Lammer's," said The Miller sharply. "I knew she was staying here with her aunt, and I came down to make sure the other night, but I never dreamt she'd plant herself on you. She was hanging round here for something, but I couldn't guess what it was."

Evans was pale, his mouth wide open.

"Wha's—wha's happened?" he croaked, and The Miller laughed unpleasantly.

"Tonight they cleared Lammer's safe and made a get-away. We'll be able to pick them up because she's got a baby."

Educated Evans opened his mouth again and tried to speak, blinked impotently and tried again.

"Miss Develle. . . "

"Mrs. Erman," corrected The Miller, and his eyes fell upon the little slumberer.

"Yours?" he asked, and Educated Evans shook his head, speechless.

The Miller walked across the room and examined the child. He saw what Evans in his agitation had failed to see. A card tied to the baby's wrist by a piece of pink ribbon, and the card was inscribed:

A little sooveneer."

Mrs. Erman was good at figures, but her spelling left much to be desired.

3.—THE MAKER OF WINNERS

The Miller would have passed the crowd at the corner of College Street, only the voice that emerged from the centre of the throng had a familiar ring, and he edged his way into the press with no great difficulty, for certain of the audience recognised Detective-Sergeant Challoner and were passionately desirous that the recognition should not be mutual.

In the midst of a cleared circle was a thin iron rod held by a small and dirty-faced boy, and attached to the rod by a gallows bracket was a spluttering naphtha lamp. And round and round the clear space in the middle of the crowd walked a man who was jockey from the waist up. The colours were familiar to The Miller. He had seen them to the fore on the day Weathervane won the Royal Hunt Cup and when London Cry won at Goodwood. Though the great owner of the colours had recently changed His trainer, there was no evidence that He had engaged Educated Evans as first jockey to the stables.

The tipster had a bundle of cards in one hand, a riding whip in the other; his jockey cap was a little too big for him, and the peak flopped down over his nose, and all that The Miller could see was a fringe of ragged moustache, the tip of a stubby nose and an unshaven chin. . . .

". . . And let me tell you people who know me far and wide that a man of my education wouldn't go lowerin' hisself to appear in public like the famous Lady Gawdiva who rode through the streets of London with nothin' on to settle a bet, if it wasn't that I can't letcher miss the most unbeatable certainty that ever looked through a bridle. Did I give yer Salmon Trout? Did I beg an' implore yer to back Charley's Mount—did I go down on my knees to yer and say 'Whatever y'do, don't leave out Twelve Pointer for the Cambridge'—did I tell you what his twelve points was . . .?"

The Miller waited through another quarter of an hour's eloquence; waited till Mr. Evans had stripped his royal livery and resumed his coat. And then:

"I'm surprised to hear you telling the tale, Evans."

Mr. Evans shrugged his narrow shoulders.

"It's common, I admit—but I got to work up my connections, Mr. Challoner. Competition's done it. Old Sam got my best customers. You wouldn't think that old pub-lizard could compete with a man like me. Why, I could talk him blind, Mr. Challoner. Where's his education? Could he put a letter together like me? Could he get a job like I got—a hundred pound job with lashin's of money besides? No! That old Sam is a low, uneducated pub-prop! But I got him. He's goin' for Lapwing to win the Newbury Cup, an' the horse don't run. I've had it from the boy that does him. Ice Box is a certainty—tried twenty-one pound better than Blue Nose. He'll come home alone."

The Miller walked on until they came to the corner of Stibbington Street.

"I don't fancy Ice Box," he said then.

Mr. Evans smiled.

"Could you fancy Twelve Pointer with six stun three? Could you fancy Pharos, the property of the celebrated Sir Derby, with no weight at all—that's Ice Box at 7-5!"

Again The Miller was thoughtful.

"I saw you with a swell in Euston Road this afternoon—friend of yours?"

Educated Evans looked important, coughed knowledgably and patently avoided the topic.

141

"He's an acquaintance—goodnight, Mr. Challoner."

"Hold hard: who is this lad you were with?" asked The Miller. "Got an idea I know him."

"He's a doctor," said Educated Evans briefly. "Doctor Walling—a client."

He seemed disinclined for further discussion. The Miller watched him turning back towards Bayham Street, his colours under his arm, using his whip as a walking-stick, and then of a sudden the officer of the law forgot that there was such a person in the world as Educated Evans, For, glancing idly up at the dark facia of a house, he saw the figure of a man walk carefully along a parapet and disappear into a top window.

It was a large house and respectable. It was owned by a Mr. Opes, a builder, who lived on the premises and had his workshops in what had once been his back garden.

The Miller crossed the road and presently a uniformed constable appeared. There was a brief consultation and the policeman went off to telephone for a few reserves.

Waiting until he had returned, the sergeant went up to the door and knocked; it was opened by a small maid-servant, who told him that nobody was home but she: the family was at the Bedford music-hall. After he had explained who he was, and had supported the young lady, who never before had felt that she could throw a faint in such safe and agreeable circumstances, he went upstairs and found, hidden in a cupboard, William Henry Smith, by trade a painter, by inclination a small-time burglar. By which is meant that he compared with real burglars as a street singer compares with Tetrazzini.

"It's a cop—I'll go quiet," said the philosophical William in plain English. "I rumbled you as soon as I took a screw through the winder. When I got my lamps on you I knew you was a busy. What'll I get—a laggin'?"

"Hope for the best," said The Miller, as he snapped handcuffs on the man (William sometimes changed his mind about going quietly).

As they walked to the station:

"I have to work for *my* livin'," said William Henry Smith bitterly. "I'm not like this here Educated Evans, that can go tellin' the tale an' the police not so much as clout him!"

One of the standing grievances of the criminal classes is the immunity of the non-criminal classes.

"What has Evans done to you?" asked The Miller, who was a tireless seeker after knowledge.

William Henry thought hard and could find no offence in the Educated Man—at least no offence that he could put into words at that moment.

"He's unlucky," he said. " It's well known all over Camden Town that if you have anything to do with Educated Evans you'll have bad luck. An' why I did a bust at that so-and-so taller chandler's house, when I've got a hundred pound job to do for a gent, I don't know," he added in despair. "When I come out of my house to have a stroll round I'd got no more idea of bustin' that house than I had of flyin'—I must be gettin' childish. But the fact is, Miller, I can't resist paripits. If I see a paripit rennin' round a house I've got to get up to it. . ."

He expatiated on the lure of parapets and threw in a remark or two about the temptation of pantry windows, and The Miller listened with great forbearance.

"What was this hundred pound job you were going to do?" he asked, during a pause in Mr. Smith's homily.

But William Henry Smith was no Squeaker.

"You said you were going to do a hundred pound job for a gentleman," said The Miller patiently. "What's the good of being silly?—I'm your best friend—"

But William Henry was deep in his gloomy thoughts.

"And there was a hundred pound job waiting for me," he repeated moodily. "A hundred pound sweet. No risk, and, in a manner of speaking, quite lawful. But the moment I knew Educated Evans was in it I ought to have run away from London, I ought indeed, Miller."

"Was he in it?" asked The Miller, as they turned into a street where the blue lamp of the station house gleamed mournfully.

"He was and he wasn't," was the cryptic reply. "He was, and yet he didn't know he was, if you understand me rightly? He's unlucky, that feller. Tipster! Why, he couldn't tip a load of dirt into a shell-hole, that feller!"

William Henry had once served in the Labour Corps in France, and his illustrations were occasionally of a military character.

When The Miller had seen his guest safely housed, and had furnished the station sergeant with a number of uncomplimentary particulars about William Henry and his past and hopeless future, he strolled home to his lodgings in Great College Street, a very thoughtful man.

Educated Evans had spoken about a hundred pounds—William Henry Smith, painter, had also spoken of a hundred pounds. Was it a coincidence . . . ?

There was at this time a celebrated race-horse named Digger Lad. He was trained in the north, and, for some extraordinary reason, he was a good horse. Everybody knows that good horses are not trained in the north. If Ormonde had been sent to a stable in Yorkshire he would have become automatically a selling plater. He would have looked round, taken a screw at the pitheads and chimneys, listened bewildered to one of the stable boys saying, "Tha knows lad an' all," and would have immediately developed boils, strangles and infantile rickets. But Digger Lad was a good horse. Even Newmarket, which, according to the touts, is entirely populated by horses that could win the Derby in a bad year, admitted that Digger Lad was a good horse, and that, if he'd only been trained in Newmarket, he would have been an aeroplane.

He was favourite for the City and Suburban. That is to say, he was favourite with everybody except the bookmakers, who had laid him at all prices from 50-1 to 9-4. With them, he was no more favourite than measles in a girls' school.

As Mr. Evans walked home to Sansovino House, his educated brain was occupied by thoughts of Digger Lad, that wonderful horse, and it is a remarkable tribute to his self-control that, though the name had trembled on the very tip of his tongue, he had made no reference to this animal of quality.

Unconscious of the doubt that he had raised in the minds of the constabulary, he reached Sansovino House, which was a room over a stable in Bayham Mews, unlocking the door, locked it again, pulling up the ruins of a mat to keep the room airtight, and lighting his oil lamp, began to put on evening dress. Which meant that after a sluice in a pint and a half of water, he changed into a pair of check trousers, put on a nearly clean collar, an Ascot tie (embellished with a large golden pin in the shape of a horseshoe, which is popularly supposed to bring great luck to the wearer), and, rubbing his boots with a towel to raise a polish, he found the white bowler hat he had purchased for a mere song, rubbed a bit of dry pipe-clay over the stains, and, taking down a pair of yellow wash-leather gloves from the line, fitted one with some difficulty upon his left hand, for they had shrunk in the process; and, after finding his walking-stick, which was under the bed, he blew out the lamp and went forth, a model of sartorial sportiness.

A penny 'bus took him to the Oxford Street end of Tottenham Court Road, alive at this hour with throngs of the idle rich who had just been turned out of the cinema houses. Passing through Soho Square, he came to a small restaurant, into which he turned. It was at the moment inhabited by a stout French lady in a dirty apron and a well-dressed man who sat at one of the tables drinking coffee. He turned his head as Evans appeared and nodded him to a chair opposite.

"Good-evening, doctor," said Educated Evans languidly, as he handed his stick to the waiter, who handed it back to him. "Sorry I'm so late. But a couple of members of the Jockey Club called at my diggings, and I couldn't get rid of 'em. They didn't half rap about the way the turf's going from bad to worse. One of 'em—Lord X.: I won't tell you his name because he wouldn't like it—said to me: 'Evans, speaking as a man of education and knowledge—'"

"Yes, yes," said the other testily. "Sit down. What'll you take? It's too late for a drink."

"Coffee," said Evans indifferently. "I've been drinking champagne all the night till I'm sick of the sight of a tumbler. As I was saying—"

"I was expecting another gentleman to come tonight—a friend of mine," said the doctor.

He was a thin-faced man with eyes that never kept still.

"But I will tell you before he comes what I want you to do. Do you know Wilmer's in King's Cross?"

"The livery and bait stable?"

"That is the place," said the doctor. "You told me you were willing to earn a hundred."

Evans nodded dumbly. He was willing to earn ten shillings at that moment.

"Now I have told you before, and I'll tell you again, the strength of the situation," said the shifty-eyed man, sucking at the stub of an unlighted cigar. "I'm one of the connections of Digger Lad."

Again Mr. Evans nodded, this time almost humbly. The very thought that he was hobnobbing with "connections" was overpowering.

"Digger Lad is arriving from the north tonight, and goes on to Epsom tomorrow," said the doctor, slowly and emphatically. "He has had a tiring journey—you know what horses are."

Mr. Evans nodded slowly.

"As a owner and trainer," said the World's Best Tipster, "I understand 'em inside and outside, up and down, this way and that way, so to speak. As the celebrated George III. said to the well-known Duke of Wellington, the highly renowned officer in the army—"

"Never mind about the Duke of Wellington," said the doctor, who was disinclined at the moment to listen to any other voice than his own. "The point is that the owner doesn't want this horse"—he looked round and lowered his voice—"doped!" he hissed.

Educated Evans bit his lip and looked profound.

"But he's got to be doped or he won't win," the doctor went on. "The owner's a personal friend of mine, but I've got to look after him for his own good, if you understand me?"

Educated Evans did not understand.

"Here's the stuff," said the doctor, put his hand in his pocket and took out what looked to be like a tiny jam tin. He prised up the sunken lid with a coin and displayed a brown treacly mass.

"A friend of mine will get the stable open, and all you've got to do is to get into the box, put your finger in that and let him lick it."

"Suppose he bites me?" said Evans, a cold shiver running down his back.

"Bite you!" said the other contemptuously. "You understand horses, don't you? Horses don't bite, they suck!"

"But they've got teeth," said the obstinate Evans. "I've seen 'em?"

"They never use them," said the veterinary authority. "Are you game?"

Mr. Evans was rather white by now. He coughed, looked helplessly up at the fly-blown ceiling.

"I suppose it's all right," he said uneasily. "I mean there's nothing wrong in it?"

"Should I—me a doctor of medicine and all—ask you to do anything that wasn't right?" demanded the reproachful doctor.

But Evans was not happy.

"How about getting into the stable?"

"He'll be taken to Wilmers' the moment he arrives tomorrow." The doctor spoke with great rapidity. "The boys will go away to get a cup of coffee, and they'll lock the stable door. A friend of mine's going to open it—he'd have done the whole job, only he don't understand horses."

The doctor might have added that he himself would have done the whole job but his ignorance of the thoroughbred race-horse was almost as colossal as William Henry Smith's.

Educated Evans took the treacle pot, put on the lid slowly and dropped it into his pocket.

"What time is this other fellow coming?" he asked faintly.

That was exactly the question the doctor was asking himself for he knew nothing about the unhappy ending to William Henry's stroll.

"I don't know," he said. "Meet me here at seven tomorrow."

The future was brighter for Mr. Evans than he had dared confess. None, seeing the man commonly, indeed vulgarly, declaiming to a circle of incredulous punters, would have imagined that fortune had again tapped timidly on his front door.

Mr. Evans smiled to himself as he clumped up the wooden stairs that led to the very door on which the fairy fingers of fortune had danced. What a triumph would be his when it came out that Educated Evans *was in with the owners!*

Old Sam...! Educated Evans grinned diabolically at the thought of his rival's discomfiture. That beer-burdened snake in the grass!

He blew in the end of his big key, inserted it in the lock and tried to turn it. But it was already turned: he had, in fact, forgotten to lock the door when he went out, and it was unfastened. He pushed open the door and stood paralysed with horror and indignation.

The oil lamp was burning smokily, and by its light he saw there was a man in the room. An ancient man with a prismatic beard. He sat in a chair, his hands clasped on his waistcoat, his mouth open, his eyes closed.

2 a.m.! Mr. Evans almost choked. Possibly he made appropriate noises. Old Sam opened one eye and waved a feeble hand.

"Come in. . . Evansh! Take a sheat. . . was yours?"

Evans strode into the room, his eyes glaring.

"Outside!" he hissed. "'Op it, you ale-eatin' perisher! You are not satisfied, you uneducated old 'ound, with takin' the bread out of my mouth, but you come a-trespassin' in my house!"

Old Sam surveyed him glassily.

"'Tain't a house, it's an aylorft," he said, and for a moment Educated Evans thought he was talking a foreign language.

The man was intoxicated. Evans shuddered at the pollution brought upon Sansovino House. And not only was he intoxicated, but he was truculently so, and, surveying him, a doubt crept into Mr. Evans's mind. He was old but muscular, and under the stimulus of strong drink old men have done terrible things. Educated Evans coughed, and his tone grew more conciliatory.

"You can't stay here, Sam," he said mildly. "I've got to get to bed."

Old Sam stared at him blankly.

"I'm staying here," he said with great deliberation, "till tomorrer.

147

I got pinched over you, and you went and give away a stable secret what I got from the boy that done him. Tomorrer, you uneducated man"—Evans gasped and turned even paler—"I'm sendin' out a tip that'll knock you silly, and I'm stayin' here to see that you don't get ahead of me."

"But, Sam," said the agitated Mr. Evans, in an even more friendly tone, "you can't stay here, old man. I've got one of my clients coming up to see me here tomorrow."

"Ha!" said Old Sam. "Your client! Walker the fishmonger. He owes! I've come for an explanation."

He found the word rather difficult to say, but eventually said it.

"When I lay in the cold prison cell—at my time of life too—I thought I'd come out and cut your throat—give us something to eat. I'm starving."

Educated Evans was being ordered about in his own house.

"My dear old Sammy," he said, "as the celebrated Michael Angelo said to the well-known Lewdcreature Burgia, it can't be done."

And to demonstrate the absurdity of the whole situation, Evans took off his coat, hung it on a peg, as though, whatever happened, he was going to bed.

"Want to fight, do you!" roared Old Sam, and staggering to his unsteady feet reached for the first missile which came to his hand, which was Mr. Evans' small but hard poker.

No horse that Educated Evans ever tipped moved faster than the World's Champion Prophet and Turf Adviser.

The Miller, strolling towards High Street, saw a shivering man in his shirt sleeves standing at the end of the mews.

". . . Half an hour ago," explained Evans tremulously. " Come into my house and threatened to murder me! After all I've done for him! The four ale I've stood him! The perishin' old beer-biter!"

"Come along with me," said The Miller authoritatively. "We'll deal with this Trojan. What's this great tip of his for tomorrow?"

"He didn't tell me," said Evans, with some asperity. "And what's more, if he did I wouldn't take the slightest notice of it." They mounted the steps together. The lamp was still burning when Evans opened the door, and Old Sam was seated at the table and was talking drowsily to himself . . . . Nothing to eat in this 'ole," he mumbled, "only bread and golden surrop, and he carries *that* round in his coat pocket!"

A cut loaf was before him, and a small open tin. There was also a half-eaten slice of bread covered thickly with a brown, treacly substance.

Evans did not faint, but somehow he knew that Old Sam would not be in a position on the following day to give a tip, good, bad, or indifferent.

4.—A Judge of Racing

The Honourable Mr. Justice Bellfont was a very human man with a wide knowledge of human affairs. If the name of Carslake had been mentioned in his court, he would not have said, "Who is Brownie Carslake?" but would have told you the position Brownie occupied in last year's list of winning jockeys, and his lowest riding weight. If he did not tell the court this aloud, he would have exposed his knowledge *sotto voce*, for he had the habit of speaking his thoughts aloud.

On Saturday meetings you could see him at Kempton or Hurst, and he had even been known to journey north to witness the field in the Manchester November Handicap emerge from the fog. He had a cousin who owned horses and a nephew who trained them. He was, in the sense of experience and knowledge, the widest judge that ever sent a lad for a stretch.

He loved horses, and even in the days when he was a prosperous junior, never had more than a pound each way on Ormonde. And if there wasn't a horse relatively as good as Ormonde in the field he did not bet at all.

He had a notoriously tender place for the little thief, and a hard surface for the clever financiers who came at rare intervals before him, and his terse "You will be kept in penal servitude for seven years," had brought distress to many a family which was living in luxury on the doings that papa had extracted from poor investors.

Therefore it was, in a sense, an act of providence that Walter Holl came before him—for Walter, though a tea-leaf, was a good fellow and a well-meaning man.

In the clear grey of morning, before the shops are open and whilst yet milkmen are lying in their beds, Camden Town is a place of solemn splendour, and even her public-houses have an especial dignity. Save for a belated cat or so making its weary way homewards after a night spent in reckless debauchery, nothing human moved in High Street. The drone of a distant newspaper van chug-chugging to Euston, the twitter of the birds in Bayham Street and the distant hoot of a goods engine at the Midland Goods Station, are the only sounds that break the sylvan stillness.

The Miller had spent the night profitably in conducting a raid upon a snide factory just off Ossulton Street, and now, at peace with mankind, he stood surveying the desert of High Street.

A figure came shuffling round a corner, saw him instantly and faded out of sight.

The Miller did not move: seemingly he had not seen the wayfarer. Presently the furtive man peeped round the corner, saw his enemy standing apparently oblivious of his presence, and, turning, walked back the way he had come, satisfied that justice was happily blind.

Mr. Walter Holl would have found it difficult to run, for he carried in his cloth bag a large quantity of lead piping and brass taps that he had acquired in the earlier hours of the morning from an untenanted house in the Holloway Road.

He was half-way back to Great College Street when he heard the softest sound behind him, and turned to meet The Miller.

"Lord! Mr. Challoner, you give me a fright! Them rubber soles of yourn ain't half quiet "

"Been shopping?" asked The Miller pleasantly, his eyes upon the bulging bag.

"Them?" Mr. Holl asked innocently as he opened the bag and displayed his loot. "They belong to a friend of mine, a plumber. He's goin' up to Scotland to do a job an' he asked me to bring the bag to the station for him—gave me a bob to do it. You see, Mr. Challoner, he got soused last night an'—"

"Come along and have a cup of coffee at the station," said The Miller, "and we'll talk over old times. How long ago is it since I took you for 'busting' empty houses, Holl? Must be nearly three years."

Mr. Holl fell in by his side, The Miller's hand affectionately gripping his arm.

"It's a cop," said Walter, with the philosophy of his kind. "I got these out of a house in the Holloway Road—Number 804, or maybe 408. It's hard luck on me, because I was goin' to get a packet out of Telltale in the Victoria Cup. I've been workin' honest for two years, but what with this here unemployment an' Lloyd George bein' the gover'ment, an honest man can't make a living."

"Mr. Lloyd George has been out of office for years," said The Miller, and Walter sneered.

"This choppin' an' changin' of gover'ments is the ruin of the workin' classes," he stated.

At the police station he was searched; before he was put into the cells he asked a special favour.

"I'd be very much obliged, Mr. Challoner, if you'd ask Educated Evans to put a piece together for me, so as, when I go in front of the old bubble an' squeak, I've got, so to speak, a full answer?"

"Can't you afford a mouthpiece?" asked the sympathetic Miller, referring in this crude way to a gentleman learned in the law.

"Mouthpiece!" Walter was scornful. "Why, all these so-and-so lawyers 'ang together. Why, I see a picture the other day of Marshall 'All an' Courteous Bennett walkin' arm an' arm together—and they was on different sides in a murder! No so-and-so lawyers for me!"

"Moderate your language," said The Miller. "I'll tell Evans, though I don't know what he can do for you except to tip that you'll get time. In which case you'll probably get off."

Educated Evans, of Tapin House, Bayham Mews (he had a disconcerting habit of renaming his residence after big race winners) was indeed a friend to the poor and afflicted, in addition to being the World's Greatest Turf Adviser.

And at that moment he was riding on the crest of a wave.

Camden Town, which had lost confidence in the man and the prophet, was slowly regaining its faith. For had he not given in rapid succession:

Argo! What a beauty!
Argo! What a beauty!
Argo! What a beauty!

... together with:

Mr. Clever! What a beauty!
Mr. Clever! What a beauty!
Mr. Clever! What a beauty!

.... to quote his own admirable literature.

It was rumoured (mainly by Mr. Evans) that the West End bookmakers were panic-stricken. People had come to his flat and paid him real money to encourage him in his good work.

The Miller walked up the wooden stairs which led to Tapin House, and found one who described himself immodestly as "The Wizard of Camden Town," engaged in the study of the next day's programme. Evans received him gravely—as a man of property would receive a bailiff, or a successful author a reviewer; in other words, as somebody who was respected but did not count.

Briefly The Miller explained the reason for his visit, Evans shook his head.

"I've given up writin' out defences for common people," he said. " I'm too busy, as the well-known Sir Francis Drakes said to the soldier when he was teachin' the young princes in the Tower to say their twice-times table. What with owners an' trainers an' what not writin' to ask me not to tip their horses, an' what with me correspondents at Lambourn, Newmarket an' Epsom sendin' me yards an' yards of winners, I've got no time to disgrace meself with Walter Holl. What's he done?"

The Miller told him, and Mr. Evans made an impatient sound.

"The man was certainly a client of mine in the past, but whether he acted honourable or not I can't tell till I've seen me books. I'll see what I can do."

"What is going to win the Gatwick Handicap?" asked The Miller.

"Blue Nose," said Evans indifferently. " I'm not troublin' about that race—it's too easy. Give me somethin' hard, like the Victoria Cup."

"Blue Nose?" queried The Miller. Evans went to his bed, turned the pillow and produced a letter.

Read that," he commanded.

The Miller read.

Dear Sir,

With reference to your inquiry, Blue Nose has done no work for six months and has a very bad leg.

Yours faithfully,

H. Haggitt.

"That Haggitt," said Evans profoundly, "couldn't tell the truth to his doctor. What's more, he owes me one. So I wrote to him, knowin' that whatever he sent me would be a lie. Blue Nose is money for nothin'. Help yourself an' don't forget I've got to pay rates an' taxes."

The Miller was impressed.

"Telltale will win the Victoria Cup," he hazarded.

Here The Miller voiced the opinion commonly held by all keen racing men. For Telltale had, so to speak, been flung into the handicap. He had been left (also, so to speak) ten minutes in the Newbury Cup and had been beaten a short head by a great horse. Ardent sportsmen in Camden Town were going down to Hurst Park in a fortnight's time to place their underwear at the disposal of the receptive bookmakers, and, if the truth be told, Mr. Walter Holl's divers larcenies and felonies had been performed or committed with the object of getting a little stock of money to invest in this gilt-edged security.

Educated Evans scratched his nose.

"He *ought* to win it," he admitted. "He ought to be able to fall down an' get up an' then win. But them bookmakers won't lay more than twoses an' more likely it'll be six ter four on the field an' twenty to one bar two. And that don't pay me an' my clients."

He looked round cautiously, though there was no danger of being overheard.

"You're in the lore, Mr. Challoner; what about Dum Spyro? He's trained by Falston—he's the nephew of Lord What's-his-name, the highly celebrated judge."

"You mean Mr. Justice Bellfont?" asked The Miller.

"That's him. Don't you ever get any tips at Scotlan' Yard? Don't judges put things in your way—they ought to. Where would they be without busies?"

The Miller chuckled.

"The judge doesn't give tips, you poor miserable man!"

Mr. Evans was deep in thought.

"If I thought Dum Spyro was on the job I'd take him to beat the fav'rite. But that Falston's so close that he's stuck together. He don't bet, but he wouldn't tell his own wife where he kept his shirts; he's that tight you couldn't open him with a pickaxe."

The Miller went away and brooded on the immediate problem of Blue Nose. He was, in a way, slightly amused by the perverted reasoning of the World's Premier Turf Prophet. So was the station-sergeant and several form- studying constables. When Blue Nose won that afternoon by the length of a street they were slightly annoyed.

Mr. Evans spent the greater part of the evening composing an address which Walter could read from the dock. He had composed many such: generally speaking, they began in very much the same strain.

"May it please your Worship. It was said by the celebrated Shakespeare, '*The quantity of Mercy is not strange*,' therefore I ask your worship, in the terrible position I find myself, an innocent man dragged ruthfully to the bar of justice, to take a lenient view of a mere bagatelle committed under the influence of drink, that well-known curse."

The three hours spent in this labour were, however, so much wasted time, as he learned on attending the police court the next morning.

"Sorry, Evans," said The Miller, but this will be an Old Bailey case. We found a lot of stolen property in his house, and he is certain to be fullied, (fully committed for trial). He tells me he did a bit of work for you in the past two years?"

This was true. Mr. Holl had earned many an odd shilling. He had run a few errands, scrubbed the educated man's floor, and once had distempered the walls of his bed-sitting-working room.

"If you go up before the judge and say a few words for him, you might save him a lagging," suggested The Miller—a scheme which at first filled the World's Champion with quaking fear, but which afterwards had certain attractions.

Educated Evans had participated in many police court proceedings, but he had never yet attained to the distinction of making an official appearance at the Old Bailey.

By great good fortune, Mr. Holl was fullied in time to catch next week's sitting of the Central Criminal Court. Kind friends, one and all, whipped round to supply the funds necessary to secure the services of that eminent barrister-at-law, Mr. Chubblechine, a very young man who knew just as much of the world as can be viewed from the quad of Caius College, Cambridge, and Pump Court, E.C.4. Educated Evans, wearing his check trousers and nearly gold horseshoe tiepin, his almost white bowler hat on the side of his head, strolled into the hall of the Old Bailey, the observed of all observers.

"It's curious, Mr. Miller," he said modestly, "how a feller gets known. All them people know me. . . I'm, so to speak, the sinicure of all eyes."

"They think you're Woddle, the forger, surrendering to his bail," said The Miller coldly. "And listen, Evans: when you get up in front of the judge, don't talk too much—it's Bellfont."

Figuratively speaking, the ears of Educated Evans pricked.

"The highly famous Lord Bellfont—him whose nephew trains Dum Spyro?" he asked, and The Miller nodded.

"That's a bit of luck," said Evans thoughtfully. "When he sees the kind of man he's got to deal with, I bet he'll ask me into his private room an' have a talk—"

The Miller's eye was cold.

"The only private room you'll ever be asked into," he said, "is one of twenty in the basement, which has a lock on it and a peep-hole where the warder can see that you're not committing suicide."

Nevertheless, Mr. Evans was not depressed.

It was two o'clock that afternoon when Mr. Holl stepped brightly up from the bowels of the earth into the dock. He pleaded "Not guilty" in a chirpy tone.

At a quarter to three, Educated Evans walked into the witness-box, and, having kissed a strange book, leant negligently on the ledge of the box.

"You are," said the youthful counsel, "a very well-known sporting journalist?"

Evans was momentarily staggered at this description.

"In a sense and in a way I am."

The saturnine figure on the bench glared at him.

"Are you or aren't you?" he rasped.

"I am, my dear lord," said Evans, and went on to answer questions which were intended to prove, beyond any question of doubt, that Walter Holl was between whiles a hard-working man, a good father and a kind and loyal friend. The counsel for the prosecution did not even trouble to cross-examine him.

"When you say you are a sporting journalist, what do you mean?" he demanded.

"The fact is, my dear lord—" began Evans.

"There is no need for you to be affectionate," said his lordship.

"The fact is," said Evans, a little wildly, "I'm what you might term the World's Champion Turf Adviser and Pronosticator. I'm the gentleman that gave Braxted at 20/1—what a beauty, dear lord Also Tarpin—"

"Oh—a tipster!"

It is impossible to convey all the scorn, derision, contempt and condemnation in his lordship's tone.

"Yes, my dear sir—my dear lord, I mean—I'm a prophet. As the well-known and highly respected John Bunions, the celebrated composer of Robinson Crusoe and his man Friday, said—"

"A tipster!"

His lordship's lips curled.

"A prophet an' turf adviser, dear my lord," murmured Evans. "The same address for twenty-five years; not one of them gone today and come tomorrer people. As the far-famed Lord Winston Churchill said, '*Jer swee*—I'm here!'"

The judge leant back in his padded chair; the cold malignity in his eyes made Mr. Evans shudder.

"You infernal rascal!" he muttered. When he was annoyed, he invariably spoke his thoughts aloud. "You robber; you ought to be in the dock!"

And then:

"You have the audacity to come here to certify a man's character!"

"Yes, my dear lord," said Evans faintly.

"You send out your inf—your prophecies as to what horse will win?"

"Yes, dear—my lord." Evans in his terror was swaying in the box.

"And you have the—really I—I am amazed at your audacity! Do you profess to be able to predict horses that will win races?"

Evans nodded—he hoped respectfully.

"I believe you are a swindler!" said the judge firmly. "I believe that you are obtaining money by false pretences."

The educated man saw the prison gates yawning wide to receive him. Cold perspiration trickled down his nose. The hands that gripped the ledge were clammy—the court spun round him.

But the unconquerable spirit which is latent in every prophet sustained him. In a last desperate effort to justify himself:

"The fact is, dear old—dear mister... my lord," he stammered, "it's easy. Now take Telltale—he can't help winnin' the Victoria Cup. . . . ."

"Not a ghost of a chance," muttered his lordship." Not with Dum Spyro in the field. . . ."

So low he spoke that only Evans heard him. Then, aloud, and with a stern look in his eye:

"Stand down, sir!" he said. "The fact that the unfortunate prisoner has nothing better in the shape of witnesses than a wretched swindling tipster, is proof of his friendlessness."

He let off Walter with three months' hard.

Evans staggered out of court like a man in a dream. The Miller spoke to him, but he did not hear. In Newgate Street he found a taxi and drove back to Bayham Mews.

That evening, Detective-Sergeant Challoner made one of his frequent calls at the Hall of the Prophet, and found Evans in his shirtsleeves struggling with the patent duplicator that a child could work. Round and round the little cylinder was turning, and with every revolution there appeared a quarto sheet, wet with violet ink. In silence The Miller picked up a sheet and read:

Educated Evans

The World's Champion Turf Profit and Racing Adviser.
Owner of the following high-class performers

under both Rules.

Raw Meat Tommy Hake Shin Sore
Eyeballs Wiggle Wag Jerusalem Moke

Educated Evans, commonly called "The Whizard of Camden Town" (same address for 30 years) has given some of the biggest selections the world has ever known.

BRAXTED 20/1! What a beauty!
BRAXTED 20/1! What a beauty!
TARPIN 11/1! What a beauty!
TARPIN 11/1! What a beauty!

Educated Evans begs to announce that one of the

BEST JUDGES OF RACING
BEST JUDGES OF RACING
BEST JUDGES OF RACING

has kindly given him the winner of

THE VICTORIA CUP

This horse has 21 lb. in hand of

TELLTALE.

This horse is trained by

A RELATION

of the best Judge of Racing and

IS TRYING.

Send T.M.O. for 5/- to Educated Evans,
Tapin Lodge, Bayham Mews.

"What is the horse?" asked The Miller.

"Dum Spyro," said Evans rapidly. "I had it from Lord Bellfont his-self—didn't you see him give me the wink?"

5.—An Amazing Selection

There is no doubt at all that Educated Evans had a soft place in his heart for ladies. And it is no exaggeration to say that ladies had a tender place in their hearts for Educated Evans.

As Miss Maudie Hallsback (the beautiful barmaid at the "Rose and Crown") used to insist:

"I don't care what you say, he's a nice man, and the way he lifts his hat to you when you meet him out, is a fair treat to see. He may be long-winded, and I dessay he is, but there's no getting away from his

157

education."

"He don't let you," said her gloomy audience; "he fairly rams it down your throat! I don't believe harf he says about hist'ry. Take that bit about Bloody Mary—"

Miss Maudie's cold eyes fixed him.

"As a bird is known by his note so is a man by his conversation," she said pointedly, and left Mr. Lew Figtree spluttering protests.

It was the same with the beautiful Miss Birdie Rothman—her that has "Birdie" in oriental diamonds right across her chest—and the same with Mrs. Grail, the proprietress of the "Egg and Duck." They all spoke well of Educated Evans. He was holding Miss Rothman spellbound one evening.

"Very few people know," he said, "that the moon is a extinct volcano. How it got up in the sky is a problem that's known only to a few of us. Take rainbows. Now a lot of people think rainbows are real, but as a matter of fact they're an optical illusion. Take Mars: there's canals on Mars owin' to there bein' no trains—everything's got to go by water. Take the stars—"

"Lord, Mr. Evans, what a headpiece you've got!" said the awe-stricken lady. Educated Evans smiled modestly.

"It's readin' that does it," he said, "an' experience. Take Camden Town. It used to be a wild jungle full of savages that painted their faces with wood—"

"It's not much better now," retorted the young lady.

Mr. Evans' dearest enemy was one Old Sam, as all the world knows. His age was variously computed between seventy and a hundred. He had the appearance of one who had been on nodding terms with Noah. If the Biblical parallel be permissible, his ark nowadays was the saloon bar of the "Red Lion," whence he sent forth his doves full of hope and confidence. This ale-sustained ancient had once been the veriest slave of Educated Evans, shuffling about Camden Town to execute his orders for a mere tuppence a time. But in the absence of Evans, Old Sam had not only blossomed forth as a tipster, usurping the position of his master, but had developed, as the result of his lucky pin-pricks, an arrogance, indeed a truculence, which ill became one of his years.

"He ought," said Evans bitterly, "to be thinking about another world, instead of which he's pinchin' Captain Coe's nap and sendin' it out as private information! But I'll do the old perisher! I've got a bit of information for the Liverpool Cup from me Epsom correspondent that'll fairly put it across him."

"It occurs to me," said The Miller, "that your style and language have deteriorated since your absence from Camden Town."

Evans coughed, a little embarrassed. Any reflection upon his diction touched him nearly and sorely.

"He's not worth any better. He's a low, uneducated, guzzlin' 'ound!"

The tenderness of heart which was Educated Evans' especial property, together with an increase in the volume of his business, led him, unwisely as it proved, to employ an assistant, Mrs. Arabella Bolton, whose husband at the time was away in the country: a thin, peaky-faced, discontented woman, with a wail against life and against that much of life which sustained her husband in his Dartmoor retreat. Evans, who subsequently had reason to be thankful for his charity, took her on out of pity, she having in her younger days been what is known as a "clerk" at Pinkses, the jam-makers. A client of his had told him about the destitute state of Mrs. Bolton, and since at that moment there was a great deal of work to be done, Evans sent for her.

"I'm sure I'm much obliged to you Mr. Evings," she exclaimed. "It's very good of you I'm sure I was offered a much better job last week but I was that sick and ill that I couldn't take it" (she spoke without any commas, full-stops or periods, and her speech in some ways resembled an Act of Parliament).

"What with Bolton took away and bringing disgrace on me which my father thank God don't know anything about it or he'd turn in his grave and two mouths to fill and his relations not allowing me a ha'penny-piece though they're well off his father being in the butchering business in Smithfield market getting his money out of selling kagmag, (also cagmag, bad meat), to poor people that it's a shame what do you want me to do Mr. Evings?"

Evans explained, and the thin-faced Mrs. Bolton sat down in the one rickety chair with a disparaging sneer on her face, and proceeded to open and sort out the letters which had arrived by that morning's post as the result of an advertisement which, in some miraculous fashion, Educated Evans had succeeded in getting into the *Sporting Chronicle*. Usually the *Sporting Chronicle* is more careful.

Mrs. Bolton lived at Little College Court, which rather suggests the shaded quadrangle of some ancient house of learning, but was, in point of fact, a *cul-de-sac* of microscopic houses, where babies were born every day and old people died every other week.

Her next door neighbour was a Mrs. Lube, who had the dubious distinction of being the granddaughter of Old Sam, who now lodged with her, and at this time was keeping her, her family, her husband and her husband's aunt. The prosperity which had come to Old Sam as the result of his miraculous tips was advertised in the sparkling rings in Mrs. Lube's ears, and in the magnificent wrist-watch she wore when she went to the pictures. She was a great friend of Mrs. Bolton's, having troubles of her own, and there were, so to speak, no secrets between them.

"Good Gawd, Mrs. Bolton" said Mrs. Lube, in a hushed voice. "You don't mean you're workin' for that old 'ound, the so-called Educated Evans? Educated, indeed! Why, he went to a Board School, as everybody knows! Giving 'isself airs and takin' the bread out of our mouths, so to speak, me an' my poor husband, my poor old grandfather, a man of his age, to be cast on the world for us to keep!"

"I've got to live," said Mrs. Bolton, hardly knowing whether she ought to defend her employer or admit his delinquencies and deficiencies right off, and ready to take either side under provocation.

"Of course, I don't think no worse of you," Mrs. Lube hastened to assure her friend. "But it's a bit lowerin' to have to work for that kind of daylight robber."

"I've got to live," repeated Mrs. Bolton. "What with my old man being put away through drink and wimmin as I shall maintain to my dying day and two mouths to fill. . . ."

"Come in and have a cup of tea, Arabella," said Mrs. Lube, as a great idea flooded her dull brain.

And in the best parlour (which was also the only parlour and had been newly furnished out of the proceeds of Old Sam's prophecies), they sat down and had a good talk—and Mrs. Lube was an expert pumper.

"Wait a minute, Mrs. Bolton. Do you mind me seeing my grandfather? He usually has a cup of tea and a bloater about now?"

Mrs. Lube hustled out of the room, went up the narrow stairs and intruded herself into Old Sam's bedroom. Here sat the prophet, looking rather like a prophet of old. He woke with a start, rubbed his bald head and blinked up at his granddaughter. She closed the door carefully, and, in a hoarse whisper, passed on the information she had gained.

". . . it's running in the Liverpool Cup on Thursday. He's had it from Epsom." Old Sam scratched his bald head.

"Paddy?" he said thoughtfully. "Never 'eard of the 'orse! Is it a 'orse?"

"How do I know, grandfather?" rasped Mrs. Lube. "I'll ask Alf when he comes home."

"What can I do?"

"Send it out, grandfather," said this representative of his progeny, who was the real manager of the business. "Spread it all over Camden Town—"

"He'll do it too," interrupted Old Sam. Mrs. Lube shook her head vigorously.

"No, he won't," she said darkly. "We'll settle his hash, grandfather. . . . . .the low, common man, taking the bread and butter out of my dear children's mouth. I'm sure it's a struggle to live. If wasn't for Alf's dole, we'd be out of 'ouse and 'ome."

Old Sam sighed. For three months he had been the most popular member of the family, but the return of Educated Evans had marked a crisis in his affairs.

"If something ain't done, grandfather," Mrs. Lube went on, and there was a note of menace in her voice, "you'll be outside the 'Red Lion' with your back against the wall, picking up a penny here and there."

Old Sam sighed again.

"Tell Alf to get it printed," he said, and was glad when the door closed after this dominating woman.

Mrs. Lube's work was not done. A shrewd and thrifty woman, she had put a bit by for a rainy day out of the magnificent receipts which had followed the point of Old Sam's pin picking the name of Charley's Mount in the Cesarewitch. Mrs. Bolton needed very little persuasion.

"Five pounds in the hand," as she said, "was worth two or three in the bush," for it was by no means certain (indeed, Educated Evans hinted as much) that she had struck a permanency at Tapin House.

That evening, Educated Evans went forth in search of the one policeman for whom he had any respect, and he discovered The Miller, standing outside the "Nag's Head," where he had been waiting for two hours in the hope of picking up an acquaintance of his, urgently wanted by Scotland Yard. Since his bird was not likely to fly thither that night, The Miller walked back down High Street and listened with scepticism larded with interest to the story Educated Evans told.

"Never mind about Roysterer, never mind about Dinkie," said

161

Evans firmly. "This horse Paddy will win ten minutes, I got him from a man who's got a nephew in the stable. And, what's more," he added triumphantly, "I've seen him gallop."

"Have you been touting horses, Evans?" asked the surprised Miller. Evans nodded.

"I go down and have a look at 'em now and again," he said indifferently, as though such events were an everyday occurrence. "Now nobody knows anything about this horse but me—"

"I seem to have observed that it's been tipped by several of the weekly papers," suggested The Miller.

They're only guessing," said Evans meaningly. " I *know!*"

"What's that woman Bolton doing with you? You're not contracting a matrimonial alliance?"

Mr. Evans turned upon him the gaze of a wounded fawn.

"I'm surprised at you, Mr. Challoner," he said. "A man of my education. Why, the Queen of Sheeney—"

"Sheba," corrected The Miller.

"Well, whoever she was—she wouldn't tempt me. Nor would the celebrated Cleopatrick, who got her well-known needle through being turned down by the highly celebrated Nero, the far-famed Italian. If Mary Queen of Scots come into my room and said, 'Evans, what about taking me to the pictures?' I'd say, ''op it,' I'm done with women! Besides, she's a nagger."

"Mary Queen of Scots?" asked The Miller in surprise.

"No, Mrs. Bolton. She's always got something to grouse about. If it ain't one thing it's the other, and if it's not that it's something else."

He certainly found Mrs. Bolton in a grumbling mood when he reached home that night. She said she was ready to drop; she'd been turning the handle of the duplicator that a child can work for three hours, and was in a condition of exhaustion.

The response to Evans' appeal had been a heavy one. There were no fewer than three hundred envelopes on the table, half of which were filled. Ever a lover of peace, the educated man gave her fair words, and, more to the purpose, a promise of overtime; and together they finished the work, stuck down the last envelope and affixed the stamps. Evans looked at his announcement again with a glow of pride.

TAPIN LODGE,
BAYHAM MEWS.
SIR,

Once more I am able to put you on to the Goods. Far-famed throughout every land and nation where the British flag is flown, the sun never sits on the name of Educated Evans, the World's Premier Prophet and Turf Adviser.
Today I send you a piece of information that
nobody else has got!
What a beauty!
What a beauty!
What a beauty!
You can go your maximum on
PADDY ★★★★
today—he will win in a canter.
Yours truly,
EDUCATED EVANS.
P.S.—Put me on the odds to 1/-.

"Rubbish and nonsense, I call it," said Mrs. Bolton.

Evans' smile was one of great superiority.

"You don't understand these things, Mrs. Bolton," he said. " Naturally the turf don't appeal to women, though I've known ladies who've made fortunes out of my high-class selections."

Mrs. Bolton sniffed. She was gathering the envelopes into packets and putting them into the pillow-slip which Evans had borrowed from her for the purpose.

"Post 'em in the High Street," said Evans.

"What about my money?" asked his assistant, more to the point. "I can't go toilin' and moilin' for a mere nothing with two mouths to fill."

Though her work was only for two days Evans generously handed her a one-pound note.

"Is the overtime here?" she asked.

"Yes, and your lodging allowance," said Evans sarcastically.

He went to sleep with a feeling that he had done a good day's work. The information he had received about Paddy was undoubtedly reliable.

He was cooking his breakfast in the morning when a small and dirty-faced boy arrived with a small and dirty-faced note. It was from Mrs. Bolton.

Dear Sir—it ran—I was took so bad when I got home last night that I can't come to work any more. Please send pound by bearer instead of week's notice.

Yours truly,

Mrs. Bolton.

"Go back to your mother," said Evans, rightly sensing the relationship of the small and grimy child," and tell her I'm Not Made of Money."

The little boy waited till he was downstairs and in the mews beyond the fear of pursuit, and made certain derisive noises which were very irritating to a man of Mr. Evans' refined susceptibilities.

He had plenty to occupy his mind until the afternoon, and then he strolled forth to get a copy of the afternoon paper. It was a little disconcerting to find at the newspaper shop a small stack of Old Sam's Midnight Specials, and to be told that Sam had made Paddy his five-starred nap.

"The perishin' old plagiariser," spluttered Evans, choking with indignation. "Why, that's the horse I sent out! He's got it from that woman Bolton that lives next door to him...."

His feelings were somewhat mollified by the arrival at that moment of a newspaper runner, and the discovery, in the smudged space, of the news that Paddy had won.

"Seven to two it is," said the shopkeeper. "I heard it on the telephone. One of the runners told me. They got that price from the blower round at the Arts Club."

Evans scratched his chin.

"The news must have got out," he said. "I reckoned it'd be ten to one."

But a shock awaited him when, a little later, he strolled into the shop of a client. "It won," he said laconically.

"What won?" demanded Mr. Harry Leek, the well-known furniture dealer.

"Paddy—I sent it to you—fear nothing!" The furniture dealer frowned.

"You didn't send anything to me," he said, "or I'd have backed it."

Evans turned pale.

"Do you mean to say you didn't get my five-pound special?" he squeaked.

But not only had this gentleman not received it, but nobody else had received it, as Evans discovered when he made a rapid visit to four or five of his clients.

Pale with fury, he half ran to Little College Court and knocked at the door behind which Mrs. Bolton had her habitation.

"Mother's ill in bed and can't see nobody," said an uncompromising young lady of fifteen.

"Go up and ask your mother what she done with them letters what I gave her to post last night," said Evans huskily.

She ain't had no letters. She's not right in 'er 'ead—she's deleerious and nobody's allowed to see her," said the daughter, and pushed the door close in Evans' face.

"Is 'e gorn?" asked Mrs. Bolton over the banisters. "Like his cheek, coming to my 'ouse!" she said, as she came downstairs, very fit and well. That serves him right for trying to sweat the poor," she said.

"What are you going to do with the letters, mother?" asked her darling child.

Mrs. Bolton ran her fingers through her untidy hair.

"They'll keep for a bit. I'll ask Old Sam."

She did not ask Old Sam because it was not her way to do anything she arranged to do. With Mrs. Bolton things just happened; and she had forgotten the fact that underneath her bed was a pillowslip full of unposted letters, when, on the Wednesday morning, she opened the door to see a familiar face.

"Good-morning, Mrs. Bolton. How's the world treating you?" asked The Miller cheerfully—and when he was cheerful something dirty was going to happen.

"Good—good-morning, Mr. Challoner," faltered Mrs. Bolton. "You're a sight for sore eyes, I must say. Is it anything about my husband you want to know?"

"No, not exactly," said The Miller, leaning negligently against the door-post. "You've been working for Mr. Evans, haven't you?"

She nodded, a sudden fear gripping her side.

"I understand he gave you some letters to post—about three hundred, each with a three-ha'penny stamp on it, which represents roughly about one pound seventeen and sixpence."

The throat of Mrs. Bolton, a comparatively honest woman, went dry.

"Yes, sir, he did, sir," she faltered.

"Did you post them?" asked The Miller carelessly, his hard, grey eyes on hers.

"Yes, sir"—how she said the words she never knew.

"Are you sure?"

She nodded dumbly.

"Ah, then, I shall have to make inquiries at the post office," said The Miller, and took his leave with a happy nod.

Mr. Bolton closed the door and, staggering up the stairs, sat on her bed. Visions of the female equivalent for Dartmoor swam before her eyes. Going to the head of the stairs she called in a hollow voice for her daughter, and Millicent—such was the name of this child—came up the stairs and listened to the horrid tale.

"Let's burn 'em," she suggested brightly. "Or"—as an idea struck her—"let's slip out and put 'em in the post tonight.

"Nobody'll see who posted 'em, and they can't bring nothin' up against you, mother." It was a wonderful idea.

★★★★★★

A gloomy Educated Evans strolled into the High Street, sad and depressed. All that morning he had avoided the busy haunts of men, gravitating, as was his wont, to the Thames Embankment; and now, with little interest in life, for he felt that his luck was baulked, he came back to the great highway with a feeling that fate had indeed baffled him.

The Miller, riding past him on his motor-bicycle, saw him, and, stopping, jumped off and came back with a beaming face.

"You old scoundrel!" he said heartily. "Fancy sending out a twenty to one winner! I've backed it, and you're on the odds to a shilling."

Evans' jaw dropped.

"Only got the letter this morning." The Miller took it from his pocket and handed it to the flabbergasted World's Champion. "You didn't tell me this horse was going for the Newbury Cup. . . . I'll see you later, Evans."

Mr. Evans walked along, High Street like a man in a dream, receiving, it seemed at every yard, the onrush of some admiring friend who crossed the road or flew from a shop to congratulate him upon his prescience.

For Paddy, who had won the Liverpool Cup at 7/2, had also won the Newbury Cup at 20/1! And the three hundred foolish people who had received the belated communication meant for the Liverpool event were blissfully unaware of what a providential tipster Mrs. Bolton was. And Educated Evans, who did not even know that Paddy was entered for the Newbury event, received the congratulations with a modest smile.

"Yes. . . I was goin' to send it for Liverpool, but changed my mind...

information pays in the long run."

6.—A Good Gallop

Alfred Robspear, a distant acquaintance of Educated Evans, called at Sansovino House very early in the morning to borrow a shilling.

He was a raw, lop-sided man of forty-five, who had been out of employment for twenty years, until a miracle happened and he discovered that by calling every week at the Labour Exchange he could draw enough money to keep his children and his favourite bookmaker from starvation.

"You don't get no shillings out of me," said Evans firmly, and went down the wooden steps to draw a pail of water for his morning ablutions.

Mr. Robspear did not immediately follow. This, Educated Evans remembered later. . . .

It was not the happiest day in Mr. Evans' life. It was, in fact, a morning of crisis when he surveyed his possessions and calculated skilfully and with accurate judgment the exact amount he could raise on his non-necessities. He had a library of books which included three annual volumes of *Racing Up-to-Date*, a turf ready-reckoner and five dog-eared volumes which had been presented to him by a client in lieu of the five shillings which Mr. Evans had earned by his gift of prophecy, and which were supposed to be valuable, one at least being yellow with age and having "f's" for "s's" in the typescript. And it is pretty well-known that ancient books with "f's" for "s's" are sometimes sold for enormous sums.

Mr. Evans sighed and, gathering together his books, tied a piece of string round them and was leaving his room to carry the volumes to Jones' Renowned Marine Store, when a thought occurred to him, and, pulling back the mattress of his bed, discovered that his best pair of trousers was missing.

Alfred Eustace Robspear was no relation to the French gentleman whose name was thus anglicised. He was not sea green nor, if his fingerprints records at Headquarters are to be believed, was he incorruptible.

Probably no black deed of his is comparable, in point of sheer infamy, with his villainous attempt to twist Mr. Evans of Bayham Mews, notorious wherever the Empire's flag is flown as the World's Premier Sporting Prophet and Turf Adviser. He carried his sorrows to Sergeant Challoner.

"Robspear? He'd rob Shakespeare, that fellow would," said Educated Evans, trembling with annoyance. "What did he do? When I gave him Marrow Bones—it ought to have won ten minutes but the jockey wasn't trying—he comes to my flat an' pinches the only good pair of trousis I've got! An' me due at the Hollyoak Whist Drive tonight to meet a young lady, a regular. . ."

He used a French expression and The Miller was startled.

"A what?" he asked, shocked. " Do you know what that means?"

"It's French for bein' half in this world an' half in the next," said Evans.

Very gently The Miller explained the meaning of the term.

"Lord love a duck!" said the agitated Evans. "I thought she dropped her eyes when I called her that."

"If she had kicked you in the stomach it would have been no more than you deserved," said The Miller severely. "Do you want to make a charge against Robspear?"

Here Educated Evans hesitated. Grievous a loss as he had suffered, he was not prepared to come copper on a fellow citizen.

"I'll reason with him," he said. "I'll talk to him in what I might term a diplomatic manner: just the same as the well-known Queen Elizabeth argued with the far-famed Spanish gentleman, Signor Armada, in 1066, causin' her never to smile again."

"There's another point I'd like to take up with you, Evans—you told me yesterday Fideles was a certainty for the Richmond Handicap at Kempton on Easter Monday. What do you know about it?"

"Fee-dellis?" Educated Evans was startled. "I didn't tell you that, Mr. Challoner. What I said was Fiddles—Bolfort's horse."

"I pronounce it a little differently, but it is the same horse," said The Miller patiently. "Have you dreamt this one or is it genuine? I can't imagine old Bolfort winning a race except by accident. He never gallops his horses and has one winner every leap year."

Mr. Evans smiled mysteriously.

"Him and me's like brothers," he said. Prophetic words!

There was a time when John Bolfort was a name to conjure with. The Bolforts had been trainers of horses since the days of Richard III., or maybe Alfred the Great (or, as some cynics say, since the times of Aethelred the Unready). Even today the word "Bolfort" against a horse's name in any programme is a cachet of its respectability, for John Felton Bolfort is a man of superior learning and eminent toniness. John Bolfort went to Eton, as all. Bolforts have done. Indeed, it is often suggested that Eton was founded by Henry VI. for the purpose of giving this great family of trainers the education so necessary to the scientific super-vision of racehorses.

Mr John Bolfort trains at Marsh in the Moor: that is to say, attached to the old manor house, where he drinks his port at a polished table, are a dozen or so loose boxes, where horses are sent to feed and canter and sometimes race. For the past twenty years he has had an average of 2.75 *per cent.* winners *per annum.* Regular racegoers leave out his horses, uttering the slogan: "When he wins I can afford to lose." And it suits Mr. Bolfort, who cares very little whether he wins or loses, having a mind superior to horses and being wholly engrossed in the study and collection of early church music. In truth his owners do not worry whether he wins or loses: they are mainly fine old country gentlemen who ride to hounds, drink port, and bemoan the passing of the Reform Bill in eighteen thirty something, which, as everybody knows, ruined England.

But if, by accident, he gets the horses of a plebeian, upstart owner who wants to know whether his horse is going to win, Mr. Bolfort shrugs his shoulders, shakes his white head, strokes his patriarchal beard and smiles.

"I can only tell you," he says, in his well-modulated voice, "that your horse is very well."

If the owner becomes a little too insistent, Mr. Bolfort writes him a letter and asks him if he will kindly take his horses elsewhere. That is the kind of man Mr. Bolfort is.

When his horses win, as they occasionally do, his is mildly surprised but the surprise on the part of the public is not so mild, because his winners invariably start amongst the "20/1 others," and low down punters, who have backed the favourite and seen it pipped a short head on the post, curse Mr. Bolfort and wish his charge had dropped dead, yet console themselves by repeating: "When he wins I can afford to lose."

He had in his stable a horse called Fideles, which common book-makers invariably called Fiddles," and Fiddles was remarkable in that it had run thirty-five times without catching the judge's eye, or indeed any other portion of his countenance. Fideles was the property of Lord Livergrome, who was a gentleman of the old school who liked to see his colours in public. It would have cost him much less to have had those same colours carried around on a pole, but he preferred to see them on a jockey's back, and paid cheerfully the most expensive entrance fees.

By the curious workings of fate, Mr Bolfort was browsing in Camden Town and was standing at the counter of Jones' Renowned Marine store and Second-hand Bookshop, examining a germ-infected copy of a very old book when Evans came into the store, nodded jauntily to the untidy lady behind the counter, and put his books on the counter.

"I've got a few odds and ends here, Mrs. Jones, you might like to buy," he said airily." Me library's getting overstocked. The books are valuable, but I haven't time to take 'em down to Christie's, the celebrated auctioneers."

Mrs. Jones, with a look of disparagement on a face that was otherwise featureless, cut the string and turned over the books one by one.

"Eightpence," she said laconically.

"Eightpence?" said the indignant Evans. "Why that there book's got 'f's' for 's's' in it."

"It's not worth tuppence," said the cruel Mrs. Jones. "What's it about, anyway? What's a madrigal?"

"A madrigal," said Evans, with dignity, "as everybody knows, is a book about lunatics: one of the most famous books that's ever been published."

Mr. Bolfort came out of his trance.

"Excuse me, sir," he said, in his gentle voice, reached for the book and, turning over the pages, uttered an exclamation.

"'Elizabethan. Madrigals, collected by Thomas Scott,'" he said. "I should like to buy that. Good gracious me it's the book I've been looking for for years! What do you want for it, sir?"

Evans coughed. He hated to say too little for fear he got it, or too much lest he be assaulted. Mr. Bolfort saved him the trouble.

"I will give you five pounds," he said apologetically, and Evans nodded dumbly.

"You are a collector, sir?" said Mr. Bolfort, ignoring the glaring Mrs. Jones, who had been robbed out of £4 19s. 4d.

"A bit of a one," said Evans, recovering his voice.

Mr. Bolfort shook his hoary head.

"Alas! I wish that I had the time to devote to that fascinating hobby," he said; " though I think I have the best collection of old English madrigals in the country. You must come down to Bolfort House one day and look over my library. I find most people are more interested in my horses than in my books."

"Bolfort House?" said Evans hollowly. "You ain't—aren't—you're not Mr. Bolfort, the highly celebrated trainer?"

The highly celebrated trainer smiled sadly. "I would rather be known for my madrigals," he said.

Five minutes later Evans walked arm-in-arm down Great College Street—with a trainer! With a man whose name appeared in newspapers, with a gentleman who could race horses every day of his life and think nothing of it.

"Yes, yes, you must see my collection," said Mr. Bolfort, who was interested in the subject of books to the exclusion of all else; who even regarded the shabbiness of his new acquaintance as a proof of his genius.

The Miller was patrolling High Street, Camden Town, next morning, when Mr. Evans crossed the road to intercept him.

"I got them trousis back, Mr. Challoner," said Evans. "It was a bit of a joke on Robspear's part. . . . it would have been awkward for me if I hadn't. I'm going down to spend a weekend with my old friend Bolfort."

The Miller looked at him suspiciously. " It's rather early in the day for fairytales," he said, " but I'll buy this one. Bolfort the trainer?"

"I'm spending a weekend with him," said Evans, coughing importantly. "as I've told you before, him an' me's like brothers. 'Evans,' he said, 'come down and see that horse of mine Fiddles.' "

Evans coughed again, this time not so importantly.

"I've been having a bit of trouble getting money in from clients—" he began.

"Why should they give you money?" demanded The Miller. "Except to get you out of the country "

Nevertheless, when Educated Evans approached him with some urgency, The Miller parted. For there was this to be said about his educated friend, that he never forgot his debts.

The money was very necessary, for the fare to Marsh in the Moor was exorbitantly high, and the walk from the railway station would have been an immense distance but for the station fly he was able to hire. The next morning Evans woke up in a four-poster bed and looked round the enormous apartment with a sense of complacency. He had spent the night before drinking port and examining books which were Greek, Sanskrit and Cuneiform to him. He had skilfully led the conversation to the subject of race-horses, and had been as skilfully led back to the matter of madrigals and Gregorian chants. But this morning he was to see with his own eyes the interior of a real racing stable.

"Do you ride, Mr. Evans? Why, of course you do," old Mr. Bolfort corrected himself. "You were telling me how you won the Bengal Steeplechase."

Educated Evans turned pale.

"I haven't had a ride for years," he said. "and I'm a bit nervous about strange horses."

"Nonsense!" said Mr. Bolfort. "I'll have a hack for you that is as quiet as a mouse."

What Evans at that moment wanted was a horse as steady as a concrete gun-platform, but this he could not state without a loss of caste.

The horse was waiting at the door. Mr. Bolfort lent him a pair of gaiters to put on over his trousers and handed him a whip. "I never use a whip," said Educated Evans tremulously.

"You'd better take a whip, sir," said the stable boy in attendance. "Old Toby shies at anything and he wants a couple of rib-benders before he settles down."

Evans took the whip in his trembling hand and looked again at the horse. It was an enormous horse: he could scarcely see over the top of it. How he got into the saddle he never knew. Before he realised what had happened, there was a huge mass of coarse hair wobbling beneath him, and he was clutching desperately to the saddle with one hand, following Mr. Bolfort's hack as it moved towards the stables, which were half a mile from the house. Happily, Mr. Bolfort was at first content to walk; but halfway to the stables he called Evans to his side, and as though the horrible beast that the World's Champion bestrode understood his words, he broke into a most uncomfortable jog-trot which jerked every atom of breath from his educated body. Thereafter, however, the ride was a pleasant one, for Mr. Bolfort was also content to walk his mount.

"You'll see some nice horses," said the old trainer; "though I must confess that I'm not as much interested in them as my grandfather was. I love to see a horse looking sturdy, with his coat shining and a little flesh on his bones. I believe in treating animals kindly, as I would myself wish to be treated."

"That's what I always say," said Evans.

He was beginning to get used to the dangerous experience of

moving through the air with his head some ten feet from the ground, and a little of the colour was coming back to his face.

"The curious thing about horses," mused Mr. Bolfort, "are the likes and dislikes they have. Now I've got a horse in my stable that simply loathes old Toby."

"The one I am riding?" asked Mr. Evans, feeling a certain amount of sympathy with anything that shared his utter dislike of the ambling beast beneath him.

"Yes, old Toby," Bolfort went on. "The horse in question is one called Fideles. The mere sight of that hack—"

He tapped old Toby on the nose, and old Toby did a violent shy, in the course of which, by some miracle, Evans preserved his seat, though not his presence of mind.

"The sight of old Toby," the trainer went on, unconscious of the panic he had aroused in the bosom of the World's Best Tipster, "drives Fideles into a fury. Now I've often tried to account for this extraordinary prejudice, but so far I have not succeeded."

"Do you mind if I get off the horse when we come to the stables—I mean before Fiddles see him?" begged Evans, large beads of perspiration on his brow.

"Certainly. You can't ride round the stables, you know," said the old man good-humouredly.

Happily there was a stable boy who seemed to understand horses at the entrance of the yard, and Evans slid down Toby's forelegs to the ground, his knees trembling beneath him, and for the space of two minutes he had the head lad to himself.

"Nice place this," said Evans conversationally.

The head lad, who had the face of an aged man and the legs of an infant, growled something uncomplimentary.

"Going to see Fiddles?" he asked, and Evans' heart warmed towards one who pronounced the word correctly. "That 'orse ought to win a race, you know, guv'nor," said the head lad, "but Mr. Bolfort won't give him a gallop—says it strains their 'earts! One good gallop, and old Fiddles would win that Richmond 'Andicap next week as sure as you're born!"

At this moment the trainer came back and conducted his guest round the stables. At the third door he paused.

"This is Fideles," he said, "and he's rather a wild fellow, so I wouldn't advise you to come inside."

He opened the top half door, and revealed a ferocious animal whose lips curled back in a sneer at the sight of the man who had so often tipped him.

"That's Fideles," said Mr. Bolfort, "Put him over the other side, boy."

It was only then that Evans noticed that there was a boy attached to the horse by an iron chain. At least, it seemed so.

"If I went into that box," said Mr. Bolfort complacently, "he'd eat me. You wouldn't be in there two minutes alive, Mr. Evans. Whoa, boy!"

For Fideles had suddenly whipped round and lashed out with his hooves in the direction of the box door. Evans made a hasty retreat.

The inspection of the stables did not take a long time. Mr. Bolfort had spoken the truth when he said that horses did not interest him as much as madrigals. With some reluctance, but with the comforting assurance that the house was very near, Evans was assisted into the saddle of his hack and he and his host walked side by side out of the gate.

"I almost think that Fideles of mine would win a race, but unhappily he is such a brute that none of my lads likes to ride him, and the boy who does him—"

"Was that the boy that does him?" asked Evans in an awed voice, thinking of the diminutive youth attached by a chain.

"That is the boy that does him. He's too light: the horse would simply run away with him. He's such a brute. . . ."

There was a clatter of hooves behind and he turned his head, and Evans, who did not dare to turn his head for fear of falling off, saw a look of amazement and horror in the trainer's face.

"Fideles!" he gasped. "He's after that hack of yours! Gallop, Mr. Evans, for heaven's sake!"

Evans screwed his head round and caught one glimpse of the ferocious horse galloping towards him, followed by three yelling stable boys, and he almost fell off his horse.

Toby did not need to have spurs clapped to him, even if Educated Evans had had spurs to clap. With an unearthly snort he bounded forward. Mr. Evans clutched his mane and held tight. The house flew past them; they were crossing a field at seventy miles an hour—or it may have been a hundred and seventy. It seemed more. A hedge loomed in front of them. Before Evans realised what had happened, he felt himself rise, fly over the hedge, still clutching the mane, his legs dangling helplessly, the stirrups striking his knees most painfully at every stride.

He heard the thunder of the hooves behind, and, more by accident than design, saw the open-mouthed fury that pursued them not more than half a dozen yards away.

Through a field of cabbages, over another fence—how he maintained his seat he never understood—into a country road, past a motor-car—or it may have been six motorcars—through a farmyard, twice round a haystack, with Fideles following, and then back towards the stable. Evans closed his eyes and waited for death as he saw his fear-maddened mount dashing, as it seemed, straight for a brick wall.

Toby stopped suddenly. Not so Evans. He described a wonderful curve through the air, and he had a sensation of flying, saw beneath him the top of a wall, then suddenly his eyes, ears and nose were filled with sharp ends of straw, and he lay half-conscious.

Two stable boys helped him up, and he heard, in a dim, dazed way, that his horse was safe. He was not wildly elated at the news.

"Is Fiddles dead?" he asked hopefully.

But Fiddles lived.

★★★★★★

On the evening of Easter Monday, Educated Evans sat in his room, a long cigar between his teeth, a look of infinite satisfaction in his eyes. There The Miller found him, at peace with the world.

"Congratulations, Evans!" he said heartily. "Fiddles won all right —I got twenties to my money."

Mr. Evans removed his cigar.

"You can thank me," he said simply. "He wouldn't have won but for me. I says to Bolfort when I see the horse, 'Bolfort,' I says, 'that horse wants a gallop. Let me lead him one gallop an' he'll win.' "

"And did he let you " asked The Miller incredulously.

Evans knocked off the ashes of his cigar. "It wasn't a question of letting," he said "The matter was took out of his hands."

The Miller did not believe him—but for once The Miller was wrong.

7.—A Horse of the Same Colour

The two-year-old Hesperus was a grey. And the two-year-old Milikins was also a grey. And both their owner and their trainer were hoary-headed men who had grown grey with artfulness.

Mr. Tooks (*the* Randolph Tooks) had two stables, one at Lambourn and one in Wiltshire, and to the Wiltshire stable he sent Milikins and to the Lambourn establishment he sent Hesperus, just as soon as he had bought these horses privately from their breeder. Only he changed their names and when the stable boys at Lambourn were talking about the amazing speed of Milikins they were in reality talking of Hesperus.

Only the astute Mr. Groom, the trainer, and the astuter Mr. Tooks knew this.

Hesperus (wrote the head lad of the Wiltshire stable) isn't worth tuppence: you can leave him out every time he runs.

He was writing to one of his punters, for naughty head lads sometimes have a few correspondents who will give them the odds to a fiver in return for information.

Milikins is a smasher (wrote a literary stable boy who supplied a plutocratic tipster with information). "We tried him yesterday at level weights with Hard Egg and Dontbelate and he smothered them.

"Be open and frank about these horses," said Mr. Tooks, the wily owner. "If any of these newspaper touts come nosing round your gallops, don't hurt 'em—give 'em a drink. We'll enter Hesperus and Milikins at one meeting, I'll send my own boys to bring the horses on to the course, and we'll skin the ring."

It is not an offence at law or by the rules of racing to call a horse by any name you wish, so long as he runs by the name he is entered. There is many a high-sounding Derby winner who is called "Bill" in the stable, and if the stable name for Hesperus was Milikins, nobody was hurt but the stable hands who, contrary to Rule 176, sub-section *v*, conveyed illicit information.

Educated Evans, the World's Champion Prophet and Turf Adviser, did not ordinarily interest himself in the thoroughbred race-horse, as a horse. To him, a horse was a name in the daily newspapers anchored to the column by a weight, the names of his owner (to which "Mr." was affixed) and his trainer, who was just Jones or Smith without any mistering nonsense whatever.

But Mr. Evans had smelt the early dawn of the gallops and seen the vast uplands of country places, and had, moreover, felt the soul-stir which comes only to those who have sat on the back of a thoroughbred hack. In other words, he had once been the overnight guest of a real trainer, and the exhilaration of the experience had got into his blood and even found its way to his legs. From Isaacs in High Street he acquired a pair of riding breeches and gaiters. He began to take an interest in the horses stabled in the mews, and would often imitate, unconsciously perhaps, the hissing noise that grooms make when they run a dandy brush over a horse's back.

But the most remarkable change that this experience of his had brought about was his passion for observation. He had been twice to Epsom and had shivered on the top of Six Mile Hill whilst innumerable horses that looked very much like one another came at an alarming pace towards him. He had been as far afield as Newmarket—and he had made one most profitable visit to a spot which was somewhere between East Ilsley and Wantage. It may be explained that none of these journeys cost money, a friend and client of his, who did odd cartage-jobs with a motor-van that he had picked up for a song, giving him a lift whenever he was going near to a training centre.

These serious preoccupations of Educated Evans had not escaped the keen eyes of Camden Town. Mr. Evans was again in favour. Even the carters at the Midland Goods Station, who had once (so it is said) bribed the driver of a shunting engine to run him over, took him to their arms. His detested rival, Old Sam, had been unlucky. Possibly he was using the wrong kind of pin to find winners, but certain it is that, when the ancient man walked abroad, his beard of many colours floating in the wind, disappointed punters said bitter things to him. The riding breeches and gaiters of Educated Evans were the final blow to Old Sam. He came to Mr. Evans' house one night, breathing hops and vengeance, but the Educated Man had gone down into Berkshire overnight.

Early the following morning Mr. Groom, the eminent trainer, rode out on to the downs, his string of horses having gone ahead of him. Cantering towards the end of the trial ground, he became aware of a figure on his misty horizon and a big motor lorry drawn up by the side of the road.

"Good-morning, sir," said Mr. Groom politely.

"Good-morning, sir," said Evans, ready to bolt.

"Are you one of those newspaper gentlemen?" said the amazingly polite trainer.

Evans, who could not tell a lie, admitted that he was.

"Ah! then you'll see an interesting gallop," said Mr. Groom. "I never object to newspaper gentlemen seeing my trials. What paper do you represent?"

Educated Evans mentioned a journal which would have reeled from Printing House Square to Fleet Street had it but heard.

"It's a good paper but the price is high," remarked the trainer.

"We're thinkin' of rejuicin' it," said Evans carelessly. "I was only sayin' to Lord What's-his-name yesterday, 'people won't pay fourpence unless you give away a pattern or somethin'—'"

"Here they come!" Groom interrupted as four dots came over the skyline and grew larger every second.

Evans knew enough about horses to see at a glance that the leader was a grey. It flashed past him four lengths ahead of the rest.

"Yes. . . very good," agreed Groom.

"No, I can't tell you its name—but it is the only grey I have in the stable. Good-morning, Mr.—er—"

"Evans," said the educated man airily. "You may have heard of me—the celebrated Educated Evans? Braxted. . . don't that recall nothing?"

"Were you named after him?" asked Mr. Groom.

The Master of Paddy Lodge, Bayham Mews, shrugged his shoulders.

"I'll write it down for you," he said, oblivious to Mr. Groom's obvious indifference.

Drawing a fat fountain-pen from his pocket (purchased only a few days before from the shilling bargain basement of Pelfridge's) he inscribed his name on a bit of paper he found in his pocket.

"Look out!"

Evans heard the warning shout and stared round. The horses had been pulled up and were returning to where he and the trainer stood. The grey, still fighting for its head, was within a yard of him, and as he looked, the animal spun round like a *teetotum*.

Pen and paper fell from Evans' hand as he stumbled back. He saw a hoof smash on the pen and a spurting fountain of green ink leap up.

"Keep away from him!" called the trainer sharply, and Evans retreated to the road. He did not even call attention to the loss of his pen.

"That horse didn't seem to like you," said the trolley driver, as his passenger climbed up.

Evans shrugged again.

"I'm cruel to horses—I admit it," he confessed. "He ain't forgot the hidin' I gave him last week."

Three minutes later he was being rattled towards Newbury, his mind seething with excitement. At the first newspaper shop he stopped and bought a copy of *Horses in Training,* and turned eagerly to that page which bore the name of Mr. Groom's charges.

"Milikins, gr. colt by Grey Fairy—Mill Girl."

Milikins! Here was a tip, not from the boy that did him, but from his very own eyes!

The Miller, who had been out of town for four days, having gone to Paris to take over the body of Harry Elbert, the well-known fishmonger who, being in a precarious financial position, had packed up a parcel of his employers' money (The Deep Sea Fisheries Limited—The Shops with the Blue Tiles) and gone abroad with the young lady from Higgins the Poulterers.

He came back and, having safely hutched Harry, went in search of Educated Evans.

That learned man he found at his home, Paddy Lodge, and Mr. Evans was engaged in the comparatively innocent occupation of frying a sausage.

"Ever heard of Ptolemy, Evans?"

The World's Champion Turf Adviser shook his head.

"Tolly Me?" he frowned. "That's one of Bennett's hair-trunks, ain't it?"

The Miller spelt the word and the face of his host lit up.

"Oh, you mean Pet-olmy—heard about him? He belongs to the celebrated Adjer Kan an' he can catch pigeons. He's runnin' in the Jubilee—"

"He belongs to quite another gentleman, he's running in the Derby, and they tell me in Paris he can't lose."

Mr. Evans sniffed and turned the sausage with his one-pronged fork.

"There's a horse in the Derby," he said, with great deliberation, " that can fall down, eat a good meal, get up an' *then* win it! This horse was tried twenty-one pound better than Sansovino, belongin' to the highly popular Sir Stanley Derby, of Derby House, Newmarket—a personal friend of mine. I've written letters to him."

"That seems a pretty slight foundation for friendship," said The Miller dryly. "Do you call all the people your friends just because you write to 'em?"

"I do," said Evans significantly. "If they act honourable. Everybody don't act honourable. Twenty-one pun' eight shillin's, a basket of greens and a gramophone that don't work—that's all I got out of three hundred clients."

"It seems a lot," said The Miller, and Mr. Evans sighed in resignation.

"I gave 'em Paddy, 20/1—what a beauty—did I or did I not?"

"You did," said the officer of the law. "You sent it out for the Liverpool Cup, but the woman to whom you gave the letters refrained from posting them till Tuesday. In consequence of which you've got a reputation you don't deserve."

Mr. Evans shrugged.

"Maybe I'll get another next week," he said mysteriously. "Maybe, when a certain horse comes home alone, I'll get a reputation that won't be deserved too! Oh, no! Oh, dear no!" ·

"I hate you when you're sarcastic," said The Miller. "Come on! What is this come-home-aloner?"

But Mr. Evans was adamantine.

"I'm sorry not to oblige you, Mr. Challoner, but I've got competition in my business. There's a certain party—no names no pack-drill—who's fairly doggin' me to get information: him an' his pretty daughter."

Educated Evans used "pretty" in the offensive sense to describe Mrs. Lube, of whom most people have heard.

It was regrettable that Mr. Evans was not of the temperament which makes secrecy possible. All Camden Town knew that the master of Paddy Lodge had a rod in pickle: its actual name he did not tell. He contented himself with "hints."

Certainly he hinted to such effect that he had aroused a considerable amount of curiosity, and at the same time had provoked mean-spirited men to discover for themselves the identity of this wonderful horse that he was giving on Thursday, and which, in two incautious moments, he had stated to one person, would win the Birbeck Two-Year-Old Plate at Gatwick, and to another, that it was a grey. When you know the race and the colour of a horse, and there are but two grey horses running, and one of those loudly advertised by every newspaper dealing with the noble sport of horse-racing, it is not difficult to arrive at a conclusion.

"That's it!" said young Harry Gribbs, examining the programme. " It's Milikins! It'll start at four to one on—that's a nice five pound special, I don't think!"

In other quarters the identity of the animal had been discovered. The Miller called round to see his friend.

"Evans, you're going to lose your connection, my lad," he said.

Mr. Evans was in an irritable, indeed a nervous, state of mind, because he had recognised his indiscretion. In the first place, his secret information was everybody's news. It would be difficult to find a weekly paper that had not put a star against Milikins, except those that had put two.

"And obviously that is the horse you have been gassing about all this week."

"That's where you're wrong," snapped Evans, and The Miller stared at him.

"But you said it was a grey; you said it was running in this two-year-old race."

"Never mind what I said," Educated Evans looked almost truculent. "Ain't I entitled to be diplomatical, the same as the well-known Gallypot, the French astrologer, who, when he was asked if the world turned round, replied to the haughty dogs of Venice: 'It do and it don't.' Ain't I entitled—good lord-'mighty!—to use discretion and artfulness and cleverness? Am I supposed to carry me heart up me sleeve?"

"Calm yourself, Horatius," said the Miller. "I meant no harm. Only everybody in Camden Town thinks you're tipping Milikins, and even Old Sam thinks you're losing your dash."

"So-and-so and so-and-so Old Sam!" said the exasperated Evans.

"Be calm, Elijah!" said The Miller gently. "And what is that horrible green stuff on your fingers?"

"It's ink that I got for me fountain pen—it won't come orf."

"Nor will Hesperus," said Sergeant Challoner, and Evans ground his teeth.

He went back to Paddy House, Bayham Mews, slammed and locked the door and sat for a quarter of an hour glaring at the notice he had run off on his duplicator.

BETTER THAN PADDY!
BETTER THAN PADDY!
BETTER THAN PADDY!

I am sending you one today which can catch pigeons. I am sending you one of the grandest horses that ever looked through a bridal! This one I have touted with my own eyes and seen all its work day by day at great expense! This one is better than Paddy ever knew how to be. He will start at 33/1 and win in a canter.

MILIKINS—FEAR NOTHING.

And don't forget your old and true and tried friend,

EDUCATED EVANS,

Paddy Lodge,

Bayham Mews.

P.S.—Beware of imitations. The police have orders to take into custody any person, old or young, who plaguerises my tips.

Evans had brought into the flat with him a bundle of weekly newspapers, purchased at the local newsagent's, and now he examined the sporting prophecies with interest and despair, as sheet after sheet revealed the implicit faith of the anonymous sporting writers in the superiority of Milikins.

We have seen Milikins do several gallops, and we know that his trainer has a high opinion of him (wrote "Bow-Wow" in the *Racing Watch Dog*) and there is no doubt that he is a certainty for his race on Saturday, and we have every confidence in giving

MILIKINS.

Evans groaned with every fresh discovery. He realised, in some indefinable way, that his very reputation was at stake. Camden Town was waiting to sneer at him, and he took a sudden and dramatic resolve. Very painfully, he wrote out a new duplicator sheet, substituting for "Milikins" the word "Hesperus." That at least was a grey and was in the same race—for he was committed to a grey.

What did the sporting newspapers say of Hesperus? Even the *Saturday Sports Herald,* whose training correspondents tip every horse in the race, had little to remark in his favour. "Ours is not good," said the local correspondent.

Others were equally offensive. Evans groaned again. There was no help for it. Better to send a wild outsider, without a possible chance of winning, than sacrifice his fame for sagacity. Setting his teeth, he finished writing on the wax paper, and the bell of St. Pancras' Church was chiming three before he climbed into bed, so weary that he forgot to take off his braces—a precaution he had never neglected before.

Was Camden Town agog at the news it had received? It was.

"Hesperus?" said The Miller, wrinkling his brows, and went in search of the tipster. But Mr. Evans had left by an early rattler for the scene of the contest.

Mr. Groom, the eminent trainer, was running both horses, he was glad to see, for a non-runner was almost as damaging to the prestige of a turf prophet as an odds-on favourite.

In what miraculous fashion Mr. Evans contrived to get into the most exclusive enclosures at a race meeting, nobody has ever discovered. He is one of the few sportsmen in the world who has had the distinction of being thrown over the rails of the Royal Enclosure at Ascot. Amongst his other battle honours is the experience of being kicked out of Newmarket private stand twice in one day. It is certain he was in the Gatwick paddock, without the title which payment usually confers upon the patrons of racing.

Miller had a day off; his motor-cycle had whizzed him into Surrey, and his profession procured him the same advantage in the matter of admission as Evan had obtained through another cause.

"What's this Hesperus you've sent out?"

" A horse," said Evans laconically.

"Does it run?"

Mr. Evans closed his eyes.

"It will run and will win by the length of the Holloway Road," he said. "I've had this horse give to me by the boy that does him, and I've brought down twenty pounds to back him."

The Miller shook his head.

"Give the money to me: I'll mind it," he said gently. "You're ill, Evans. The truth is, you intended giving Milikins, and when you found everybody else was giving it, you switched over."

Mr. Evans raised his shoulders in patient protest.

"Them that laughs last laughs least," he said cryptically.

It was true he had as much as £25 in his pocket. It was quite untrue that he intended risking so much as a penny upon Hesperus. What he did design was a plunge upon Milikins, that would bring some solace for the losses he would sustain over his idiotic tipping.

Just before the 4.15, he was leaning on the rail, watching the horses parade. There were two greys, but which was Hesperus and which was Milikins, he did not know. Educated Evans never recognised a horse until the jockey got up.

Just as the numbers were going into the frame, The Miller came hurrying to Evans and led him to a quiet corner of the paddock.

"Evans," he said, "there's some talk about these horses being mixed up: that Milikins is really Hesperus, and Hesperus Milikins. You told me you saw a trial?"

Evans nodded importantly.

"Then you can tell one horse from the other. Which of those two greys won the trial?"

Evans glanced back at the saddling ring, where the horses were slowly walking. Beyond the fact that they were two greys, he was quite unable to distinguish the trial winner, for two horses, as I have remarked, looked as much alike to Evans as two pairs of boots of similar make and size.

And then there flashed across his mind a recollection of the alarming incident which had marked the end of the trial.

"Here, hold hard, Miller," he said agitatedly. "I can tell you in a twink!"

He hurried back to the ring, followed by Mr. Challoner, and presently the greys came along, one following the other. Evans glared down at their feet, and then, with a gurgle of joy, he pointed.

"That's Milikins," he said. "See them green spots on his legs? . . . . My fountain-pen. . . ."

Incoherently he told the story of his loss, which was now to prove his gain.

"That's Milikins," he said. "He'll win by the length of Tattersall's... that horse is money for nothing," he went on, forgetting his role of prophet, forgetful of three hundred unfortunate people whom he had begged and implored to back Hesperus. ". . . that horse could stand on his head and win."

"You daylight robber!" said The Miller softly. "Then you were bluffing?"

Evans threw out his hands in protest.

"A man of my position has got to fyness," he said simply, and The Miller was in too much of a hurry to ask for an explanation.

Evans went back to the ring again. There were the green spots on the grey's fetlock. He smiled triumphantly, and, clutching his £20 in a hot hand, he hustled his way into Tattersall's and, taking £35 to £20, climbed up the stand to see his money come home.

"I've got to get it some way or the other, Mr. Challoner," he said to The Miller, who joined him. "Self-preservation's the first law of betting, and —"

"They're off!"

The start was a straggling one, but Hesperus—even Evans recognised Hesperus now —jumped off in front, was a certain winner at two furlongs, an assured winner at four furlongs, and actually did win by ten lengths.

"Hesperus?" said the dazed Evans. "The—the thieves and robbers! They've been and run them horses on me!"

And then it slowly dawned upon him that, however much his pocket might have suffered at Gatwick, his reputation in Camden

Town was considerably enhanced. Well, well," he said tolerantly, " it's a case of information *v.* guesswork. If I'd stayed at home I'd have made a lot of money. I knew they'd rung this horse, and if you hadn't put me off it—"

The Miller gave him one glance, which would have withered an ordinary man. But Evans was no ordinary man.

Said Mr. Groom, the trainer, to Mr. Tooks, the owner:

"Did you see that ugly little devil looking at the horse's legs? He's a tout or something and came up to my gallops. What did he do? Why, he dropped some green ink on Hesperus. I guessed he'd been sent to find out which was which, so I cleaned Hesperus—and a devil of a job it was—and put a few green spots on Milikins. Artful, eh? I tell you these newspaper chaps want a bit of beating!

8.—MIXING IT

Every great man has his sycophants, partly because, realising their greatness, they cannot hear too much about it, and partly because flattery produces largesse in some shape or form.

Educated Evans was a great man: he was the World's Champion Prophet and Turf Adviser, which in itself is a distinction that many a man would give his head to possess. He was also a scholar and an authority on all sorts of esoteric subjects.

You could never floor Evans with any kind of question, historical, astronomical, biological or anatomical. He was the only man in Camden Town who knew what an appendix was for.

And Abe Slow was his most vocal admirer. Abe was a bookmaker who had fallen on evil times owing to his honesty. He used to admit this.

"If I'd thieved same as..." (he named quite a number of limited liability bookmakers, and named them libellously) "I'd be walking about in my Rolls-Royce car, but, Mr. Evans, believe me or believe me not, I'd rather have my ear cut off than fiddle."

Evans believed him. At that particular moment he believed anything, for he was in his politest mood. A high stool was under him, the shining counter of the saloon bar of the "Blue Horse" was before him, and within earshot was the loveliest barmaid in Camden Town—Miss Bella, she with the diamond ear-rings and the wrist-watch.

"Very true, very true," said Evans, condescendingly and loudly. "How true it is, as the celebrated Mikel Vally, the well-known Eyetalian artist, said, 'Honesty's a good servant but a bad master,' which reminds me."

The beautiful barmaid was wiping a wine glass, breathing upon it to obtain a better polish, but she was listening and Evans raised his voice still louder.

"Travellin' as I have in all parts of the uncivilise' world, Africa, Orstralia, Wantage an' other wild spots, I've often seen things that people don't know, such as lions, tigers, ostridges—where we get feathers from—kang'roos, elephants. . . ."

The beauteous Bella stifled a yawn and walked to the other end of the counter to serve a customer. Mr. Evans shrugged his thin shoulders, and from there on the conversation became normal.

"I've had my ups and I've had my downs," Abe went on, "but if I'd 'a had a gentleman like you behind me I shouldn't be in my present position—good health, Mr. Evans."

Mr. Evans nodded as his beer flowed down another man's throat. He knew, but preferred not to know, that Abe was once a street-corner bookmaker, with a limit of tenses and a strict all-in rule for doubles, trebles and accumulators. Even these restrictive regulations had not averted ruin in the year that Humorist won the Derby. Abe had paid out £47 10s. 0d. over that race without a murmur—partly because the two chief winners were Lew Davis, the celebrated middleweight, and Alf Sossino, who had done two stretches for biting policemen, and partly because he was an honourable man. This latter cause was, however, the smaller part.

"Have you thought any more about that idea of mine?" asked Abe, as he wiped his mouth.

Evans had thought a great deal. That idea of Abe's was in a way rather intriguing.

"A man in my position—" he began, but Abe arrested his objection eloquently.

"You've got the capital, you understand the game, you've got the information," he said rapidly. "I've got what you might call the book-keepin' ability. It's money for nothing, Mr. Evans. All you've got to do is to stand up an' the money rolls in. You know the ones that are dangerous, all you've got to do is to say polite, 'Very sorry, my book's full,' an' lay the duds!"

"It's rather low," murmured Educated Evans, half convinced, "standin' up on a race-course an' makin' a exhibition of yourself."

Abe grew more voluble, more urgent as he saw his great idea gaining ground.

"Everybody knows you by name, Mr. Evans," he said. "People will simply flock round you. . . "

The truth must be told: Educated Evans was seriously considering the possibility of "mixing it." To tip with the one hand, and to make a book with the other. It was delightfully simple and had been done before. And the prospect of standing up on Epsom Downs and shouting the odds was not altogether without its allurement.

Ever a dreamer, he had visions of a palatial establishment in Shaftesbury Avenue and a big rosewood office where he could sit smoking expensive cigars and drinking port wine, whilst an army of clerks dealt with stacks of bets, mainly losing ones.

"I'll do the clurking, you'll take the money—give me a quarter share in the book an' pay my expenses, that's all I ask, Mr. Evans," pleaded Abe. "You'll come home at night with your pockets full of gold an' silver . . . "

"I'll think about it," said Evans.

He had already decided when strife disturbed the harmonies of Brisl Villa, Bayham Mews, N.W. It was due in the main to A Certain Woman. To make the situation perfectly clear to every reader, there were in Camden Town two Turf Prophets, one known wherever the Union Jack flies, and the sun never sets, as the World's Champion the other (this is the view of the said World's Champion) a miserable old man, or an usurper; a pub-propping, uneducated old bounder named Sam.

The straw-chewing representative of the Criminal Investigation Department whom Camden Town called The Miller, listened sympathetically to Educated Evans.

"She came round to me an' asked me what I meant by takin' the bread out of her children's mouth by givin' winners—Dio-meeds, what a beauty!"

"Long odds on," murmured The Miller, "if you refer to Diomedes."

"I can't help the price," retorted Educated Evans briskly. "That horse was give to me by the brother of the aunt of the boy who does him, but it got out."

"And what did you say to Mrs. Lube?"

"I merely told her that business was business an' that what her grandfather did was nothin' to do with me. She asked me if I wanted to see her and her children in the workhouse an' her husband rejuiced to workin' for his livin' like a common lab'rer. I told her I didn't care.

187

And that's the result!"

He fingered his cheek tenderly. The skin beneath his left eye was slightly swollen and very blue.

"If she hadn't been a lady I'd have sloshed her!" said Evans, his voice trembling with pardonable annoyance. "But like King Alfred the Unready, I turned again an' counted six. I wouldn't hit her back even if she'd have let me. I sort of looked at her contemptchus."

"Where were you then?" asked The Miller.

"Under the bed," said Evans. "I had to go somewhere so that I didn't let my temper get the better of me. I ordered her out of my room. But the woman's got no sense of dignity."

"Take a summons," suggested The Miller, in his best judicial manner.

Evans coughed.

"I thought of doin' it an' told her so, an' she got the poker an' started waggin' it under the bed. But she didn't get me—I was firm with her."

"What on earth did you do?" demanded the astonished Miller.

"I got farther under the bed," said Evans. "I beat a strategic retreat like the far-famed Hinderburg, the highly celebrated 'Un. An' she got frightened after a bit. I told her what I thought of her—"

"After you found that she couldn't reach you with the poker?" asked The Miller.

"It may have been before or it may have been after," said the diplomatic Evans. "I told her that she wasn't educated an' ought to be ashamed of herself. An' she began to see that she had a pretty hard nut to deal with an' got out."

"I'll talk to her," said The Miller, who was something of a peacemaker.

"Don't tell her I told you." Educated Evans was alarmed. "I don't want her cumin' round here—I won't be responsible for what happens."

"To whom?" demanded the police officer sardonically.

Mrs. Lube, the granddaughter of Old Sam, Tipster and Ale- Eater, was a woman of great character and determination. She had for a brief period enjoyed considerable prosperity as a result of her relative's successful prognostication. But the return of Mr. Evans to the scene of his earlier activities had coincided with a slump in Old Sam's powers as a prophet. There was a great uneasiness in the Lubian household. Mr. Lube, her husband, was worried and irritable. He came home from the "Blue Peter" as many as three times a day to inquire into the sale of Old Sam's Midnight Special, a little blue card printed locally and enjoying (until Evans's return) an extensive sale at tuppence. On the back of this card and printed in very big type was the announcement:

Old Sam's Friends in the Training stables often send him a
11th hour tip which is sent by telegram to all clients who act
honourable and send 10/- by T.M.O.
Eventually—why not now?
Send today—without delay.

It must be admitted that the latter urgent request was a blatant plagiarism, being pinched from the literature of Educated Evans, who in turn had lifted the phrases bodily from a highly respected turf accountant.

When The Miller called at the little house where Old Sam slept and had his meals, Mrs. Lube was on the point of leaving for the pictures—the lure being those stupendous super-films (then showing) "Only a Mother: the story of a Wasted Life," and "Silk Garters—a story of Stage Life and Intrigue."

Her face fell at the sight of The Miller. "Come in, Mr. Challinger," she said graciously.

Sergeant Challoner, who was accustomed to having his name mutilated by people who invariably chose the wrongest pronunciation, followed her into the over-furnished parlour.

"Now, Mrs. Lube," he said genially, "what is all this I hear about your going to see Evans and raising a fuss?"

Mrs. Lube blinked twice.

"As Gawd's my judge and if I drop dead this minute an' never utter another syllable, I've not so much as spoken an 'arsh word against the Dirty Dog!" she said tremulously. I went up to see him as one lady to another gentleman an' all I said, without the word of a lie, an' if I die this very minute, was: 'Excuse me, Mr. Evins, but do you realise what you're a doin' of to a poor old man that 'asn't got your 'ealth and strength,' I says, an' taking the bread out of my children's mouth,' I says, 'with your low common tippin, and sayin' "Beware of spurious imitations," 'I says, 'an' look here,' I says, 'I know enough about you to get you ten years,' I says, an' with that he ups an' insults me about my lodger!"

"You surprise me" said The Miller. There had been certain rumours. . . "I am surprised," he said again, and Mrs. Lube nodded.

"And he called my poor dear grandfather a beer-bitin' old 'ound! So naturally bein' a woman with feelin's, I handed him one!"

"Naturally," murmured The Miller.

"An' the low, cowardly, sneakin' so-and-so—excuse my language, Mr. Challinger, but I'm a woman and have got my feelin's—he got under the bed and yelled murder! If I'd only got at him with a—with my hands, I'd have skull-dragged him!"

Thereupon The Miller began to speak, no longer affably, but in the ominous fashion of detective sergeants, and what he said left Mrs. Lube unrepentant but in tears.

She had recovered by the time her grandparent returned from lunch at the "Red Lion," his nearly white beard waving in the breeze.

". . . only a couple of pints, Agartha," he protested, "an' one of them was give me."

"Now listen to me, grandfather," said his buxom descendant. This has gone on quite long enough. How many midnights do you think you've sold today—ten! You've got to rouse yourself up, gran'father; you've got to bustle round. I've got two Mouths to fill and All talks about sellin' the harmonium. Me and him and you are goin' to the races tomorrow an' you've got to hang round and Hear Something."

"Races?" gasped her aged relative. "'Orse races? I don't know nothing about 'orses. I'd get run over."

"You're goin' to the Epsom races tomorrow," she said firmly. "I'm not goin' to allow that low, common potherb to say you don't know nothing about a horse except that he drinks water—that's what he said, grandfather, when he was under the bed—an' I'm goin' to take you down tomorrow. Alf's borrowed a horse an' trap an' Charlie Luce, the sign-painter, is getting some placards painted to put on the waggonette. Alf says it's the only thing to do. He's a racin' man. He says you've got to advertise. All you've got to do is to sit round wearin' a top hat—I got one from the rag-shop for fourpence. Alf will do the talkin'."

Old Sam was mollified.

"I can sit round in a top hat all right," he said, "if it fits."

"It's got to fit. I can put a bit of paper under the lining," said the determined female; "and we'll have a few bottles of beer in the trap."

"Ah!" said Old Sam. Epsom grew suddenly an attractive place.

Two mornings later, all the street in which Old Sam lived gathered to see the resplendent waggonette which was to carry him to the field

190

of victory.

"Now understand this," said Alf, the oracle, as he doffed his collar. We've got to give a winner today or we're out!"

"What's going to win this race?" asked Mrs. Lube.

"I don't know. Taping's a certainty, according to the papers, but it's no good giving short-priced horses. What we want is a sign. I dreamt last night of boiled mussels: is there a horse called Boiled Mussels running?"

They searched the programme, but if Boiled Mussels existed his owner had neglected to enter him for any event that day.

"What about asking Mr. Dimitri?" suggested Mrs. Lube helpfully, and her husband turned on her a disapproving eye.

"I don't want no lodgers interfering with my business," he said coldly.

Mr. Dimitri was a shipping clerk employed by an Athenian firm, and occupied the room next to Old Sam. He was, it must be confessed, a constant source of friction between husband and wife, for he was young, fairly good-looking, and had nice manners.

"I thought of asking him to come down with us," suggested Mrs. Lube.

Her husband's eyebrows rose.

"If he goes, I stay at home," he said, and Mrs. Lube, who could be very violent, became so.

"All right, all right," said Alf, in alarm, for he had, on more occasions than one, been forced to take the cover which had so well served Educated Evans. "Don't let's have any argument."

And so Mr. Dimitri, who had already arranged to go by train, being a thrifty Levantine, leapt at the opportunity of being conveyed free of all charge to Epsom Downs, with the chance of cold meat sandwiches and bottled beer thrown in. Thus they progressed through Streatham and Ewell, the cynosure of all eyes, and thus they came, Mrs. Lube furtively holding her lodger's hand (for her husband was driving and her grandfather was asleep) to the Downs.

To Educated Evans, the day on which the Great Metropolitan Stakes was decided had been a day of splendour and glory. For the first few minutes of his experience, he was embarrassed, alike by the new patent-leather satchel he carried over his shoulder, and by the bundle of tickets which he gripped in his moist hand. But the novelty appealed to him. The result of the first race, in which, by some miracle, nobody amongst his ever-growing list of clients backed the winner, no less than the delightful consequence of the second race, where the only person who did back the winner never troubled to claim his money, gave him a confidence which might have had disastrous consequences, but for his attendant book-keeper.

"Don't go shouting twenty to one the field, Mr. Evans," begged Abe, beads of perspiration on his face. "It's all right now, because they think you're kidding."

"What shall I say?" asked Evans.

"Say 'Five to one bar one,'" said the practical Abe.

"What do I bar?" asked Evans, interested.

"Anything they want to back," said Mr. Slow.

He had behind him, supported on two sticks, a banner, painted overnight:

EDUCATED EVANS

The World's Famous Turf Accountant.
No way barred. No Limit.
Same address for Fifty years.

And possibly it was true that his fame had gone abroad, for a stream of punters flowed steadily in his direction, and his satchel grew heavy with illicit silver. Mr. Evans went home that night from Tattenham Corner Station, sitting on his bag, and spent a delirious hour counting his gains.

"What do you think of it, Mr. Evans?" asked his partner anxiously.

"Money for nothing," said Evans. "If Screw had won instead of Brissell, I'd have been able to retire. We'll settle up tomorrow, Abe."

Mr. Abe Slow looked dubious.

"Better settle tonight," he suggested. "That's the custom in the profession."

Educated Evans gracefully bowed to the custom and paid out one quarter of his winnings.

He was now so engrossed in his new occupation that he almost forgot to send out his Five Pound Special, and would have done so for the City and Suburban had not The Miller happened along providentially.

"Taping is a cert," said Evans. "It's waste of money to send it out."

It was fortunate for all concerned that, having passed this piece of information on to one who received it with every evidence of scepticism and scorn, Evans had not time to set in motion the duplicator which a child could work, and Camden Town was deprived of an excuse for blasphemy.

A fair morning, with a chill wind blowing; the green, rolling Downs, and a sky flecked with light, vaporous clouds; and a song in the heart of Educated Evans.

The crowd was bigger than on the previous day. New clients recognised him with a smirk. One helped to erect the banner with the strange device, and was rewarded. Evans examined the book with a professional air, rustled the cards between his fingers, and:

"I'll lay on the City! Four to one Taping, four to one Taping. Ten to one De Orsey, ten to one De Orsey..."

And then he stopped, as his eyes fell upon a horrific sight. Near to his pitch a waggonette was drawn up, and its emaciated horse was being released from his work of bondage, preparatory to his being allowed to feed, free of all cost, on the grass provided by the Epsom ratepayers. It was an ancient waggonette; the weather-worn sides were covered with linen streamers, excitingly inscribed; whilst diagonally, and supported by two clothes-props on the waggonette, was a banner even more urgent and boastful than Mr. Evans's.

EDUCATED SAM

The One and Only
Camden Town Turf Prophet and Adviser!
Inventor of the Midnight Special.

PADDY

What a beauty!
What a beauty!
Beware of Imitators!!!

The placards on the sides were to the same effect.

"Educated Sam!" gasped Evans, growing purple. " Look at the old perisher!"

Seated in the back was the patriarchal figure of Sam himself, his whiskers crumpled on his bosom, his mittened hands clasped on his stomach, a hat a size or so too large crushed down over his ears, for he was sleeping peacefully, despite the proddings of a red-faced female in black silk.

"Wake up, grandfather," she said sharply. "You're 'ere."

Old Sam opened his eyes and stared round.

"Wake up, grandfather. Look, there's the race-'orses!"

He glowered owlishly at the course, where half a dozen gaily attired riders were cantering up towards the five-furlong post.

"Got the cards ready, grandfather " Mrs. Lube was visibly agitated. "Go on, Alf, say a few words."

All was a stocky man with ginger hair and a drooping ginger moustache. He was something of an orator, having sold patent medicines in the public streets in the days of his youth. He got up on the driving seat and became talkative, and Evans listened spellbound.

"Educated Sam!" he groaned hollowly. "Well, of all the sauce...!"

And then a brilliant idea struck him.

"Friends one and all!" His strident voice might have been heard in the grand stand, half a mile away. "This boozing old 'ound is trying to rob me of my living! He's no more educated than I—than you are. I'll lay twice the market odds against anything he tips."

Mrs. Lube listened aghast. She climbed up the waggonette by the side of her drowsy ancestor.

Go on, grandfather," she hissed. "Tip something."

Old Sam pondered a moment, stroking his beard.

"What's running?" he asked cautiously.

Alf, the barker, turned with a marked card.

"That sounds good—tip that"

"Not for this race, grandfather," his intelligent granddaughter protested. "Tip it for the City. If you give one for this race and it don't win, you'll get no more customers."

"What about Taping?" asked Alf anxiously.

"Look at 'em conspiring together!" sneered Evans raucously. "They've never so much as seen a race-horse wag his tail...!"

So excited was he that he did no business on the first race, which was well for him, for a hot favourite won; and little business on the second race. It was only when they began betting on the City and Suburban that he came to realise his vanishing opportunities.

"What about De Orsey?" asked Old Sam. He won a race the other day."

"A selling race," said Alf.

"He won a race," said the old man doggedly. " I see it in the paper. De Orsey!"

Alf and his wife exchanged glances.

"Taping won a race, too," said Alf.

"And it's easier to write, grandfather," said Mrs. Lube, who did most of the clerical work.

"De Orsey," murmured Old Sam, and dozed off again.

Suddenly Mrs. Lube uttered a squeak and pointed to their guest. "Greek. . you married?"

Mr. Dimitri's mouth was full of sandwich, but he shook his head.

"Greek Bachelor!" screamed Mrs. Lube, purple in the face. "Go on, Alf—bark it!"

Alf was a good barker, and an example of his style may not be out of place. . .

". . . You see before you one of the grand old men of the turf. He's looked after more 'orses than any trainer going (which was true, for, in the days when horses were not a novelty, Old Sam drew water for them at the Red Lion for a penny a time, until some interfering society put on a horse trough, thus robbing the poor of their livelihood). "Take a look at him, and tell me, ladies and gentlemen, if a man like that could tell a lie! Old Sam is one of the most famous educated men in the country. He's writ books—"

"You're a liar!" roared the exasperated Evans from his pitch. " He can't write his own name, the thievin' old gin-hawk!"

"He's writ books," said the unperturbed Alf, watching with some satisfaction the spectacle of Educated Evans dancing from one foot to the other in his impotent rage. " And they've been bought and sold, as is well known. He's come down here to give you the winner of the City from information received. . . ."

When the first of the tips came to Educated Evans, he laughed long and scornfully.

"Greek Bachelor? I'll lay you fifty to one," he said recklessly. "I'll lay anybody fifty to one Greek Bachelor!" he roared. "I'll lay 'em a hundred to one Greek Bachelor. That horse ain't got no more chance of winning this celebrated race than the far-famed Cleopatra, the well-known needle-maker. I'll lay any price you like Greek Bachelor—"

"Here, what are you doing?" asked Abe, in a ferocious whisper. "You can't go laying fifty to one against horses."

"I'll lay a hundred to one," said Evans rashly. "Come on—roll up. . . an 'undred to one. . .!"

★★★★★★

Evans in the days of his youth had been a runner. He did not run as fast as Greek Bachelor, but he beat his field by a longer distance. He ran into the landscape, so to speak, and by-and-by that portion of the howling mob which had not taken his satchel and divided his money, gave up the chase and went back to the sport of kings.

Abe Slow, who, belying his name, was just behind him, shouted the news, but still Evans ran and did not stop until he staggered up to the gates of a great mansion. Here he collapsed, and when Abe came up to him Mr. Evans was receiving first-aid from two uniformed attendants.

"What's this place?" he gasped, as he opened his eyes.

"Banstead Lunatic Asylum," said one of the men.

Abe Slow's lips curled.

"You don't want to go no further, Evans," he said bitterly. " This is your natchral 'ome!"

9.—THE FREAK DINNER

All the world knows Frithington-Evans. At least, all the sporting world knows him. Even his educated namesake had heard of him. Mr. Frithington-Evans was an extremely rich young man, an owner of race-horses and a pet of a certain class of people who did not work for their living, and who were sometimes described as "the smart set," occasionally miscalled "society," but more frequently referred to as "that lot."

Mr. Frithington-Evans had so much money that he could have well afforded to race his horses honestly. But deep down in the slither of spirituality which he called a soul, he had a rooted objection to anybody making money but himself and his friends. He was by nature suspicious, changed his trainer as a rule twice a year; and when he found that somebody was backing his horses, employed a detective agency to discover who this miscreant was, and if, by any chance, the unfortunate punter happened to be in Mr. Frithington-Evans' employ, he was summarily dismissed.

Amongst his friends was Lady Mary Herban, a beautiful young lady, who was received in the homes of all broad-minded people. They qualified for this description when they received her. It was after Mr. Frithington-Evans had won a nice little race in the north, with a horse that had 21 lbs. in hand, and which started at 100/8, that Lady Mary suggested the dinner. Frithington-Evans wriggled and complained about the expense.

"Don't be a mean little devil, Frithy," said Lady Mary severely. "You backed that horse s.p. with every unfortunate bookmaker in England—"

"I put you in," he pleaded. "You won a packet!"

"I know you put me in, and now you can stand the dinner. We'll have a real racing dinner, with jockeys and bookmakers, and have canvas stretched on the dining-room walls and painted to look like Pontefract race-course."

Frithington-Evans turned pale and rattled his keys.

"That'll cost a lot of money," he. said. "And I hate freak dinners anyway! Look here, Mary, let's wait until—well, I've, got a nice little coup that's likely to come off at Chester."

"We'll have it now," said Mary scornfully; and since they were very good friends indeed (Lady Mary's husband being abroad and wholly indifferent) the dinner was arranged.

It is very trying for a man of delicate susceptibilities to meet the rebuffs and insults of common people, and the other Mr. Evans never displayed his fine qualities to greater advantage than when he met with a smile, in which contempt and mysterious understanding were blended, the ill-printed placards which decorated almost every newsagent's shop in Camden Town:

IF YOU WANT THE BEST TIPS
OLD SAM HAS THEM!

Greek Bachelor!
Greek Bachelor!
Greek Bachelor!

£100,000 paid to any Charity if it can be proved that
Old Sam did not tip Greek Bachelor for the City and Suburban.
Don't go to Educated Welshers—
Go to the Grand Old Man of Camden Town.

Educated Evans could not afford to smile. Indeed, it was a painful physical effort to smile at all. Nevertheless, he met these vulgar attacks upon his probity with a loftiness which did credit, as some said, to his noble spirit, but, as others claimed, to the thickness of his hide.

"Mixing it, Mr. Challoner," he explained sadly, "always leads to trouble. As Looey the nineteenth, him that had his napper cut off in Paris, France, said as he was ascending the scaffold: 'They may 'ang me, but they can't prove I killed the little princes in the Tower.' And that's my position, Mr. Challoner. I'm being persecuted like the celebrated Hougemonts, who was massacred in Bartholomew's Hospital; but I'm too much of a gentleman to mind. It's breed that counts every time."

"It was very unfortunate," said The Miller sympathetically. "But whatever induced you to make a book?"

Mr. Evans made a gesture of indifference. His brave heart would not allow him to reveal the despair which had settled on him. For the story of his Epsom folly had run like wildfire through Camden Town. Clients had written him insulting letters; he had been ordered out of the saloon bar of the "Red Lion" by a flaccid landlord who had uttered, in stentorian tones "We don't want no welshers here." Even his thick-and-thin clients had deserted him.

"The public's fickle," he said philosophically. "And after Paddy! What a beauty, what a beauty And Dio-meeds!"

Evans went home with an aching heart to Brisl Manor, still over a stable in Bayham Mews, locked the door and sat down in the airless, ill- furnished room, his head between his hands, his bruised spirit incapable of initiating the least movement. He heard the sound of light feet on the wooden stairs outside, but did not raise his head. There came a knock, and another and, arousing himself, he walked apathetically to the door, pulled back the bolt and flung it open.

"What do you want—" he began, but got no farther, and stood staring at his visitor.

She was slim and very pretty, and dressed with a simple elegance that took Evans's breath away. He did not recognise Lady Mary Herban, because he was no student of the illustrated weeklies which portray the higher branches of society in their moments of ease and recreation. If he had been such a student he would have seen pictures of Lady Mary, sitting on a shooting stick, pigeon-toed, at point to point meetings; he would have seen her smiling in groups; he would have seen studio portraits of her singly; in fact, it would have been very difficult for him to have missed Lady Mary, who appeared in these high-class publications almost as frequently as the advertisements of ladies' underwear.

Her smile was a dazzling one; she exuded a faint perfume which went immediately to the head of this educated man.

"May I come in?" she asked sweetly.

"Certainly, ma'am," stammered Evans, and she followed him into the bare room.

"You are Mr. Evans, aren't you?"

He nodded dumbly.

"I am Lady Mary Herban, and I am wondering if you can help me."

"Certainly, my lady," he gasped, when he could find his tongue at all.

"We are giving a racing dinner on Monday, and we are having a representative of everybody in the sporting world. We have a book-maker who will lay us the odds, and we thought it would be an excellent idea if you would care to come as a tipster!"

Evans coughed. The word chilled him.

"I'm not exactly a tipster, me lady," he said. "I'm what you might term a Sporting Prophet. This is what you might call my office." (The tumbled bed belied him.)

"We would pay you well, Mr. Evans," said her ladyship, who was quite indifferent as to whether this was the office or the *boudoir* of the world's most famous turf prophet. "The dinner will be at my house, 104 Grosvenor Square, and we're having the room arranged like a race-course. Everybody will wear morning dress, and Lord Ferrerby is bringing two horses with their jockeys. We do so hope, Mr. Evans, that you will be able to help us."

The head of Educated Evans was in a whirl. He expected the day to produce little more that would assuage his misery; and here, by some beneficent workings of providence, he found himself plunged as if were into the vortex of high society.

"I'll certainly do anything I possibly can. You'd like a tip for the Derby? Zionist is a cinch. That horse could fall down, get up and then win. Don't talk to me about Picaroon; don't talk to me about El Sassik; don't talk to me about Aon—whatever his name is. Zionist, who belongs to the celebrated Adjer Kan, could fall down—"

"I know, I know," said Lady Mary soothingly. "Then I take it you will come, Mr. Evans? I will give you five pounds now and five pounds on the night. Here is the address. When you arrive at the house will you ask for my butler, and he will take you to a room where you can dress. We should like you to wear something rather loud. You don't mind, do you?"

Evans did mind. He hated loudness. He preferred, and said so, to wear his check trousers and a classy green tie, with horseshoe complete. To his surprise, Lady Mary agreed that that would be a more suitable costume.

As she was taking a graceful *adieu*:

"Hold 'ard, my lady. You don't mind me saying that I've been engaged as private tipster to your ladyship?"

"Not at all." Lady Mary seemed to be delighted at the prospect. She hated publicity but liked to be talked about.

For an hour after she had left, Mr. Evans sat trying to put in order his scattered thoughts, though it was rather like trying to catalogue the sparks at a fireworks display. And then the possibilities of this adventure began to take hold of him. There would be present at the dinner loftily owners, possibly aristocratic trainers, certainly a jockey or two. He might stock himself for a year on the information to be gleaned at that remarkable banquet.

Putting on his hat, he hurried forth in search of his oracle and The Miller, who had had a pretty unpleasant morning at the police court, was not at first in a mood to advise him.

"Lady Mary Herban!" he said. "That woman would raid herself at a night club to get her name in the papers!"

Educated Evans began to look upon life from a new angle. The jauntiness returned to his step; the smile which greeted the placarded slanders of Old Sam became natural. Here he was, private turf adviser to the aristocracy! He had been chosen, of all the thousands of members of his profession, to represent the fraternity. It was not unpleasing.

He made at least two visits to Grosvenor Square, and from the opposite side of the street regarded with rapture and awe the magnificent mansion which held so rare a jewel as Lady Mary Herban, and in which he would figure, to the confounding of his detractors and the utter annihilation of his senile rival. Such things are reported in the newspapers. On the following morning he would see:

> Amongst those present at Lady Mary Herban's select and aristocratic party was the well-known Educated Evans, whose celebrated tips are all the go just now. Mr. Evans, a tall, good-looking man in the early forties, replying to the toast of his health, said—

The relatives of Old Sam, not unnaturally jubilant at the turn of fortune's wheel, had at the same time no doubt about the elasticity of their enemy.

To them came a distorted rumour of Mr. Evans' noble patronage.

"That feller would swank hisself into Buckin'ham Palace," said Mrs. Lube, granddaughter and manager of the aged Sam. "Alf, don't let him out of your sight! If he's goin' to a lord's party, as he says he is, he's bound to get soused and you ought to be able to get anything out of him!"

"He ain't goin' to any party!" said her husband contemptuously. "It's all talk!"

But Mrs. Lube was not of that opinion.

The Miller says he is—he told a lady friend of mine. Alf, that man would swank hisself into the Bank of England. Watch him!"

Little did Mr. Evans know that from thence onward he was under observation.

It was seven o'clock on a pleasant spring evening when he descended the area steps in Grosvenor Square (Mr. and Mrs. Lube watching furtively from the corner of the square) and was received somewhat haughtily by Lady Mary's butler. Lady Mary's butler, Simmings, was less impressive than ordinary by reason of the fact that all the servants of the house had been ordered to array themselves in sporting attire. And Mr. Simmings was certainly too stout for a jockey.

"Come in, come in," he said testily. "Henry, show this man up to the dressing-room... lot of stuff and nonsense! I never heard of such rubbish in my life. . . ."

Henry, who was also dressed as a jockey, and rather fancied himself, for he was thin and had legs like straws, led the way up the stairs into the big hall.

"Want to see this show before it starts?" he asked, and, pushing open the door, Evans saw an amazing sight.

The room had been converted into a race-course. The table, which ran down the centre, was covered with green cloth, and a winning-post had been erected at one end where Lady Mary was to sit. The walls had been converted by the scene-painter into an idealised race-course. The floor was covered by a rough green cloth; a judge's box, real rails and a saddling bell had been added to the usual garniture of the room.

"They talked about bringing 'orses here," said Henry, "but they can't get 'em up the steps. You're a tipster, ain't you? What d'you know?"

Evans thought it was a moment to assert his dignity.

"I'm Mr. Evans, the celebrated Turf Adviser," he said, with a touch of *hauteur*, "and as the celebrated Richard Cower de Lion, the well-known Gay Crusader, said to his brother, the Duke of Clarence, who was drownded in a bottle of claret: 'You keep your place and I'll keep mine.'"

The impressed Henry handed him over to one of the servants hired for the day, and who alone were dressed like civilised waiters. He was taken up to the third floor, where, as he understood from Henry, he was to wait until he was called for. The gloomy, middle-aged man who escorted him to his room had views of a communistic, not to say

201

bolshevistic, type.

"If the money these 'ere *burjoises* were spending on this kind of muck was give to the poor, comrade, this'd be a land fit for 'eroes to live in. But the day is coming," he added darkly, "when the *burjoises* will know all about it—"

"Who are they?" asked Evans, a little hazy.

"It's them that's got what you ain't got," was the cryptic reply.

Henry, the jockey, came up to see him, and Evans learned that he would not be required until half-past nine, when the dinner was over, and he was left to rehearse his speech, which began:

"Ladies and gentlemen,—Education, as everybody knows, is one of the grandest things in the world, and I stand before you today, an exposition of erudition and brainwork versus guesswork and picking 'em out with a pin. . . ."

From below, when he opened the door, came the sound of revelry and laughter. The dinner had begun, and he paced the little room, repeating his speech, stopping now and again to fasten his white spats, which constantly came undone... There was a knock at the door: it was the socialistic servant, and he had in his hand a telegram.

"They ain't half goin' it downstairs," he said gloomily. "Wine flowin' like water! Little do they know what's waitin' 'em! This is for you."

Evans took the telegram from his hand: it was addressed "Evans, 104 Grosvenor Square." He opened it in wonder. Only The Miller knew he was attending this dinner party.

The wire was addressed from a little training centre west of Newbury, and it had been handed in at one o'clock that day, but apparently had been readdressed.

Evans, 104, Grosvenor Square. Tried Longlegs a certainty advise you run him Wednesday and have a good bet.

It was signed with the name of Mr. Frithington-Evans' latest trainer.

For a long time the educated man did not understand his good fortune, and then he began a frantic effort to lick down the torn flap.

"This is for another gentleman," he said, " not for me. Take it down to him."

"One of the *burjoises?*" asked the waiter, with a sneer.

"He's worse than that," said Mr. Evans.

Longlegs! he thought, as the door closed upon the hired waiter. What a chance to rehabilitate himself with the sceptics of Camden

Town! He had hardly reached this conclusion when the door was flung open violently, and a red-faced young man exploded into the room.

"Here, you fellow, what the devil do you mean by opening my telegrams?" he demanded wrathfully. "This was addressed to me."

"My name's Evans too," said Mr. Evans gently. "Perhaps we're related. We've had some very flighty people in our family, my uncle Joe—"

"Did you read it, confound you!" roared the agitated Frithy.

"I certainly read it—" began Evans.

"Oh, you did, did you?" said the gentleman between his teeth, and, before Evans realised what had happened, the door had slammed and he heard the click of a turning lock.

Frithy flew downstairs. Lady Mary was waiting in the hall.

"Why on earth did you dash away? We're only just beginning—"

"That—that—" spluttered Mr. Frithington- Evans, pointing dramatically up the stairs, "has got the best thing of the year in his possession! Do you realise what that means, Mary? He'll spread it all over London. The damned thing will start at six to four. . . oh, my God! why did I come to this party?"

She saw that the situation was a serious one. Mr. Frithington-Evans was in danger of losing money.

"What can we do?" she asked, for she also spelt life with an £. "He's got to be kept there until the race is over. Under no circumstances is he to be allowed to leave the house or use the telephone. You've got to put a servant on to watch him day and night. As for that cursed trainer, I'll fire him as soon as the race is over. The fool, to wire!"

He conveniently forgot that he had left strict instructions that the result of the trial should be sent to his house in Berkshire.

Evans waited with growing impatience for the summons that came not. As the horror of his position gained on him, Educated Evans grew deathly pale.

Outside in the dark of Grosvenor Square two people were in earnest conversation. It's makin' a fool of me," said Mr. Alf Lube bitterly, "bringin' me here an' keepin' me without so much as a drink —what for?"

His lady wife answered with ominous calm. "He'll come out in a minute, oiled to the world," she said malignantly, "an' if he's got information we'll get it, Alf. I'm not takin' risks—I've got two mouths to fill an' grandfather might pop off any day."

"It's makin' a fool of me," said Alf, but wisely uttered no other protest.

It was nearing midnight, and Evans was lying down on the little bed, when a step outside the door brought him to his feet.

"Are you awake?"

It was the socialistic waiter, and the hollowness of his voice through the keyhole sent a shiver down Evans' spine.

"They're goin' to do you in," said the voice pleasantly. "That *burjoise* that the wire was meant for says you've got to be kept here for a week—they're goin' to starve you to death, comrade."

"Are they—comrade?" quavered Evans.

"The best thing you can do is to tie your sheets together and let yourself down to the street. Me and a couple of comrades will stand underneath and catch you if you fall. Long live the revolution!"

"What revolution?" asked Evans.

"Wot's coming," said the waiter, and immediately crept away.

Evans opened the window and, looking down four storeys, withdrew, dizzy. To knot three sheets together and lower yourself from a fourth-storey window is a very easy matter in books; but when there are no sheets, the difficulties increase. Moreover, Evans had never knotted anything together in his life.

Another simple plan was to climb up to the roof, tap the telephone wires and call the police; but as against this, he couldn't climb, and he had never tapped anything except an old friend in his more impecunious moments.

Midnight came one o'clock struck—two. And then, looking out of the open window, by the light of a street lamp he saw two people. They were the comrades who had come to catch him when he jumped, he guessed. Nevertheless, he did not jump.

And then a brilliant idea struck him. Pulling a paper from one pocket and a pencil from another, he wrote:

Please take this to Sergeant Challoner, the well-known Miller.

And, underneath:

Dear Mr. Challoner—This comes hoping to find you quite well as I am not. Longlegs is a stone certainty for the Leigh Handicap. Would you kindly oblige by asking somebody to send this for me to all clients, old and new?
Yours truly,   Educated Evans.

Wrapping the paper around half a crown, he threw it, and had the satisfaction of seeing one of the watchers pick it up. . .

Mr. and Mrs. Lube hurried home with the paper which had fallen into their hands, and half an hour later were reading the message. When they had finished:

"A trap," said Mrs. Lube. "The artful old rat! He spotted us watchin' and tried to catch us. This letter goes round to The Miller—we'll send a boy with it. Let 'em send it out! Longlegs—I'll give him Longlegs!"

Mr. Lube pocketed the half-crown and felt that he was in some measure repaid for his vigil.

And when, two days later, Longlegs won at 100/8, and Mr. Evans was released from captivity with a ten-pound note and a warning to keep away from Grosvenor Square, there was rejoicing in Bayham Mews.

"And let me tell you, Evans," said The Miller firmly, "that you'll get me hung if you send me letters like that. What do you think my inspector would say?"

"He'd say 'What a beauty!' Mr. Challoner," said Educated Evans.

10—THE USER OF MEN

By some miracle, Educated Evans had recovered his prestige in Camden Town. Possibly it was the reaction from the failure of Old Sam, that ancient impostor, whose Midnight Special had napped six successive odds-on chances, only one of which succeeded in finishing in the first three.

It was significant that a certain railway Goods Yard, which is a solid body of public opinion, had turned to Evans after the remarkable victory of Longlegs at Chester, and that not only had they paid for this incomparable selection, but many of them had acted honourably afterwards.

Evans had received two large Scottish salmon, with their labels obviously torn off, a bushel of apples with a label pasted over, and a small case containing three bottles of invalid wine. And then Siezem had won at Warwick at the surprising price of 100-6, and Siezem had been the Double Nap Fear Nothing Help Yourself Midday Special of Educated Evans.

"I got it from the boy who does him," said the exultant man of learning. "I've had that information locked up, so to speak, in my bosom for munce and munce. I've been waiting for him, I've been watching his gallops, and at last I says, 'Today's the day.'"

"The story you told me last night," said the patient Miller, "was that you got so fed up with trying to find a winner that you shut your eyes and stuck it with a pin. But perhaps you're more truthful when you're sober?"

"I had two half-pints last night," said Evans reproachfully. "It's the 'eat makes me go funny like that."

Down in the little street where Old Sam had his habitation there was a great deal of heartburning, and not a little wrath. There was also a crisis.

Mrs. Lube was in her most vixenish mood. Not so Old Sam, who sat before the empty fire-grate, his eyes closed, humming snatches of songs, the most modern of which was " Tarara-boomdeay!"

"I'm surprised at you, grandfather," said his exasperated relative. "Sitting there as drunk as a lord and not caring whether me and my two poor children are in the workhouse. Why don't you go and find things?"

"Greek Bachelor—what a beauty!" murmured Old Sam. "What a beauty, what a beauty!"

He repeated "What a beauty!" about forty times, until his voice sank to nothingness and his head followed suit. Mrs. Lube looked at her husband.

"I've got forty pounds," she said deliberately.

Her husband started.

"You never have? Then a sense of his wrongs came uppermost. "And last week I asked you to lend me—"

"I've got forty pounds, saved—from the wreck."

She nodded at the wreck, who, blissfully unconscious of this un-complimentary reference, was sleeping noisily.

"And I've got something to do with my money besides givin' it to you to guzzle away. I'm going to take him into partnership."

"Who?" asked her lawful husband, his mind flying instantly to a certain undesirable Greek lodger.

"That Evans." The words almost choked her.

"Give him money?" All Lube was incredulous.

"I'm goin' to take him into partnership. He's doin' too well. That's what Mr. Elmer of the 'Red Lion' said to me: 'Why don't you go into partnership? What's the good of competition?'"

Her husband had only the vaguest idea of what constituted a part-nership, and what mysterious ritual preceded its creation.

"There's no sense in scrappin' with him. What we've got to do is to make a partnership, get his addresses, make as much use of them as we can, and then—"

She snapped her fingers tragically. The outlook for Educated Evans was not a promising one.

To approach her victim was a delicate business. Mr. Evans saw her coming up the steps and locked his door. It was difficult to negotiate an amalgamation of interests through the little window which looked out on to the landing, with half the inhabitants of Bayham Mews forming an interested audience.

"I don't want no truck with you, Mrs. What's-your-name," said Evans, pale but determined, and keeping at a reasonable distance from the open window, which, fortunately, was too small for an ample lady to climb through.

"Let bygorns be bygorns," pleaded Mrs. Lube. I want to live in 'armony. Forty pounds is forty pounds—"

"Forty pounds—ha ha ha!" Evans' laugh was sardonic and scornful. "Forty pound for half a share of my business! What I'm gettin' thousan's an' thousan's for! Woman, you're mad! Go away before I forget I'm a gentleman!"

Mrs. Lube swallowed something.

"Think it over, Mr. Evans," she said, with a grimace which was intended as a smile.

Evans pointed to the steps.

"Go!" he said dramatically.

Every man's favourite dream usually centres around easy money. Educated Evans used to dope himself to sleep with a story of his own creation.

It was about a foreigner who had robbed a foreign bank, had escaped to London with negotiable property in a large handbag, and, in a moment of mental aberration, had deposited the bag on Educated Evans' doorstep, and, having thus disposed of his ill-gotten wealth, went away and drowned himself. Better men than Educated Evans will read this and start guiltily.

And now, it seemed that the dream of years was to come true; for fate, in a sealskin coat, had descended upon him, and the days and hours he should have spent analysing the relative merits of thorough-bred race-horses, were occupied in the compilation of balance-sheets. Thus:

	£		£
Rent of premises and so forth	2,000	Fees from clients	50,000
Cost of telegrams	3,000	Presents from ditto	75,000
Office staff and bonuses	6,000	Managing Director's commiss. on above	12,500
Upkeep of motorcar	1,000		
Expenses of managing director Including cost of furnished flat in Park Lane	5,000		
Balance in hand	120,500		
	£137,500		£137,500

It was not a balance-sheet which would pass the average auditor, for Evans had put at least one item on the wrong side of the sheet.

There is no doubt that money in large quantities could be made, and there is less doubt that Mr. Evans, given the necessary capital, would make it.

Mrs. Lucy Tarbet could provide that capital. She had wealth beyond imagining. Two resplendent public-houses, house properties outside of computation, money at the bank, jewels rare and costly, a little flat of her own in the most elegant part of Regent's Park. It seemed that Mr. Evans' dream had come true.

"Yes," said Mrs. Tarbet, with a bland smile, to her nearest and dearest friend, "he is a funny little fellow—common as dirt, but quite comic in his way. Mind you, he's got a headpiece all right. But he's like the rest of them, my dear" she sighed very heavily, as only a stout lady can sigh—"he's after the money!"

"I can't see how you can take up with a common man who's only a low, vulgar tipster, Lou," said her friend, who had almost as many diamond rings as Mrs. Tarbet, and owned quite a number of greengrocer's shops in the north of London.

"I've not taken up with him," said the amiable Mrs. Tarbet. "I'm not taking up with any man, not after my experience with George. Men! I use 'em, my dear! Come upstairs and see my new dress. I got it from Way's and it's a dream. . . ."

★★★★★★

On the following Saturday The Miller was talking with the official on duty at the members' entrance at Hurst Park, when a man walked briskly past them. He wore a peaked cap, around the band of which were the words "Hurst Park Race Club," and he carried in his hand an important-looking blue envelope.

"Who is that bird?" asked the discreet detective.

"I don't know—one of the ground men, I expect," said the officer.

The Miller passed through the motor enclosure on the heels of the messenger, followed him across the course and over the members' lawn into the paddock.

Still the man with the blue envelope walked on, until he disappeared in an outbuilding. The Miller waited. Presently the man came out, minus his envelope and wearing a crushed-looking trilby hat.

"Good-morning, Evans."

Mr. Evans was momentarily startled.

"How long have you been on the staff of this race-course?" asked The Miller sternly.

For a second the educated man was embarrassed.

"It's a mild form of deception, if I may use the expression," he said, "but nobody loses nothing by it. If I didn't get into Tatt's this way I shouldn't come in at all, so, in a manner of speakin', the stewards don't lose so much as a tosser. There's a horse in the first race that's money for jam. I've had him from the boy who does him. He was tried with the celebrated Golly Eyes an' walked away from him. Mugman's the name, help yourself but keep it dark."

The Miller sighed.

"Evans, I'm compounding a felony by not pinching you—my kind heart will be the ruin of me. I suppose you've got a collection of cap-bands and use a different one for each horse?"

"All except Ascot," confessed Evans modestly. "It's one of the best lot of cap-bands you ever see. I call 'em my members' badges."

"What was in the envelope?"

"Nothing," said Evans shamelessly. "It's got 'To the Secretary—Urgent' on it. Nobody don't dare stop you if you've got that. It's as much as their job's worth."

Here, the representative of the law thought, was an opportune moment to deliver a lecture on morality. Evans listened meekly.

"I quite agree with you, Mr. Challoner, an' I won't do it again. Honesty begins at home, as I always say, an' as the famous Lord Wolsey—him that haunts Hampton Court—said, 'If I'd only looked after myself like I've looked after other people, I shouldn't be drawin' the dole.' That's a nice-lookin' horse, Mr. Challoner!' "

He pointed to an animal which was being led round by a groom.

"He looks like Zionist to me—I'd recernise the horse anywhere—I see him do a gallop up at Wantage. Funny how some people can recernise horses an' other people can't—that's Zionist all right."

"To be exact, it is the starter's hack," said The Miller patiently.

"Is that so?" Evans was respectfully interested. "I didn't know the Adjer Kan had sold him. It only shows, Mr. Challoner, what horses come down to. As the highly respected Dr. Johnstone said, 'The more I see of horses the more I like dogs.' That's a funny-lookin' horse goin' into the ring. I wouldn't back her with bad money. Look at her feet—look at her ribs!"

The Miller consulted his card.

"That is Mugman. Presently we shall see him fall down, get up and *then* win! he said quietly.

Mr. Evans coughed.

"Looks ain't everything," he said, very truly.

"How is business, Evans?" The Miller was kind enough to change the subject.

"Not so bad." Mr. Evans was surprisingly indifferent. "Camden Town's no good to a man like me. I'm thinkin' of takin' a office at Newmarket an' doin' things on the big scale. Advertisements everywhere—balloons over Epsom—sanwidge men with boards up an' down the West End."

"Indeed!" Mr. Challoner was politely sceptical. "Have you come into a fortune?" Evans considered this question.

"In a sense—yes," he said, and went on: "You haven't seen my young lady about, have you?"

He grew rosy under the stern eye of his companion.

"Did she have a cap-band too?" asked The Miller. "Or did she wear the cap and apron of a tea-room waitress "

"Her? Evans was slightly amused. "She's got money of her own—an' what a lady! Manners! You never saw manners like 'em. Talks French better than a Frenchman. Hongri, the celebrated French waiter, said that he don't understand some of the words she uses. That's class. Here " His voice sank. "I'll introduce you!"

A lady was approaching them. She was, The Miller guessed, lingering in the thirties, and she was, not to put too fine a point on it, on the stout side. Without being pretty she was pleasant; the pink of her cheeks was a deep pink.

"Mrs. Tarbet, *permittez moi* to introduce you to my friend, Mr. Challoner," said Evans, who had evidently acquired the French language.

"Excuse fingers," said Mrs. Tarbet briskly. "I've just been eating fish. Ain't it hot? You're here, then?" This to Evans, who smirked foolishly. "I been lookin' all over the place for you. What's goin' to win this first race? Mugman? Don't make me laugh. I've got a tip for Ooji from one of our customers. So long! I'll see you at Assizes."

With this bright quip she passed on.

"She's never, so to speak, at a loss for an answer," said the admiring Evans. "Witty? She'd make a cat laugh!"

"Barmaid?" asked The Miller, who was not easily amused.

"She owns property," said Evans impressively: "two public-houses an' a block of flats!"

"And you come into the last category," said The Miller, who occasionally employed words which were more Greek than French to Educated Evans.

A few minutes later he joined the lady in the sealskin coat.

"Who was that bird you introduced me to, Evans?" she asked, a little resentfully. "Don't go introducin' me to your race-course friends, I beg."

"He's one of the stewards," exaggerated Mr. Evans, and the lady was mollified. They had met at the cinema; she had trodden on his toe by accident (for she was ladylike and would not descend to a vulgar subterfuge) and at his invitation they had supped together at Isaacs' Fish Bar. She was a widow and lonely. She admired cleverness and education. Mr. Evans had the goods. He was both clever and educated. At Isaac's fish bar she learned for the first time that the world went round the sun once in twenty-four hours, that people used to be hung at Marble Arch, and that Ormonde won the Derby in a snowstorm and had to have butter put on his feet to help him slip round Tattenham Corner. She was also instructed in medieval history, and discovered that B— Mary, Queen of Scotch, was not all that a lady should be, and that Julius Caesar, the far-famed Italian, signed the Magna Charter and laid the foundations of the Rules of Racing.

Nevertheless, being a monied woman, she was not willing to submit her intelligence to the domination of any man, however learned.

"Come along and see this race, and we'll have a chat afterwards about The Business. I don't want to put my money into anything that I can't see my way out of."

The moral position of Educated Evans was strengthened when

Mugman scrambled home a head in front of the horse he had backed. Even Mrs. Lucy Tarbet was impressed.

"Logic an' deduction an' information *v.* guesswork," murmured Evans, surreptitiously tearing up the ticket which, if the second had won, would have brought him five very necessary pounds. "That horse was sent out to three thousand clients. . . ." Then, remembering that she would certainly want to see his books, "or, rather, would have been sent out, only I was in such a hurry to meet you that I only had time to send thirty wires. If I had a bit of capital. . ."

He enlarged upon the prospects. Mrs. Tarbet listened thoughtfully.

"How much do you want?" she asked. Evans dared not say, in case he put the figure too low.

"Thousands," he suggested.

"Fiddlesticks" said Mrs. Tarbet scornfully. "I wouldn't mind putting fifty pounds into it."

The hopes of Educated Evans fell with a dull, sickening thud.

"Fifty!" he laughed hollowly. "Why, fifty pounds wouldn't go no-where!"

She nibbled the end of her glove, frowning. "Do you know any other horse that's going to win today?" she asked.

Evans smiled.

"Brass Nail is a stone certainty," he said. "The common people will back Blue Nose. An' in the last race High Up can't be beat. I got him from a servant girl who's got a sister who walks out with the head lad."

"I'll tell you what I'll do," said Mrs. Tarbet. "Just wait here."

She hurried into the ring and came back with a smile of triumph.

"I said I'd put fifty pounds into your business. Well, I've put it on your horse! We'll see what happens. I've got ten to one with my friend Mr. Izzy Friedman."

Evans looked at her wildly.

"What do you want to waste money like that for?" he blurted.

"Waste?" Mrs. Tarbet's eyebrows went up.

"Well, not exactly waste," said the palpitating Evans. "But putting all that money on. . . it ain't much, but it might do a bit of advertising."

"Don't let us discuss it," she said coldly.

He followed her, a miserable man, back to the ring. His misery was not long-lived. Brass Nail made all the running and won by a neck.

"Well, perhaps you're right after all," he beamed. " Five hundred and fifty—you can do a lot with five hundred and fifty."

"Ye-es," said Mrs. Tarbet thoughtfully. " Tell me that bit about High Up again."

"You're not going to back another horse?" said Evans, in alarm. "With five hundred and fifty we could do some advertising. . . "

She made an impatient noise.

"Don't let us talk business, please, Mr. Evans," she said, and he was crushed to silence.

Just before the last race, she found him leaning miserably over the rails of the saddling ring.

"I've just seen a friend of mine, and he says that High Up hasn't got any chance at all."

"I don't care nothing about what he says," said the wretched Evans. "If you're going to back horses, back 'em! If you're going to tip horses, tip 'em! You can't mix it. I've tried. What I say is this: put two hundred pounds into advertisin', put two hundred pounds into a office; put a hundred into expenses, keep fifty for yourself. . . . ."

But he was addressing the air. Mrs. Tarbet was making her rapid way back to Tattersall's.

He roused himself sufficiently to stroll into the ring, climb to the top of the littered stand, and watch a race which had no more interest for him than the golden dome of the stewards' stand. He didn't even know the colours of High Up, and until he saw the number in the frame and consulted his card, he was not aware that High Up had won. And then, with a wildly beating heart, he dashed down into the ring.

"What price was that?" he asked, almost incoherently.

"Four to one," somebody told him, and he flew through Tattersall's into the paddock, searching vainly for his *inamorata*.

She was standing talking to a number of obese friends when he flew up to her, his face beaming.

"You was right after all, Lucy," he said.

She transfixed him with an icy stare: obviously she was in a very bad temper.

"Mrs. Tarbet, if you please," she snapped. "Please go away. I don't want to hear any more about your beastly horses. If you don't go, I'll call a policeman!"

Evans reeled back, pallid of face, as these words fell from the fresh red lips of the User of men. He tried to speak, but she silenced him with a gesture, and dejectedly he slouched across the paddock, his hands in his pockets, the picture of misery.

He was wandering towards the open horse gate, and as he was half-way between the unsaddling ring and the gate, the horses were coming in. And between the jockeys on the first two there was something like unpleasantness. Evans heard. . .

". . . you bored me out from the rails, you dirty dog. . . . Of course I'm going to object. . . ."

An objection! Evans was electrified. This fat vampire had friends in the ring. At the word "Objection!" she would fly to one of her book-making pals and save her money. Hell hath no fury like a turf prophet scorned. He would be avenged on this woman. Instantly, as the idea took shape, he turned and raced across the paddock. Mrs. Tarbet was still talking to one of her friends, and at the sight of the dishevelled Evans her face clouded.

"Excuse me, Mrs. Tarbet, for one minute. I've something very important to say to you," he begged urgently. "It's not about business, it's about somethin' that's goin' to happen next week. . ."

Excuse me," she said frigidly to her friend, and consented to walk with Evans out of earshot.

What wild story he told her, he never remembered. It was evidently something fascinating, for she listened open-mouthed, her attention so concentrated that she never heard the cry of "Objection!"

There was no need for her to go into the ring. She had arranged for her money to be sent to her by cheque.

After about five minutes. . . .

"I don't know what on earth you're talking about, Evans," she said raucously. "You're simply wasting my time with a lot of nonsense about a horse that'll run on Wednesday. I don't want any of your tips, and I don't want any more to do with you. You're simply coming after my money, and I can't stand spongers."

Evans could swallow the insult and smile. He must keep her engaged in conversation so that there was no possibility of her saving her money. The red flag was flying but this Mrs. Tarbet did not notice. And then a blessed word reached him. Somebody shouted "Sustained!" and the faint sound of it came to his ears. At that moment Evans was magnificent.

"Thank you very kindly for your attention, Mrs. Tarbet, and I can only say, in conclusion, that, having done in your stuff, we'll cry quits."

"What do you mean—'done in my stuff,' you guttersnipe?" she asked angrily.

"Your horse is disqualified," he hissed. "Rat's Tail has got the race on an objection!"

"High Up disqualified!" she shrieked. "My Gawd! I backed Rat's Tail!"

11.—THE LADY WATCH DOG

Satan, the original labour exchange for Idle Hands, put it into the heart of Alf Lube that the diamond-encircled wristwatch worn by Mrs. Arabella Fich, the proprietress of the "Three Dogs" public-house in Stibbington Street, could do him a bit of good. Mrs. Fich was an absentminded woman and had the habit, when she assisted in the bar, to put her watch on a little shelf at the back of the bar. A man (said the Evil One) with a long reach and a walking- stick, could hook out that watch without the slightest exertion.

One Thursday evening, when trade was very bad, Mr. Lube turned into the saloon bar and found its other occupant a solitary man sitting on a high stool and thoughtfully regarding a glass of whisky and water. Mr. Lube's lip curled.

"Hullo, Evans," he said coarsely. "Been welshing lately?"

Educated Evans regarded him with the look of a wounded fawn.

"Politeness costs nothing," he said mildly.

"Been down to Epsom lately?"

Mr. Evans did not reply.

"I wonder a man like you's got the nerve to show himself in a bar parlour," nagged Alf. "Here, missis, give me a small bitter. I can't afford whisky—I don't welsh."

"Nor work," said Evans, still regarding his glass.

Mr. Lube's chubby face darkened.

"I don't welsh," he said.

"Nor work," said Evans absently; "not since you come out of stir, anyway."

It was true that on three occasions Lube had been put away for trifling offences. But to be told by a man like Evans....

"You're askin' for it!" he said, breathing through his nose. "I've killed men for less than that!

Evans lifted his glass, smelt the contents and drank leisurely.

"You're an uneducated man," he said, after the last gurgle, "and if Old Sam wasn't keepin' you, you'd be in Pentonville. As for your wife—"

"Don't say a word against my wife!" hissed Mr. Lube, making a fear-inspiring grimace and edging closer.

"I'm sorry for you, Lube," said Mr. Evans, getting down from his stool. "You can't help your misfortune. Buy yourself a drink."

He put down sixpence on the counter and walked out. Lube glared after him, pouched the sixpence and drank his bitter bitterly.

He was not a fighting man. And Evans had spoken the truth. The Lube family was at the point of crisis. That very night his wife had refused him a shilling, though she knew that his dole was due on the morrow. Moreover, she had refused him the wherewithal to go to Kempton.

His eyes, roving the bar, rested on the sparkling watch half hidden from view between two claret glasses. He knew a fence at Finsbury who would give him at least a fiver for that. Mr. Lube hesitated. It was so long since he had broken the law that he had almost acquired the habit of honesty. The four ale bar was empty; the barmaid was at the other end of the bar, her back towards him, engrossed in a book. He lifted his walking-stick tentatively, laid it on the counter, stretched... The watch dropped in his pocket. In a few seconds he was in the street.

"What's the matter with you, Alf?"

Mrs. Lube was engaged in preparing a rough balance sheet of Old Sam's Midnight Special when her husband came in. One glance at his face told her everything, for his was an easy face to read.

"Nothin'." He was very jerky of speech. "Thought I'd go up an' see a friend of mine at Finsbury—"

She held out her large hand.

"Drop," she said tersely.

Alf spluttered, bullied, lied, but in the end the watch was lying in her palm.

"Mrs. Fich's," she said calmly. "You're a nice father of a family, I don't think!"

He tried to bluster his way out. By accident he touched the right note.

"It's that 'ound Evans—he got me wild, the way he talked about you an'—an' the lodger. He said no wonder we tipped Greek Bach-elor...."

Mr. Dimitri, the nice-looking Greek lodger, had departed from the home of the Lubes after a terrific scene. Alf felt he might put into Mr.

Evans' mouth some of the private thoughts on the subject which he had not hitherto dared to express on his own behalf.

"Oh, he did, did he?" said Mrs. Lube, grey with fury. "An' you sat round an' said nothing! A dam' fine husband you are!"

One lie was as easy as another. Alf described how he had caught the traducer by the throat and shaken him sick. His wife did not believe him but was appeased. She looked at the watch again.

"He was in the bar when you went in?" she asked. "Now you go up to bed and keep your big mouth shut, or I'll take the rollin' pin to you like I did last Good Friday!"

Alf meekly obeyed.

Mrs. Lube decided to make a call on Educated Evans next day, and she did so at a moment when the World's Champion Prophet and Turf Adviser was engaged in the case of Henrietta Bowsome.

Educated Evans had never heard of Henrietta Bowsome, and might never have heard of her, for he seldom read anything else in a newspaper than the columns in which racing correspondents explain why their selections did not win the day before; but it happened that he was in attendance at the police court, a client of his having fallen into grievous error.

Educated Evans, because of his erudition and his well-known gifts in the matter of terminology, had prepared the defence which was read from the dock and instantly recognised.

"I think," said The Miller *sotto voce* to his *protegé* as they walked out into the lobby, "that if it hadn't been for that defence of yours, young Herbert would have got off. As it is, he's going to do three months. Why don't you change your style?"

Evans raised his eyebrows and said nothing. It was useless to argue with Sergeant Challoner in his more aggravating moods.

"Is Henrietta a client of yours, by the way?" asked The Miller.

"Henrietta? I don't know the gentleman."

"It's a lady, to be exact," said The Miller, and described Henrietta's weakness. She was a "shopper." It was her custom to walk into one of those crowded departmental stores which ornament Oxford Street, carrying on her hands a large muff. A pillow muff is a very convenient appendage to a lady with a weakness for acquiring property in the Homeric manner, for what Henrietta

. ...*thought she might require*
She went and took.

217

Interested, Mr. Evans strolled back to the court, in time to see a very pretty, well-dressed girl step blithely into the dock, nod smilingly to the unresponsive magistrate, and glance round the court with the air of one who was visiting her old home and was gratified to discover that nothing had been changed. And at the end of the evidence....

"Really, Henrietta, I don't know what to do with you," said the magistrate, leaning back in his chair and taking off his *pince-nez*. "You are incorrigible!"

"It is very difficult for me to find work with my record," said Henrietta. She had a soft, cooing, almost pathetic voice.

The magistrate shook his head.

"The missionary can do nothing with you. This thieving—"

"*Kleptomania*," murmured Henrietta. "It runs in the family. My father was a tax-collector."

The magistrate gazed sternly round the court.

"I will not have any laughing in this court," he said. "This is a very serious matter, and unless you can find somebody who is willing to employ you and be guarantee for your good behaviour, I shall send you to prison with hard labour."

He waited expectantly.

"I will," said Evans huskily.

He had had no more intention of intervening in this case than he had of kissing a policeman.

The magistrate put on his glasses again, the better to observe the philanthropist.

"Oh, you're Evans, aren't you?"

"Yes, my lord," said the educated man.

"Is he a householder "

The Miller came to the rescue here, inwardly cursing his friend, and explained that Evans certainly was on the voters' list.

"But what on earth can you do with this girl? Are you an employer of labour?"

Evans nodded dumbly. In justice to him, although he was acting on impulse, he was prompted by the subconscious knowledge that he needed assistance in the great and beneficent work of conveying to the sporting public information which even owners and trainers did not possess. For Evans had had the good fortune to tip a 20/1 winner at Sandown Park. On this particular day it was difficult, if one tipped a winner at all, not to tip one at a long price, for it was that Black Thursday when hundreds of punters, great and small, spent their evenings filling up petitions in bankruptcy.

The magistrate heaved a deep, dissatisfied sigh.

"All right; she'll be bound over in the sum of twenty pounds on your recognisances, Mr. Evans." And his tone suggested that he would have added: "And I wish you joy of your bargain," but he was a kind-hearted man and did not wish to depress unduly one who had undertaken a task of such magnitude.

"You've done it, my lad," said The Miller under his breath. "This is going to cost you twenty of the best and brightest. She'll be up again before the old man within a week."

Evans was too interested in his new responsibility to heed the warning.

She was a pretty girl, this Henrietta, in a pinkish way, with a trick of showing her white teeth, for she was easily amused. For the moment she was a little scared too, for she had served one period as a guest of the proprietors of Holloway Castle, and had no desire to repeat her experience.

"I don't know what makes me do it, Mr. Evans," she said, as they walked towards Bayham Mews together. " But somehow, when I see loose property laying around, I've got to hook it or die."

"You listen to me, Henrietta," said Evans soberly, and in the manner of a father, "and you'll not go far wrong. Come to me for advice. If you find the temptation a-overcomin' you, out of business hours, just pop round and see me."

She looked at him in surprise.

"But I shan't have to pop round, shall I?" she asked. "Aren't you going to give me some work?"

"There's plenty of work," said Evans enthusiastically, "and what's more, you'll be well paid for it. Can you typewrite?"

She said she thought she could.

"It would teach me to spell," she said. Later he discovered how bad a speller she was.

"You stick to me, Henrietta," he said, in his best parental manner; " never say a word of what goes on inside my office, be my watch dog, and you'll make money. I'll show you the office."

The office had an occupant. Mrs. Lube, in her best clothes and wearing all the family jewels, was sitting in the one chair, fanning herself with the afternoon paper. Her manner was gracious; she even smiled, though the smile vanished and a look of surprise and understanding came into her bulgous eyes when the girl followed Evans into the room.

"Good-morning, Mr. Evans," she said sweetly.

Evans left the door wide open and stood at a respectful distance.

"My dear grandfather sent me round to ask if you'd be good enough to tell him what you're sending out for the Chester Cup," she said, almost apologetically. "He says he wouldn't like to send the same horse because people might talk."

Evans was thunderstruck. This advance from the enemy's camp was amazing. He could hardly believe his ears.

"Eh . . well, Mrs. Lube . . . to tell you the truth, I was thinkin' of sendin' Laberens, belonging to the well-known Rajah of Ranji, the celebrated cricket-ball thrower."

Again Mrs. Lube smiled.

"It's so good of you, Mr. Evans," she said, as she rose to go. "Perhaps you'll slip round an' have a sociable drink one day?"

She was gone before he recovered from the shock.

"Me have a drink with her!" he said at last. "Would I take a sitlitz powder from the hands of the celebrated Lewd-creature Burgia, the female Crippen of Rome, Italy?"

"Who is she?" asked Miss Bowsome curiously.

"She's Nothing," said Evans, and changed the subject. "This is my little den," he explained. " I've thought out some of the best winners here that any man's ever found. In that there corner by the fireplace I got the idea for Braxted—20/1, what a beauty!—on that table I writ or wrote 'Taping—Fear Nothing!' I lay on that bed an' thought out Paddy —20/1, what a beauty. . . !"

Henrietta looked round the historic apartment without any visible signs of enthusiasm.

Where's the other room?" she asked.

"What other room?" demanded Evans.

"Where do I sleep?" she demanded, her innocent eye on his.

Evans stared at her.

"Ain't you got a home?" he asked.

"Of course, I haven't got a home," she replied scornfully. What's more, I can't get lodgings. I've got such a bad name that nobody will trust me in Camden Town."

The colour left the cheeks of the World's Greatest Tipster.

"You can't stay here," he squeaked.

"This is my room!"

She sat down in the one chair and folded her arms.

"I've got to stay here," she said steadily. "You're in charge of me: the magistrate said so. Besides, how can I keep honest if I'm away from you? The moment I get out of your sight I shall be pinching something; I can't help it, Mr. Evans!"

Educated Evans took half a cigar from the mantelshelf with a hand that shook, and lit it unsteadily.

"This is a nice thing!" he said, in a tone which meant that it was anything but that." I've got myself into a nice kind of trouble through helping young women, I must say!"

"Haven't you got any place where you can sleep? she asked innocently. "Couldn't you take lodgings?"

Evans grew testy.

"I can't have you sleeping here, getting me a bad name," he said, with vigour and vehemence. "It's ridiculous an' absurd. Why, I'll have people pointing the finger of scorn at me, as though I was one of them celebrated *pashers* of Hindustan."

Her eyes lit up.

"With divans and things," she breathed, "and beautiful Indian curtains and wonderful Persian rugs on the floor! Like the pictures!"

Evans staggered.

"I'm not a *pasher*, and I never will be a *pasher*," he said sternly. "Nobody's ever breathed the breath of scandal against me. I'm like Caesar's celebrated friend, Cleopatra, whose well-known needle we all admire—see Shakespeare—"

"Couldn't you sleep out somewhere?" she interrupted his discourse to ask. "It's so easy for you, Mr. Evans."

Her voice had in it that note of pathos which so thrilled him.

"I'm a poor girl—lonely and friendless, with everybody's hand against me, Mr. Evans. I'm not educated like you are, Mr. Evans. I know I shan't be reformed—I've tried to be. But give me a chance, Mr. Evans. If I could only raise enough money to get to Canada, I might marry a farmer and live in the country where there's nothing to pinch but corn."

The upshot of it was that Evans took a room with his friend, the motor-lorry man. It was not an arrangement exactly pleasing to him, as he told The Miller that night when they met in the High Street outside the cinema.

"You're a fool," said The Miller. "And what's more, you're going to get a bad name. That girl can't help stealing. Her parents were that way. She can hardly write her own name and her general education is nil!"

"She's fond of poetry—she told me so," said Henrietta's defender stoutly.

"Pah!" snarled The Miller. "Poetry!"

Early the next morning, as he was strolling to the station, he was intercepted by Mrs. Lube, who had heard, it seems, the plaintive outcry of the landlady of the "Three Dogs" and had certain information to impart... .

At that moment, when The Miller and the voluble Mrs. Lube sat in the inspector's room, Evans entered Bayham Mews, determined to regularise an intolerable situation. The lorrydriver's bed was hard. Mr. Evans could not bring his mind to the contemplation of the thoroughbred race-horse in an alien atmosphere. Henrietta must find lodgings. He had practically arranged this.

But when he got to his "office" the girl was not there. The bed was neatly made; the floor was brushed; the hearth tidied; but Henrietta had vanished.

On the table was a note.

Dear Mr. Evins.—Fairwell, Try to fogit me.
The ruleing pasions very strong
If you carnt go write you must go rong.
    Yours truely
    Henrietta.
P.S.—Excuse speling the potry was on a sell door at Holleway.

Evans breathed a sigh of relief. For the moment he thought nothing of the possible estreatment of his recognisances.

He had taken up his pen to indite a frenzied appeal to the speculative classes, when he heard men coming up the stairs. The Miller came in first, and behind him was a man whom Evans recognised as a detective-constable.

"Sorry to disturb you, Evans," said The Miller. "You were in the 'Three Dogs' the other night?"

Evans was shaking.

"Yes, Mr. Challoner," he said.

"Whilst you were there, Mrs. Fich lost a wrist-watch the value of which is over £150. It was stolen from a shelf behind the bar. There is information that you left the bar hurriedly, and I have a warrant to search your room."

Educated Evans said not a word, but stood like a man in a dream, watching the systematic combing of his room.

"Nothing here," said The Miller; "not that I expected to find any-thing."

He lit a cigarette and, as he did so, asked carelessly:

"Mrs. Lube been in your room lately?"

"Yesterday," said Evans. "I found her here when I got back from the court."

The Miller smiled grimly.

"Where is Henrietta?" he asked.

"Gorn," said Evans, and showed him the letter.

The Miller read it carefully.

You found a winner when you took that girl," he said.

When he left Zionist House, he went straight back to Mrs. Lube's home.

"Thank you for the information, Mrs. Lube," he said dryly; "and I'll tell you straight away that when your husband says that he saw Evans reaching with a stick, I don't believe him."

"Did you find the watch, Mr. Challoner?" she asked anxiously. "An' did you pinch the thievin' hound?"

"I didn't find the watch," said The Miller carefully, "and Evans didn't find it."

"Did you look under the mattress?" asked the agitated woman. "That's where thieves hide property."

"And that's where they find it too," said The Miller cryptically.

12.—THE JOURNALIST

Mr. Frithington-Evans had a colt, Sunsweet, by Sunstar out of Tof-fee. It was trained by an old stud groom who knew more about horses than most trainers.

From time to time Mr. Frithington-Evans sent a good handicap-per to Shropshire to try this wonderful two-year-old, and every trial aroused joy in the shrivelled soul of this rich young man, who was a sportsman by profession and a gentleman by custom.

It was arranged that the horse should be brought to Alexandra Park, where the opposition was unimportant, and by skilful organisa-tion, Mr. Evans secured 1752 bookmakers' accounts. Some were in his own name, some in fictitious names. In defiance of the laws of racing he advertised through a trusty agent and in this way obtained accounts to reach the total given. On the day of the race the wires would be sent from a hundred sub-post offices in London, each batch being preceded by long-winded telegrams addressed to himself, the idea being to delay the despatch of the wires. It was what Mr. Evans called a "coop." Unfortunately. . .

Mr. Frithington-Evans was by nature and inclination a twister. He twisted Lord Bascom (Viscount Bascom of Bascom) to the extent of fifteen hundred pounds. Not that Frithy needed the money. He had so much that he was ill with it, but it was his nature to twist.

Lord Bascom was very annoyed, and with good reason, when, at their club, Frithy coolly denied that he had ever promised to put a monkey on Longlegs for his friend the first time he was trying.

"Imagination, dear old thing," he said coolly. "You're dreaming!"

Now, although Lord Bascom was an extremely wealthy man (he was chairman of fourteen colliery companies) he was also an extremely mean man. And he hated losing fifteen hundred pounds.

"You're a dirty skunk," he roared, and one of these days I'm going to get even with you!"

Mr. Frithington-Evans grinned, and that grin cost him a lot of money.

"You blabbed Longlegs all over the place—and I only got three to one to my money," he said.

His lordship did not call him a simple liar. He added something.

"Didn't you kidnap a dirty tipster, and didn't he manage to get the news out of the house that Longlegs was a certainty? Why the man didn't bring an action against you for illegal imprisonment, I don't know. You've caught me, Frithy, and I shall catch you or my name's not Bascom!"

Good luck!" said Frithy cheerfully, having no fears.

Lord Bascom went back to his office, red in the neck and breathing vengeance stertorously. It had been on the tip of his tongue to talk about a certain horse called Sunsweet—for his lordship lived in Shropshire, near the secret training quarters, and the best of servants talk. And then by chance there fell into his hands a copy of an unique publication. . . .

There was no greater admirer, nor more consistent supporter, of Educated Evans, than Mr. Bert Sybil, the printer. He did everything for Evans except lend him money; and in justice to our friend, such a request never came from the World's Champion Prophet and Turf Adviser. He had even expressed a willingness to print Mr. Evans' tips at cost price, but, as Educated Evans pointed out to him, the inspiration for his selections came so late in the day that it would be a waste of money to put them into cold type.

Evans was working late one night, revising his tattered list of clients, when Mr. Sybil called upon him, and the visit was a little surprising, because Evans believed that Mr. Sybil was a wealthy man who could well afford the services of a professional mouthpiece. As it happened, he did not come in search of advocacy.

"Heard about my trouble, Evans?"

"Yes, Mr. Sybil. Sit down, won't you?"

Evans himself sat on the table, placing the only chair in the room at the disposal of his visitor. Mr. Sybil sighed.

"I'm afraid I'm for it this time," he said. "Trade's bad, or I wouldn't have taken on the job. You're a man of the world and you understand that."

Evans understood and sympathised. For the third time in three years Mr. Sybil had been summoned by the police for printing the tickets of an illicit sweepstake. He had been fined large sums, and had had ominous warnings.

"I'm afraid they're going to put me away this time, Evans," said Mr. Sybil, gazing reflectively at his cigar. "I've been in before, but nobody knows that but you and me. I tried to straighten The Miller, but he wouldn't be squared. Now the point is, what's going to happen to the business when I'm away? I've got a sort of manager, but I don't trust him any farther than I can chuck him. I'm not married, I've got no relations, and there's nobody in Camden Town that I can put in charge. Do you know anything about printing?"

Evans' first inclination was to give a history of the printing art from its inception by the celebrated Klaxon in 1066, but on reflection he decided to deny all knowledge of the trade.

Mr. Sybil smoked thoughtfully for a long time without speaking.

"You know enough about it to pay the wages bill, I suppose? I've got a dozen contracts that'll keep the works going till I come out. What I want is somebody to keep an eye on it as if it was his own. I don't mind paying two or three pounds a week," he added suggestively.

Although Educated Evans knew nothing about printing, he knew a great deal about two or three pounds a week, and after two hours spent in instructions and warnings, the arrangements were made, and Mr. Sybil's foresight was justified when, on the following morning, he was sent to two months' in the second division.

"It's a bit hard on me," complained Evans to his chief confidant.

"What with the rush of business and the lies that Old Sam and his grand-daughter's tellin' about me, an' Ascot comin' on, I haven't got any time to mess about with printing businesses. I've got all my work cut out gettin' lists."

Addresses are the life-blood of the tipster. There are many eminent firms of publishers which issue classified dictionaries of various trades. You may discover at a glance all the ironmongers and most of the linen-drapers who do business in England. You may, by the turning of a page, have revealed to your eyes the directors of public companies. But up to date, nobody has published a volume indispensable to every turf prophet—a Dictionary of Mugs.

There goes on a trade in addresses which is a lucrative one. One tipster, having exhausted his credit and the patience of his clients, will sell his list to another of his profession, who, employing a new method of approach and a new appeal to the credulity of his clients, may revive in their bosoms the hope and faith which are so essential to the well-being of the turf prophet.

"If I can only get a list or two, Mr. Challoner, I'll be playing banker at the well-known Monte Carlo."

Now The Miller, like most officers of the Criminal Investigation Department, had an extensive knowledge of the queer trades of London; and the list-touter was a familiar object on his mental landscape. And he knew that these evil men sometimes produced lists which had been assiduously copied from reputable directories, and were of no more value to a hard-working turf prophet than a copy of the *War Cry* would be to a system worker.

"Who is offering you a list?" he asked, and, after a second's hesitation—for Evans had a natural objection to supplying information to the police:

"Joe Liski," he said, and The Miller smiled.

"Joe couldn't fall straight if he fell out of a balloon," he said picturesquely. "Take my advice, Evans: let. Mrs. Lube buy all the lists she wants, and you stick to your own. Why don't you advertise "

Mr. Evans closed his eyes.

"As the celebrated Queen Elizabeth said to Cardinal Rishloo, when he asked her why she didn't get married: 'Ask me another.' Them newspapers are too particular, and they're very expensive, Mr. Challoner, and they want to know all your private affairs—"

"Such as whether the winner you say you sent out, you actually did send?" suggested The Miller, and, as Evans evaded the question, he was probably right. "Why not start a newspaper of your own? You've got the business."

The idea only then dawned upon Educated Evans.

"A paper?" he said thoughtfully. "Bless my soul! *Evans' Weekly*, or the *Educated Magazine!*"

As soon as he could, with politeness, shake himself clear of the Miller's company, he hurried to the little side street where Sybil's Electric Printing Works were situated. The foreman and manager, a thin, shifty man, was surprisingly helpful.

"You could do it for about seven pound a week," he said, after making rough calculations on the back of a bazaar bill. "You want a fellow on a bicycle to take the papers round to the shops—what are you going to charge for it?"

"Half a crown?" suggested Evans.

The printer took a pinch of snuff—printers who do not take snuff have no right to the title.

"What about tuppence?" he said brutally, and added: "I don't mind doing this job: it'll liven things up a bit. It hasn't been the same place since the governor's been away. We never had a week pass that the police didn't come in, and that prevented you feeling dull."

The scheme now took definite shape, and Evans applied himself to his new avocation with tremendous intensity.

The magic of printer's ink was in his blood. For three days he neglected all business, whilst he moved deliriously through the grime and ruin of a jobbing printer's office. For there is this about all such places: that they have the appearance of having survived a bad earthquake which was accompanied by a phenomenal shower of soot.

The news came to the Old Sam faction in the nature of a shock.

"'Im with a paper!" said Mrs. Lube, aghast at the suggestion. "I'll believe it when I see it."

She saw it soon enough. The first number of *Evans' Imperial Racing Guide and Backer's Friend* appeared on the Tuesday. It consisted of four very small pages, but there was meat and drink in every line. One column was headed:

WHAT I SAW WITH MY OWN EYES.
By Educated Evans, the World's Premier Prophet and Turf Adviser.

Down at Kempton the other day I had a good look at Fluky Jane. She wasn't trying a yard. Where were the stewards?
★★★★★★

How long will it be before Mr. Frithington-Evans, the celebrated owner of Longlegs, is warned off? This man is a curse to the turf, besides being a low-spirited hound.

******

I understand that a great coop is intended with Mugman. This horse won at Hurst Park when I tipped it. What a beauty! What a beauty! But his trainer ought to be warned off for the way he ran at Sandown.

******

Mr. Challoner, the celebrated detective officer, who is highly respected by Camden Town, as all the world knows, has his eye upon a certain beer-eater who calls himself a turf prophet. If this man had his rights he would be doing time.

Styme, the foreman, read these notes with great relish.

They're a bit personal, ain't they, Mr. Evans?

"They've got to be," said Evans, who had sat up all night in the printing office in order to get the first copy of the paper. "I'm goin' to clean the turf. Many a horse sent out by me has had his head pulled off as soon as it was known that Educated Evans had give 'im!"

Mr. Styme scratched his chin thoughtfully.

"Well, the old man's inside and he can't see it," he said with satisfaction. "But didn't there ought to be some tips in the paper?"

Evans gasped. He had forgotten the tips!

Mrs. Lube read the paper from title to imprint. It was not the reference to her sacred grandparent that really annoyed her, so much as certain paragraphs marked.

PERSONAL CHIT-CHAT AND CAMDEN TOWN GOSSIP.
(By Educated Evans, the World's Champion Prophet and Turf Adviser.)

The goings on of the lower classes is getting worse and worse. The Greek Bachelor having been kicked out of its lodgings, still meets the fair English lady at the cinema, as I have seen with my own eyes. . . .

Mrs. Lube choked, went purple, crushed the paper in her hand and flung it into the grate; thought better of it and smoothed it out, and, grabbing her hat, pulled it viciously over her head. She dashed into the kitchen, selected a small but heavy rolling-pin, put in the market bag and went out in search of Evans.

Mr. Evans saw her coming; barricaded the door, and conducted his

228

negotiations through the window, keeping well out of sight and out of reach.

You dirty, slanderous, perjurous 'ound!" screamed the enraged female. "Open that door to me and I'll. . ." She enumerated the various portions of his anatomy on which, given the opportunity, she would experiment.

"Go away before I send for the police," shouted Evans.

"I'll 'police' you, you perjurous. . ."

She had a large supply of adjectives, and Evans, listening, realised that journalism had its drawbacks and its dangers. Happily for him, "Evans' Imperial Racing Guide and Backer's Friend" enjoyed a strictly local circulation, and other gentlemen who might have had just cause for resentment at his exposure of their weaknesses were blissfully ignorant of the charges brought against them.

When Mr. Evans got home that night he found a man sitting on the bottom step of the wooden stairs which led to his room. At first anticipating violence, he put himself in an attitude of defence.

That you, Evans? growled a voice. "What the devil do you mean by keeping me waiting here? I told you I should come at ten o'clock."

"Me, sir?" said Evans. "Nobody told me nothin'. Come upstairs."

He recognised, by the acerbity and haughtiness of his caller, that he had a gentleman to deal with. The mystery was explained partially when he found a letter which had evidently been pushed under his door. The visitor also found an explanation, for he snatched the letter from Evans's hand.

"I want to talk to you, and I can only spare five minutes. Are you the owner of this rubbish?"

He produced a carefully folded copy of Evans' Imperial Racing Guide and Backers' Friend.

"I'm the owner and I'm not the owner," said Evans, temporising. "All the nasty things in that paper was written by a friend of mine—"

Never mind who wrote it. A lot of it's true. You know Frithington-Evans, don't you? Of course, you're the fellow that he locked up in his room? Why the devil didn't you sue him?"

"Could I?" said Evans, with a new interest in life.

"Of course you could, you fool!" said his lordship. "You could have got a couple of thousand pounds out of the little beast! Now I want you to do something for me. When does your paper come out?"

"Any day," said Evans, recklessly disregarding the regular habits of well-conducted weekly newspapers.

"I'll tell you something. I'm going to spoil Frithy's little joke. He's no relation of yours?"

"No, thank Gawd!" said Evans, and his pious denial aroused the first sign of pleasure that the visitor had displayed.

"Well, now, listen. Get out a new paper, and put in a paragraph something like this: 'Sunsweet will win at Alexandra Park.' Send it out to all your friends—the more the better—and there you are. Now how much will it cost?" He took out a pocket-book.

Evans wasn't quite certain whether to say £2 or £5.

"Will a hundred do?"

Evans, speechless, nodded.

"Now how many people can you send this out to?"

Evans thought.

"About two thousand," he suggested.

"Humph!" said his lordship. And then an idea struck him. "Come to my office in the morning, or rather, to the office of a friend of mine, and I will give you a list of people to whom you can send this paper. But mind you, you've got to keep in the paragraph about that scoundrel being warned off! If you can think of anything worse to say, don't hesitate to say it. Here is the address: if I'm not there—of course I shan't be there," he added hastily, " because it's not my office—ask for the secretary."

He wrote down the address on the blotting-pad and left without further ceremony. All that evening he sat up, till two o'clock in the morning, compiling a list of people to whom the reference to Mr. Frithington-Evans, and particularly the reference to Sunsweet, would bring joy and profit. It was not a long list, about two hundred in all.

At three o'clock the next afternoon, Mr. Evans, having made the necessary alterations in his paper, came into Basinghall Street, passed the imposing portal, and knocked at the door of the room to which he had been directed. A harassed secretary appeared.

"Lists?" said the gentleman with a frown. "Oh, yes, you're the man Lord Bascom was expecting."

He went to a telephone and Evans heard him.

"Man come for the list... yes, my lord, Evans... on your desk? You don't mean... all right, my lord!" The latter rather hastily.

Lord Bascom! Evans knew the name, and remembered dimly having had the nobleman pointed out to him on a racecourse. So he was under the distinguished patronage of Lord Bascom! He glowed.

Presently the secretary returned with a large roll of paper.

"Bring this list back when you've finished with it," he said.

It was an enormous list: it contained nearly five thousand names, and Evans had to recruit all sorts of odd labour to prepare the wrappers. He spent the greater part of the night superintending the new edition. All unnecessary paragraphs, save that relating to Mr. Frithington-Evans, were deleted, and, in large letters:

Under the patronage of his Lordship, Lord Bascom, Educated Evans, the Wizard of Camden Town! The World's Premier Prophet and Turf Adviser! Braxted—what a beauty!

His lordship has give me a tip which same will be sent for 10/. T.M.O. addressed to H. Evans, Greek Bachelor House, Bayham Mews. This is a beauty! It can't be beat! Given to me by one of the world's grandest old sportsmen, God bless him!...

Evans was too much of a professional to send out Sunsweet or any other sweet without making sure that he got something out of it.

Lord Bascom had been called away into the country, so he never saw, until it was too late, the unauthorised use of his name. Had he known that the document supplied to the wretched tipster was a list of the shareholders of his company, he would have died on the spot.

Old Sam and his coterie read the "come on" and wondered how long it would be before Evans was putting out his tin at Dartmoor.

"It's forgery, that's what it is," said Alf. "It stands to reason that no gentleman's going to have anythin' to do with a tyke like that...."

The Miller saw the paragraph and was really alarmed. He hastened round to Bayham Mews and found Mr. Evans entirely surrounded by telegraph envelopes, and huge stacks of money orders piled up on the table.

"It's rolling in—Sunsweet, help yourself," said the exuberant tipster. "Twelve hundred an' forty-two pounds ten up to date, Miller!" He was hysterical with joy. "They're comin' in faster than I can open 'em!"

"Did he give you this tip? asked The Miller.

"He certainly did," said Evans, in his most rollicking manner. "That Sunsweet will win this afternoon by the length of a street. What a beauty, what a beauty!"

It was only by accident that Mr. Frithington-Evans learned of the tragedy, and immediately burnt the telegrams he was sending and sent away his messengers. Blue and red with rage, he stamped up and down his expensive drawing-room, and visited on the head of his groom-trainer the piled-up wrath which properly belonged to Educated Evans.

"We'll run the damn thing and run it down the course," he said. "Where's the horse?"

"On the course, sir," said the shivering groom, "in charge of Mr. Thomson, your trainer."

Mr. Evans seized the telephone directory and searched. There was only one number for Alexandra Park, and this he called.

"I want to talk to Mr. Thomson, who is in charge of my horse," he said. "I am Mr. Frithington-Evans."

"Wait a moment," said a voice.

Five minutes passed, and then somebody asked:

"Is it about Sunsweet?

"Yes, it is." Anger made Mr. Frithington-Evans incautious.

" Now listen, Thomson: that horse is to run but it's not to win—do you understand—"

"Wait a moment: I think you've made a mistake," said the voice at the other end of the line. " We couldn't find your trainer. It is the senior steward speaking."

Frithy did not collapse.

"Oh—yes," he said, more mildly. "I—er—meant to say that my horse isn't running."

"You horse *is* running, Mr. Frithington-Evans," said a very stern voice, "and if it can win, it will win, Mr. Frithington-Evans!"

"Yes, sir," said Frithy.

He looked at his watch: it was too late to rewrite his wires, and his messengers had departed.

"What a beauty! What a beauty!" murmured Educated Evans.

"Hold up," said The Miller, and pushed him against the wall. "Where's your key?"

"What a beauty! What a beauty!" murmured Educated Evans, and began to sing.

"The trouble with you, Evans," said The Miller, as he dragged him up the stairs and flung him on to his bed, " is that you can't carry corn. A little success drives you mad."

"What a beauty! What a beauty!" murmured Evans, and, so murmuring, fell asleep.

Good Evans!

To Brownie Carslake
A great jockey and a good friend

1.—A CHANGE OF PLAN

It was when an excited and vengeful client demanded what the so-and-so and such a thing Mr. Evans meant by sending out three selections for one race, that the educated man laid down his system of ethics.

"Tippin'," he said, "is ta'tics. You start out to do one thing an' do another. Bettin's a battle. You got to change your plans the same as the celebrated Napoleon Bonaparte, him that was killed in the Battle of Waterloo."

This philosophy he impressed upon a Miss Casey, with disastrous effects. As to Miss Casey. . .

To sit beside a beautiful lady in the pit of the Lyceum is indeed a privilege. To feel her small hand steal into yours in the excitement and emotion occasioned by Miss Frederick's acting, is thrilling. Educated Evans had both these experiences. The lady was young. Her face was as fresh and as sweet as a pansy. She had red lips and large grey eyes... presently to be blinded with hot tears at the pitiable plight of Madame X.

Evans returned the grip of her hand and reeled.

"Whatever will you think of me?" she asked penitently as they came out of the theatre.

"My opinion of you," said Mr. Evans passionately, "is the same as the well-known Henry the Eighth had for the far-famed Joan of Arc."

"Oh, go on!" said the delighted Miss Casey. They went to a famous corner shop *café* and Evans blew a dollar on coffee and doughnuts and a box of chocolate tied up with blue ribbon —which was Miss Casey's favourite colour.

Mr. Evans agreed to meet her in Hyde Park the following evening, and went home walking on air.

A week later Mr. Challoner ("The Miller" to the *cognoscenti* of Camden Town) called on the educated man. And the real reason for his call was an article in a certain weekly publication. The article was entitled "Fortunes from Tipping," and the paragraph ran:

"Another turf prophet who has amassed wealth is Mr. Evans, the well-known racing man of Camden Town. Although Mr. Evans lives in unostentatious surroundings, it is no secret that his fortune runs into five figures."

"Did you supply that information?" asked The Miller sternly.

"It's publicity or press work," murmured Evans. "I had a chat with the reporter—met him up West —"

"Five figures!" said The Miller, shocked.

"Ten pun' nine an' eleven," said Evans calmly. "Write that down an' if it ain't five figures nothin' is."

He had been putting the finishing touch to a neat little sign on the door—an oblong of wood on which was painted the new house title.

No directory of Camden Town would reveal the whereabouts of "Priory Park" but for the fact that on all circulars to clients, old and new, Mr. Evans added more concisely, "Bayham Mews, N.W."

"You've got a nerve," said The Miller with that reluctant admiration he offered to the successful criminal. "So far as I can remember, your tip was Asterus."

Educated Evans closed his eyes, a sure sign of offended dignity, and began to search the one drawer of an article which served as desk, counter, dressing-table, stand for duplicator, and occasionally seat. From the litter the drawer contained he produced a hectographed sheet.

"Read," he said simply.

Detective Inspector Challoner read.

EDUCATED EVANS!
The World's Chief Turf Adviser
(Under Royal Patronage)
To all clients I advise a good bet on ASTERUS
At the same time I am warned by my correspondents that

Weissdorn is greatly fancied and that King of Clubs will be on the premises. At the same time what beats Melon will win and Priory Park will run forward.

"He ran forward," said Mr. Evans with even greater simplicity.

"Most horses do," said The Miller, "unless they're clothes horses."

"I also give Sprig—what a double!"

"Sprig? You lie in your boots!" said the indignant Miller. "You said that the Prince of Wales had given you Thrown In!"

Evans shook his head.

"Sprig," he said. "I've got documents to prove that me Ten pun' Special to all and sundried was Sprig—fear nothing."

The Miller did not argue. Mr. Evans' Ten Pound Special was his favourite myth. Like Mrs. Harris, there was no such thing.

Once upon a time Mr. Evans had announced his intention of sending out such a startling service, and had offered it for a beggarly quid a nod, but nobody coughed up and the service fell into disuse. For why, argued the regulars who followed Educated Evans to their ruin, pay a Bradbury for a ten pun' special when you could get his five pound guarantee wire for a dollar—and that on the nod?

"Them Lubeses is givin' me trouble, Mr. Challoner," said Evans, shaking his head sadly. "I've done me best to educate the woman but she's like the far-famed horse that could be led to the slaughter but you couldn't make him think. Never since the days of Mary Queen of Scotch—her that invented the well-known Johnny Walker—has there been a lady like Mrs. Lube—an' when I call her a lady I expect to be struck down for perjury."

The Miller lingered on the first step of the ladder by which Mr. Evans reached Priory Park.

"It's malice an' libel this time—an' mind you, Mr. Challoner, I haven't said a word about her new lodger—but she's takin' the name of a young lady in vain—as good a young lady as ever drew the breath of life!"

The Miller came back to the room.

"You interest me strangely," he said. "Who is the unfortunate female honoured by your attentions at the moment?"

The face of Mr. Evans went pink; his manner grew haughty, almost cold.

"She's in business down the West End an' it's purely planetic."

"What-ic?" asked the puzzled inspector, and then: "Oh—you

mean platonic?"

"It's spelt both ways," said Evans, unmoved. "The Germans call it one thing and the French another. The whole proceedings are accordin' to what you've been brought up to. I call it planetic."

The Miller did not dispute this shameless change of pronunciation but pursued his inquiries.

"I am anxious to know," he said, "because my experience is that women only get hold of you to twist you—what is she after?"

Evans smiled.

"We got an infinity for one another," he said. "She's in lingery."

"Let us be delicate," said Mr. Challoner.

"I mean she's in a lingery department of Snodds and Richersens, the well-known high-class ladies' underwear and knick-knack shop—see advertisements. I met her the day I brought off All Green—fear nothin'—what a beauty! In fact we was seein' the well-known Miss Palling Frederickson, the far-famed scream actress at the Lyceum. I lent her a pocket-handkerchief to wipe away her tears."

"You lent Miss Frederick—?"

"No—Her. Miss Casey. She's Irish on her father's side, but her mother's quite a lady. Them Lubeses see me with her at the cinema and put it around I was adoptin' her. An' I've had anomalous letters callin' me body snatcher."

"From which I gather that she is young," said The Miller.

"Twenty come the 19th of April," said Mr. Evans. "And what an education! She knows Romeo and Julia, Switzerland, where all the well-known winter sports go to, hist'ry grammar an' she can knit ties."

"Has she got medals for these accomplishments?" asked the sarcastic police officer.

"Cups," said Evans, and added "She can play the pianner with two fingers."

Mr. Evans could afford a little light recreation. Since the five-figure episode he had struck a vein of fortune such as comes to few tipsters.

He had not only tipped three winners off the reel, but he had, with unexampled recklessness or courage, backed them. As Mr. Issyheim said when he reluctantly counted out note after note into the trembling hands of the world's supreme prophet and turf adviser, all the miracles were going against the book.

Mr. Evans had a new suit—or practically so. It was, in hue, violently blue, the trousers were slightly long in the leg, even when painfully

236

braced, but the general effect was distinctly classy. A new white bowler hat and a necktie usually sacred to the officers of the 10th Hussars completed the pleasing picture when, on a bright spring morning, Mr. Evans journeyed by 'bus to Paddington Station.

A neat little figure awaited him in the booking-hall. Awaited? Nay, came running towards him.

"I've bought the tickets!" she said excitedly. "Oh, Mr. Evans, I've got so much to tell you!"

He winced at the sight of the briefs—they were first-class; but her next words reassured him.

"I insist upon paying for the tickets, Mr. Evans—I'm rich!"

He smiled tolerantly. Nothing made Mr. Evans smile so tolerantly as somebody else paying.

"They wouldn't give me special tickets," she said. "I told them you were a member of the Jockey Club—"

"In a sense," said Evans hastily, as he hurried her to the platform. "It's not generally known. I do a lot of secret service work for the old club—that's why I usually go into the silver ring. Me an' Lonsdale's like brothers—good mornin', me lord!"

He lifted his hat graciously to a hurrying race-goer. The hurrying race-goer nodded and said "Hullo, face!" and passed on.

"Lord Lashells, the far-famed husband of Princess What's-her-name," explained Evans casually.

They had a carriage to themselves. The Miller, walking along the platform, paused at the door but thought better of it.

"Now!" said Elsie Casey as the train started. "What do you think of this?"

She produced from her bag a long envelope. It had been heavily sealed in wax. Pulling out a letter, she handed it triumphantly to Evans. The letter-head ran:

John Dougherty, Solicitors, Ballyriggan, Co. Wexford.

Dear Miss Casey,—We have had a communication from Heinz and Heinz, Attorneys, 175 Fifth Avenue, New York, of which we hasten to apprise you. By the will of your uncle John Donovan Casey (deceased) the sum of $100,000 and the residue of his estate (proved at $1,757,000) is bequeathed to you. . ."

Evans gasped and the lines swam before his eyes. In his agitation he held her hand.

... absolutely. The attorneys inform me that it will be necessary that you should go to New York at once. As I know you are in possession of the necessary funds, it is not necessary to offer you an advance on account of expenses. Our Mr. Michael Dougherty will join you at Queenstown.

"Well, well, well!" said Evans. But apparently it was not well.

"You see, Mr. Evans, I've been rather a fool—I didn't want my people at Ballyriggan to know that I was a shop girl, and so I—well, I swanked. You'll never understand that."

Mr. Evans understood perfectly.

"You got your position to keep up," he said, "the same as me. Everybody's swankers. Take Pharer's daughter, her that said she found the well-known Moses in the bulrushes, take Queen Elizabeth, the far-famed verging queen, take B—Mary, her that done in her little nephews in the Tower. . . ."

He talked all the time, and his busy brain was working overtime. He saw the fulfilment of his ambitions. He would buy Swan and Edgar's and put up a twenty storey building with Educated Evans picked out in black marble. He'd have a grand dinner room and invite the trainers, who, under the influence of generous wines, would put him on to the goods. His advertisements would cover front pages.

EVENTUALLY—WHY NOT NOW?
EDUCATED EVANS
Piccadilly Circus
(same address for thirty years)
Our £50 Special runs at Windsor.
(Cross all cheques "Bank of England")
Verb Sap.
(Enough Said).

In this exalted mood came Mr. Evans to Newbury.

"Don't waste your money," said the young lady anxiously.

But nothing would hold Mr. Evans.

"I got a horse in the first race that can't lose unless the stewards are cuttin' it up. I got him from the boy that does him. He's been tried better than Pri'ry Park—an' there's one in the three o'clock that could fall down, get up an' then win. I got him from me man at Lambourn. I got agents everywhere."

"Don't lose your money,' warned Miss Casey. . . .

£80 to £20 the first winner, 100-15 the third, 200-25 the fourth.

Returning by train, there was little opportunity for confidences. At the little restaurant near King's Cross Mr. Evans bought a bottle of wine and they talked. From this man of the world she had much advice.

"Don't be puttin' your money in banks," he said. "Hand it over to some educated person of experience. Look how banks fail..."

He explained his own methods of securing his wealth; showed her the pocket inside his waistcoat.

"Now about this fortune of yourn, Miss Casey. I can let you have the money to get to America—"

"I wouldn't dream of it!" she said instantly, and the little nagging worry that had gnawed at Evans' heart all day vanished. "I've got enough and more than enough—but you are a darling."

Evans closed his eyes and breathed through his nose. Nobody had called him a darling for years, though Mrs. Lube had once addressed him as "a pretty beauty." Probably she did not mean it.

"I should so love to see your office," she said suddenly.

Mr. Evans coughed.

"It's not much to look at," he admitted, "but if you go puttin' up skyscrapers you only attract a lot of undesirables, as the saying goes. They just call in for a drink an' that's where your profit goes."

Nevertheless, he allowed himself to be persuaded.

"What a dear little room!" She was bright-eyed and ecstatic. "I suppose you keep your race-horses in the stables downstairs?"

In the stables downstairs was a Ford van, the property of a provision merchant, but Mr. Evans did not think it necessary to explain this.

They sat together, he smoking one of her scented cigarettes, and they discussed the future.

"I'm rather young to marry," she said, "but I should feel safe with you, Algernon. And having all this money. . ."

"Qui' ri'," said Mr. Evans thickly.

Two days later The Miller, strolling up West and entirely out of his own division, was called upon to assist two policemen in the arrest of a certain Mr. Albert Ugger, on a charge of working the confidence trick on an unsuspecting American. Mr. Ugger was ferociously intoxicated, but under the beneficent influence of The Miller, whom he recognised, he went quietly.

"Wimmin's ruined me, Miller," he said as they marched him to Vine Street. "I got a mug taped up Camden Town way—a feller called Evans. He's got lashin's of money accordin' to the papers. . . ."

The Miller was a fascinated audience.

". . . So we put Polly Agathy on to him—she's twenty- eight but looks a kid... and what do you think she done on us? Gave him a doped fag and skipped out with four hundred quid that she took from his pouch. Is that right —I ask yer?"

The Miller began to understand why for the past two days no selections had been flowing from the anguished tenant of Priory Park.

2.—Mr. Evans Does a Bit of Gas Work

Mr. Siniter was wider than Broad Street. He was very rich and he trusted nobody, least of all jockeys. But he thought he could trust Lem Dooby, one of the smartest lads that ever left Australia for the good of the English turf. That a jockey could not trust him will be made clear.

Lem had rather a pretty wife. Saul Siniter had a soft place in his heart for beauty, married or unmarried; and Lem's wife had a weakness for good dinners, theatre parties, and those expensive but inconspicuous articles of jewellery that a very rich bookmaker could, with propriety, send her on her birthday.

One day, when Lem was riding in the North, Mrs. Lem and Saul dined magnificently, danced till three o'clock in the morning, at which hour Saul saw her home.

"I'll tell you the truth, Saul," said Margarita, which was her name: "I'm rather worried about Lem. He's one of those quiet people who say nothing and think a lot; and if he should hear—"

"Don't worry about Lem," scoffed Mr. Siniter, who was a very tall, handsome man with the manners of a duke—such dukes as have manners— "Unless you go talking, Lem will know nothing. Anyway, I'll write to him tomorrow, and tell him I took you out to dinner, so there's no secret about it."

Which was very true. There was no secret at all about the dinner part of the evening or even the dancing part.

Mr. Siniter, for all his bulk and his strength and his notorious *savoir faire*, was a moral coward, of the type to whom worry and suspicion were more potent poisons than strychnine and arsenic. For the moment, however, he saw no cause to worry; he had a horse that was saved for one of the big handicaps, and which he had backed at ridiculous odds; he had a certain winner in Hot Feet when the moment arrived to let his head loose; and he could contemplate the future with equanimity.

Before Hot Feet ran at Hurst he had a little conversation with Lem Dooby, who was a very nice little man without vice or temperament.

"Lem," he said, "I don't want you to win this race. . . . yes, I know they'll make him favourite, but seven to four is no good to me. I've told everybody to back him and the next time we'll get a good price. You'd better get caught flat-footed at the start, and the further you're left the better I shall be pleased."

Lem nodded.

But he was a man who had many friends, in all circles of society; and as he was going into the ring he saw a nobleman for whom he had ridden and who he knew was in that select circle which supplies the stewards of meetings all over the country.

"I want to talk to you, Dooby," he said, and led the jockey aside. "You must tell nobody, not your best friend, what I'm telling you, but there's been a lot of talk about the way Siniter 'rubs out,' and they're watching your running today very carefully. In fact, one of the stewards will be down at the elbow to see the start. You can make any excuse you like to Siniter—and I know I can trust you not to tell him the truth—but I don't want to see you stood down."

Lem, who was a wise lad, touched his cap and went into the saddling-ring.

The story of Hot Feet's possibilities was already public property in Camden Town.

★★★★★★

The Miller met Mr. Evans at the corner of Bayham Street.

"One of these days," he said savagely, "you're going to get me hung; and if you don't get me, you'll get yourself hung. What the devil do you mean by calling up the police station and telling the sergeant that you had something hot and extra for me?"

Evans shrugged his shoulders.

"You've been a good friend of mine, Mr. Challoner," he said, "and I wasn't going to let you out of this coop. I got it this, mornin' from a feller that does a lot of betting at the club, an' I promised him I wouldn't tell a soul."

"And you sent it out to your forty-three thousand clients, I presume?" said The Miller.

"Five hundred an' seventy-four," confessed Evans, in a modest vein. "I've been sendin' a army of messengers all over Camden Town puttin' them on to Hot Feet."

"A bookmaker's horse," said The Miller coldly. "It's the sort of

241

stumer that bookmakers put around. Hot Feet! Cold Feet would be a better name for him!"

Mr. Evans smiled cryptically.

"He's been tried forty-one pounds—" he began.

The Miller silenced him with a look.

Apparently the legend that Hot Feet was a stumer, and that Mr. Evans was the misguided, perhaps the all too willing, victim of a penciller's machinations, was for some extraordinary reason general throughout Camden Town. When Mr. Evans, took the air at midday in the High Street he was accosted every few yards by sceptical clients.

"What's this Hot Feet you've sent me, Evans? Siniter's horse! I'm surprised at you sendin' a wire like that. He was beat a short head at Hurst and he'll be rubbin' out today."

Mr. Evans closed his eyes and looked pained.

A few yards on he met Mr. Harriboy, the far-famed fishmonger and poulterer.

"I've got your message, Mr. Evans, but I can't see Hot Feet winning. He's a bookmaker's horse, and everybody knows he'll be rubbing out, today."

Now "rubbing out," as the initiated know, is the art of discouraging backers from putting their money on horses that seem to have an outstanding chance. And this art is very widely practised. Today you are a short head behind a good winner; next week your horse starts at 6-4 and finishes a bad fourth; and this may happen on his next outing, until newspaper tipsters and wily punters grow weary of supporting this erratic animal; and then he pops up at a price remunerative to all concerned. And Mr. Siniter was one of the best-known "rubbers out" of form.

"I can only tell you," said Mr. Evans patiently, "that he's On the Job. If there's any man in Camden Town who can teach me my business, let him come forward or for ever hold his speech. I'll allow him ten points for education an' then beat him. I'm like the far-famed salamander, I've got eyes in the back of me head—I've got to, Mr. Harriboy, to live."

Mr. Harriboy shook his head.

"I'm not backing your horse today, Evans," he said definitely.

And others had formed a conclusion as definite; and when, that afternoon, Hot Feet won at 7-1, there were sore hearts in Camden Town.

"It's Evans' fault," said Mr. Harriboy to a disgruntled friend. "If he'd only told us what he knew, instead of chucking his weight about up and down High Street, I'd have been on that horse."

After the race Lem got down to meet his enraged owner.

"What the hell do you mean by winning?" hissed Siniter. "Didn't I tell you that I'd not backed the horse? Didn't I ask you to start flat-footed?"

"I was left, but I couldn't hold him in," said Lem, and for two pins would have told him the strength of the position, but loyalty to his aristocratic friend kept him silent.

Mr. Siniter went away from the course a very thoughtful man; and two days later, when he met Margarita, expressed his suspicion.

"Lem's got something at the back of his mind. I don't think you and I had better be seen out together so much. I'll have to find another jockey."

Now Margarita was not a nice woman, but she had a curious sense of loyalty.

"You'll do nothing of the kind," she said. "Lem never did a crooked thing in his life." Mr. Siniter grew purple.

"He's not going to ride Blue Tick!" he stormed. "I've backed him to win me three thousand and I'm taking no risks."

She smiled.

"You don't know what risks you'll be taking if you put down Lem," she said significantly.

He very wisely did not ask questions. And later that day it came to his ears that one Educated Evans had sent Hot Feet to 49,732 clients, of which five had backed the horse and fifteen hadn't.

Mr. Siniter trusted no detective. He himself went in search of Educated Evans and found him engaged in the preparation of his morning advice.

"Sorry to intrude on you, mister," said the temporarily genial Siniter.

He looked round the apartment. It did not seem the kind of place from which 49,732 letters were likely to be addressed, but you never know what tipsters can do at a push.

"I've come to thank you for your tip on Hot Feet," said Mr. Siniter, and put a five-pound note on the table. "You sent it to a friend of mine, but I backed it. Now if you ever have any tips from this stable—"

"I have 'em every day," said Mr. Evans with a quiet smile. "There's nothin' that twistin' Siniter does that I don't know."

Siniter swallowed something.

"You knew that Hot Feet was going to win?" he said, maintaining his calm with difficulty.

Evans nodded.

"Information *v.* gaswork," he said. "I got a boy in the stable, and Dooby—"

"Ah—you know Dooby, I suppose?"

Evans smiled again.

"Me an' him's like brothers," he said. "I met him at the Jockey Club in Park Lane. He reminds me of the celebrated Fred Archer who rode the far-famed Eclipse when it won at San-down Park in 1795—I don't know whether it was the fourth or fifth of May."

"You know a lot about Mr. Siniter's horses?" Educated Evans was amused.

"Everything," he said. "Take Blue Tick—him they lay 7-4 about in the Epsom Handicap—not a yard!"

Mr. Siniter heard and perspired.

"What—who told you?" he demanded, trying to smother his wrath.

"Information," murmured Evans. "That race is a squinch for Dew-flower—tried two stone better than Lopear an' walked it!"

When Mr. Siniter got home he summoned Lem by 'phone.

"Dooby, I'm putting up another jockey on Blue Tick. I don't think you understand the horse, old man."

Dooby understood. He was one of those little men who were treacherous to others and never imagined he would be suspected of treachery.

"Certainly," he said. "Now who shall we put up? What about Jim Gold?"

Now the name of Jim Gold had also occurred to Mr. Siniter, but the mere fact that Dooby suggested it was quite sufficient to put him off.

"No, I can't have Jim: he wouldn't ride one side of the horse," he said. "I don't mind any other jockey—bar Slick Markey."

Here again Lem understood. Slick Markey was as crooked as a flash of lightning. Even jockeys, who never give one another away, admitted that Slick was mustard. He was one of those clever jockeys who got twenty-five mounts a year and was popularly supposed to be in everybody's pocket but his own.

"No, I wouldn't advise you to take Slick—he can't help thieving any more than I can help scratching my head. What about Tommy Lutter?"

Mr. Siniter hesitated. It had been on the tip of his tongue to mention the same jockey.

"No," he said, "he doesn't understand the horse either. I don't care who rides him, but the only thing I bar is Slick."

"Naturally," murmured the sympathetic Mr. Dooby.

He went away without having discovered a solution to the pressing problem. By midnight Mr. Siniter had worked himself into a condition of nervous prostration, and at that hour he called up some one who was nearly a friend.

"I want a jockey to ride my horse Blue Tick," he said. "I don't think he'll win, but he's a curious horse to ride and I'd like to have the best man available."

His friend, who was also an owner, thought for some time.

"Isn't Dooby riding—no? Well, what about Joe Ginnett? He hasn't a mount. Funnily enough, I saw him tonight in Camden Town—"

"Oh, did you?" said Mr. Siniter loudly. "Well, he won't do! Can you suggest anybody else?"

After a long pause.

"I don't know. . . of course you can't have Slick: he's impossible. If he knew you'd backed the horse he'd stop it, and if you hadn't backed it he'd win. And he's in the pocket of. . . " He libelled half a dozen perfectly respectable but eminent pencillers of Tattersalls. "The only man I can suggest is Callison. He's a friend of Dooby's—"

"He won't do either," said Mr. Siniter promptly. "Sorry to bother you, old man—I'll think it out."

"Anyway, don't take Slick," came the final warning.

Mr. Siniter, in spite of his agitation, smiled.

Time was growing short. The next day he made another attempt. One jockey after another came up for review—none could be trusted. At eleven o'clock that night he rang up Slick Markey and offered him the mount.

Secretly, and in an assumed name, he had become one of Mr. Evans' subscribers. The morning post brought a communication from that genius.

EDUCATED EVANS,

The World's Premier Prophet and Turf Adviser.

KEEP OFF BLUE TICK!

KEEP OFF BLUE TICK!

KEEP OFF BLUE TICK!

Information *v.* Gaswork.
Straight from a reliable source.
My information is that

BEGGAR BOY

is walking over for the important event as advertised in all
leading papers.

Mr. Siniter wiped his perspiring brow. Somebody knew more than he; there was a conspiracy amongst these jockeys. What a fool he had been to put up Slick, the most notorious crook of all!

To change him now was neither possible nor desirable. There was only one thing to do. He sent secret instructions to his commission agents to lay Blue Tick, and drove to the course with the full assurance that he had taken the only wise course.

Before the race he interviewed the wizen-faced jockey with the shifty eyes.

"I've laid off all my bets on this horse," he said, "so you can handle him gently."

Slick nodded—he was a man of very few words, and they were mostly unprintable.

There was a big field. Mr. Evans, lounging against the rails, waited with a calm air of assurance for his unbeatable gem to materialise.

He never could read a race, and never learnt to look at any of the horses except the one he had backed—and usually he confounded that with another.

There was no mistaking Blue Tick: he was a grey, and the flamboyant colours of Mr. Siniter could not be mistaken nor confounded with anything more delicate. They lay in the centre of the field, about third for most of the journey. In the last furlong they drew to the front. . . .

Blue Tick won, hard held, by three lengths.

"Information *v.* gasworks," said Evans bitterly. "It almost makes you give up trying to find 'em!"

Mr. Siniter watched the horses come back to the paddock like a man in a dream. And it was a pretty bad dream. He saw Dooby, who rode one of the last division, slip from his horse and unsaddle, and as the little man passed him Mr. Siniter noticed in a vague kind of way that he was beaming.

"I'm glad you won, guv'nor," said the jockey. "I think anybody could have won on him. He had us beat from start to finish. I hope you had a good win. My missus had eighty pounds on him."

Mr. Siniter recovered his voice:

"Who told her to back it?" he asked hollowly.

"Old Slick Markey, just before he went out," said Lem. "It's given me another idea of old Slick—first time I've known him to do the straight thing."

3.—Education and Combinations

Mr. Evans had concluded his ablutions and had hung the towel on the bed-rail to dry. The yellow sunlight which slanted through the open window proclaimed the coming of spring; the piles of unopened letters that covered the table proclaimed the Turn of the Tide.

Until the small hours of the morning he had been turning the handle of the Duplicating Machine that a child could work, and littering the bed was his latest *pronunciamento*.

EDUCATED EVANS

The World's Premier Prophet and Turf Adviser
(Thirty-five years at the same address)

STICKY BOY (7-1) What a beauty!!
STICKY BOY (7-1) What a beauty!!
STICKY BOY (7-1) What a beauty!!

Once more the well-beloved Evans has done the hat trick by
giving a 7-1 winner—nothing else mentioned
Information *v.* Gaswork!
Now I want all clients new and old to roll up in their millions
for the grandest winner that ever looked through a bridle!
This one will win the
Newbury Cup
He's been tried unbeatable!
He's been tried unbeatable!
Eventually—why not now?
Eventually—why not now?
Send P.O. 5s. for this Guaranteed £5 Special to Educated
Evans, Myra Gray Mansions, Bayham Mews, N.W.

Mr. Evans picked up a hectographed sheet and read it with satisfaction. He had struck a blow at the very heart of his enemies. Seven successive three star naps had Old Sam sent forth in his Midnight Special, and each and every one of them had gone down the sink.

He heard footsteps on the stairs, but did not turn round, even when a shadow came into the room.

"Good morning, Mr. Evans."

The educated man spun round and his face went pale. Standing in the doorway was Mrs. Lube, and in her hand a large bunch of primroses.

"Many happy returns of the day, Mr. Evans, an' let by-gorns be by-gorns."

Once you knew Mr. Evans' birthday it was well-nigh impossible to forget it, for he first saw the light on April 1st in the year—well, never mind about the year.

"Um—same to you, Mrs. Lube."

He took the flowers gingerly, expecting them to explode at any moment.

"May I come in, Mr. Evans?"

He indicated a chair and watched her warily, ready to jump at the first sign of a poker. But not only was Mrs. Lube unarmed, she was disarming.

"I daresay you wonder why I come, Mr. Evans," she said. "After all the bickerin' an' unpleasantness we've had and what not. But what I say is live an' let live, but I've been talking it over with my dear gran'father an' my dear husband an' I says 'What's the use of us tryin' to down dear Mr. Evans?' I says, 'the only thing to do,' I says, 'is to get him to help us,' I says."

Evans found his voice gruffly.

"I got nothing to give away," he said.

Mrs. Lube swallowed something.

"Yes, you have, Mr. Evans." She was very earnest, or appeared to be. "You've got education. I says to my poor dear gran'father, 'What's the use of our goin' on as we're goin' on without education?' "

Educated Evans coughed and fingered his chin importantly.

"I says," continued Mrs. Lube, "the only thing is to throw ourselves on his mercy an' for me to ask him to educate me."

Mr. Evans coughed again.

"In a manner of speakin' you're right," he said. "Take biology an' science. What's water? In French it's 'O.' In science it's H.3.0., in German it's something altogether different. Take the world, which revolves or turns on its axle once in every twenty-four hours, thus causin' the stars to shine. Take history. The War of the Roses was caused through Lancashire beatin' Yorkshire and *vicer verser*, which is Latin. Which brings us to Julia Caesar, the far-famed wife that was always suspicious of her husband owin' to his carryin' on with Lewdcreature Burgia the female Crippen of Italy. Where's Italy, you ask me? That's geography again and brings us to the question of Mussel Enos, the far-famed Fassykist."

Mrs. Lube blinked rapidly.

"My poor brain!" she said disparagingly. "What a headpiece you've got, Mr. Evans!"

"Take botomy, the science of vegetables," said Evans, warming to his subject. "By studyin' the ways an' means of flowers we arrive at zoo-ology or caterpillars which change into butterflies by metamorphious methods commonly called hibernation. . ."

Mrs. Lube stayed two hours and had a grounding in erudition.

"It's your idea, Elfred," she said to her husband on her return, "and if it turns out that I've bin wastin' my time on that old so-and-so, I'll have something to say to you!"

"We've got to do something," said Alfred.

Detective-Inspector Arbuthnot Challoner was taking what was literally and figuratively a constitutional. In other words he was engaged in the improvement of his system by the exercise of his limbs and the improvement of Camden Town by the employment of his senses.

He called at the Blue Pig, to the embarrassment of a young married gentleman who had left his wife chargeable to the Parish of St. Pancras; he looked in at Hookey's Coffee Bar and Good Pull Up for Carmen and found Spicey Brown and Cully Parks intent upon dominoes—they invariably planned their busts over a game, and used the pieces to model the house they intended to burgle.

("Say that double-six is the front door," Cully was saying when The Miller arrived, "and that four-one is the pantry winder, all we gotter do is to get down the area an' the job's as good as done. . . .")

The pieces were swept into confusion on The Miller's approach, and two innocent men greeted him with sycophantic pleasure.

Mr. Challoner's next call was at a fried-fish shop off the High Street, where one who was born Lieverbaum but was now styled Leverbrown carried on a small spieling club in the back parlour.

Comparatively speaking, Camden Town was law-abiding and almost chaste.

"All the boys have gorn racin', Mr. Challoner," said Lieverbaum, rubbing his podgy hands. "It's a blessing this racing, ain't it? Keeps the boys out of mischief, yes? An' what with Edjercated Evings doin' so well—three winners right orf the reel—the man's marvellous. The bookmakers are doin' rotten."

He spoke feelingly, for Mr. Lieverbaum was notoriously an evader of the law, being a ready money bookmaker, and had been three times convicted.

The Miller stopped long enough to warn him against this practice, and resumed his stroll. And then, turning past the Nag's Head in the direction of Regent's Park, he beheld a sight which left him dazed and gasping. There flashed past him one of those handsome limousines which can be hired by the mile or by the hour, and wedged on the back seat thereof was Mrs. Lube, a white-bearded old gentleman, and Mr. Evans of Myra Gray Mansions.

The Miller's first thought was that his unfortunate friend had been kidnapped, and his hand strayed to his pocket where he kept his whistle. In another second the car had vanished in the direction of the park.

That evening, being off duty, he made a call in Bayham Mews and found Mr. Evans pressing his best trousers.

"Good evenin', inspector—mind you don't knock over them flowers." He hastily saved the jam jar full of primroses and put it on the mantelpiece. "They were sent to me by a friend."

"Mrs. Lube?"

The Miller meant to be ironical. He was staggered when Mr. Evans nodded.

"We're goin' into partnership, me an' Old Sam," he said calmly. "The man's got his points, but, as Amelia says—

"Who's Amelia?" demanded the baffled detective.

"Mrs. Lube—we're like brothers and sisters."

The detective looked at him suspiciously. "What's the idea?" he demanded.

"Education an' combinations," said Evans profoundly.

"Let us keep the conversation clean," said The Miller.

And then Evans explained. It was, he said (untruthfully), his own idea. By some curious workings of chance, which even The Miller had observed, it fell out that luck balanced up and down. When Old Sam's Midnight Special was successful, Evans was unsuccessful. When Evans' fortune hit the beam, gloom reigned in the house of Lube. Why not therefore conclude a secret arrangement? Both parties to work independent one of the other and to pool profits. In this way, the misfortune of Old Sam would be relieved by the swelling coffers of Educated Evans. On the other hand, when the fickle goddess had deserted Evans, his exchequer would be supplied from the surpluses which came from his rival.

"Umph!" said The Miller. "That won't work!"

Mr. Evans could afford to smile.

"As a matter of fact it's workin'," he said simply. "We've both had a good week, but he's had better than me an' sent me four pun' six an' ninepence difference."

It appeared that Mrs. Lube was keeping the books, that Mrs. Lube's cousin was acting as accountant, and Mrs. Lube's sister-in-law was preparing the balance sheet, and the money was to be kept in Mrs. Lube's bank.

"It's a hundred to one against you, Evans," said The Miller ominously. Evans smiled again.

If it was not to be registered, the partnership was to be a very high-class affair. It was Mr. Evans who suggested the telegraphic address, "Evanlube, London," and in his enthusiasm paid the two guineas required by the postal authorities. "Not," said Mrs. Lube, "that it makes much difference, for all the telegrams we shall ever get." Still, it gave the firm an importance when added to Old Sam's flamboyant note-head with a rubber stamp.

The week that followed was a tragic one for the followers of Educated Evans. He gave four £5 Specials that failed to finish in the first nine. His unbeatable cert for Friday (widely circularised) was a non-runner. On Saturday he called at the Lube household confidently, for Old Sam had had a wonderful run, including two 100-8 winners.

There was no accident about this except the fluke of Alfred finding Mr. Dewbring, a watcher of horses at Carshott. It happened that the three trainers at Carshott were enjoying the fruits of their industry and cunning, and sending out winners almost every day.

Evans knocked at the door with a gay heart and was admitted. Mrs. Lube received him in the parlour and her manner was as distinctly cold as Evans' was distinctly genial.

"I've had a temp'ry setback in fortune," he said breezily. "As dear old Hamlet said, you can't win all the time."

He produced from his trousers pocket a very small bundle of Treasury notes, mostly, as Mrs. Lube saw with a discriminating eye, green.

"Two pun' six," he said cheerily, and placed it on the table.

Mrs. Lube's lips tightened. With some reluctance she produced her books.

"That's seven pun' five I've got to pay you," she said ungraciously. "What with all this money goin' out an' none cumin' in and five mouths to fill, the instalment on the pianner due next week, I dunno, I'm sure."

What she did not know she did not specify.

"I got something up me sleeve for Tuesday, Amelia," said Evans darkly as he pocketed his money. "Something that could fall down, get up an' then win. I had it from the boy that does him—a girl named Jackson who's keepin' company—"

"I dunno, I'm sure," said Mrs. Lube again, and with those cryptic words dismissed the partner in her new business.

On the following Tuesday Mr. Evans started badly. He sent out Bollybill "tried 21 lbs. better than Coronach," and Bollybill finished a bad last. On the Wednesday he pleaded with all clients new and old to go for Snatcher. "This horse" (to quote his own words) "is a Rod in Pickle. He's been brought over specially from Ireland for a coop." Snatcher was seventh in a field of eight. On the Thursday The Miller met Mr. Evans at the entrance of Bayham Mews.

"I've just headed off a small deputation that was calling upon you. I don't know whether I oughtn't to have pinched them for conspiring to murder."

Evans smiled tolerantly.

"What's one man's meat," he said, "is another man's poison, which is French for chickens. My dear old partner Sam has brought home two eight-to-one shots. Next week it'll be my turn. Mr. Challoner, I got a horse for you on Saturday. He's a stone pinch. I had her from the boy—"

"If I were you," interrupted The Miller gently, "I should lose that boy."

On the Thursday afternoon Mrs. Lube made up her mind. The telegraphic address was expunged from the notehead, and a penny postcard sent to the local post office informing the official in charge that "Evanlube" might in the future indicate Evans, but it did not indicate Lube.

"Nobody sends us telegrams," explained Amelia to her husband, "except Mr. Dewbring, and he puts our full name and address."

"What are you going to do?" asked Alf.

Mrs. Lube smiled unpleasantly.

On the Friday afternoon she came to Myra Gray Mansions, and there was something very determined in her mien.

"Good afternoon, Amelia," began Evans. "You're just in time for a little bit of education. Take astronomy or the heavens—"

"We've had enough 'eavens, educated an' uneducated," said Mrs. Lube, "and I'll thank you not to call me Amelia. Me husband objects. How have you done?"

Too well she knew how Mr. Evans had "done."

"I don't suppose I've took a couple of pounds," said Evans cheerfully, "but luck will turn—"

"So will worms," said Mrs. Lube. "You don't think me an' my poor dear gran'father's going to keep you in idleness an' losin' our connection what we've built up through information v. gaswork?"

"Here, hold hard," said Evans, stung to annoyance by this gross plagiarism.

"You don't suppose,' Mrs. Lube went on, "that we're goin' to put your measly two pounds to our fifty day after day an' week after week an' year after year an' keep you in the bread of idleness with five mouths to fill an' my poor dear gran'father gettin' older every day?"

"Who ain't?" asked Evans loudly. "That's the evolution of nature, as I've told you till I'm sick of telling you. It's due to the subcutaneous tissues and bones—"

"Never mind about bones," said Mrs. Lube, even more loudly. "You'll soon be gnawin' them if this goes on."

She planked a piece of paper on the table. "There's five pounds— that's your share, and the partnership's over. We're not goin' to be ruined by educated has-beens and whatnots."

Evans turned pale with fury.

"You come to me for education—" he began.

"And we got it," said Mrs. Lube. "The partnership's over."

Evans watched the departure of the lady from the top of the steps, walked back with a shrug, and applied himself to the task of composition.

That night, from information received, there was delivered by hand, or posted, to all clients old and new an important statement.

Educated Evans is once more Educated Evans. Partnership with Uneducated People Dissolved and Abolished.
Educated Evans, the World's Premier Turf Prophet and Adviser to the Nobility (by request) begs to announce that he has taken away his valuable advice from the so-called Old Sam (lately assistant and messenger boy to the well-known Educated Evans) and now henceforward and herewith is on his own. Clients new and old who have received Educated Evans'

beauties can now have a horse that he's been keeping up his sleeve till he'd dropped all his low connections.

WET WHITE.

WET WHITE.

WET WHITE.

All clients new and old are advised to have their limit upon this unbeatable gem, especially kept up the sleeve of Educated Evans. No connection with any other business, no longer adviser to Old Sam.

Great minds think alike. That evening Mrs. Lube was turning the handle of a rotary machine which announced to the world that:

We have dismissed our assistant tipster, E. Evans, having no use for same.

"Do you think," asked Alfred Lube thoughtfully, as they sat at breakfast and he read Mr. Evans' flamboyant claim, "do you think he's got anything up his sleeve?"

"His sleeve?" scoffed the infrequent partner of his joys. "He's had nothing up his sleeve, not even a shirt!"

Yet Wet White won; and on the Monday, at a Midland meeting, Too Gladly won at 100-6 and was Evans' special three-star help-yourself selection. And on the Tuesday Wiggletoe won, and was Mr. Evans' confident and unbeatable gem. And on the Wednesday up popped Small Schweppe in a two-year-old seller. Popped was hardly the word, since he exploded at the brilliant price of 20's.

Mrs. Lube put on her hat and went out to interview Evans.

"Fair's fair all the world over, Mr. Evans," was her opening. "Me an' my dear gran'father have got the idea that we've been a bit hasty—"

And then she stopped. On the table was a telegraph envelope addressed to "E. Evans, Esq., Myra Gray Mansions, Bayham Mews." And by its side was a telegram, but the address was different: it was simply "Evanlube London." Slowly there dawned upon the good lady the horrible revelation. She had transferred the telegraphic address without realising that she had been receiving Evanlube wires all the time! She seized the telegraph form and read:

Blinkeye certainty tomorrow.—Dewbring.

"A gentleman at Carshott," said Evans. "He's been sending me winners all the week. I don't know why. What was you saying, Mrs. What's-yer- name?"

But Mrs. What's-yer-name was speechless.

4.—THE OTHER LUBESES

Educated Evans, being by nature gallant and by predisposition romantic, imagined, in the purity of his mind and the loftiness of his soul, that he might do almost anything that would be reprehensible in other men.

A lesser man might have thought twice before taking Millie Ropes to Lingfield. Millie was a little on the notorious side. She had left the bar of the "White Cow" with suspicious suddenness. There was a lot of vague talk about marked half-crowns. And she had subsequently disappeared from London, returning at the end of six months with a very small baby that she said belonged to her sister Annie, who had to leave England for Australia. Millie Robes was frankly an indiscretion on Evans' part.

"It's all over Camden Town, is it?" he said defiantly to a well-meaning friend. "Well, is it all over Camden Town that I give Orbindos— fear Melon—nothin' else mentioned? Is it all over Camden Town that I give Funny Freak—100-6 beat a head—hard lines? Is it all over Camden Town that I give Priory Park before the entries come out? I don't take no notice of what common people say about us. I'm like the well-known an' highly respected King Edward the Professor, who picked up a lady's garter an' shoved it round his neck, hence the celebrated sayin' '*Hony swar kwee maly pense*'."

But Millie was not the only brick that Mr. Evans dropped. Was he not seen at the Hialto Cinema with Mrs. Alf Ibbidino? And was not Lou Ibbidino (her husband was in the ice-cream business) a lady about whom the tongue of gossip wagged slanderously?

"She's a Satisfied Client of mine," protested Evans when The Miller reproached him. "What was I to do when she asked me out to see the pictures?. . . I *know* she's Livin' Apart. . . . I know all about the barman at the Green Moon. . . but, Mr. Challoner, I'm like the famous wife of Julius Caesar, the well-known King of Italy, I'm never suspicious."

Too well was Educated Evans doing for the Lubes to ignore this opportunity. Old Sam's Midnight Special announced

OLD SAM
(The Moral Tipster)

83 years old and never got anybody into trouble.
Patronise the Man who Gave Myra Gray.
Old Sam gives tips that children can read.

Evans complained bitterly about this—his chief complaint being that Myra Gray was a figment of Lubean imagination.

But after a while the reflection upon his character began to get on his nerves. People began to stop him in the street and ask him not to speak to their wives. A woman who occupied a room in the mews told him he ought to be ashamed of himself—a man of his age. And behind it all was the crude propaganda of the Lubeses—apocryphal stories related to the hushed denizens of bars by Alf Lube, scandals proclaimed over the tea table by Mrs. Lube. Even Old Sam, that patriarchal man, made insulting references to the moral probity of the educated man.

"You've got to live it down," said The Miller.

"Live what down?" wailed the agitated Evans. "I done nothing— me character's bein' demobbed by them Lubeses and if I don't take 'em into court my name's not Evans!"

One day business took him to a foreign land—Camberwell, S.E. He had to interview a friend who had settled in this strange country. This friend had a wife whose sister was walking out with the brother of a head lad in a Wiltshire stable, and the possibility of obtaining direct stable information was not to be missed. They had completed their business, and it had been arranged that anything the wife's sister told the wife about what her young man's brother had told her young man should be communicated by the husband to Evans at the earliest possible moment. And after Evans had told his friend to ask his wife to tell her sister to ask her young man to tell his brother that Evans paid heavily for news, the party was adjourning when he received a very staggering piece of information.

"I wonder, Mr. Evans," said his friend, "whether you know of a job for my sister-in-law? She's been offered a place up your way, but she wants a little extra work to keep her going. She's as nice a young woman..."

Evans listened with closed eyes, framing the while a polite regret that he could not furnish the necessary employment.

"I've got meself into too much trouble lately min' to bein' kind to wimmin," he said, shaking his head. "There's a certain party in Camden Town who's cast more aspiration on my character than the far-famed Lewdcreature Burgia, the well-known female Crippen of Italy. But I might hear of something—what's the name of your lady friend?"

His friend gave it, and the educated man staggered.

"What?" he said incredulously. "Goo' lor'!"

His brain worked rapidly.

"I'll engage her," he said excitedly. "Two pun' ten a week if she'll come and do a bit of racing with me."

"She's highly respectable," warned the friend. "So am I," said Mr. Evans.

Thereafter life ran with greater smoothness at Orbindos Manse— which, despite the ecclesiastical and evangelical character of the title, was the one room above a stable in Bayham Mews which was the *pied à terre* of the World's Turf Adviser.

Prosperity was revealed in the two flower-pots topped with the blazing blue of hyacinths, in the gold lettering on the door tablet, in the new green and magenta tablecloth.

"Good heavens!" said The Miller, stopping in the doorway to survey the unexpected grandeur.

Mr. Evans smirked in a self-deprecatory way.

"I got a young lady who comes in an' does," he said simply.

"Does what?"

Evans shrugged.

"Does for me. I got no time nowadays to go messin' about makin' beds and fryin' sausages."

The Miller turned the straw between his teeth.

"Attractive?" he asked.

Evans' shoulders went up and down.

"I scarcely notice the girl," he said indifferently. "Her name's Mrs. Lube—"

"Eh?" The Miller's eyes opened. "Not your hated rival—and you let her come here?"

"She don't have any truck with Old Sam," said Evans, avoiding the visitor's eye. "As dear old B— Mary said to Cardinal Rishloo, the famous French poet, when she had her uncle chopped in four pieces for encouragin' Lady Jane Graves, 'Relations are best apart.'"

The Miller nodded slowly.

"I think you're mad!" he said.

"I'm quite 'in sansitas,' to use a foreign expression," said Mr. Evans calmly. "As a matter of fact she ain't any relation at all. But her name's Mrs. Lube and she's partially a widder—her husband havin' run away with another lady. I pay her two ten a week an' she's worth it."

News travels fast in Camden Town. Mr. Alf Lube, supporting the bar of the "Grey Squirrel," heard a whisper.

"Here, what's that?" he demanded.

"He's goin' about with Mrs. Lube—that's all I know. He was down at Kempton—or was it Plumpton?—with her. Harry Gribble, the bookmaker, said Evans introduced her in a gentlemanly way an' she took seventy-five shillin's to five Cats Eyes an' drew."

Alf went purple.

"That's a lie!" he said. "And for tuppence I'd give you a punch on the nose."

His informant laid two pennies on the counter and uttered truculent words. Apparently Alf neither saw nor heard. He dashed back to the headquarters of Old Sam's Midnight Special.

"Here!" he demanded wrathfully. "What's all this about you an' Evans? Here's me workin' me brains out tryin' to think winners an' you gallivantin'. . ."

After he had picked himself up and Mrs. Lube had thrown the broken chair into the scullery—she always used a chair as a weapon in her more distraught moments,

"I'll go an' see Evans," she said, and went in search of the bag in which she did her shopping. In was the only bag she had in which she could carry a poker.

Mr. Evans was not in when she bounced into his room. There was in his place a neat little woman in a print dress.

"Where's that. . .?" Mrs. Lube described the educated man vividly.

"Moderate your language," said the calm guardian of Evans' home. "I'm a respectable woman an' not used to common talk. What's more, I don't want to lose me temper and slosh you one."

Mrs. Lube gasped as an idea flashed on her. "What name do you call yourself?" she demanded.

"Lube," said Mrs. Lube II. "I call myself that because it was me husband's."

Mrs. Lube I. stood petrified.

"Your real name. . . no relation to me?"

"Gawd forbid!" said Mrs. Lube II.

Mrs. Lube staggered down the stairs a broken woman. Half a dozen people saw her leave. Half a dozen broadcasters spread the tidings. So it *was* true. . . .

People who scarcely knew Alf Lube came up to him and gripped his hand sympathetically. Perfect strangers offered him beer, and women came to their front doors to see him pass, shake their heads sorrowfully and say "Poor feller!"

As to Emma (which was one of her Christian names, the other being Amelia), she explained the matter to her husband.

"Another woman called Mrs. Lube, eh?" he said, with cold politeness. "Oh, yes, I dessay. . . ."

"Go an' see for yourself," hissed his partner. Alf Lube said nothing, but looked murderous.

Detective-Inspector Challoner thought it necessary to warn his friend.

"Personally," he said, "I have no very strong feelings in the matter. We haven't had a good murder in Camden Town for years, and I should know who did it, because I happen to have heard that Alf Lube was trying to buy a German revolver that Joe Carter brought back from the war."

Educated Evans turned pale.

"Is it my fault," he demanded, "that people talk about me an' her? Ain't they been talkin' about me for munce and munce, a scandalisin' an' deprecatin' me? As the well-known an' celebrated Cleopatra, her that hid Moses in the bulrushes, said: 'You can't do nothin' if you can't prove nothin'.'"

"We shall see," said The Miller ominously.

He left Mr. Evans very thoughtful, though not for long. Mrs. Lube II. was a cheery soul, a lady of thirty-five; rather, as The Miller had supposed, attractive. She dressed neatly and took an intelligent interest in racing, so that Evans was more or less justified in adding to his circulars:

"Address all communications and other postal orders to E. Evans, Orbindos Manse, or to my private secretary, Mrs. Lube."

He had arranged to take his lady friend to Sandown. If the truth be told, Mr. Evans did not find his deception a very irksome one. Mrs. Lube II. was a presentable lady, who agreed with almost everything he said.

On the way to Sandown he explained to her the new move.

"You be my secretary, Mrs. L.," he said. "I'll give you another ten shillin's a week for that."

She brightened at the prospect; and there was room for improvement, for all that morning she had been glum and depressed—in fact, Mr. Evans had the suspicion, when she arrived at the Manse, that she had been crying. She had had some bad news, she told him when he questioned her, but she made no attempt to inform him of its character.

"Naturally"—Mr. Evans pursued the topic as the train sped to Esher—"you haven't got my education. I don't suppose you ever will. Take the two seasons, flat an' jumpin'—they're caused by the world going round on its axle or orbit. The farther you get away from the sun the colder it gets, which is natural, hence the National Hunt Committee an' the so-called sport of gentlemen. Take chemistry, botomy and syntax. Take mathematics or decimals. Take algebra, invented by the far-famed Euclid. Take hist'ry. . . ."

Fortunately the train had reached Esher station before Mrs. L. could take anything more than a passing interest in the scenery.

Mr. Evans had come down laden with information, but his star was not in the ascendant. There is no doubt that Guggs should have won the first race if he had been trying. But he wasn't trying.

"He ought to have won ten minutes," said Mr. Evans hotly. "I had him from a friend of mine whose wife's sister is keeping company—"

Only then was he dimly aware of the presence of Mr. Alf Lube. The man was watching him evilly. When Evans walked into the paddock Mr. Lube followed, muttering incoherently.

"You're looking pale, Mr. Evans," said Mrs. L.

Evans smiled a sickly smile.

"I just remembered a client I didn't send Guggs to. We'll keep him anyway!"

His unbeatable selection in the second race should have won pulling up, instead of which he was pulled up before he won.

"Tut, tut!" said Evans impatiently, as he glared through his glasses at the offending horse. "There's a bit of dirty work there."

He feared dirty work elsewhere; kept an apprehensive eye over his shoulder for Mr. Alfred Lube. Never once did he miss his shadow. As Evans was standing by the ring marking his card, a hateful voice spoke at his elbow.

"You'll go on till you go off!" grated Mr. All Lube.

"I don't want any talk with you, my friend," said Mr. Evans loudly.

Mr. Lube laughed harshly. Later, Evans saw him in the bar, drinking whisky feverishly, and suggested to his companion that they should go home by the next train. But the fire of racing was in her and on her disappearance into the ring to battle with bookmakers, Evans thought it was an excellent opportunity to explain the situation to the disgruntled husband of Mrs. Lube I.

He saw him emerge from the bar, met his murderous scowl with a smile, and was about to approach him when his arm was caught in a firm grip and he was swung round.

The man who confronted him was six feet in height and terribly broad. He had a strong, brutal face and light blue eyes that glinted murder.

"Here," said the stranger. "I see you talkin' to a lady just now—Mrs. Lube."

Evans opened his mouth but no sound came.

"She's my wife," said the giant fiercely. "I admit I done wrong, but a lovin' wife ought to take her husband back. When I see her this mornin' she wouldn't—someone's come between us. What is she to you?"

Mr. Evans' mouth was dry, as the stranger urgently rocked him to and fro, and then inspiration came.

"Excuse me," said Evans, with what dignity he could summon. "I know nothing about the lady in question—she's a mere friend or client. I'm Educated Evans, the far-famed Turf Prophet. If you're Mr. Lube then I have been mistaken an' I apologise. That's the gent. who calls himself Mr. Lube." He pointed at the glowering Alf.

Mr. Lube II. released his grip.

"Who—him? . . . Calls himself Mr. Lube. . . ."

Evans waited till the battle joined and sped blithely to the pass out gate. He did not even turn his head to see the result of the contest, but it was a satisfaction to him to see the motor ambulance speeding round the course towards Tattersall's.

5.—MR. EVANS PULLS OFF A REAL COOP

The Miller regarded his unfortunate friend with a stern but pitying eye.

"A tipster is a rogue until he starts backing his own wayward fancies," he said, "and then he qualifies for admission to the mug class."

Evans shifted uneasily under the other's gaze.

"It was give me by the boy that does him," he pleaded. "This here horse was tried twenty-one pound and a beatin' better than Coronach. He could have fell down, got up an' *then* won. If he'd been trying—"

"It wasn't the jockey, it was the judge," said The Miller gently. "If *he'd* been trying hard he might have seen your unbeatable gem.

But he's only human, Evans—he couldn't see so far down the course. Evans, I think you had better stick to motors."

Mr. Evans ignored this insulting reference to a certain licence he held, sighed, and then, with a start of alarm, saw The Miller take from his pocket a hateful green paper.

"What them Lubeses say don't mean nothing to me," he said loudly. "Mrs. Lube is no better than a lady ought to be. Old Sam's Midnight Special!" he sneered. "It ought to be called 'The Lodger's Moonlight Sonata.' She's worse than the far-famed Kate Webster that cut up her mother an' put her in a biscuit box. She's as two-faced as the well-known weathercock on St. Pancases Church. That woman would take away a man's character an' never think twice about it. She's—"

"Leave the poor woman alone: listen and weep," said The Miller as he read:

<blockquote>
Who sent three horses for one race?
EVANS!
Did they win?
NO!
Was they placed?
NO!
Is that education?
YES!
</blockquote>

Stick to Old Sam, who only sends one winner and that wins.

"That's what I call vulgar," said Evans hotly. "I wouldn't have that woman's disposition for ten million pounds. Education! Ain't I the only man that could ever ask Datas a question that could never be answered? Didn't I stand up for two hours and twenty-five minutes in Hyde Park one Sunday night and argue about drink till a policeman come an' moved me away? I don't mind Old Sam: he's not right in his head; but this here Mrs. Lube, I'm going to bring an action in the High Court an' I'm consultin' me solicitor this mornin'. I wouldn't be surprised if she didn't get ten years."

Yet, for all Mr. Evans' righteous indignation, there can be no question whatever that he had fallen into grievous error over the Stanborough Handicap. For, having sent out overnight Waxy, he had received information by the first post which induced him to change his selection to Fairy Feet, and at the eleventh hour, as the result of an urgent communication which had come to him from the sister of a girl who had got into serious trouble with a head lad, he wired all his important clients that Funny Harry was walking over for that same race. And, as The Miller rightly and properly said, not one of those horses had finished in the first three, or, for the matter of that, in the first five.

Now a man may make mistakes and be forgiven. It was not the first time that Mr. Evans had had the misfortune to tip more horses than one in a race; but on all these occasions Camden Town had forgiven him and offered him one more chance. But whether it was due to the wide publicity which the Lubeses gave to his unfortunate mistake, or whether for some more esoteric reason, Educated Evans encountered a stone wall of hostility, and within three days of his *faux pas*, his clientele had been reduced to three persons, one of whom suffered chronically from delirium tremens. The other two never paid, so they didn't count.

Evans for once was sensitive to popular disapprobation. He sought vainly to justify himself, made a rapid circuit of his houses of call, was frozen out of three and physically thrown out of the fourth. Misfortunes never come singly; and it was Mr. Evans' misfortune that he had ventured not only his reserve but his very rent money on Funny Harry, and it was a ruined man who pored over the evening newspaper, hoping that some misprint or a chance prick in the programme would act as a revelation from heaven and furnish him with the necessary means of rehabilitation.

Tragic indeed is the lot of him who, falling from a high estate, of which he was the admired darling, discovers himself lying in the mud, a door-mat on which the unworthy feet of sometime clients might be wiped, a gibe for Lubeses of both sexes.

Mr. Evans felt his position acutely during those seven tragic days which followed.

If he could only have persuaded one of the old reliables to come back and act honourable, he might have mounted again to his former eminence but with a unanimity which was terrifying, Camden Town refused to recognise the genius and integrity of him who had once been its pride.

He buttonholed Mr. Hackitt, the eminent fishmonger and poulterer.

"I've got a horse in the Lingfield Plate——" he began.

"Keep it there," said Mr. Hackitt roughly, disengaging himself. "He'll feel lonely without his two pals, won't he? You usually send three, don't you, Evans?"

"All I want to say to you, Mr. Hackitt," pleaded Evans; but long before he could frame his justification and apology, Mr. Hackitt had disappeared into the fish mortuary which he called a shop.

He tried with the landlord of the "White Hart" over a friendly whisky and soda which he could ill afford, and at that hour in the morning could hardly digest.

"I got one for the Lingfield Plate, Mr. Long," he said confidentially. "It was sent me in a curious way."

"I dessay," said Mr. Long, wiping the zinc-topped counter mechanically. "And I expect you'll send it out in a curious way, but I'm not going to back it in any way. A man who sends one horse I can stand, but a man who sends three—and I got 'em all—is, a man I never want to see in my house."

By the end of the day all Camden Town knew that Mr. Evans had something unbeatable, something remarkable, something that could fall down, get up and then win the Lingfield Plate. Men told each other this fact with a quiet, sneering smile. It is true there were one or two weaklings who were almost inclined to subscribe, but the scorn and contempt of their fellows made them change their minds.

In perfect justice to these hard-shelled gentlemen, it must be confessed that Mr. Evans had no unbeatable selection for the Lingfield Plate; he had hardly looked at the entries. Yet, in a mysterious way, his fate was bound up with three young men who were very greatly interested in a horse entered for that affair, and by the queer workings of Providence he was brought in touch with them.

It was evening and rather sultry. A heavy shower had fallen on Camden Town, making the roads greasy. He was walking along Hampstead Road when he saw a big car coming at a little above regulation speed in the direction of the West End. It tried to pass a taxi, skidded on the tram-lines, did a graceful *chassé* towards the pavement, hit a lamp-post, and in some miraculous fashion came to a stop by the kerb without having sustained any greater damage than a smashed mudguard.

Before the crowd gathered, Evans went up to the window, and the first thing he realised was that the young gentleman in evening dress who was sitting at the steering wheel was slightly the better for drink. He was very cheerful, very talkative, and in fact was screaming with laughter, as at a great joke, when Evans approached. His companions were a little better, or a little worse, according to the view you take of intemperance.

Now, if Evans had never driven a car, he had driven one of those motor-lorries which Mr. Ford, a well-known American, had introduced to our long-suffering country; and in his pride and skill he had acquired for himself a driver's licence. He saw at some distance an approaching policeman; and whatever you might say about Mr. Evans, you must admit that his mind worked quickly.

He opened the door of the saloon and stepped in uninvited.

"Hi, outside you, old fellow!" said the driver. "You're right!" hissed Evans. "And if that flattie comes up you'll be pinched."

The driver was not so unsober that he did not recognise the truth of this unknown intruder's prediction. In an instant he made way, and by the time the policeman came up, groping in the region of his pants for a pocket- book, Mr. Evans was sitting nonchalantly at the wheel.

Happily for him, he was not recognised by this young constable, and after taking the number of the car, examining Evans' licence, which he had with him, carefully examining the lamp-post, the car proceeded.

"Where are you going?" asked Evans, starting the car with a grind of gears that set the occupants' teeth on edge, and certainly did much to sober them.

"We're going to St. Jamesh Street," said the young man, who was now thoroughly alert.

"And I'm dashed obliged to you," he said, after the exchange had been made. "Come along and have a drink."

In the palatial flat of Sir Henry Llewellyn Creen (for this proved to be the name of the driver) Mr. Evans explained his vocation. He did not notice the three men look at one another significantly, and if he had he would have thought nothing more than that they were impressed by this chance meeting of one whose name was famous throughout the north-west district of London.

In the course of time he was dismissed, with a £5 note which he twice refused, until he was quite sure they weren't trying to take a rise out of him. The three young gentleman sat round a table and discussed the great event of the morrow.

They were all fairly well off, and one of them owned a certain horse, Dictonite, a maiden four-year-old that had run six times as a two and had never been placed, had not run at all as a three, but as a four-year-old had been got ready for the Lingfield High-Weight Plate. It had not only been got ready, but every substantial bookmaker in the United Kingdom had also shared in the process.

There was in course of preparation amongst these young bloods the colossal coup of the year. The race was to be run at 2.20, and at

2.15 1,270 telegrams were to be handed in at fifty post offices in various parts of England. They had borrowed names and they themselves had opened accounts wherever accounts could be opened; and their secret had been so jealously guarded that nobody, with the exception of their trainer and their trainer's head lad, was aware that Dictonite was "walking" the Lingfield Plate.

They did not need the money, but they wanted the rag, and the organisation of the coup had occupied three months which otherwise would have been spent in evading boredom.

They talked of Dictonite over a bottle, and then they talked of Evans over another bottle; at the third bottle they got back to Dictonite. And then the young baronet, who was the head of this lively gang, rose unsteadily to his feet.

"Boys," he said thickly, "we'll do this bird Evans a turn! Le's go roun' and see him and tell him to send out Dictonite to all his pals."

And they were in that state of mind that none of them recognised that the carefully laid plans of three months were on the point of going assy-tassy.

It was late at night when they clambered into a taxi-cab, and a quarter of an hour later, after considerable search, Evans' flat was located, and they were thundering on the door.

Mr. Evans rose hastily and admitted his visitors.

"'Slike this, ole feller," said Sir Henry gravely. "You're a goo' chap, we're goo' chaps. You're a tipshter, we're tipshters. You shend out Dictonite tomorrow morning... money for nothin', old thing... got many clients?"

"Fourteen thousand seven hundred and fifty-one," said Evans wearily.

"You shend Dictonite, old cock. . . ."

"You'd better go home," said Evans, whose first thought when he had seen them was that they had called for the return of his £5 note.

"You shend Dictonite," said Sir Henry Llewellyn Creen again, and with this piece of profound advice they took their leave, each having in his bosom the glow which comes to drunken men who have done somebody a good turn at their own expense.

But the morning brought recollection, repentance and something like dismay. The elder of the three dashed into Sir Henry's room and woke him.

"I say, we were awfully pickled last night, but did we go round to that damned tipster and tell him about Dictonite, or did I dream it?"

The youthful baronet rose and rubbed his hair.

"We did, by gad!" he said. "Wake up, Winkie, we'll have to have a council of war."

Winkie, the youngest of the three, was dragged from his bed, brought to consciousness with a cold-water sponge thrust into his face, and pushed into a chair at the council board.

"There's only one thing to be done," said the penitent leader. "What can we do? What lunatics we were!"

"I'll tell you," said his second-in-command. "Let's send this bird a wire asking him to keep his mouth shut and not to send the horse, and we'll give him the odds to a pony."

The wire was sent over the telephone, and three gloomy young conspirators went to their baths and bathed and dressed.

"If this feller sends the tip, it'll cost us about twenty thousand quid," said Sir Henry Llewellyn Creen, over his meagre breakfast. "Let's go and see him."

They went in a body to Bayham Mews, but no response came to their knocking. A taxi-driver, about to venture forth with his machine, volunteered the information that Evans had left early. "I see him comin' down the stairs as the telegraph boy arrived—"

"Did he get the telegram?" asked Sir Henry eagerly. "Thank heaven for that!"

They drove to Lingfield with a lighter heart.

Mr. Evans had received the telegram. If the truth be told, he had left early in order to avoid an interview with his rapacious landlord, to whom he owed four weeks' rent. He had met the telegraph boy, had taken the telegram from him and thrust it into his pocket. It was his practice to receive, three mornings a week, a wire from his correspondent at Lambourn: but as the last four wires he had had from that quarter demanded payment for past work, he had got into the habit of leaving such messages unopened.

He had a yesterday's railway ticket for Lingfield which he had scrounged from a disgruntled backer who had succeeded in evading the collector, and, after chewing off the date, he made his way to Victoria and eventually reached the course. Only very few intimates know how Mr. Evans succeeded in reaching Tattersall's. He had three methods, and none of them had ever failed.

He was leaning disconsolately over the rails, watching the horses go down to the post, when he heard The Miller's voice.

"Had a bet, Evans?" asked Inspector Arbuthnot Challoner.

Evans smiled wanly.

"I got a horse in this race that couldn't lose," he said. "Pinpoint— help yourself. You couldn't put me off it. Three young swells came round to my flat last night and tried to stuff me with a horse called Dictonite—"

"Dictonite?"

The Miller looked at his card, then consulted his book of form, then shook his head.

"Not a earthly. That horse couldn't win a race—"

He stopped here. The field had started on its homeward journey. He had not even troubled to examine the colours of Dictonite, so that when the brown and purple jacket went past the post two lengths ahead of its fellows, he was under the impression that it was something of Jack Jarvis's .

"This horse Dictonite—" he began.

"It won," said The Miller.

"Did it?" said Evans, aghast. "Bless my heart an' soul. An' to think I had that horse give me by the owner. Tut-tut! When your luck's out you can do nothin' right. Now I've got one for the next race, Mr. Miller—"

But The Miller didn't wait to hear.

Evans strolled disconsolately into the paddock. He heard, with a shudder, that Dictonite had started at 100-6.

"What a nearly beauty!" he moaned.

And then he saw approaching him the young man whom he had displaced at the wheel on the previous night. The young gentleman beckoned him aside and Evans went.

"Did you send this horse out?"

It was on the tip of Evans' tongue to enumerate the number of clients to whom this gem had been sent, but second thoughts were best.

"To tell you the truth, sir, I didn't," he said. "I gathered you didn't, from the price," said Sir Henry cheerfully.

He dived his hand into his pocket, produced a wad of notes and thrust them into the palsied hand of the World's Champion.

"Here the odds to a pony each way, as I promised you in my wire. Good fellow!"

He patted Evans paternally on the back. Evans held on to the railings with one hand and to the banknotes with the other. It was not until the numbers went up for the last race that he was sufficiently recovered to make his way to the railway station.

And that night all Camden Town knew that, though they had rejected the priceless information which Mr. Evans had been prepared to give them, he himself had packed up a parcel. For did he not stand at the bar of the "White Hart" that night and insolently demand of the landlord that he should change a £50 note, and threaten him with the loss of his licence unless he did so?

6.—The Nice Minded Girl

There is no doubt at all that Mr. Nobbs, the celebrated trainer, was hot, and less doubt that Mr. Snazzivitz, his chief and principal patron, was even hotter. Mr. Snazzivitz was so hot that when he went for an insurance on his new cabinet works at Bethnal Green, the insurance manager sent for the police.

They were both hot and patient, and that made them even warmer. Mr. Nobbs was quite content to run a horse down the course one day a week for the whole of the season, and pop him up at Warwick at 100-7 in the last week; the identical animal having finished tailed off last time out. And he felt no shame when he read in the morning newspapers that his horse had made every yard of the running and had been well backed.

There were many people who thought Mr. Nobbs would be better off in another world, and bitter statements were made about the purblindness of stewards; but Mr. Nobbs was never warned off, for he had an explanation up one sleeve and an alibi up the other, and the only time he was ever called before the local stewards, he told such a pathetic and plausible story that there was some talk of raising a subscription for him, though it came to nothing.

It was the privilege of Educated Evans, the World's Premier Prophet and Turf Adviser, to know the barber who shaved Mr. Snazzivitz whenever he was in town. And whenever one of Mr. Snazzivitz's horses was on the job, the fact was whispered into the barber's shell-like ear for his own information and guidance, repeated to Educated Evans, and by him circulated the wide world over. So it might be said that the confidence of Mr. Snazzivitz was only partially respected.

One afternoon Mr. Snazzivitz met his trainer, the eminent Mr. Nobbs, at lunch, and Mr. Nobbs was both querulous and accusative.

"We ought to have got twenty to one about that horse yesterday, Snazzivitz," he said. "I didn't have a penny on him on the course; I told nobody, and even the stable lads didn't know he was going to run; and yet money started rolling in for him ten minutes before the off. Five to two is no good for me—"

"It doesn't fill me with the wildest enthusiasm, my dear," said Mr. Snazzivitz, who didn't talk quite as good English as I have made him talk. "It must be that so-and-so barber of mine. I only heard this morning that he's a dead pal of that so-and-so-Evans, the Camden Town tipster."

"Change your barber," suggested Mr. Nobbs.

"I know a better way than that," said Mr. Snazzivitz, an unholy smile on a large and cherubic face that was sprinkled with large and prominent features.

"They've spoilt one of the best coups we have ever had, and I'm not going to let 'em down as lightly as that. I'm the sort of man, Nobbs," he went on, "that never forgets a friend or forgives an enemy. I'd work my fingers to the bone to help them that help me, and to destroy them that did me down. That's the kind of man I am!"

Mr. Nobbs knew the kind of man he was without being told. He was the kind of man who, if you sent him in the ring to back a horse for you, returned you the starting price and pouched the difference for Mr. Snazzivitz was so rich that he couldn't afford to be honest.

Educated Evans occasionally employed female labour. He had not been very fortunate in his selections, it is true, but such was his faith in human nature, and so high was his regard for the female of the species that he never entirely lost hope. So there came to be installed at Forseti House the beauteous Miss Marie Rose, who was fair and slim and had wonderful blue eyes and arched black eyebrows—all of which were attached to a body of singular attraction, so far as could be seen; and as she dressed in the mode of the day, quite a lot was visible.

She was the niece of Mr. Rose, the cheese-monger, who was a great admirer of Educated Evans, and dreamed dreams of giving over the sordid cheese and butter business and embarking upon the romantic adventure of an s.p. book. And since she was likely to be the only person he would trust, he was desirous that she should become acquainted with the peculiar technology of the racing world. And he had another reason for getting her out of the house.

"I trust her with you, Evans," he said, "and I wouldn't trust her with anybody else. She's a nice-minded girl, high-spirited and all that sort of thing, and she was brought up in a convent."

"With the monks," nodded Evans.

"I don't know nothing about monks," said the cheese man. "But

270

she knows practically nothing of the world, and I want you to stand between her and, so to speak, temptation. I know you're all right, because no girl would look twice at you without laughing: you've got such a good-natured face," he added, and the ruffled Evans was hardly appeased.

He was enunciating his philosophy one morning, what time she folded with nimble fingers the announcements which were to gladden the hearts of all clients new and old.

"I dare say, Miss Rose," said Evans, "that I sort of puzzle you at times. Not that you ain't well educated, but you haven't got my experience and savvy fair, to use a foreign expression. I dare say sometimes you don't follow my reason and logic, but you'll get used to me in time, Miss Rose. I'm like the well-known William the Silent, the highly-celebrated Emperor of Germany; I don't talk unless I have to."

"Education is a wonderful thing," sighed the young lady. "I often wish I'd gone on to the sixth standard."

"It is wonderful and it's not," admitted Evans modestly. "You get a bit fed up with people pointing you out in the street and saying 'That's him!' But you've got to put up with that. The way they come to me to settle bets is getting a public nuisance. Do you know the date of the Great Fire of London?" he asked, closing his eyes and raising his eyebrows.

She shook her head.

"No, I'm only twenty-one," she said. "I don't quite remember; it must have happened when I was a baby."

"1643," said Evans rapidly, "during the reign of the great Queen Anne, known as the virgin queen because of her friendship for the great Duke of Marlborough, the ancestor of Winston Churchill, the highly celebrated naval man. The last time the Thames was froze over was in 1472, the year we defeated the Germans at the Battle of Trafalgar Square—see Lord Nelson."

"I wish I knew as much as you," said Marie Rose wistfully.

"You can't," said Evans. "It's not given to everybody. It's a gift, the same as a voice for singing purposes. All my work is brain work. I've got to carry things in me head that'd drive you silly! When did Eclipse win the Derby?"

"Last week?" she hazarded, having only a vague knowledge of the sport of kings.

"In 1872," said Evans with even greater rapidity. "It was run during a snowstorm, and Jack Jarvis, the celebrated trainer, put a ball of butter in the horse's hoofs so that he'd slide round Tottenham Corner. Eclipse was the half-brother to Bayardo, from which the mighty Bart Snowball is descended. See Stud Book!"

His further lesson in ancient history was interrupted by a tap at the door. Evans himself opened it and saw a resplendent gentleman smoking a large cigar and wearing what appeared to be the entire contents of Sam Isaacs' jewellery store.

"Name of Evans?" he asked.

"Yes, I am Mr. Evans," admitted the educational authority.

The newcomer swept the room with a glance in which contempt, amusement, resentment and disgust were unskilfully blended.

"I'd like to have a word with you when you're alone," he said.

Evans looked at the young lady, raised his eyebrows with great significance—he had very flexible eyebrows—and she took a hasty departure.

"Now, Mr. Evans." Mr. Snazzivitz sat down uninvited on the only comfortable chair in the room. "You've probably heard of me. My name is Isidore Snazzivitz."

"The celebrated owner?" asked Evans, interested. "Who trains with the well-known Mr. Nobbs on the far-famed Berkshire Downs?"

"That's me," said Mr. Snazzivitz. "You've been sending out a horse of mine. I'd like to know where you got your information."

Evans knit his brow.

"I send out so many horses," he said. "Perhaps, if you'll kindly name the animal—" He paused inquiringly.

"Bluebottle," said Mr. Snazzivitz, and a look of intelligence came to Mr. Evans' already intelligent face.

"Bluebottle? I seem to remember the name... yes, yes, I sent it out on my five-pound special. I had it from one of my touts."

"You had it from my barber—that's who you had it from," said Mr. Snazzivitz unpleasantly. And then, remembering his mission, he forced a smile to his face. "Now look here, Evans, you're not a bad fellow; I've heard a lot about you; and if you ever want a tip, come straight to me. Don't go messing about with my barber. I'll tell you anything I know and anything that's going. Here's my address"—he produced a large card with a floral decoration in the corner—"I only live five minutes' walk away," he said. "Never hesitate to come and see me, and maybe I'll put you on to one or two good things. You're interfering with my business, Evans, and that's a fact. What chance have I of getting a job home when you're circulating it round Camden Town? You see what I mean?"

Evans saw what he meant. Such condescension from a real owner was most overpowering. He could only bow.

"That's a very nice girl you've got. Where did you get her?"

"She's a friend of mine," said Evans, with a certain amount of dignity. "I never give away the names of the staff."

Now Mr. Snazzivitz had come with no other idea than to take a firm grip of a possible cause of annoyance, for he had many horses due to win, and, so to speak, his winter's keep was looming ahead. And it was vitally necessary that no so-and-so tipster should send his so-and-so horses (as he himself tersely described the situation) and spoil his something-or-other market. Which was a feeling very right and natural, and held in common with other speculative owners, trainers, jockeys and jockeys' valets. But he was a susceptible man, and the sight of those blue eyes and that rose-and-milk complexion, that svelte form and other appendages peculiar to radiant femininity, shifted, so to speak, his angle of vision.

The next morning he called again. Evans saw him coming down the mews and uttered a few words of warning and admonition to his assistant.

"You want to be careful about that man," he said. "I'm so to speak responsible for you to your uncle. Ever heard about the gipsy's warning? I'll get you a copy this afternoon. If he asks you to go and have a bit of dinner with him, just be 'aughty—like that!" Evans gave an imitation of a haughty young lady of twenty-one, a piece of acting that must have made Mrs. Phelps turn in her grave.

"I wouldn't dream of going," said the girl. "Who is he?"

"His name is Snazzivitz," said Evans rapidly, for the man was coming up the stairs. "He's a horse-owner and a rooey."

"What's that?" she asked, in open-eyed wonder.

"A man that don't know when to stop," said Evans.

"What does he do for a living?" asked the girl.

"Backs horses. But the bookmakers are getting wise," said Evans, "and they're closing his accounts. He used to have about four hundred, but they're shut down now, and he's always on the look-out for mugs to open accounts for him."

"How perfectly dreadful!" said Marie.

It was perfectly true that Mr. Snazzivitz was that kind of man. He was the greatest job merchant of his year, and when he wanted to back a horse he used not only his own accounts, but he had a large list of friends who for a consideration would lend their names and accounts for his purpose. Thus, if you are John Jones and have an account with Macpherson the eminent bookmaker, you could by arrangement lend him a wire addressed to your bookmaker, and at the psychological moment he would back the horse for £5, the odds to £1 being yours, the odds to £4 being his; and if the horse went down, which it never did, he would refund you the £4 you had lost.

"Does he get a lot of money that way?" she asked wistfully.

"Packets," said Evans.

"How wonderful!" breathed the girl. "I mean, how dreadful to take it perhaps from the poor bookmakers and to deprive them as it were of sustenance for their wives and shoes for their little children I wonder he can sleep at nights."

"I don't know that he does," said Evans.

And then Mr. Snazzivitz came in.

"Talking about horses," he said, his eyes on the peerless Marie, "I've had a tip for one that's going at—er—er—er Lingfield on Saturday, a horse called Heah."

He did not take his eyes from the girl. Evans was annoyed. He was annoyed because there was no meeting at Lingfield on Saturday, and because Heah had already won there.

"Good morning," said Mr. Snazzivitz. He was not speaking to Evans.

The girl raised her timid eyes from her work and dropped them again.

"That's a funny job you've got," said Mr. Snazzivitz in his most amiable tone. "We shall have to improve on that, eh, Evans?"

"This is my business," said Evans loudly, "and I'd be obliged if you didn't speak to the clurks."

A look passed between the two. Evans, unused to the artfulness of courtship, saw nothing. Did she scribble "8 o'clock, Cobden Statue" on her blotting-pad? If she did, she scribbled it out again, because he could see nothing but wriggly lines when he examined the pad later. At any rate, Mr. Snazzivitz did not prolong his stay.

He was a youngish man, and people who wanted to be in his good books, or men and women of defective vision, might describe him as handsome. Mr. Evans, returning from a heated argument at the "Bull and Crow" with Lube on the ethics of tipping, had occasion to walk through Mornington Crescent, a somewhat deserted residential thoroughfare; and there he had the shock of his life. A man and a girl were walking in front of him, arm in arm, their heads together, their pace leisurely. Evans gasped.

"Good God!" he breathed.

He had a good mind to go back and challenge Mr. Snazzivitz, reprimand the girl, wave her dramatically in the direction of the cheesemonger's, and send her home. But he did not.

The next morning, when he went to his office, Miss Marie Rose was not there. Instead was a little note in which she said that she found the work was rather heavier than she had expected, and with her uncle's permission she had decided that a woman's place was at home.

"Education's wasted on that girl," said Evans bitterly to The Miller at the first opportunity. "That man's no better than the celebrated Looey the Nineteenth who used to chase nimps through the glades of Fountingblue. I'm going straight to her uncle."

"I shouldn't if I were you," said The Miller. "That young lady can take care of herself."

"She went to a convent—" began Evans.

"She was also chucked out of the convent for teaching the younger students the game of banker," said The Miller.

"But her uncle sent her to me because—"

"Her uncle sent her to you," said The Miller patiently, "because she tossed the errand boy for his salary with a two-headed ha'penny. If you can teach her anything, you might send the subject along to me, will you? That girl will do anything for money except work."

Yet she was a good girl, as she told the discomfited Mr. Snazzivitz, when he offered her almost everything in the world, except a marriage certificate, to share his life and fortune.

"I will do almost anything for you, Ronald," she said, with sweet childish impetuosity, "and haven't I already opened twenty-five accounts for you in dear uncle's name? At least, on dear uncle's noteheading? And there'll be another thirty by tonight's post. You can't ask me to do more than that."

"I love you—" began Mr. Snazzivitz.

"I know, and I love you dreadfully," said the girl, shaking her head, a tear trembling on her eyelids. "But we must be sensible, mustn't we? I don't even mind being married at a registrar's office; you can always get the photographers there, and I make an awfully good photograph. But this idea of a Bloomsbury flat is so dreadfully vulgar and shocking that I cannot let myself think about it."

275

Mr. Snazzivitz was content to wait. They dined that night at the Laurence in Wardour Street, and they supped that night at the Boolum Club, and they lunched next day at the Empress Club, and went to a *thé dansant* at the Regent Palace, and dined at the Worlingham—in fact they were quite a lot together. And all the time one of Mr. Nobbs' charges, a noble animal called "Button Boots," was nearing perfection.

On the night before the Hurst Park meeting Mr. Nobbs came to town and saw Mr. Snazzivitz.

"This horse," he said, "could pull a 'bus and win. You haven't been to that so-and-so barber of yours, have you?"

"I'll so-and-so watch it!" said Mr. Snazzivitz luridly.

"Then we ought to get 100 to 7 for our money. Have you opened any new accounts?"

Mr. Snazzivitz nodded.

"A friend of mine has opened sixty," he said complacently...

The next morning The Miller met Mr. Evans and made a suggestion.

"Button Boots?" said Evans dubiously. "He hasn't been placed all the year, and he's been running in selling plates. You don't expect him to win a good-class race?"

"There's a whisper round the town."

Evans smiled sourly.

"That Snazzivitz couldn't win a race," he said definitely. "He won't have no luck for the rest of the year. He's a kidnapper, a snake in the grass and a rooey! I'd like to do him a bad turn, but—"

When The Miller had gone, Evans sat down to consider the matter. He had no very definite views on the race. Why not send out Button Boots, if only to annoy the man for whom he had conceived such a deadly hatred? To think, with Evans, was to act. To all clients new and old the message went forth.

SIR,—Have a good win on
BUTTON BOOTS.
This horse has been tried to be 21 lbs. in front of the highly celebrated Pickaboon. Help yourself, and don't forget your old friend Educated Evans.

And Button Boots won—at a modest price, it is true. For there was an illusion in Camden Town that Evans knew all about Nobbs' horses, and his fame as an informant in the matter of these animals had spread to the very end of the world, which is somewhere beyond Croydon. He was reckoning the possible revenues from his success when the door was flung violently open and the innocent girl came in. Her eyes were blazing, her cheeks were white.

"Did you send out Button Boots?" she hissed. "Yes, Miss Marie," said Evans, rising with politeness. He was always a gentleman.

"Then what in hell do you mean by spoiling my market?" she howled at him.

She left Evans staggering and dazed. As she turned out of the mews she was met by Mr. Snazzivitz.

"Oh, here you are!" he said, relieved. "You got those wires away? It was a rotten price—I don't know why—but so far as I can make out, you'll be sending me a thousand pounds on Monday—"

"A thousand buck-rabbits!" said the blue-eyed child with startling malignity. "It ought to have been three thousand if that pie-faced mutt had closed his big mouth! And listen, Mr. Snazzivitz, I'm English, and my motto is '*What I've got I hold.*' If you ever get any money from me, book the address—I'll be writing from a high-class lunatic asylum!"

7.—THE MUSICAL TIP

It is a curious fact, that must have impressed itself upon the observant, that people who move in an environment of splendour seldom realise their own good fortune.

For example: there are men and women who live at those earthly paradises, Blackpool and Southend, all the year round and are unconscious of the blessing. There are coarse stage hands who see Gladys Cooper every day of their lives and do not swoon with ecstasy. Similarly, Sir Boski Takerlit knew and entertained some of the wisest trainers that were ever licensed by the Jockey Club, and yet profited not by so much as a penny from the priceless information which came his way.

"Rubbish and nonsense!" he used to say of racing. "Dommy rod! Der man dat bags horses is a stubid ass—hein?"

How he came to know these trainers at all is a long story but may be briefly condensed. He was an authority on the musical comedy and operatic world, and when he wanted to put a girl in the chorus in a small part his recommendation was almost a command. And there were many naughty trainers who, quite unknown to their wives, were interested in furthering the stage ambitions of pretty young ladies in whom they took more than a fatherly interest.

Lady Takerlit was not so well known to all who go racing as, say, Old Kate. In fact, for certain reasons she never went racing at all, because, to her husband, racing was anathema. He was a popular musician and had been knighted. It is a well-known fact that any man who wags a baton before a hired band playing somebody else's music simply can't escape being knighted. Round about New Year's Day the Flying Squad scour London to find a bandmaster who isn't a Sir, and, clubbing him into insensibility, they tie a Garter round his neck, hit him on the head with a sword and his name henceforth is Sir Mud.

Sir Boski Takerlit was a rich man, having recomposed several popular tunes of the '60's. Her ladyship (as she was often called) was a democrat. That is to say, she was happiest when she was in the company of her intellectual and social inferiors. They were sometimes difficult to find, for this is the truth: Sir Boski, in a moment of temporary insanity or spiritual exaltation (one is sometimes mistaken for the other) married his housemaid. She was pretty and once upon a time had been slight. She was still pretty when, an optimistic circular having come her way, she wrote to Educated Evans.

Dear Sir,—Please send me your 5 pound special. I inclose p.o. for 2s. 6d.
Yours truly,

Lady Takerlit.

She always signed herself "Lady Takerlit." Otherwise, as she said to her husband: "How the hell would they know I was a lady?"

Mr. Evans sent his £5 Special for 2s. 6d. The usual price was 5s., but he never returned money. And the horse he sent was a winner.

She wrote:

Thank you, dear Mr. Evons! I back Marked Marble and as you say, What beauty! Pray pop round one day to tea. The buttler will show you in.
Yours truly,

Lady Takerlit.

She usually referred to her buttler in such letters.

Evans popped round to Micklesfield Square. He was met on the doorstep by Sir Boski Takerlit, who glared at him.

"Who der plazes are you?" asked Sir Boski. "Mr. Evans, of Masked Marvel Mansions," said the educated man; "commonly known as the World's Champion Turf Adviser

"Tibster!" roared Sir Boski. "So id is you that has let my wife as-dray! Gid oudt!"

Evans got oudt.

He did not know that Sir Boski was both jealous and mean. This he learnt later when her ladyship called on him one dark evening.

"I don't really know how I can look you in the face, Mr. Evons," she said. "I don't reely! The way my husband went on to you is simply disgraceful and disgusting."

She looked round the little room; to her it seemed agreeably cosy, for in truth she was rather overawed by the magnificent Victorian surroundings in which she moved.

"Good idea having your office over a stable—I suppose you keep your horses downstairs?" she said.

Evans inclined his head gravely, though in truth the only animal beneath him was Ford Van (by Rattle out of Detroit).

"You've no idea how near he is, Mr. Evons, and him with money to burn and everything. If I didn't make a bit of pin money now and again I don't know where I'd be. But don't send me any more—he opens my letters. I'll pop round and see you, and now and again I'll be able to give you a tip."

"My ladyship," said Evans, with old-world courtesy, "the pleasure will be yours."

He kissed her hand. He had seen pictures of people kissing the hand of royalty and he thought it was the right thing to do. Unfortunately, at that second the door was opened and Bogey Jones appeared. He had come to borrow the *Sporting Chronicle*. It was an embarrassing moment, but Evans, quick-witted, thought of an expedient to get rid of the visitor: he had reason to regret his intelligence.

★★★★★★

"Them that acts honourable *is* honourable!" said Educated Evans emphatically. "An' them that *don't* act honourable would pinch the nails out of a orphan's boots an' sell 'em to blind men for cloves!'"

"Which, reduced to the language of Camden Town, means that you've been had," said The Miller unsympathetically. He was chewing a straw that he had abstracted from a truss at Morley's, the Corn and Flour Merchants. "Anyway you're a Can—nobody but a Can would trust Bogey Jones."

"I don't know what you mean by Can, Mr. Challoner," said Evans with dignity. "I've never got hold of the low talk that abounds or percerlates through Camden Town. Bogey is a tea-leaf: we all know that, but tea- leafs act honourable in their sportin' transactions—see Palmer, the well-known Rugby doctor who poisoned his bookmaker rather than knock him."

"Rugeley," murmured The Miller.

"Wherever it was. Bogey Jones is a Twister. If he ever gets married he'll have a family of corkscrews."

"Perhaps he'll return the money," suggested The Miller.

Mr. Evans made a noise like a meditative duck.

"As the well-known W. Shakespeare said to Lord What's-his-name—him that got his napper cut off for takin' a liberty with Queen Elizabeth, the so-called Vergers Queen because she used to go to church so often—"

He paused, having missed the path. "Shakespeare," prompted The Miller.

". . . As he said one day when him an' David Garrick the well-known artist who painted Lady Godiva, The Woman They Couldn't Shingle, her that did the bare-back ride down Coventry Street to advertise the Back Ache pills—"

He reached a cross road.

"Shakespeare," murmured The Miller.

"As Shakespeare said—you can't expect nothin' from a pig but a grunt."

Evans took out the stump of a cigar, sneered at it and put it back in his face.

"I'll *get* Bogey," he said.

"In the meantime you've been got," said The Miller gently, "and it is your own fault." Inspector Challoner reproved him. "Imagine a man like you, as wide as Broad Street, giving Bogey a five-pound note and asking him to bring you the change in the morning. It is inexplicable!"

The Miller had a line of classy words of four and five syllables that was the admiration of High Street, Camden Town.

"It may be ines—what you said," retorted Evans hotly, "but the money's gone."

The Miller frowned and eyed him curiously.

"There is something at the back of this act of guileless trust on your part," he said. "A woman!"

Mr. Evans went red and spluttered.

"A woman!"

"A lady!" protested Mr. Evans passionately. "A lady of title an' as pure as a driven snowball! If you want to know—"

"I don't—" The Miller's manner was pointed. "Scandal has never interested me."

Evans looked round as though he expected to discover an army of secret service agents waiting to note his words.

"I gave that fiver to Bogey to Save a Woman's Name."

"And you got no change," said the practical officer. "I don't think that you came off very well."

Evans shrugged his shoulders.

"It was the Price I Paid for Honour," he said mysteriously.

The Miller was thoroughly interested.

"If you'll stop talking like the pictures and get right down to solid earth, I'll give you a round of applause," he said.

But Mr. Evans smiled cryptically.

"Aristocracy," he said simply.

★★★★★★

Evans learned by accident that her ladyship had been ordered by her indignant husband to close her two modest bookmakers' accounts (the accounts were modest, not the bookmakers), and then one night there came to him a mysterious message.

Dear Mr. Evons,—I must tell you somethink of great importance. My husband will be out tonight conducting his orkystra. Expect me about 10.

Yours truly,

Lady Takerlit.

P.S.—Don't let anybody come popping in after I pop in.

At ten o'clock that night a mysterious figure might have been seen flitting into Bayham Mews. It was not seen as a matter of fact, because it was a rainy night and nobody was particularly interested even in mysterious figures. But Evans waited at the top of the stairs. The light was turned low in his room, and he experienced all the agreeable sensations of a conspirator. There was, too, a thrill in it.

Her ladyship mounted the stairs cautiously, as she had become a woman of weight, and panted into Mr. Evans' bureau in an agitated state. Evans closed the door—the curtains were already pulled—and then he turned up the light.

"Oh, Mr. Evons"—she was on the verge of tears—"I feel I've got to speak to a Man about his Goings On! I'll divorce him, Mr. Evons! I won't be trod on like a worm. I've stood it long enough."

"It's a long worm that has no turning," said Evans seriously. "What has his lordship been doing, my ladyship?"

She sat down breathlessly on a chair, and as breathlessly related the story of a letter, discovered by accident, as all such letters are discovered, whilst she was searching his pockets for papers of a greater monetary value.

"I'll divorce him before the Lord Chief Justice his own self!" said her ladyship tremulously. "He's a low, common Hungarian from Austria, and I bemeaned myself by marrying him! I'll get almony out of him, too. This comes of his mixing up with low, common chorus-girls. All musical people are alike, Mr. Evons: they don't know where to stop, and even if they do, they don't."

Evans listened gravely, shook his head, uttered tut-tuts of surprise and horror, and when she had exhausted her denunciations of musical genius, she unburdened her soul on a matter which was much more important.

"I told you I'd give you a tip, Mr. Evons, and I will," she added vehemently. "We had one of them—those, I mean: forgive me being unladylike—trainers up to lunch today, and whether Boski's told 'em or not I don't know, but they never speak about horses in front of me. But I did hear something." She nodded more emphatically than ever. "It's going to win at Newbury. It's the biggest certainty of the year. In fact, Mr. Evons," she said, "this horse can't lose. You never heard of a horse like that?"

Evans had heard of horses like that, and had frequently described them in his optimistic circulars.

"Did you hear the name, my ladyship?" he asked:

She shook her head.

"No, that's where the—where my husband was artful. The only thing I know is this"— she spoke slowly and deliberately—"the horse runs on Wednesday, and the name of the horse is the name of a piece he's playing as an extra on Tuesday night at the Queen's 'All—Hall, I mean; I'm so upset that I don't know even how to speak grammar. That's what Boski said when they whispered it to him."

"It'll be on the programme," said Evans thoughtfully.

She shook her head.

"No, they never put the names of the extras on the programme, but it'll be after the third piece is played. He's bound to get an encore, and then he'll play this other piece. It's operatic —that's all I know."

Evans considered.

"The Merry Widder?" he said.

She didn't think it was the Merry Widder.

"'I'll take you back if you want to come back?'" suggested Evans, going rapidly through his repertory.

"Is there a horse called that?" she asked.

Evans had to admit there wasn't.

"We'll easily find out. Go to the hall the night before, and anybody will tell you what it is. And, Mr. Evons, will you put a ten-pound note on for me?"

She produced the ten-pound note. Evans waved it aside and continued waving until she showed an inclination to replace the money in her bag. He stopped it half-way.

"I'll learn him!" said her ladyship, quivering with annoyance. "The Pretty Beauty!"

In this vague and unsatisfactory way did Educated Evans become possessed of the gem of the year.

She left him in a studious mood. She was going to divorce her husband; and her ladyship had looked kindly upon him. There was an understanding between them...

Evans walked to the wall and looked into the four square inches of cracked mirror. He wasn't bad looking, he confessed; he was on the right side of fifty, and he was a man of fame and education.

The next day he sounded The Miller as to the propriety of marrying a *divorcée*.

"Not that I'm a marrying man," he said, "and as for titles—bah!" He snapped his fingers. "I don't want to marry just for the sake of being Lord Evans...."

The Miller explained gently that marrying a knight's lost lady would not entitle Mr. Evans to a seat in the House of Lords.

"Wouldn't it?" The educated man was obviously disappointed.

"I suppose," said The Miller. "you thought it would look fine on the circulars.

LORD EDUCATED EVANS,
The World's Champion Turf Prophet.
Address all money orders
c/o the Lord Chancellor.

.... But it can't be done."

Evans shrugged.

"I'm a Socialist meself," he said, "practically red. Me an' Sakker—

what's his name—are like brothers."

He did not tell his friend anything about the musical horse. Indeed, he kept his secret locked in his own narrow chest; for secrets have a habit of leaking out, and the Lubeses, who ran Old Sam's Midnight Special, sent forth from day to day crowds of spies and informers to discover and anticipate the substance of his £5 Specials.

Mr. Evans knew nothing about music, except that it was a pleasing noise made by barrel organs. And naturally he was not particularly well versed in operatic selections. He looked up the newspaper, saw that Sir Boski Takerlit was conducting the New Brighton Symphony Orchestra, but the programme told him nothing. He had never heard of a horse called "Three Dances from Henry VIII.," nor did he know of any animal who answered to the name of "Rachmaninoff's Prelude." He settled himself down to prepare for the great coup, got out his circular complete, leaving only a space into which he would insert, by means of a rubber stamp, the name of this unparalleled quadruped.

The Miller met him when, arrayed for the evening, with his pockets stuffed with handbills advertising his virtues as a finder of winners (for, as Mr. Evans argued, you never know what business might be brought in by a few bills dropped judiciously in a public place) and wearing the famous plaid trousers and gold pin, he sallied forth to an evening's entertainment.

"Music?" said The Miller incredulously. "I didn't know you had any tastes in that direction —or are you going to take a peep at the injured husband?"

"I'm going to get a little information," said Evans mysteriously. "And as for music, it's education, ain't it? The well-known and highly respected Mozart who wrote the Moonlight Sonata—"

But The Miller had passed on.

He found the Queen's Hall, a handsome place of entertainment, crowded when he arrived and, with great reluctance, paid for his seat.

"If you *are* Press," said the manager, "I'll admit you, but what paper do you represent?"

"I won't argue," said Evans loftily. "What's the cheapest seat you've got? For two pins I wouldn't go in and report your music at all."

Eventually he found a seat at five shillings on the floor of the house, and made his way in with a look of disparagement on his face. He was fortunate enough to get an aisle seat in a row half-way between back and front, and for an hour he listened uncomprehendingly to a succession of musical acrobatics. Standing on a little platform in front of his orchestra was Sir Boski Takerlit, whom he recognised instantly.

"A bit of swank, ain't it?" he asked his neighbour, an aesthetic young man with horn-rimmed spectacles. "Him standing up there so that everybody can see him?"

The young man was startled and made no reply.

"It's what I call gettin' yourself in the limelight," said Evans, warming up on the subject. "It's pushin' yourself forward."

The young man maintained his silence but edged a little farther away from the companion which the booking-office had thrust upon him.

"It only shows what a dirty dog he is," said Evans. "He don't play nothin', he simply sits up there an' chucks his arms about, and when people clap he starts bowing an' scraping as if he did it all."

"I don't wish to speak with you," said the young man in a very elegant voice.

The applause that greeted the third piece was deafening. Evans joined in, because he was anxious that the encore should be given.

There was no announcement: the piece started with a thunderous beating of drums. Evans in frantic anxiety turned to the studious young man.

"What's the name of this bit?" he asked. The young gentleman ignored his insistence. "Do you mind tellin' me what's the name of this song they're playing of?" quavered Evans. The young man turned in a fury.

"If you don't leave me alone I'll send for an attendant and have you turned out," he said.

People were scowling at the educated man and twisting their necks round and glaring at him, in the way typical of all music-lovers. Evans began to perspire.

Eight hundred and four envelopes, all addressed and all stamped. Eight hundred and four circulars, ready to receive the imprint of this gem of the year. And what it was, heaven only knew!

And then a wild resolve came to him—an inspiration. He rose and walked swiftly along the aisle. Before him was a short flight of steps leading to the platform, and above this two more steps to the rostrum where Sir Boski, unconscious of the coming interruption, was waving his baton ecstatically. In a stride Evans was on the platform; in another, he was peering over the shoulder of the outraged conductor.

Low murmurs arose from the hall; a voice cried "Chuck him out!"

And then he saw the word on the top of the page...

Fortissimo!

With a chortle of triumph he turned as a red-faced attendant grabbed him by the collar and dragged him to the aisle. He had a dim vision of royal-looking personages surveying him with amused interest. And then another hand gripped him and he was dragged towards the door. One disengaged hand he thrust into his pocket, grabbed a bundle of handbills and flung them wide. A few seconds later he struck the pavement of Wigmore Street with a dull, sickening thud.

Mr. Evans rose with a beatific smile, waved a cheery hand to the attendant, and shuffled off. The musician's secret was his!

★★★★★★

The next evening The Miller came to see him.

"Yes, yes, I know Fortissimo won. But, you poor piece of cheese, Fortissimo isn't the name of a musical piece, it's a direction meaning 'louder.' Obviously the horse was Lohengrin—that was the piece they played. And Lohengrin was pipped on the post by a short head. . . *Fortissimo!*"

Evans closed his eyes and smiled.

"What a beauty, what a beauty!" he murmured. "Straight from the trumpet's mouth!"

8.—Psychology and the Tipster

Mrs. Lube had a cousin, a young man who had done well for himself. He was in fact an educated man, being one of those teachers at elementary schools who do so much to imbue the young idea with ultra-Socialistic principles. When the Lubeses talked of Cousin Arthur they did so in hushed tones. His portrait hung in every Lube parlour, including the parlour of that Lube who had been sent to Canada by the late Dr. Barnardo.

Cousin Arthur very infrequently visited his relations, for he lived in a magnificent semi-detached villa at Streatham, but when he did he gave ample warning and the parlour was dusted, the loo-table polished and a fire was lit. This latter being an important event, for, as everybody knows, the fire is never lit in the parlour except on Christmas and Boxing Days, for which occasion all the antimacassars are removed and carefully folded away.

He came after due notice and was received in the manner of a reigning prince paying a state visit to a feudal dependant. That is to say, Mrs. Lube bought crumpets for tea and a bottle of Gilbey's port wine—the genteelest of all refreshments.

Arthur Stickleburn was a young man who wore pince-nez, a little yellow moustache, a red necktie to proclaim his abhorrence of capital, and a heavy gold watch-chain to emphasise his affluence. He had a ready smile, was affable to Mrs. Lube, gravely respectful to Old Sam (who sat in a corner, his hands clasped over his stomach and his beery eyes glued to the bottle of port), and comradely to Mr. Lube.

After they had thoroughly and exhaustively discussed all the relations who had died since they met last, and what sort of funerals they had had, Mrs. Lube told him some of her troubles. And in the front rank of these was Educated Evans.

"And of all the perjurous hounds that *ever* lived, Arthur—if you'll excuse my language—there's nobody like him. An' me strugglin' on with three mouths to feed, and him a bachelor, makin' money hand over fist an' gettin' winners. . . ."

Cousin Arthur was amused.

"Educated, is he? In what direction—philosophy, science, archæology, philology—?" None of these sounded familiar to Mrs. Lube. She explained her difficulties.

"H'm! I seem to remember having heard of the fellow," mused Cousin Arthur, stroking his weak chin thoughtfully. "I wish I could spare the time to deal with this person. Educated! I don't suppose he has ever read a line of John Stuart Mills or heard of the Binomial Theorem."

"Whose horse is that?" asked Mrs. Lube hopefully.

Cousin Arthur smiled.

"It is not a horse—it is a Calculus," he said, and then, after frowning consideration "Psychology is what you want," he said. "Fortunately that is my pet study. Tell me something more of this man and I may get his Psychology."

Mrs. Luke shook her head.

"You'd never get anything out of him," she said. "He's so mean, he uses his tea-leaves twice!"

Cousin Arthur explained, as far as she was able to comprehend, just what he meant. He elaborated his plan, grew enthusiastic with its growth.

★★★★★★

A week later the news went forth to Camden Town of Mrs. Lube's dire straits, and naturally Detective-Inspector Challoner, who was the repository of all fairy stories, came to learn of her domestic trials.

There comes to most men to whom fate has been unexpectedly kind, a large and glowing sense of benevolence. Toby Walker, drawing fifty shillings from Issy Issyheim over a successful up-and-downer, enters the saloon bar of the "Red Lion," nods genially to the assembled company, and the glad cry of "What's yours?" falls upon grateful ear-holes. Mr. Issy Issyheim, on his annual visit to Monte Carlo, struts forth from the *Cercle Privée* and throws a *mille* note to a chance acquaintance with a nod and a smile; one suspects M. Blanc, the guv'nor of the rooms, to disperse his doings in a similar glad spirit of munificence.

Educated Evans was in that mood which is so acceptable to the importunate ear-biter when the news of the Lubeses' misfortune came to him. He had sent out three winners in succession, and the majority of his satisfied clientele had acted honourable. With crinkling banknotes in his pouch and the peace of God in his heart, he strolled forth into the snowy wastes of High Street, Camden Town, reconciled even to the inevitable abandonment of the Windsor meeting. And opposite the "Nag's Head," whom should he pop up against but The Miller, a frozen straw gripped between his teeth and his face a little redder than usual.

"Heard about Mrs. Lube?" asked The Miller.

"I don't want to hear anything about them Lubeses, Mr. Challoner," said Evans loftily. "They take the low road and I take the high, as the good book says, an' we never meet. Socially they're not in my set. As Richloo, the celebrated French clergyman, said to Cardinal Valtaire when they was in France: *'Demi-tasse, demi-monde,'* which means that one half of the world don't know how the other half drinks and the other half don't care."

"She is ill," said The Miller, a little dazed by the erudition of his learned friend.

"Poomonica?" asked Evans, interested.

"No, not pneumonia—if that is what you mean—nervous breakdown. Old Sam's broke, and her husband's run away with the barmaid at the 'Cow and Garter'."

"Not the red-haired one?" Evans was fascinated by the news.

"I don't know the colour of her hair," retorted The Miller impatiently. "But she is certainly—Mrs. Lube I mean—down and out."

Evans made a faint tut-tutting noise.

"It had to be," he said complacently. "I kill all competition. Information *v.* gaswork. Knowin' *v.* pickin' 'em out with a pin. I got one that's runnin' on Tuesday that's past the post! Tryin' for the first time since last year's National. This horse is fourteen pound better than Ruddygore an' ten pound better than Silvo—an' he's in a seller! I got him from the boy who does him."

Mr. Challoner's concern for the unhappy Mrs Lube momentarily evaporated.

"What's this—Ned Carver?" he asked, with provocative sarcasm.

"Ned Carver's gone to stud," said Evans, unperturbed by the implied scepticism. "So has Bart Snowball and Sergeant Murphy."

The Miller explained certain reasons why none of these horses was likely to make successful sires.

"It's a shame to treat horses like that," said Evans severely. "Anyway, this horse I'm tellin' you about is goin' for the coop of the year. You know Sarkles the trainer—he's hot. Whenever a horse of his wants a poultice he just leans against 'em."

"Sarkles? Then it's Bonny Whitelegs you're talking about?"

Evans wagged his head in annoyance.

"I ought to wear a muzzle," he said; "but you'll keep this to yourself, Mr. Challoner? This is the biggest coop that ever looked through a saddle. Keep it quiet and we'll get eightses to our money."

The Miller made a mental note and reverted to the subject of Mrs. Lube.

"Yes, I know that she is no friend of yours," he interrupted Mr. Evans' protest, "but she's a woman."

"So was Lewdcreature Burgia, the female Crippen," said Evans bitterly. "So was Cleopatra, whose needle we all admire; so was B— Mary who done in the princes in the well-known Tower by pourin' poison in their earholes! So was Catherine, the celebrated Queen of Russia, who massacred all the inpatients of Bartholomew's Hospital because they wouldn't have any truck with the Hugenuts; so was Mrs. Manning, who was hung in a blue silk dress at Horse-monger Lane Gaol for murderin' her nine little children—see Dickens!"

He might at that moment wash his hands of the Lubeses, dismiss them to the outer oblivion, shrug them into the infinite spaces where wander The People Who Don't Count; but in the cosy comfort, not to say fug, of his bureau at Desert Chief House, and what time he smoked a good cigar before a blazing fire, the thought of his sick enemy came back to him and his conscience stirred uneasily.

On his new table were stacked five hundred and forty stamped, addressed envelopes. Into these shortly would be inserted the circular

289

already printed, advertising the merits of Bonny Whitelegs. In his sky-rocket a wad of notes rustled musically every time he crossed his legs. And in that dark and saddened home lay a woman deserted by the man to whom she had given her hand and confided her destiny.

Evans sighed. And then a formless thought took shape.

He went out into the chill night with a basket, and procured from Higgs's, the grocers, a jar of invalid jelly, a dozen new-laid eggs, a packet of oatmeal and various other luxuries associated in his mind with the effective treatment of sickness.

★★★★★★

In the kitchen of Mrs. Lube's house sat Old Sam, Young Alf Lube and the partner of his joys and sorrows. Old Sam was asleep, and, by the happy smile that transfigured the patriarchal face, it was easy to suppose that he was dreaming of strong drink.

"It's a bit rough on me," grumbled Mr. Lube, "poked up in the house all day and night waitin' for Evans to come—a silly idea I call it."

Mrs. Lube bridled.

"What about me?" she demanded. "Every time there's a knock at the door do I have to go into the parlour an' lay on the sofa or don't I? Answer me."

"Silly idea!" gloomed Alfred. "As if this Sy—whatever the word is—is goin' to bring Evans here. An' what about my reputation? Me supposed to have run away from you with a common barmaid!"

"You seem to bear up all right," she said.

"Do I? Suppose *she* gets to hear of it—what's she goin' to say?"

Mrs. Lube stiffened.

"She—which 'she,' I'd like to know?"

Alfred Lube was embarrassed.

"Well... whoever it is. I don't know her myself, never so much as said 'How d'ye do' to her. But she's got her feelin's, the same as the rest of us."

"Barmaids haven't got any feelin's," said Mrs. Lube, her suspicious eyes on her husband. "You seem to think a lot about what she'll think, Alfred!"

He closed his eyes wearily.

"Whose idea was it—did I say anything about runnin' away with barmaids? Wasn't it your cousin Arthur with his Sy—something?"

"Don't speak a word about my cousin," she said with acerbity. "This sy-sausagy, or whatever it is, can't be wrong. He couldn't har-

290

bour a wrong thought."

"What's it mean?" demanded Mr. Lube.

"Findin' out—it's a new way," said Mrs. Lube, and at that moment there was a gentlemanly knock at the door.

It was opened to Mr. Evans by a small boy who wore a black tie. Evans thought for a moment that his purchases would be on his hands.

"Mother's ill," said the sepulchral child. "So's grandfa'r."

A husky voice from the parlour asked "Who is it?"

"Mr. Evans, Mrs. Lube," said the educated man loudly.

"Come in."

Mr. Evans removed his hat reverently and tiptoed into the parlour. On a sofa drawn up by the fire lay Mrs. Lube. She wore her oldest dress and there was a bandage round her head.

"Come in, do, Mr. Evans," she moaned. "I suppose you've come to gloat over me?"

"Far be it from me to gloat," said the virtuous Evans, "but as an educated man it's me duty to do unto others as I'm done by. I've brought you a few things."

Mrs. Lube glanced sideways at the articles which her visitor put upon the table, spreading them out so that none might escape her attention.

"Set down, Mr. Evans—Willie, go out into the kitchen and don't make a row or I'll break your neck!"

Willie withdrew and slammed the door. Mr. Evans sat on the edge of a chair, a look of condolence and sympathy on his face.

"We all ought to stand together," he said. "Misfortune, as the saying goes, makes cowards of us all. What's the matter with you, Mrs. Lube?"

"Internal," she said.

Evans coughed and was silent He was not a family man.

"I don't think I'm Here for Long," she added. Evans made a noise expressing his sorrow. "Well," he said, "we can't expect to live for ever. You've had your life—what are you, Mrs. Lube, about forty-five?"

"Thirty-three!" she snarled. "What's the idea of forty-five?"

She mastered her emotion with an effort, but Mr. Evans was not put out.

"I suppose you get light-headed when you're ill," he said. "I remember you twenty years ago an' you was no chicken then. Anyway, you've had your life—we all have to go sooner or later. Lube's run away?"

291

She nodded: she could not trust herself to speak.

"I think it must be with the red-haired one," meditated Evans. "I always guessed there was something wrong ever since I saw 'em coming out of the pictures together."

Mrs. Lube sat up suddenly.

"When was this?" she demanded fiercely.

"Must have been a month ago," said Evans. "But don't agitate yourself, Mrs. Lube—after all, he's a younger man than you—"

"He's four years older!" she stormed.

"Men keep young longer than women," said Evans soothingly. "As the well-known Julius Caesar the Eyetalian said—"

"Never mind about him!" interrupted Mrs. Lube. "You say you saw him with a barmaid at the pictures, do you—the dirty dog!"

"Set your mind on Heaven," said the educated man gently. "You know the worst, Mrs. Lube. He's gone—forget him. Can I do anything for you?"

It was then that Mrs. Lube remembered that she was being far too energetic for a person *in extremis*. She accordingly relaxed into her role of interesting invalid.

"No, Mr. Evans, there is nothing you can do for me," she said faintly. "I'm sure I'm much obliged to you for the 'am—"

"Jelly," murmured Evans.

"You're very kind. Before I passed, as it were, I'd like to have sent out a winner—but what's the use? We're ruined, me an' my poor dear grandfather—no clients—no money for paper, no stamps—nothing. I don't want to send it out, only just to know it."

Evans considered the matter deeply. Here was a woman, in a manner of speaking, on the very edge of Tophet. Basely deserted, starving, as it were, and wanting one gleam of sunshine which he was in a position to radiate. And yet—

"How's Old Sam?" he asked.

"Ill in bed—not expected to recover—business gone, Alf gone—everything gone," she wailed.

Evans took the plunge. Leaning over her, he hissed

"Bonny Whitelegs—help yourself an' tell the angels!"

She opened her eyes wide.

"Him?" she said doubtingly.

"Got it from the boy that does him—a lad called 'Orace—nex' Wednesday. Keep it to yourself, Mrs. Lube, an' have a real good win. You ought to have a bit of money to leave to your children!"

Mrs. Lube breathed deeply.

"Oh, if I could only believe that," she whispered, "I'd pass peaceful! You sendin' it out, Mr. Evans?"

"Tuesday night—late," he said briskly. "Now don't leave it to him an' his carroty girl, Mrs. Lube. She's had enough from what I've heard. Three pun' ten he paid for the di'mond bracelet she was wearin' of when I see her last—an' the hat he bought her at Stibbinses!"

Mrs. Lube was very pale; her eyelids fluttered furiously.

"Bracelet. . . ." Her voice sounded strangled. Mr. Evans thought the end was near. "Hat. . . three pun' ten!"

She's wandering, thought Evans, and tiptoed out of the room.

The door had hardly closed upon him when Mr. Lube, smoking a cigarette before the kitchen fire, heard his wife's firm footfall in the passage. And then the door opened and she entered.

"Did you find out anything—" he began, and then he saw her face, and, swift to move, dodged the jar of invalid jelly.

★★★★★★

On the Thursday:

"Mrs. Lube has made a good recovery," said The Miller.

Educated Evans looked at him pained—for the time being speechless.

"And Bonny Whitelegs—what a beauty!" said The Miller. "I had forty pound to five. And I presume that all clients old and new received this gem?"

Evans shook his head and found his voice.

"At three-thirty on the afternoon of Tuesday the fourteenth *ult*," he began dreamily (and obviously it was a bad dream), "I was sittin' or reclinin' in my chair when I had a telegram—'Don't send out Bonny Whitelegs, Horace.' I ought to have known," he mused, "that it was a swindle or imposture, but me bein' what I am, I put it aside an' said 'Another day.' An' he won. . . an' the Lubeses sent it out to all clients new an old. An' Alf Lube sent the wire from Marlborough because a friend of mine see him gettin' into the rattler at Paddin'ton with a black eye an' a lip as big as a cushion. . . my horse. . .!"

"Mrs. Lube—" began The Miller.

"Is alive." Evans nodded gravely and pointed to the black armlet about his sleeve. "She's alive—ain't I in mournin'?"

9.—The Showing up of Educated Evans

It was unfortunate that Mr. Yevers, the landlord of the "Cow and

293

Garter," loathed Educated Evans with a deadly loathing. Mr. Yevers himself was an uneducated man. At best he could only affix his name to the south-east corner of a cheque with the very greatest labour. As for reading, when anybody pointed out a paragraph in the newspaper he invariably replied: "Read it out—I've mislaid me glasses."

His career had been a romantic one. Starting as a small boy, penniless and friendless, he had worked his way up to be first the barman and then the manager of the biggest house in North London. And as this was in the days before the coming of the cash register, Mr Yevers had diligently acquired sufficient money. With his savings he purchased his master's business (when that gentleman went into Carey Street as a result of his carelessness and the dishonesty of his subordinates), and by the application of his industry and a little fencing on the side, he attained to wealth beyond the dreams of actresses.

He was a self-made man, and had nobody else to blame for it.

He hated Evans primarily because of his education, but particularly because Evans, in an argumentative moment, had unconsciously betrayed Mr. Yevers' shortcomings.

It was over the old vexed question as to when the Thames was frozen last, and on what date a coach and four was driven across at London Bridge.

"I remember it as a boy," said Mr. Yevers, who never would admit that anything happened before he was born.

"You're mistaken, sir," said Evans, courteously enough. "It was in 1452 in the reign of Good Queen Anne, the celebrated dead lady—"

"I remember it as a boy," asseverated Mr. Yevers hotly.

"If you can read—" began Evans, meaning nothing ill.

Mr. Yevers went a dark blue and pointed to the door of the saloon bar.

"Get out of my house before I kick you out!" he said.

And because great minds brood upon little things, Mr. Yevers brooded upon the affront which had been offered him by a man who, as he rightly said, hadn't as much brass to his name as Mr. Yevers took in the bottle and jug department in one day.

"How was I to know he couldn't read or write?" protested Evans to The Miller. "The ignorance of the lower orders is simply remarkable and stupefying. I've no desire to hurt the man's feelings. He's a bung, an' I can't say anything worse to him than that."

"You've lost a client," said The Miller.

Evans smiled sardonically.

"Three times a year, and I have to take me winnings in beer, which is repugnant to me, being a gentlemanly spirit drinker. Or a bottle of port wine from the wood and made of it! I've wiped him off me books."

The Miller, the champion pacifier of Camden Town, succeeded in reconciling the ruffled Mr. Yevers. Unfortunately for all concerned, the reconciliation coincided with a period when things were going badly with Mr. Yevers. He had in two new barmen and a sub-manager in a month. But such is the mechanical mind of the present generation that the seemingly insuperable difficulties presented by the cash register were overcome by all three of them, each in his own way. And then, in a moment of insanity, Mr. Yevers decided to have a plunge on a horse whispered confidentially across the zinc.

He went down to Lingfield to see the horse run; was genial, almost convivial, until...

As the field came into the straight with Jiggling Jimmie ten lengths ahead, Mr. Evans turned to his companion with a shrug.

"Information *v.* gaswork," he stated briefly. Knowledge v. pickin' 'em out of a hat! As I told you, Mr. Challoner, this here Jiggling Jimmie could fall down—"

"He has!" said The Miller.

Mr. Evans opened his eyes arid glared through his glasses.

"That ain't Jiggling Jimmie. . . yes, it is . . no, it ain't. . . yes, it is."

"Shall I say 'when'?" asked the sympathetic Miller. "Tough luck, Evans!'

Tough luck it was, for Jiggling Jimmy, having fallen and dislodged his rider, was still leading the field as it passed the post.

Educated Evans threw his race-card on the asphalt of Tattersall's, jumped on it, lifted his nose in a bitter sneer, and sent his glasses back in his case with a crash; it was the gesture of a defeated warrior sheathing his sword.

"That horse was tried twenty-one pound better than Jerry M. and two stone better than Tom Pinch," he began. "An' to think that—what did win it?" he asked suddenly.

"Cat's Eyes," replied The Miller, and Mr. Evans breathed heavily through his nostrils.

"Old Sam's Three-Star Nap!" he said hollowly. "Is that luck or ain't it? Was Cat's Eyes on the map? I'm asking you."

"I heard you," said The Miller, as they made their way towards the rattler. "It is sad—but it is racing, Evans. Such things happen."

295

Evans had forgotten all about Mr. Yevers' existence in the passionate despair of the moment, and when that blue-faced man confronted him on the platform he was dumbfounded by the injustice of the attack.

"Tipster!" he roared. "You bring me down here and make me have monkeys on horses that can't stand up on their own legs! Why, Old Sam's worth a million of you—two million," he amended generously.

In the face of such vulgarity Evans could merely shrug his shoulders.

"Speaking as an educated man—" he began.

"You're a fake!" howled Mr. Yevers, shaking his fist in the face of erudition. "You don't know nothing about nothing and never did!"

A most persistent patron of the "Cow and Garter" was one Old Sam, editor of the Midnight Special, whose three-star nap had won the race. To him Mr. Yevers confided his woes in the condescending way which publicans have with their moister clients. Old Sam sighed and shook his head in his melancholy way.

"You'd better by half have stuck to me. What won the race, Mr. Yevers?"

"Cat's Eyes."

"That's a good horse," nodded Sam soberly, though he wasn't. "As nice a horse as ever looked through a collar."

"You tipped it," said Mr. Yevers.

Old Sam scratched his nose.

"Did I?" he said. There was a note of genuine surprise. "Why, of course I did! Bless my soul, I've give so many winners that I don't know what I tipped."

"As for his education!" said Mr. Yevers.

Sam smiled.

"He gets it out of a book," he said confidentially. "I know: he used to be a partner of mine. He gets it all out of a book. Not his ideas at all."

Now the idea of showing up Educated Evans might have gone no further but for the fact that Mr. Yevers was called away to a sick relation in a little country town; and as the man owed him a bit of money, and, moreover, since there was no written acknowledgment of the debt (this was the principal cause of anxiety), Mr. Yevers thought it advisable to call on his relation and secure from him an acknowledgment that at any rate his executors would honour....

This took time, because the sick man was also a very obstinate man, and one of the symptoms of his disease was an extraordinary lapse of memory, so that he could not recall any time when he had ever borrowed money.

The matter satisfactorily settled, Mr. Yevers found time hanging on his hands, and went into a small music-hall. And there he saw on the stage the most charming young lady, who answered the most abstruse and difficult questions fired at her from the audience with an alacrity which almost suggested that she had some good friends in the audience. He asked the man on his right the name of the lady, and learnt that she was Lizo, the Human Encyclopaedia, and later, having a drink at the bar with the manager, he learnt that Lizo wasn't as successful as he would have expected her to be.

"It's out of date, that sort of turn," said the manager. "People are not interested in ancient history since the War."

An idea flashed through Mr. Yevers' mind. He learnt the girl's salary, and interviewed her in a dressing-room and discovered to his joy that she had once graced the private bar of a high-class establishment in the West End.

He engaged her on the spot.

★★★★★★

The "Cow and Garter" was not a House that was a particular favourite of Educated Evans, and even the arrival of Miss Betty, the new and even more golden-headed-than-usual barmaid, did not attract him, though the fame of her spread throughout Camden Town. For beauty, as Mr. Evans remarked originally, is but skin deep and very often not that.

"What's comin' to young ladies nowadays, Mr. Challoner, I can't understand," he said in despair. "What with paint and powder an' doin' up their eyelashes with blackin' an' jinglin' their hair and what not, they beat me!"

"I wonder," mused The Miller, "if you are as good a judge of beauty as you are of horses? Because, if you are, I shouldn't like you to pick out a wife for *me!*"

Evans smiled tolerantly.

"Wimmin don't like me—I know too much about 'em. Take Hist'ry—"

"If you are going to talk about B— Mary. . ." expostulated The Miller.

"I ain't," Evans shrugged. "There's others, an' as the widely advertised Shakespeare says, 'I've learnt about wimmin from all of 'em!' Take the well-known—"

"Not Lewdcreature Burgia!" begged The Miller. "Let that poor lady rest in her marble tomb—"

"Lipsus lazily—not marble," corrected Evans. "She was buried in Westminster Abbey by the side of her dear old father in 1684—correct me if I'm wrong. Her last words was 'You'll find Callis engraved on me brain'—her end was peace."

The Miller fanned himself vigorously.

"No," Evans went on, "I'm referrin' more to such wimmin as—"

"Cleopatra," murmured The Miller, "whose needle we all admire!"

Mr. Evans' annoyance was not wholly without cause.

"I'm thinkin' of wimmin like Bore-de-Syer, the well-known Roman queen that fought the ancient Britons in a chariot with mowin' machines tied on the spokes! What a woman!"

"Ah!" agreed The Miller densely. "A friend of yours?"

Educated Evans could only make impatient noises.

"Anyway, I don't get lured up to no public-houses by females," he said. "I got my reputation to lose."

"May I suggest," said The Miller, with infinite gentleness, "that you not only lose it, but that you tie a brick round its neck and drop it into the Regent's Canal? So that it doesn't come back. As to the new Circe—"

"Pardon?" said Evans.

"Temptress," amended The Miller, "her chief interest to me is her education. She is one of the best-read girls I have ever met and she has a memory like a loose-leaf ledger. I confess that she staggered me when she told me the date the police force was founded."

"1743," murmured Evans, "by the celebrated Lord Copper—it used to be Peel, I know," he added to The Miller's correction, "but he changed his name for family reasons."

"Her education," went on The Miller, "is rather remarkable. People are talking about it. Yevers says he had her schoolmaster in the saloon bar the other day and she fairly staggered him."

"Anything staggers a schoolmaster," scoffed Evans. "Besides, how can a bit of a girl be educated? Where's her experience? Where's her man-of-the-worldness? Take geography diamonds come from Asterdam—very few people know that. Sugar comes from Demerare, coffee comes from Africa, cotton comes from Liverpool and dear old Dixieland—see song. Take mathematics—"

"Eh?" said The Miller.

"Take mathematics," said Mr. Evans calmly. "What about algebra? What about Euclid? What about isosceles triangles—that's geometry: you do it with a compass. I got a prize for it at school. Take physics. What makes a seidlitz powder go fizz? Very few people know that. It's the combustion of the blue with the white..."

Curiosity and tentative invitation extended at third hand, plus the fact that several people had told him about the young lady at the "Cow and Garter," eventually induced Mr. Evans to make a call.

Mr. Yevers was standing in the bar, a sardonic smile upon his face, as Evans strolled in with a certain *hauteur*. To his surprise, the landlord came towards him.

"Let bygones be bygones, Evans," he said thickly. "'Ave one on the 'ouse."

"Port wine," said Evans, "or maybe a glass of sherry white wine—as seck as possible. Seck's Latin for sweet, hence the word seckarine."

This was a challenge, delivered alike to the awe-stricken habitués of the "Cow and Garter," who had gathered to witness this Homeric contest, and to the beautiful lady who was regarding him with the speculative eye of a gladiator confronted with a large and unshaved lion. Mr. Yevers looked round at her, frowned significantly. Here was her quarry.

"Sherry," she said, in a clear, loud voice, "comes from Jerez, pronounced Hreth, in the south of Spain. '*Sec*' means 'dry.' Sherry was first introduced into England in 1642."

"'41," murmured Evans. "The first lot was brought here by a gentleman named Williams." He was on the point of saying "a particular friend of mine," but checked himself in time.

He glanced round the saloon bar, stared insolently through the windows.

"Looks like snow," he said; "which reminds me that the Thames was froze over in 1714 and a coach and six horses drove across at Wapping Stairs."

"The Thames was frozen over," said the belle of learning, "in 1742 at Richmond Bridge, and a whole ox was roasted on the ice near Putney in 1831."

"'32," murmured Evans; "and it wasn't a whole ox, it was half an ox. It was the year that Diomedes won the Derby."

He thought this would stagger her, but she was a girl not easily staggered.

"Diomedes," she said, "is a bay colt by Argos-Capdane. He is trained by H. Leader and owned by Mr. Beer. As a two-year old—"

"I'm not talking about that Diomedes, there's another," said Evans loudly. "You've got 'em all mixed up. I'm talking about the horse that won the Derby in 1784, owned by Lord What's-his-name and ridden by Fred Archer, the well-known but late jockey."

She was staggered by this, but came again nobly.

"Fred Archer was born—" she began.

"Everybody knows that," said Evans. "What about Socrates, the well-known poet and Eyetalian, the fellow that double-crossed the well- known Rubicons—him and Julius Caesar was like brothers. So was Mark Antony, the highly celebrated friend, Roman and country-man.

"Shakespeare—" she began.

"Never mind about Shakespeare," said Mr. Evans, holding tight to his vantage. "What about Brutus, that chewed tobacco?"

"Tobacco—" began the girl.

"Never mind about tobacco. Did he or didn't he? Didn't Julius Caesar, when he lay a-dyin' on his couch on the Plain of Nervy, say '*Et chew, Brutus?*' Is that hist'ry or making it up? And what about Cleopatra, who was stoned to death by rats? What about her needle, which we all admire, covered over with hydrostatics, which I used to be able to read when I was a boy, as everybody knows, though I've got out of speaking Egyptian, though I still know a few words, such as '*ooka*' and '*wookha*,' which means 'male' and 'female,' as there is in every country throughout the British Empire, on which the sun never sets. Which brings us to Australia. The finest horse that ever came out of Australia was Carbine, by Musket out of Woodbine. He ran in seventy-five races and was only beaten once, his jockey havin' a packet on the second. Take Flemington race-course, the finest course in the world, where the Viceroy's Cup's run. Which brings us to the question of Ireland."

Hebe made her supreme effort.

"Ireland was conquered by Richard Strongbow in 1066—"

"I know all about that," said Evans. "He landed in Galway 'Ar-bour on the thirteenth of July at seven o'clock in the morning. It was raining," he added. "Which brings us to the question of how many pennies put side by side would reach from here to the moon. Very few people know this. The moon is an extinct volcano, entirely sur-rounded by ether. Chloroform was invented by Dr. Lister by accident whilst trying to discover the secret of gunpowder. In 1635: I am not sure of the exact date. Talking of doctors reminds us that Lewdcreature Burgia, the female Crippen of Italy, who poisoned the little princes and buried 'em under the stairs where the Marble Arch now stands, was one of the most educated women of the day. Her husband was the well-known Leonardo D. Vincey, the celebrated picture-taker, whose portraits we all admire, both in the British Museum and otherwise. The British Museum was founded by an old sailor who wanted the people of London to have a place to go into when it was wet."

The female encyclopaedia lost her head.

"Look here, Mr. Whatever-your-name-is," she said hotly, "all these dates and things you're giving us are wrong. You know they're wrong. And all my dates are right: I got them out of the *Encyclopaedia of General Knowledge*, and learnt the 2,000 pages by heart."

Evans smiled.

"I wrote it," he said simply.

10.—THE SUBCONSCIOUS MIND

The eternal quest for education led Mr. Evans into many strange experiences. There was a Cult that had meetings in a tiny hall in Stibbington Street, and the educated man was for some time a regular attendant.

"What is this I hear about your going to the meetings of The Children of the Sun?" asked The Miller.

Mr. Evans smiled.

"It's learnin'," he said simply. "I gotta sub-conscience."

"A what?" asked the startled officer.

"A sub-conscience—it's workin' all the time. It's due to the sun."

"But you never see the sun in Camden Town."

"I go racin'," said Evans. "When a man gets a sub-conscience he gets Revealations. Things come into his mind. It's in a book. Sometimes when I'm walkin' about I get a sub-conscience of what I'm goin' to have for dinner; sometimes I get a sub-conscience that I'm goin' to meet you. It's astral."

"Whatal?"

"Astral—somethin' to do with flyin'," said Mr. Evans.

"Kite-flying?"

Mr. Evans smiled again indulgently.

The life of a prophet, even a world's champion prophet, is not all jam. He is at the mercy of temperament—temperamental horses, temperamental jockeys, and last, but by no means last, temperamental clients. No client of Educated Evans better fitted this description than Moses Smike, the owner of Smike's Renowned Fish and Chip Restaurant, whose establishment was off Great College Street, Camden Town.

And yet Mr. Evans had undoubtedly been the salvation of the man. As long ago as Braxted (what a beauty!) and Eton Boy (given from the weights some clients got 33-1), he had encouraged Mr. Smike in the pursuit of easy wealth. Only the other day, when Mr. Smike had some difficulty with the wholesaler who supplied him with plaice and skate, it was the Educated Marvel who found him Obscotch (8-1) and Bunions (11-2), and thus rescued him from an appearance in the Bankruptcy Court.

"I wouldn't mind," complained Mr. Evans, "if the man would say a thing an' stick to it. But when he says 'There's a tenner for you, Evans,' an' when I call for it there's only a middle piece and 8s. 3d. in coppers, I consider he's not acting honourable. And coppers is low—with all due respect to you, Mr. Challoner, an' meanin' nothing against rozzers."

Detective-Inspector Challoner took no umbrage. He was in his most cheerful mood that morning, and the straw he chewed was whiter and more imposing than usual.

"Smike's going to be married," he said, and Evans uttered a tut-tut of surprise and disapproval.

"Why, he's an old man! It'll be like the celebrated Mr. May marryin' the well-known Miss December!"

"To be exact, he is about your age," said The Miller. "Anyway, I shouldn't be surprised if he made amends by asking you to the wedding."

Evans brightened visibly.

"Perhaps he'll give me a weddin' present?" he said.

The Miller explained that the giving of wedding presents was the privilege rather of the guest than the host.

"That's a silly idea," said Educated Evans. "Anyway, the most he'll ever get from me is my Sealed £10 Guarantee Coop wire—that's worth a dollar of anybody's money."

The bride was Miss Emily Jane Loocood and she was supposed to be of French origin. She had been an assistant at Mr. Smike's fish establishment for six years.

"And about time he married her," said Evans scandalously. "That's why they call 'em December an' May marriages—they're spliced in

December an'—"

"Don't let us be uncharitable," said the Miller. "Anyway, May is a lucky month to be born in."

To the wedding Mr. Evans was invited. It occurred on a Sunday so as not to interfere with business, a brief honeymoon ("totally unnecessary," said Evans) was to be spent at Brighton, and the Happy Pair would be back in time to open the shop on Tuesday and receive the felicitations of all old customers.

As a wedding feast it was, from Mr. Evans' point of view, a failure, for not only was Mrs. Lube present in startling magenta, but Old Sam, his whiskers dry-cleaned and wearing a frock coat and white tall hat, was amongst the guests. Mrs. Lube was unaccountably friendly.

"I hope, Mr. Evans, you're going to let bygones be bygones," said Mrs. Lube.

"I hope so, I'm sure," said Evans stiffly.

"Remember what you owe to my dear gran'father that brought you up when you hadn't got a penny piece," said Mrs. Lube sweetly.

Evans choked and gurgled.

Old Sam! Who used to run errands for him! A holder-up of public-houses, waiting for a horse-drawn vehicle to pull up so that he could earn a penny by holding the head of an animal who wouldn't have run away if he could.

"I beg your pardon?" he said hotly. "That old—your gran'father was a mere menial and dependant. I said 'go' and he goed—'hither' and he hithered—"

Mrs. Lube smiled.

"Your memory ain't as good as it was when you was young," she said cryptically.

Possibly it was the effect this outrageous statement had upon Mr. Evans that put into her head the idea which, subsequently, was to cause the learned man so much acute mental distress.

"I can only say," he exclaimed in wrath, "that I'm sorry for your education. You're like the celebrated orsstretch that puts its head in the sandy desert every time somebody tries to take a rise out of him. You remind me of my old friend Cardinal Rishloo, who made the celebrated French Revolution because he couldn't find how the dumplin' got into the apple!"

"You're very strange, Mr. Evans," she said, her hazy ideas taking a very definite shape: "strange in your manner. It must be goin' to these meetin's in Stibbington Street. You're very strange."

303

"I'm treatin' you like a lady," said Evans, "an' I dessay that seems strange to you."

The Miller was not at the wedding, and to him Evans related the events of the afternoon.

"You shouldn't have gone," said The Miller. "You know that Smike and the Lubes are thicker than thieves."

The wedding coincided with a period of great activity at Masked Marvel Mansions. The Lincoln weights were out, and Mr. Evans had heard of a horse at Newmarket that was being specially got ready for the race. Moreover, to meet current demands and to satisfy the cravings of his clientele for their daily heart flutters, he had secured one of the grandest bits of information about a horse running at Hurst Park that ever came to mortal man.

The information came, as all good things in life come, by the veriest accident. He was racing at Sandown one day and heard two men talking about Suggo. Now Suggo, as everybody knows, is not the name of a new soap powder, but the registered title of a thoroughbred racehorse in one of the hottest stables at Epsom. There isn't a cold stable at Epsom, but this one was so hot that steam heating was a superfluity.

"Not today!" grunted one of the men. "Hurst—keep it to yourself."

Evans went along, and by the aid of his card and the number on the attendant's arm, identified Suggo, who had a careless look in his eye which suggested that this intelligent animal knew that he was not being called upon for any supreme effort at the moment. In the race Suggo was never wholly visible. He was eighth, ninth or tenth till the field came into the straight, and then, moving up to make a show, he finished a respectable fifth.

Consequently, a few days after the wedding, Mr. Evans was in a position to send out to all clients new and old the following:

EDUCATED EVANS'
MYSTERY HORSE!!!
What a beauty!
What a beauty!
Educated Evans, the World's Champion Turf Adviser and Racing Prophet,
begs to advise the following:
MONEY FOR NOTHING
This horse has been tried to beat the best horses at Epsom.

SUGGO on Friday.
Help yourself and roll up with your T.M.Q.'s for 10s. for
ONE THAT WILL WIN TEN MINUTES
on Saturday.
P.S. This horse has been Revealed to me.

"What on earth made you put that?" asked The Miller.

"To make it mysteriouser," said Evans complacently. "The public likes mysteries. An' I've gotta sub-conscience about this horse."

He went down to see the race. This time Suggo led the field for half the journey and then fell back, a beaten horse.

"Rapped himself," said the trainer glibly.

There was another Hurst Park meeting a few weeks later, and he had arranged that in this race Suggo should not rap himself or do anything to himself except get his head in front at the stick.

Mr. Evans accepted defeat with the philosophy of one to whom adversity was no stranger

"Can't give 'em winners every day," he said when he saw The Miller that night; "but I got one for Monday that will Doddle It!"

To all clients (new and old) he despatched the following Hurry Up message:

EDUCATED EVANS
Owing to his last selection Wrapping Himself
(hard lines, hard lines),
Mr. Evans, the highly celebrated Turf Expert,
begs to send his friends one and all
MOUSE HOLE
for the Littlehampton Hurdle on Monday.
Go for your summer's keep.
P.S. This horse is a Revellation!!

In the race Mouse Hole found its namesake and crawled into it, finishing last.

And then a sinister rumour flashed around Camden Town. How much Alf Lube had to do with it, to what extent it owed its circulation to the affected concern of Mrs. Lube, how far certain disgruntled publicans, whose word is law, assisted in its promulgation, is a matter for investigation.

The Miller, in the course of his business, had to make a few inquiries concerning the whereabouts of two motor rugs which had been absentmindedly abstracted from a garage; and in the course of these inquiries he came into contact with Toby Lyons, one of Evans' biggest and fastest supporters.

"Poor old Evans!" said Toby, shaking his head mournfully. "That only shows you what education'll do for you, Mr. Challoner."

"What's the matter with Evans?"

Toby smiled sadly.

"Goin'," he said significantly. "It's too much readin' that clogs up the headpiece, and naturally the brain won't work."

"Do you mean he's mad?" asked The Miller, aghast.

"Revelations," murmured Toby. "According to what I hear, he sits in a trance and hears ghosts tellin' him what's going to win."

Everywhere The Miller went he heard the same story. In some subtle and pernicious manner the authority of Educated Evans was being underpinned and undermined. He took the trouble to call on Mr. Evans, and that gentleman smiled at his warning.

"It's only the lower orders, the riff-raff and the what-not," he said. "I don't take no notice of what uneducated people say about me. If people are like the well-known wife of the celebrated Julius Caesar, suspicious of everybody, well, let 'em be! See what they say about you, Mr. Challoner."

"What do they say about me?" asked The Miller, interested.

"They say you've got three rows of houses out of the money you've done hooks out of! I always say: 'You're misjudgin' the man. I don't suppose he's got more than a row anyway.' "

"Thank you for your enthusiastic championship," said The Miller sarcastically. "Now take a tip from me, Evans—cut out The Children of the Sun and the subconscious mind, and keep to your old method of finding winners—putting all the names in a hat and sending out the first one you draw."

Mr. Evans was not offended.

He went to the "Cow and Garter" that night with the idea of establishing beyond any doubt his complete sanity. Mr. Yevers, the inimical landlord, was confined to his bed with an attack of gout, and the encyclopaedic barmaid had been replaced by one of greater beauty but less erudition. He could not but observe that, when he entered the bar, silence fell upon the *habitués*.

"Good evening, friends all," he said in his genial way, as he ordered his whisky and soda. "The weather's mild for this time of the year. We shall soon have spring here."

Everybody agreed.

"Spring," said Evans, "is caused by the world rotating on its own equinox, thereby not only causing day and night, but also summer, autumn, Christmas and other seasons, the snow on the North Pole meltin' an' bringin' about the floods, causin' great damage to life and property, see Sunday papers."

Toby, who was in the bar, answered him, and his voice was gentle, almost pleading.

"Don't you think, Mr. Evans, it'd be a good idea if you gave up studyin' for a bit?" he asked. "It can't do your brain any good havin' all these thoughts in your mind."

Evans surveyed his whisky with a mysterious smile.

"You can't be educated without thought, Toby," he said. "Take Biography or the study of insects. Microbes cause all diseases such as headache, earache, ingrained toenails—which brings us to the question of electricity—which causes both lightnin' and lamps. Electricity can be caused by water

"By dynimos," said a husky voice in the background. It was Hoggy Main, who for three days shovelled coal in a firehouse. "Dynimos and wires."

"Dynamos are turned by water," said Evans. "By coal," said Hoggy. "I oughter know—"

Somebody whispered a remonstrance to him and he was silent.

"Of course they're turned by water, Mr. Evans," said Toby soothingly. "Everybody knows that."

"Everybody don't know that," said Evans, irritated. "Only a few people, which brings us to the question of the human figure, composed of heart, lungs an' important blood vessels, which together with bones and muscles makes man, woman an' child."

Everybody agreed with him at once. The barmaid stood at a respectful distance behind the counter, ready to fly, for she had heard of Mr. Evans' strange disorder.

"What about the sub-conscience mind?" asked the irrepressible Hoggy.

"Shut up," said Toby. "Don't annoy the man. You oughter be ashamed of yourself, Hoggy."

Mr. Evans waved aside the defence.

"The sub-conscience mind," he said, "as everybody knows except the ignorant an' the common, is due to the brain actin' without people thinkin'."

"And I convinced 'em," he told The Miller. "Nobody so much as argued with me. It's brains that does it."

But a change was coming over the fortunes of the World's Champion. First his local, and then, as rumour reached them, his more distant clientele, grew shy of his appeals. It is true that he gave three losers in succession and two of them started at odds on; but the foundation of their scepticism was planted deeper than in the vicissitudes of a prophet's fortunes. His temper was not improved by the fact that he could not walk abroad without being confronted with the poster advertising Old Sam's Midnight Special.

HARDNUT! HARDNUT! HARDNUT!
5-1. What a beauty
OLD SAM'S DOUBLE NAP!
Information *v.* The sub-conscience mind.
P.S. Keep away from the Bogey Man!!

One old-established client wrote

Dear Sir: Hearing you have gone wrong in your head, please take my name off your list and oblige.

He sent a winner to his dwindling clientele, but it was not of a price calculated to re-establish confidence. In a fit of despondency, through which ran the red thread of panic, he sat down in his little room one night to study the programme of the coming Saturday, and as usual he limited his study to the race which had the fewest entries, because, as he argued rightly, the smaller the field the smaller the chance of picking the wrong 'un.

This race, however, did not promise well. Bogey Boy was a certain runner, would start at 6-1 on and doddle it. Mrs. Lipski, another prominent jumper, might possibly beat him, but wasn't by any means a certain runner. At the bottom of the little handicap was a horse called Iron Face. He didn't remember having seen the name before, and disconsolately he went back to Mrs. Lipski, turned up his tattered book of form, scanned the training intelligence of the *Sporting Chronicle* and eventually made up his mind to risk Mrs. Lipski. She would at least be 7-2 against.

In no happy frame of mind he drew a wax sheet towards him and wrote laboriously, and had reached the line: "This one has been sent to me by my correspondent as the coop of the century," when—Iron Face!

It came to him like the thunder of drums. Iron Face would win that race. A revelation. . . his sub-conscience mind!

Iron Face would win: he knew it as certainly as if he were watching the horse walking into the winners' enclosure.

All of a tremble, he threw aside the wax sheet and started another.

Educated Evans has had a tip straight from his
Sub-conscience Mind!
A Revellation! A Revellation!
This horse will start at an outside price and Can't be Beat.
Old and new clients all, you will never get
another chance like this.
IRONFACE
IRONFACE
IRONFACE.

The morning after he sent out the revelation, The Miller came tramping up the stairs.

"Evans, you're going to let yourself in very bad unless you drop this revelation stuff," he said. "Iron Face is an old crock that has never jumped more than two fences in his life. He's up against the best 'chaser in the Midlands. . ."

Evans closed his eyes.

"Sub-conscience mind," he murmured. "Help yourself an' don't forget I've got a mouth."

Later he met Mr. Izzy Izzyheim, the famous turf accountant.

"You're a regular money-getter to me, Evans," said Mr. Izzyheim with great joviality. "If Camden Town only stands you for another three months, I'll be getting that new Rolls I promised the missus."

Mr. Evans shrugged his thin shoulders.

"There's things you don't understand, Mr. Izzyheim," he began.

"How much money have you got?" asked Izzyheim, his eyes glowing at the prospect of easy wealth. "Because I'm willing to lay you all you have at s.p. and never send a penny to the course,"

It needed but this to spur Evans to a frenzy Diving his hand into his pocket, he brought out a disordered collection of Treasury notes and postal orders; put his hand into another pocket and produced a ball of paper which, unwrapped, proved to consist of five £5 notes.

"Thirty-eight pun' ten," said Mr. Izzyheim gravely. "It'll just about pay my expenses to Brighton for the weekend."

He had one or two sycophantic clients with him, and these were amused. At that moment The Miller came up and Mr. Izzyheim hastily pocketed the ready.

"I've just laid our friend s.p. to thirty-eight ten against his sub-conscience horse," he said, and The Miller shook his head in despair.

"Evans," he said, as he walked with him towards the Cobden statue, "do you know that half the people in Camden Town never see you without tapping their nuts?"

"Let 'em!" said Evans defiantly.

He went hot and cold as people pointed to him, walking down the High Street that afternoon, and in a state of misery retired to his room and sat in the growing darkness, his head between his hands, deploring the insanity that had led him to parting with his capital. With bitterness in his heart he cursed The Children of the Sun; cursed the sub-conscience mind...

A hasty step on the stairs, and The Miller burst in.

"You lucky brute!" he said. . . . "Three runners. They laid seven to two on the favourite, seven to two against Mrs. Lipski, and they both fell and your hair trunk won at thirty-three to one!"

Evans raised his haggard face.

"What a beauty! What a beauty!" he said hollowly. "Sub-conscience mind *v.* pickin' 'em out with a pin!"

11.—MR. EVANS HAS A WELL-SCREWED HEAD

As the field came round the pay gate turn, Mr. Evans stood on one leg with a look of exquisite agony on his face, for Theoline lay last but one and "Theoline: go heavy" had been his £5 Special, his £2 Guarantee and his £10 Occasional Beauty.

As the field breasted the hill Theoline was absolutely last.

"Not a yard!" said Evans bitterly.

As the horses came opposite the silver ring a change occurred—out of the blue shot a bolt, and Theoline, threading his way through beaten horses, came with one effortless run to win in the end in a hack canter.

"That Lappy's the best jockey in the world," said Mr. Evans to his companion. "He's what they call in the French language a *'Multum in Palmo,'* which means that he's there if he's wanted. He reminds me of the celebrated Bill Archer."

Mr. Iggson, his friend, was both polite and flattering.

"It's a licker to me, Evans," he said, "how you do it. You've got your head screwed on the right way."

Educated Evans purred: he was still purring when the red flag went up. After that he purred no more, for Theoline was disqualified for boring.

"What a jockey!" he said savagely as they made their way across to the station. "There ain't no jockeys nowadays—only butcher boys an' what-nots! Did you hear what I said to him when he came out to ride in the next race? That Lappy can't ride one side of a horse nor the other side either. He ought to be warned off."

At that moment Mr. Arthur Lappy, speeding towards London in his Rolls, was expressing the same opinion to the pretty young lady who sat by his side. He was a fair-haired young man with rather a nice voice, for his father had been a fairly rich trainer and Arthur Lappy had enjoyed the luxury of a tutor. And he had other hobbies besides racing. Millicent Drace (which was not her real name) was most anxious to talk about these, and listened with some impatience to her companion discussing quite another subject.

"Did you hear what that poor little devil said when I came out of the weighing room?" he chuckled. " 'Butcher boy!' And I am!"

"Who was he?" asked Millicent, who wasn't interested.

"A little tipster from Camden Town—a chap called Evans. Poor little blighter!"

Millicent sought to bring the conversation to the subject of emeralds. She had seen Evans: she had also seen Mr. Iggson and had been more interested in that prosperous figure than in his companion. But for the moment . . . emeralds.

"You shall see them one day," said Arthur Lappy, and forgot all about Evans in the discussion of his expensive hobby.

For he had a passion for the green stones. Some jockeys collect stamps, some bookmakers' bills, some children, but Arthur Lappy collected emeralds, as his father did before him.

He had a flat in Half Moon Street, a house in Newmarket and a shoot in Norfolk, for Arthur's income was a very large one, and he had had several big strokes of luck, and he never wasted what he won. He was chary of speaking about his collection to strangers, but Millie was no stranger. He had known her three weeks, having met her at a party given by an actor friend, and because she never betted and never asked him for a tip, he knew that her heart was pure.

★★★★★★

Mr. Evans, as the race special thundered towards London, elaborated his views on bad jockeys.

"It's ridin' flash that does it, Mr. Iggson," he said. "These here

311

jockeys go dissipatin' up in the West End when they ought to be in bed dreamin' how they can help the public. They're like the celebrated candle that burns at both ends. It's havin' no education that does it. They're ignorant. Ask Lappy where the North Pole is an' what would he answer? Ask him about Julia Cæsar an' he'd be flummoxed. Take foreign languages—suppose you said to him '*Polly voo Francy*' he wouldn't understand plain English."

No doubt Educated Evans had reason for his sourness. Theoline was his eighth consecutive loser.

Well might Old Sam's Midnight Special chortle with joy.

> Don't be robbed by so-called Educated
> Amatchers, come to Old Sam, The Expert.
> (Same address since 1869)

"Don't worry," soothed Mr. Iggson. "You'll come out on top—you've got your head screwed on the right way."

It was natural that Mr. Iggson should comfort his unhappy friend. Even on ordinary occasions this stout and red-faced man never failed to favour Mr. Evans with a friendly nod whenever education walked the pavement before Iggson's Fresh Vegetable and Seasonable Fruit Store, though, as sometimes happens to a world's champion prophet and turf adviser, luck ran a little churlishly.

"You can't find winners all the time, Mr. Evans," said Mr. Iggson pleasantly. "Don't worry—you go on trying to find 'em and go on backing 'em! You're a man who's got his head screwed on the right way."

This was a favourite saying of Mr. Iggson's, and the highest praise he could bestow on any man—that he had his head screwed on the right way.

The very next day he stopped Mr. Evans as he was passing the shop.

"I've got a thing here that you'll understand, Mr. Evans. I'm an uneducated man myself, but you with your headpiece will see what it is in a jiffy. It's art."

"Art," said Mr. Evans profoundly, "is paintin', the same as the well-known Lanspear, him that did pictures of dogs by hand. Or it's statures, the same as the far-famed Ajax defyin' the lightnin' in Hyde Park, or it's musical pieces—see Moseark."

Mr. Iggson inclined his head.

"This is a stature," he said, and led the way into the back parlour.

On the mantelpiece stood a piece of bronze—the figure of a woman in long flowing robes.

"I bought it at the Caledonian Market, and according to certain things that's been said, it's art of the best quality."

"It's Venus," said Evans, eyeing the statuette with a frown. "The Venus de Marlow by the celebrated Michael Angleol."

The inscription on the bottom said "Hebe."

"That's Roman for Venus," explained Evans. "I've been thinkin'," said Mr. Iggson, "that if anything happened to me I'd like you to keep that. Accordin' to what I've heard it brings luck—especially if you keep it in a box under the bed and don't tell anybody you've got it."

Evans smiled.

"I'm not superstitious meself," he said, "an' I don't believe in mascots. All you got to do if your luck's out is to carry a bit of coal in your pocket an' spit every time you see a peebald horse."

"I'd like you to have it," said Mr. Iggson solemnly, "when I'm gorn."

Mr. Evans murmured a polite hope that the day would be long deferred, and returned to answer certain abusive letters that had come to Goodwin Chambers in the past twenty-four hours.

A few nights later as Mr. Evans sat, a brooding, unhappy figure, examining the day's results, and wondering what perverse fate had induced him to change his mind and send to all clients old and new Black Velvet (down the course), when he had woken up with the fullest intention and determination to send French Star (won 100-7), a whistle from the mews below brought him out into the open.

"Only one for you," said the postman as the educated man flew down the steps. "It's a wonder to me you get any after the stumers you've been lumbering on to the working classes."

"No insolence, my man," said Mr. Evans haughtily. "It's the like of us taxpayers that keeps the likes of you postmen."

He took the letter upstairs and opened it. It was written on aristocratically thick notepaper and had an embossed heading.

"If Mr. Evans will call upon Mr. Arthur Lappy at 7.30 tomorrow night, he may hear of something which may be of assistance to him."

Arthur Lappy! The far-famed jockey! Educated Evans was in a twitter of excitement, and scarcely remembered how the next day passed. At 7.30 to the second he rang the bell against the polished door of Mr. Lappy's flat, and was admitted by a magnificent footman in uniform—for Arthur had the aristocracy complex which has ruined so many young jockeys.

He himself was sitting in his den, a handsomely furnished apartment, a little overloaded with the objects of art which he had acquired in his extensive travels; for Arthur in the off season was a great globetrotter.

"You're the man who called me a butcher boy," said Mr. Lappy with a grin, "and I admit I rode like one."

For certain reasons he was in an exalted

Haroun al Raschid mood, at peace with the world, his heart charged with a benevolence which, to do him justice, was not unusual, even if it was a little more intensified that night.

"I'm going to give you a winner, but I'm not going to make a habit of it. Range Rider will walk the three o'clock race on Friday."

"Do you ride it, sir?" asked Evans humbly.

"No, I don't."

Arthur nodded.

"I often wonder how you fellows get a living," he said.

Mr. Evans coughed.

"Personally speakin'," he said, "I don't understand meself how the lower orders, the hoi polloi, or what I might term the uneducated masses, manage to exist. Take art—"

He stopped suddenly. When he raised his eyes he saw on the mantelpiece the exact counterpart of Mr. Iggson's statuette.

"Good lord!" he gasped.

Arthur Lappy was quick to notice his surprise.

"Have you seen one like that before?" He lifted the bronze figure down. "I bought that in Milan. There used to be a pair, but a servant I had pinched one."

Mr. Evans was momentarily embarrassed.

"I can't exactly say I've seen anything like it," he said discreetly, for Mr Iggson had a private reputation.

There was a ring at the bell, and Arthur rose quickly.

"You clear out," he said, and the reason for the hurry became apparent to Mr. Evans when a radiant young lady passed him in the hall, leaving behind the faint fragrance of those flowers which only the Paris perfumer knows.

An industrious man was Educated Evans that night. To all clients ancient and modern went forth the joyous tidings.

Educated Evans

Goodwin Chambers
Bayham Mews
Still the World's Chief Prophet!
Still the World's Chief Prophet!
Still the World's Chief Prophet!
Educated Evans has received from an inspired quarter a
winner that can't lose.
A winner that can't lose!
A winner that can't lose!
Information *v.* Gaswork
All clients who have acted honourable are advised to go
for a big stake on
RANGE RIDER

There was something so definite, so cocksure about this missive that even that astute judge of men and horses, Detective-Inspector Challoner, was impressed and came up to see Evans.

"Where did you get this?" he demanded. Evans smiled.

"One of me correspondents at Lambourn—"

"It's not trained at Lambourn anyway," said The Miller, eyeing the prophet with disfavour. And then, abruptly: "Is it from one of your dupes? I saw you at Sandown with them."

"Mr. Iggson," said Evans with dignity, "is one of my highest respected clients."

The Miller chewed on his straw thoughtfully. "Did he introduce you to the lady?"

"There wasn't a lady," said Mr. Evans.

"I'm inclined to agree with you," replied The Miller cryptically, but did not explain his mystery.

It is a curious fact that all Mr. Evans" tips were not backed by the people who purchased them.

After a big win there was a surprising number of clients, especially those who had soberly and solemnly agreed to remit the odds to five shillings, who had forgotten that the horse was in the first race, or hadn't had the money to bet with, or hadn't received this letter. But this day, as he walked through the High Street, Camden Town, made splendid by a glorious and unusual sun, he was intercepted every few yards by earnest men who assured him they were going to back Range Rider, and that this was the last chance that he'd ever get any so-and-so money out of them if it didn't win.

Four o'clock brought the happy result, four-thirty the surprising price; for at the last moment money had come into the market for three horses, and Range Rider had started at 100-9.

Mr. Iggson was the first to congratulate his friend.

"I've always said. . ."

Mr. Evans went cheerily back to the flat, in thorough and complete agreement that his head *was* screwed on the right way, and that he lay under an everlasting debt of gratitude to that great and supreme artist of the pigskin, Mr. Arthur Lappy.

That night. . .The young woman from Iggson's made a call upon Mr. Evans: she chose the wan hour of 2 a.m. and was unconscious of the unseemliness of it all.

"Good Gawd!" exclaimed Mr. Evans testily as he opened the door and peered forth into the rainy night. "What's all this about?"

A small, squeaky voice answered him.

"It's Evie—the girl from Iggson's, Mr. Evans."

"Wait a tick," said Mr. Evans modestly, and put on his trousers in the dark,

He lit a lamp, straightened the couch on which, a few minutes before, he had been dreaming that the City was won by a horse with an elephant's head, and, opening the door, invited Iggson's girl inside.

She was neither young nor comely, but she had always been Iggson's girl—a general servant by day and a seller of potatoes in the busy hours of Saturday night.

"Mr. Iggson is in trouble," she said in a hushed voice.

Words and tone told the dire story. Mr. Evans made a clucking noise to express his astonishment—he was in truth staggered. It was common talk that Iggson did not confine himself to the sale of greens, and that, beside the trade in apples, he did a little buying "on the side."

If you found a "clock" or a bit of jewellery and casually mentioned the fact to Mr. Iggson in the privacy of his back parlour, you were certain of collecting a bit of money and no questions asked.

But Mr. Evans was not a common man. He believed the best of horses and men—especially horses. He never gave credence to the stories which came to him, but at the same time he had ears to hear and heard.

None the less he was shocked.

"That's bad news." he said, and added politely "The worst news since the Great Fire of London in 1848 that burnt down the Thames

Embankment."

"I see a fire engine as I was coming along," said Iggson's girl conversationally, but returned to the cause for her visit. "They come an' took him out of his bed—The Miller an' two 'busies,' an' Mr. Iggson got a chance to speak to me just as they was searchin' his room an' he said, 'Take that stature orf the mantelpiece in the bedroom to Mr. Evans an' tell him to keep it for me till further orders.'"

She groped in the big, soddened bag she carried and produced the "stature."

"Good lor'!" said the startled Evans.

Never in his wildest moments had he dreamt that the statue would come to him in such circumstances.

The tragedy of Iggson did not disturb Mr. Evans' rest. He accepted other people's troubles with the greatest philosophy. Iggson was a man of some property and could pay for a mouthpiece—he would not at any rate require Mr. Evans' services as legal adviser.

Evans put the statue under the bed and slept the sleep of the completely satisfied.

He had reason for his satisfaction, for the next morning's post brought the most generous acknowledgments of the service he had rendered to a world of suffering punters (bookmakers in Camden Town pay out overnight). New orders rolled in all the morning, and the heart of the educated man swelled with joy and gratitude to his benefactor.

And then he remembered the statue. Obviously it was the one that matched Arthur Lappy's—what a chance of paying back the man who had re-established him in the estimation of Camden Town.

To think, with Mr. Evans, was to act. Wrapping the statuette in a piece of white paper, wrapping that again in brown paper and tying it carefully, he waited till night, and, going down to Half Moon Street, he deposited his burden on the mat before Mr. Lappy's flat, rang the bell and made a hurried exit. Only the words "From a Friend" were inscribed upon the parcel for Evans had no desire to complicate the case against the erring Iggson. No doubt, he reflected, Iggson had "fenced" the little bronze piece from the jockey's defaulting servant.

When he got back to the flat he found The Miller waiting for him.

"Did Iggson's girl come here the other night?" he demanded.

"No," lied Evans. "What's the trouble, Mr. Challoner? When I heard he was inside you could have knocked me down with a feather."

"Emeralds is the trouble," said The Miller grimly. "We've got Iggson and we've got Lappy's old servant, but we haven't got the girl yet."

Educated Evans dithered but did not swoon. "Lappy's old servant?" he said hollowly. "What's he got to do with it?"

"They were Lappy's emeralds," said The Miller, unusually communicative for a police officer. "Apparently his servant had been pinching things for years and fencing them with Iggson—that's how he got to know there were emeralds in the flat. Twelve thousand pounds' worth."

Mr. Evans spent an unhappy night.

For three weeks he avoided High Street, Camden Town, and lived hourly in expectation of arrest as an accomplice.

One satisfaction he had—he had returned the statue.

And then the miracle happened. Mr. Iggson, brought up at the Old Bailey, was acquitted for lack of evidence, and came back almost triumphantly to Camden Town. The first intimation Evans had of the joyous news was the sight of the smiling Iggson standing in his doorway.

"Well, Mr. Evans, I'm out. All the lies and perjuries of these busies didn't get me put away."

Evans was overjoyed, and said so.

"Yes, I thought you would be. You're a man with his head screwed on the right way and you know a thing or two, Mr. Evans," said Iggson. "And if you don't mind, I'll take that stature."

The face of Mr. Evans dropped.

"I gave it away," he said.

"You what?" shrieked the greengrocer. "Give it away. . . who did you give it to?"

"I give it back to the bloke it was pinched from," said Evans, pale but determined. "As an educated man I couldn't do anything else—"

★★★★★★

It was lucky for all concerned that The Miller had followed Mr. Iggson into Bayham Mews.

"What was the trouble, Evans?" asked The Miller curiously.

Mr. Evans was dabbing his nose with an ensanguined handkerchief.

"I'm not at liberty to discuss the matter," he said. "I tried to do this low feller a favour an' he hadn't got the education to see it."

The Miller was looking at him oddly.

"I'm not going to ask you any more questions, Evans, but I've got an idea that somebody left a statuette on Lappy's doormat, and if you're the man Lappy owes you a bit. For inside that statuette were twenty-five emeralds worth twelve thousand pounds.'

Mr. Evans gaped at him.

"Inside?"

The Miller nodded.

"The inside is hollow, but you don't notice it if the head's screwed on the right way."

12.—THE TWISTING OF ARTHUR COLLEYBORN

One of the hardest things that any trainer can attempt is to speak encouragingly about any horse he trains. Everybody knows Colleyborn. He is one of those honest fellows with a shining face that everybody likes. He never bets and never encourages his owners to bet, and yet in some miraculous way he is a very rich man.

It is true that he has been known to encourage his brother- in-law to bet.

To the owner of Boopah he wrote:

"Your horse is very well, but there are other horses in the race quite as well. I am afraid of Mawky's horse and I rather imagine Sir Peter Booley's horse may be fitter than we think. I should have a little bet each way if I were you."

On the other hand, he wrote to his brother-in-law, Mr. Willie Yegley:

Dear Bill,—Get me a monkey on Boopah, and this time keep the wires back till a quarter of an hour before the set time. We ought to get tens to our money. Thank you for the cheque over Mouldy Boy. Kind love to Cis.

Arthur.

Now Mr. Colleyborn was terribly susceptible to the charms of what is sometimes described as the fair sex but is as often as not brunette. And amongst the many pretty ladies who had driven to town in Mr. Colleyborn's Bentley for a show, a bit of supper and a dance, was a certain Arabella, who was acting at the time as the assistant of a Cambridge doctor. That is to say, she assisted him by making out patients' bills and typing the evidence he gave whenever he was called upon to swear that the gentleman who ran his car into a lamp-post and wanted to fight a policeman was not drunk but was suffering from temporary dementia.

In course of time Mr. Colleyborn and his lady friend parted. He did not ask her for the return of his presents, because he had given her nothing more substantial than a Good Time.

Soon after this Miss Arabella went back to London to another job, and there the matter ended, for Arabella married—unhappily, as it proved. But the lady never ceased to ascribe the cause of her misfortune to the dirty, low and underhand treatment she had received at Mr. Colleyborn's hands.

And then fate threw this vengeful lady into association with Educated Evans. And this at a moment when Mr. Arthur Colleyborn was preparing several winters' keep.

The racing world had been greatly mystified by the eccentric running of Grub Alley, the four-year-old son of Fleet Court out of Mudslinger. Grub Alley was (according to various journalistic estimates):

(a) A good horse,

(b) A rogue,

(c) Touched in his wind,

(d) Unreliable.

There were shrewd people who thought that he was being "fiddled" in preparation for a big handicap. Certain bookmakers who had no illusions and knew Mr. Colleyborn better than his owner, issued urgent warnings to their clients not to lend their names. Grub Alley's owner, a bewildered man who never betted, was told by Mr. Colleyborn that one of these days the horse would surprise everybody, and was content to let nature take its course. So were the turf prophets, who, having tipped him a score of times, left Grub Alley severely alone. Which is just what Mr. Colleyborn most earnestly desired.

Grub Alley was in the Newshire Handicap with 7.6 when the curtain rang up on this present drama of Misplaced Confidence.

Educated Evans was a philosopher in all matters except love. When Eros aimed his tender dart at Mr. Evans' simple heart (which is poetry but isn't intended to be), his judgment went out to 33-1 others.

"To anything in skirts," said The Miller, shaking his head sadly, "you are Blackberries on a Country Road."

"This young lady," said Mr. Evans soberly, "is Educated. I admit she rather resembles the Venus dee Milan—but beauty's only skin deep as the far-famed Cardinal Garnet Wolseley said. She knows more a bout anatomy an' bones than any lady I've ever met. She was clurk to a Harley Street specialist who lives in Newmarket an' what she don't know about blood capsules and other well-known microbes ain't worth talking about."

"Does she know anything about horses?" Mr. Evans smiled pityingly.

"She lived in Newmarket an' nearly married three trainers," he replied crushingly.

"And she preferred to marry a gentleman who is doing twelve months for assaulting the police," said The Miller.

Mr. Evans was covered with confusion.

"I'm doin' my duty by her," he said.

"That's what I'm afraid of," said The Miller cryptically.

Was it entirely for her intellect or her helplessness that Mr. Evans attached himself to Arabella Louker? She was pretty—whether like the Venus de Milo or not is a moot question. Nobody ever saw that lady wearing clothes.

They had met by accident, which was the only possible manner Mr. Evans ever met anybody. She was waiting for a 'bus and he was waiting for a 'bus, and he said it was a fine day and she agreed. Then she said that the way 'bus conductors treated people was a positive disgrace and he agreed. She got off at the Cobden statue and so did he. He asked her to have a cup of tea and she said she would like one. And that is how it all happened.

Mrs. Lube, who loathed Mr. Evans and spoke of him disrespectfully on all occasions, referred to Arabella as "Evans' latest pick up," and expressed her amazement that a girl so singularly attractive should so descend the scale of taste.

"From what I hear," she told her husband, "Evans is giving her work to do at the office. I wish I knew the girl: she might like to pick up a pound now and again."

"I could easily get to know her," said her husband hopefully.

The suggestion was not well received. "Wimmin have been your ruin," she said. He looked at her thoughtfully and was inclined to admit the truth of this. But he didn't, for obvious reasons.

Mrs. Arabella Louker was a nice girl, a pleasant companion and an engaging talker. She had been secretary to a Newmarket doctor when Joe Louker crossed her path. She was on the point of returning to the medical profession at the moment Mr. Evans dawned rosily upon a dreary world which was mainly populated by landladies who wanted their arrears of rent, and gentleman acquaintances who were anxious to contribute to her support.

"What I like about you, Mr. Evans," she said once, "is that you don't insult me. I've got so tired of walking out with gentlemen and having to dodge round back streets so as not to meet their wives and children."

"I'm a man," said Evans impressively, "not like the well-known Crippen. I always say that if education does nothin' else it teaches you to respect ladies. As the highly celebrated Queen Elizabeth said to the renowned Duke of Wellington—"

"What about Newmarket?" asked Arabella, who was not especially interested in the great figures of history.

"I'll run you down tomorrow—I've ordered me car for six," replied Evans. "Not that I think you'll get anything out of Colleyborn. If I could only find out whether he's working a coop with Grub Alley, it'd mean a fortune in my pocket, Miss Arabella. Bee Face is a stone pinch with him out of the way—"

"He'll tell me the truth or I'll wring his false heart from his body," said Arabella sombrely. "Oh, if I only knew how to get my own back with that false-faced hound!"

On this evening Mr. Alfred Lube made a great discovery and came post-haste to the Headquarters of Old Sam's Midnight Special.

"That girl he's walkin' out with is a married woman. An' she's a friend of Colleyborn. Her an' Evans are gain' down to Newmarket to see Colleyborn. She knows him an' I'll bet they're after Grub Alley."

"By train?" asked Mrs. Lube.

"They've hired Winkworth's Ford."

Mrs. Lube thought rapidly.

"You go down by train an' don't leave 'em out of your sight," she said.

★★★★★★

And the next morning. . . .

Brightly fell the morning sunlight athwart the one window of Adam's Apple Orchard, Bayham Mews. There was no sound in that salubrious *cul de sac* but the impatient kicking of the hungry horses and the chirping of famished sparrows.

Mr. Evans turned uneasily in his bed and half awoke with that uneasy sensation of impending unpleasantness peculiar to gentlemen incarcerated in Pentonville Prison who have an urgent appointment with the executioner at 8 a.m.

This unease brought him to wakefulness, and he sat up, blinking. His table was piled high with the envelopes he had addressed on the night before; the duplicating machine that a child could work (but never had) rested on the floor; the wax sheet was already written which, properly placed in the duplicator, would enable him to announce to all the world that Bee Face had been tried two stone better than Cresta Run, and if a boy could only ride him, would come home alone for the Newshire Handicap.

"Good lord!" gasped Mr. Evans, remembering, and threw his shivering legs out of bed, covered them decently with his best trousers, which he drew from under the mattress, where they had been carefully laid the night before, and began his preparations for an early morning breakfast.

When the sticks were burning and the kettle making unhappy moaning sounds, his spirits revived. By the time he had shaved and had a sluice he was ostensibly like himself.

He heard the thump and splutter of the hired motorcar at the end of the mews, swallowed his breakfast hastily, buttoned his collar and put on his classiest tie, and though a walking-stick is not a particularly useful piece of equipment for a motorcar journey, he took his nearly gold-headed cane from the corner and, going out and locking the door, made his way to the covered Ford.

He picked up his lady friend ten minutes later (she was surprisingly punctual), and in two winks, as it were, the car was bumping through Epping Forest.

Mr. Evans seized the opportunity to explain the growing importance of exact information on the Newshire Handicap. There was reason enough for his anxiety. The Newshire Handicap had suddenly become an item of important public interest by reason of the fact that the wealthy Australian owner of one of the candidates had, under the influence of good cheer and other refreshment at a public dinner, announced that he would give the whole of his winnings (if he won) to the hospitals; and for the first time in its history the Newshire Handicap was the subject of ante-post betting. Which meant that there was as much dead meat in that race as any of the Spring handicaps.

The Newshire Handicap had also been a subject of newspaper comment and analysis. More than this, Mr. Evans had received inquiries from his clientele concerning this event.

"I know Colleyborn," said Arabella. "He's the sort of man who gives nothing away. If I could tell you, Mr. Evans, what I've done for that man, you'd be surprised—typed his letters, *et cetera, et cetera*, and all I got was a seven and sixpenny dinner and a four shilling bottle of

Beaune! I've not so much as had a ring or a bracelet watch out of him. And if he's going to work one of his dirty tricks on the public, and I can get the news beforehand, it'll break his 'eart—heart, I mean."

"If it comes to presents—" began Evans, in a munificent mood, but she was one of those girls who listened best when she was talking herself.

"I wouldn't have married but for him," she rattled on. "I said to him: 'Arthur, if I leave you, you'll rue the day.' I said to him: 'Arthur, I'm going to get my own back on you if it takes me twenty years.'"

"What did he say?" asked the interested Evans.

"He just sneered," said Arabella, "and scoffed."

"A man like that ought to be pole-axed," said Mr. Evans passionately. "He's worse than the well-known Edward the Eighth who had ten wives and had their heads cut off and hung up in a private room. He's worse than the far-famed Looey the Nineteenth, him that got into trouble over Lewdcreature Burgia, the female Crippen of Italy."

"He's a dirty dog," said Arabella expressively, in the language of the twentieth century.

Newmarket bounced into view at last. Strings of horses wandering aimlessly about the Heath; tiny boys in tight leggings; bored trainers following their strings home, and discussing loudly the new show at Drury Lane and other sporting matters.

"There he is," said Arabella suddenly. "Stop the car."

The car needed very little encouragement. It stopped. Arabella got out and walked towards a rather red-faced, youngish-looking man who was striding across the Heath on the way to the town. Unhappily for him, he was not mounted.

"Oh, there you are!" said Arabella's voice, and Mr. Evans thought he heard a groan.

He watched them strolling about the Heath, saw Mr. Colleyborn's arms raised in frantic protest, saw Miss Arabella shake her fist under his nose.... Evans sat and purred. Never had he seen racing information being extracted in such a picturesque manner.

After a quarter of an hour she walked rapidly back to the car.

"You wait in the town and have a bite," she said. "Me and Colleyborn's going to talk things over."

"Does he know who I am?" asked Mr. Evans, in some alarm, realising the terrible things that had happened to touts at Newmarket. (He had once been shown a mound of earth which was locally called the Ditch, but which a trainer had told him was a secret burial place of murdered watchers.)

"Yes, he knows who you are. You don't suppose I've got any secrets about my friends?" she said. "But Mr. Colleyborn's a very nice man and you needn't be afraid."

Mr. Evans found an eating-house.

When he had finished and got back to the car, the driver handed him a note.

"A boy left it with me to give to you."

The epistle ran:

"Dear Mr. Evans, I've had a very long talk with Mr. Colleyborn, and he's realised what a terrible mistake he made by giving me up. He says that Grub Alley won't finish in the first three, but the other trainer's told him that Bee Face is a certainty. I'm sorry I can't come back with you, but Mr. Colleyborn wants me to type a few letters for him, and for old time's sake and because of the past I am willing to forget and forgive."

With this information in his inside pocket Educated Evans sped back to London, a happy man.

Alfred Lube, who had watched the arrival of the car, who had seen the coming of the note, who had been a witness of that poignant scene upon the Heath, also sped back in greater comfort.

"It's all right, Emma," he reported breathlessly to his wife. "That girl's got the information for Evans, and we ain't goin' to be caught this time."

Wherefore did Old Sam's Midnight Special come out flamboyantly, recommending all clients old and new to go their limit, have their shirts on, and generally to support Grub Alley (there were ten stars against Grub Alley).

A more dignified communication was that made by Educated Evans.

EDUCATED EVANS,

The World's Champion Prophet and Turf Adviser.

KEEP OFF GRUB ALLEY!

KEEP OFF GRUB ALLEY!

KEEP OFF GRUB ALLEY!

Mr. Evans has been advised by his Newmarket correspondent
that BEE FACE could win the Newshire Handicap

with 11 stone.

DON'T BACK GRUB ALLEY!
DON'T BACK GRUB ALLEY!
DON'T BACK GRUB ALLEY!

He was not unnaturally annoyed when Grub Alley won at 7–1.

Annoyance and resentment went hand in hand on this occasion, and he carried his sorrows to The Miller. Inspector Arbuthnot Challoner listened unsympathetically.

"Your so-and-so tip cost me two pounds," he said savagely. "Arabella twisted you, you poor mutt! And she's received the price of her villainy! I saw Colleyborn's Bentley outside Woolworth's yesterday."

13.—The Kidnapping of Mr. Evans

There was a certain head lad who had a number of private clients. Which is not allowed by any of the rules of racing.

He was a purveyor of very excellent information, but he had few clients, and those did not advertise him, for a very obvious reason.

Then one day he came from the country to Camden Town to stay with a sister who had done very well and married into the laundry trade, and to her he poured forth the sum of his trouble. "I had three winners last week and got nothing out of it," he complained. "Now if I only had a bit of money and could advertise in another name—"

"What about the Lubeses?" asked his sister suddenly.

She knew Mrs. Lube personally. They shared in common an immense admiration for John Barrymore in Tragics and Charlie Chaplin in Comics.

"Her grandfather has got a paper—I bet he'd do something for you."

The head lad cogitated this, "What about this chap Evans?" he asked. His sister turned up a nose that was by nature tip-tilted.

"Him!" she said scornfully. "He made us pay for a shirt he said we lost! I wouldn't have dealings with a common man like that."

So the introduction to the Lubeses followed. Mrs. Lube came to tea and met the head lad, whose name—well, never mind his name. At first the conversation was general. Then the head lad casually mentioned his profession; then he remarked on the valuelessness of watching gallops if you can't make money out of them.

Mrs. Lube listened and quivered. She stayed after tea and came again that night, and she and the wicked head lad talked head to head and the conference was in every way successful.

A week after this, Mr. Evans was watering the geranium that represented the garden of Abbot's Speed House. He was in a complacent frame of mind. He had sent out one horse that had won at 6-4 and one that had been short-headed at 100-8. Hard lines! Hard lines!

It was not his custom to purchase Old Sam's Midnight Special.

"Why should I throw away threepence on *his* Five Pound Special?" he was wont to remark. "When I got information of me own *v.* pickin' 'em out with a pin?"

It was The Miller who brought the most sensational issue of the *Special.*

"Good morning, Evans," he said pleasantly. "Seen this?"

Evans' lip curled.

"I never read muck," he said.

"That is why your messages to the deluded public are so full of spelling mistakes," said The Miller, and placed before the educated man the *Extra Special Issue.*

It was printed on green paper—which Evans wouldn't dream of using because it was notoriously unlucky. Evans picked it up and his eye was arrested by the hysterical headline.

Secret Information by the Grandest Informer who will give
Winners Galore! No more Educated 6-4 chances! No more
swank bluff and babble! No more Educated Humbug by a so-
called 'prophet'! News that nobody knows! Not winners you
get from the newspapers!
Next Wensday!
Next Wensday!
Next Wensday!
The winner of the Colebeach Handicap!
Can't lose!
Can't lose!
Can't lose!
Send T.M.O. 10s. to Winner Mansions, Little Hillington Street.
Old Sam's Grand Winner!

"This," said Evans rapidly and indignantly, "is mere stuff and nonsense and uneducated twaddle! This is mere playgaring and sheer swank! This man Old Sam is a mere beer-eatin' patrician that ought to be in an asylum for goats. Education! Look at the spelling—look at the vulgarity and commonness of it! He's worse than Charlie Peace the far-famed inventor of the Chamber of Horrors; he reminds me of the man they couldn't 'ang; he's—"

"What is the source of this interesting information?" interrupted The Miller. "Do you know anything about the winner of the Colebeach Handicap?"

"Do I know?" scoffed Evans. "Ain't I had Hambone from the boy who does him? Ain't I seen him with my own eyes beat Abbot's Speed in a trial?"

"No," said The Miller, "you haven't."

But Mr. Evans was not abashed.

"I got this horse from a gentleman who goes to the same barber as the owner; this Hambone could win this race an' laugh at the rest. He could win on a tight rein or a loose rein. He could get left at the post an' then trot it."

The Miller listened patiently.

"Hambone was scratched this afternoon—now tell me another lie."

But it took more than that to upset Mr. Evans. "Scratched—tut-tut! An' yet, after what the owner told me, I ought to have expected it. 'Evans,' he says, 'I don't know whether to run this horse in the Colebeach or keep him for the Royal Hunt Cup,' he says. So I says to him: 'Whatever you do, me lord, don't show the horse up'—an' he's took my advice."

"You don't know anything about the Colebeach Handicap," accused The Miller wrathfully. "Until you saw this paper, you had no idea that there was such a race."

Evans closed his eyes, hurt but dignified.

"I was goin' down to Newmarket specially to see it run," he said.

"It's run at Haydock Park," said The Miller unkindly.

Mr. Evans might dismiss the frenzied claim of Old Sam lightly, but in his secret heart he was troubled and uneasy. Never before had Mrs. Lube made so confident a statement. He sensed, behind the blatant claim, the very core of sincerity.

That night he pored over the entries. Elbowed, Mognato, Binny Bird, Sweep, Obah, Lucy Lala. . . .

He paused at this. Lucy Lala was trained in a little stable that sometimes sent out two winners a year, but sometimes didn't. The trainer trained a few horses, as he told everybody, for his own amusement and the amusement of his friends. Apparently they had an enlarged sense of humour, or else they got a lot of fun out of paying their training bills.

Evans shook his head. No, that couldn't be it. He went further.

Happy Grin, Yangtse, Mogador, Bony Bertie . . .

He conned and conned till his eyes ached. And as he studied and thought, he reached a conclusion. It must be Yangtse.

He began laboriously to inscribe a *pronunciamento* which commenced:

Information from my new special and secret watcher. . .

He finished his work and went abroad for refreshment. In the meantime Mrs. Lube snatched the still wet sheet from her grandfather's hand. She, too, had been working a duplicator and had not observed the entrance of her ancestor.

"You're not supposed to read that, gran'father," she said sharply.

Old Sam, who could read just well enough to decipher "Lucy Lala" in big black type, murmured his apologies.

"Is that the horse you sent us?" he demanded.

He addressed the head lad, who, with Mr. Alfred Lube, were the other occupants of the kitchen.

"Take this two shillings and go out. Gran'father," said Mrs. Lube tartly. "And don't go stickin' your nose into business that don't concern you."

When he had gone the head lad emphasised the wonder of his tip.

"I saw this horse tried—it's the biggest pinch that ever looked through a bridle, and if it don't bring you—us—in a thousand pounds, I don't know what will."

He spent the evening telling them how fortunate they were in having met him. And whilst this was going on there was another and less pleasant meeting.

It is a fact that Old Sam, who occasionally described himself as the Seventh Wonder of the Sporting World, but who, in more modest moments, was content with the less provocative title, "The Wizard of Camden Town"—this Old Sam was normally a gentle, almost humble soul. Ere his masterful granddaughter had forced him into the hazardous business of anticipating the intentions of clever stables, he had been content to hold up one wall of the White Hart, which feat he accomplished by the simple process of standing outside the hostelry all day and applying his back to it; in this status he was affable, courteous, ready for the price of a pint (which before Hell Broke Loose in Europe was 2d.) to run an "arrand" or keep an eye upon a taxi whilst its owner had one, and sometimes two, inside.

But when Old Sam, through the strivings and pushings of Mrs. Lube, developed into the proprietor of Old Sam's Midnight Special he was no longer normal. For normality to Old Sam was a condition of mild fuddlement, beer being the instrument of his semi-insensibility. Prosperity brought spirits; spirits aroused in him a fierce pugnacity which was not consonant with his advanced age. So that he never met Educated Evans in the street but that he hurled upon that man of singular erudition the most opprobrious and bitter gibes.

Evans bore his trials with a certain haughty dignity, until one day he was passing a quiet evening in that same White Hart. He was, in point of fact, instructing the mind of Miss Eveline, the new barmaid, whose mind was not quite as plastic as a large piece of wood.

". . . take botomy. Tomatoes are fruit—very few people know that. Take apples—or *pomme de terres*, named after the celebrated racehorse that I give when he won at Ascot, or it may have been Goodwood, what a beauty! Take the day an' night, so called because the world, which is the shape of a orange, revolves round the sun once in twenty-four hours. Take Shakespeare, him that wrote the pieces which we all admire—"

"Take Shakespeare!" grated a hateful voice. "You couldn't take Shakespeare if they paid yer!"

Evans turned his head slightly and looked significantly at the barmaid.

"He's had Enough," he said meaningly.

"You couldn't take Shakespeare from the Cobden stature to the Euston Road," sneered Old Sam as he lurched to the bar.

"An' there ain't a 'orse called Shakespeare. Don't take none of his tips, miss, or you'll die in the work'us. A double scotch and a splash, miss."

Despite Mr. Evans' warning, the young lady with the diamond brooch served the old man deftly.

"You're a swindlin' 'ound," said Old Sam with great gravity. "You're a common pinprickin' perishin' piecan."

He tossed down the fiery liquid. Mr. Evans ostensibly ignored him.

"You're one of those people that can't find winners—Lucy Lala—what a beauty, what a beauty!"

"Eh?" said Evans, instantly attentive.

As instantly, as his ghastly error came to him, was Old Sam sober—

and Old Sam sober was a gentle soul.

"What was I a-sayin' of?" he quavered, passing his hand before his eyes. "Did I say anything I oughtn't to have said, Mr. Evans?" Evans' soul was filled with a great exaltation. "You said Lucy Lala!" he said.

Which was a great mistake on Evans' part. He saw Old Sam reel from the bar, and waited only till the door swung close before he followed. Little he imagined, as he worked feverishly at a new composition advising all and sundry to

Bet blind on
LUCY LALA
Don't take notice of previous messages sent in error.

. . . .that old Sam, rather tearful, was facing his enraged relatives with the story of his blunder.

Midnight was striking when a knock came to the door of Mr. Evans' flat. A diminutive boy in leggings was revealed in the lamplight.

"Are you the celebrated Educated Evans, the World's Champion Turf Prophet?"

He seemed to be recalling a sentence well learnt.

"That's me, my boy," said Evans graciously. "Lord Iggerman wants to see you urgent," said the youth.

Evans gasped. Lord Iggerham was one of the greatest of the owners.

"To see me?"

"Yes, sir; he says he don't want you to tip a horse of his."

That was quite understandable. Evans saw nothing remarkable in the request.

"Very good, my boy—where is his lordship?"

"At the Midlands Goods Yard," was the staggering reply. "He's in his special train."

Evans was intrigued. He followed his guide through the streets— but it was some distance from the goods yard that the special train was waiting, and to reach it involved dodging officious railway foremen and traversing a bewildering maze of railway lines. And in truth, his lordship's special train had the appearance of being a string of horse boxes.

The lad climbed up and opened a door.

"In here, sir," he said.

Mr. Evans swung himself up to the dark interior of the small compartment in which stable boys usually travel. As he did so, the door closed with a crash and he heard a key turn.

He tried to open the windows, but they were fast.

In the darkness Mr. Alf Lube and the head lad watched happily.

"He's all right," said the head lad, before climbing into another coach. "When we get to Salisbury I'll have the coach shunted—you needn't worry about him."

Mrs. Lube was waiting for her husband.

"I've been in his room," she said, "an' the low common swindler was sendin' out our horse! This'll learn him a lesson!"

★★★★★★

At four o'clock the next afternoon Mr. Evans woke from an exhausted sleep to hear the door unlocked.

"Hullo—what are you doing here?" demanded a railway man suspiciously.

"Where's this?" demanded Evans.

"Salisbury—hop it!"

Evans crawled out and made his way to the nearest bar. If there was a law in the land, the Lubeses should sleep that night in Albany Street Police Station.

The plot was clear—they were stopping him sending out Lucy Lala .. if only he hadn't sent out a horse at all for that race! Yangtse! What a horse to send!

All night long he'd been remembering that Yangtse was touched in the wind and couldn't gallop on hard going and didn't like left-hand courses and wasn't any good over a mile.

A newspaper boy shouted his wares, and Evans with a sinking and bitter heart went out to buy a paper. He opened it slowly and saw the headline:

A TRAGEDY FOR BACKERS.
Yangtse wins Handicap at 20-1;
Lucy Lala, a hot favourite, finishes last.

Mr. Evans drew a long breath.

"Information *v.* gaswork," he murmured, and went inside again to refresh.

14.—Educated Evans Declares to Win

Mr. Evans had many detractors. He had some admirers who stuck to him through thick and thin: men who could see no wrong in him.

For example, one Harry Wissell was such a man. He was a good-looking and athletic young man who might have broken into the most exclusive circles, instead of which he broke into houses, occasionally with profit to himself—occasionally to disappear from town into what is euphemistically called "the country."

The secret of his adoration of the educated man was no secret to police headquarters. During one of the periods of his retirement Mr. Evans, who was a kind-hearted man, had come to the rescue of Wissell's aged and ailing mother. In other words, he had paid her fine when she was charged with:

(a) Being drunk and disorderly.

(b) Assaulting Police-Constable Jones in the execution of his duty.

(c) Doing wilful damage to the extent of 13s. 4d. by tearing up the blanket with which she was supplied in the cell.

Moreover, Mr. Evans had written her defence, which she read from the dock and which began:

"Your Worship, Situated as I am, the mother of a large family, I feel my position acute. For years I have suffered from giddiness, pains in the head, rheumatism and other excruciating pains too numerous to mention ... ."

Anyway, she was fined, though the magistrate expressed his doubt as to whether he was wise in loosing her upon an unoffending world.

Mrs. Wissell gained a certain sanctity soon after the release of her son by falling in the Regent's Canal and drowning herself; and Harry never forgot what he owed to his benefactor.

"Mr. Evans," he said on one occasion, "if I could do you a turn I'd walk from here to Highgate Archway on me bare feet."

And he meant it. He did many a good turn to Mr. Evans, notably when young Mr. Lube, flushed with wine and victory (for Old Sam's Midnight Special had given three winners in succession), made disparaging remarks about the educated man. It was unfortunate for him that Harry was present.

"Educated Evans?" said Alf Lube, smiling pityingly. "Why, he ain't a man, he's no better than a bit of horse-radish! Education! I could talk his head off, before witnesses or private—!"

"Here!" said Mr. Wissell.

Alf looked round, but did not recognise danger.

"I'm talkin' about Educated Evans—" he began.

"You called him a bit of horse-radish," said Harry.

The landlord, recognising the symptoms, leaned over the zinc bar.

333

"Outside! he hissed.

They went, Alf Lube unwillingly. He returned to the bosom of his family that night slightly altered.

"And that's what I'd do to anybody who said a word against you, Mr. Evans," said Harry.

Evans grasped him by the hand.

"But if you see Mrs. Lube you might tell her that I knew nothing about it."

"If I see Mrs. Lube she'll be sorry," said Harry ominously.

Mr. Evans almost wished they would meet.

His friend had expressed only one regret: he could not help Mr. Evans in his own particular business.

"I don't know no racin' people, Mr. Evans," he said regretfully. "I wish I did."

"Don't worry, Harry," said Educated Evans, with a quiet smile. "I know 'em all. Take Lord Durby: him an' me's like brothers. When I take off me hat to him he takes off his hat to me. Take the celebrated Lord Wool—what's his name—him that invented Johnny Walker. I've slept in his park often an' often. Take Steve—I don't know his brother Pat so well—me an' Steve often meet in the Jockey Club."

"You do get about, don't you?" said his admirer, awe-stricken.

Evans smiled.

"It's education," he said simply. "It's knowin' hist'ry an' breedin' an' geography."

"If I ever get hold of a winner—" began Harry.

Mr. Evans was amused.

A week later he was wishing somebody would get hold of a winner—for they had succeeded in eluding his own grasp.

So sure had Mr. Evans been that a certain thing would happen at Epsom that he had painted a new signboard for his door—"The Priory Park." In a fit of great depression he had painted this out, and was half-way through his task of transforming that lordly demesne into "Embargo Chambers," when The Miller, whose other name was Detective-Inspector Arbuthnot Challoner, came in unobserved and stood silently regarding the artist's efforts.

"You're a bad sign-painter but a first-class liar," he said.

Mr. Evans started and turned, blinking up at the newcomer.

"Bless me life and soul, Mr. Challoner!" he said mildly. "You creep in and out like the celebrated Shylock Holmes, of Upper Baker Street, N.W. You remind me of the far-famed Lady Macduff, who walked in

334

her sleep—see Shakespeare."

"I'd hate to tell you what you remind me of," said The Miller gently, and added: "You gave Priory Park for the City and Suburban."

"The eleventh hour wire—" pleaded Evans.

"Was Priory Park," said the remorseless Miller, "and your fifty-ninth second tip was that same dilatory animal."

"I got to get me living," said Evans, and went on calmly with his fraudulent sign-work. "Them Lubeses tipped Kinnaird. If you find winners by gaswork you're bound to be right sooner or later. My information was that Priory Park couldn't lose."

"My information was that it did," said The Miller, "and I backed him on your advice! Men have been certified as mentally unsound for less."

Mr. Evans paused in his work and smiled.

"I got one for you at Newmarket next week that'll come home by himself. This horse has been tried—"

"Is it Call Boy?" asked the ruthless Miller. Mr. Evans admitted it was.

"How do you get hold of these stable secrets?" asked the detective-inspector with an exaggerated expression of surprise.

Evans was not embarrassed.

"I got it from a chap who knows the chauffeur who drives the car of Mr. What's-his-name, the celebrated author of the play that the owner of Call Boy acts in. It's all about crooks."

"It's a pity he doesn't know you, Evans," said The Miller, who was in his sourest mood. "He could write a play about you."

Mr. Evans smirked.

"I was thinkin' of goin' on the stage," he said surprisingly. "I happen to know a young lady who's an actress—at least, she's not exactly an actress but she does the young ladies of the chorus."

"Robs them or robes them?" asked The Miller, interested. "You mean she's a dresser?" Evans nodded.

"It must be a wonderful life," he said, rising stiffly. "Her father keeps the 'Grey Dog' down at Lambourn—well, he don't exactly keep it, but he's got a job there. I never had such information in me life," he said enthusiastically. "I got a horse running at Newmarket next week that could fall down, take a nap and then win. There's another horse that I got for Chester that's Home. Did you want to see me about anything, Mr. Miller?"

The Miller wanted to see him very badly about something. Harry

Wissell, notoriously a client of Evans, had vanished from London as though the ground had opened under him and swallowed him up. And coincident with this disappearance came a complaint from the Berkshire police that Highlow, an historic mansion, had been broken into and an article of value, to wit a nearly gold pencil, had been removed.

"Have you seen him lately?" asked The Miller.

Evans shook his head.

"No, Mr. Challoner."

"Well, you'd better give him a wide berth." warned The Miller. "The Berkshire police are pretty certain it was he who broke into Frithington-Evans' place. He didn't pinch much, which was remarkable. Frithington-Evans was in the next room—you know him, don't you?"

Evans knew him very well.

Mr. Frithington-Evans was one of those rich men who hated spending money. His meanness, his general unpleasantness, have been canvassed in earlier adventures. He changed his jockeys monthly and his trainer every half-year, and lived the tortured life of one who was certain that he was being robbed all the time by somebody or other.

It fell to Mr. Challoner to call upon this gentleman, for he had a very wide acquaintance with the methods of the suspected man.

"Yes, sir—it looks like Wissell's work—he always lifts casement windows off their hinges."

Mr. Frithington-Evans stood by during the inspection, biting his nails.

"Why the devil don't you catch him?" he demanded irritably. "That is your job, my friend.' '

"So I'm told," said The Miller coolly.

You must remember that he was once a public school boy and monied insolence neither rattled nor impressed him.

"Don't be impertinent, please," snapped Frithington.

The Miller almost lost his inspectorship and Mr. Frithington-Evans as nearly gained a thick ear.

"He must have broken into the very next room to the library where I was sitting," said the aggrieved young man.

"Were you alone?"

"I was not alone: I had my trainer, Mr. Bluson, here, and we were discussing—er—business."

All the racing man in The Miller ached to ask him whether the business had to do with a certain maiden race at Newmarket in which Mr. Frithington-Evans had two horses, called Blain and Woggle, engaged. That morning there had appeared a paragraph in the papers that Woggle was a doubtful runner, having picked up a nail at exercise. But Blain looked to have a. rosy chance. Mr. Frithington-Evans became communicative.

"To tell you the truth, Inspector, we were discussing a horse of mine—if you were a betting man I would advise you to back it—it is called Blain and it will win on Friday."

The Miller murmured his gratitude.

Soon after he went back to town to look for the missing Mr. Wissell.

★★★★★★

Evans was dozing when the gentle knock came to his door.

"Who is it?" he asked.

"Harry— Wissell, Mr. Evans," came the whispered reply.

Evans got out of bed and opened the door. "Seen The Miller?" he demanded.

"I ain't," said Bill, "but I don't mind seein' him. I got a alibi the size of a house. I bin stayin' with a friend at Brighton as I can prove on me oath. . . ."

His voice sank to a whisper. . . Mr. Evans listened eagerly, punctuating the story of Harry Wissell with innumerable "Bless my soul's" and "Good gracious me's."

★★★★★★

Mr. Frithington-Evans was not a very popular man with the rulers of the turf. There was one noble lord who, besides being a steward of the Jockey Club, had the dubious advantage of being related by marriage.

His lordship was a man with a grim sense of humour, and he had one hobby—he collected the literature of advertising and other tipsters.

On the morning the Highstreet Maiden Stakes was decided he met Mr. Frithington-Evans strolling in the paddock.

"Good morning, Snoopy." By this pet name was Mr. Frithington-Evans called in the secret circles of his family. "Are you running Blain in the Maiden Stakes?"

"Yes," said Snoopy. "I was hoping to run both, but Woggle picked up a nail at exercise—"

"I read the paragraph. Why run him if he's unfit?"

Mr. Frithington-Evans shrugged his shoulders.

"He is only short of a few gallops and it will do him no harm to see a race-course," he said. "Blain is a two-stone better horse, and of course I am declaring to win with him. That is, if Woggle runs. I'm not so sure. My trainer said he'd come to a decision this morning and send him on by motor-box. He hasn't arrived yet."

"Humph!" said his relative. "Lexleigh was asking me whether he should back him."

"You can tell Lord Lexleigh with my compliments," said Snoopy, with his sweetest smile, "that he can back Blain without the slightest fear. I have been carefully through the list of runners, and I'm perfectly sure there's nothing in the race that can beat him."

"Humph!" said the steward again, and went on his way.

Mr. Frithington-Evans had not many friends, but there was still a large number of people who did not know enough to keep away from him, and from the paddock to the private stands he was stopped every few yards, and to all and sundry, friends, semi-friends, nearly enemies and the loathsome, he told all he knew (as he said) frankly and without reservation.

When the numbers went up into the frame, a board was also hoisted:

Mr. Frithington-Evans declares to win with Blain.

Blain carried his first colours, was ridden by his stable jockey; and Woggle, who did appear after all, had up a stable lad and the second colours. Blain opened at 7-4, and was a tight 11-10 chance when the tapes went up.

Nobody noticed Woggle, for he was running on the stand side, until the field came into the dip, and then he was seen; but for all his second colours and his stable-lad rider, he was four lengths clear of his field. It was more nearly six lengths when they passed the post.

"Extraordinary!" said Mr. Frithington-Evans to the nearest scowling acquaintance. "I have never been so shocked in my life. I had my usual pony on Blain. We tried them twenty-eight pounds—"

"I don't believe in fairies," snarled his acquaintance.

To the paddock, after the "All Right" had been called, came Snoopy's lordly relative, and, taking him by the arm, he led him into a quiet corner.

"Great surprise for you, eh? Terrible shock and all that sort of thing?"

"I assure you, sir—" began Snoopy. "Read this."

The steward took from his pocket a document which was soon to be added to his historic collection. Frithington-Evans frowned and read.

EDUCATED EVANS.
EDUCATED EVANS.
EDUCATED EVANS.
The World's Winner Finder and Outsider Discoverer.
A COOP.
A COOP.
A COOP.
Today everybody will be on Blain!
It will be Old Sam's Midnight Special!
WHAT IGNORANCE!
WHAT IGNORANCE!
WHAT IGNORANCE!
The real pea in the basket is WOGGLE, who never picked up
any nail at exercise, and will arrive in a motorcar after racing
starts. His well-known and highly famous owner,
Mr. Frithington-Evans (no relation to undersigned) will
declare to win with Blain, and Woggle will pop up. Help
yourself, and don't forget the family motto of Educated Evans
is "Information *v.* Gaswork."

Mr. Frithington-Evans turned white and red.

"That damned burglar must have told him!" he gasped, and in the agitation of the moment did not realise his self-betrayal.

★★★★★★

"Yes, I backed it," said The Miller slowly, "but I'm very anxious to know who was your informant. It wasn't by any chance a larcenist who has succeeded in persuading some Brighton friends to perjure themselves, was it? He didn't glue his ear to the keyhole while Mr. Frithington-Evans was discussing matters with his trainer, did he? Come across, Evans. I'd like to know all about it."

Mr. Evans closed his eyes ecstatically.

"Information *v.* gaswork" he murmured, and added: "What a beauty!"

15—FOR EVANS' SAKE

Detective-Inspector Challoner strolled along the Hampstead Road, his hands behind him, a new straw clenched between his teeth, and an introspective frown on his face.

Nevertheless, he could notice the approach of Joe Maycart, and observed with satisfaction that, at the sight of him, Joe did not recall a previous engagement and turn back, nor did he cross the road to avoid meeting with this representative of the law. Instead he quickened his step and appeared eager for conversation.

"Lor'lumme, Inspector," he said breathlessly, "you seen Evans?"

"Not for two days—why?"

Mr. Maycart's eyes bulged.

"He's gotta fur-line' coat! Fur all round the collar—an' gloves! When he come into the 'Cow an' Garter' last night, everybody took off their 'ats!"

News, indeed, but:

"Is there any particular reason why he shouldn't wear a fur-lined coat?" asked The Miller blandly. "Has anybody lost one?"

"Oh, no!" Joe made haste to free himself of the imputation that he was "nosing" on any man. "It's straight—he must have bought it off a man up in Caledonian Market. They say that Mrs. Lube's linin' Old Sam's ulster with an 'earthrug. But Evans—what a lad!"

The Miller had no intention whatever of visiting the home of learning that morning, but curiosity to examine the cause of such local excitement brought him to Masked Marvel Mansions.

He discovered Mr. Evans in his shirt sleeves, for the educated man was turning the handle of the Patent Duplicator that a Child could Manipulate, and it was hot work.

On a peg driven into the wall hung The Coat. The very sight of it was enough to induce a mild perspiration.

"Business is doin' well," said Evans, pausing to wipe his forehead. "I'm just sendin' out to 3,742 clients the glad tidings about my Lincoln horse—Cora: fear nothing!"

"Where did you get the coat?" asked The Miller, examining the garment curiously.

"Sable," said Evans calmly. "Used to belong to the Grand Duke what's-his-name; sable or muck-squash."

"Muck-squash, I should say," said The Miller; "raised in a rabbit hutch. What's the idea? It's getting warm."

Evans raised his shoulders and smiled.

"I've a position to keep up," he said simply. "'*As a bird is known by his note so is a man by his apparelations*'—Shakespeare. All celebrated people are classy dressers. Look at Bo Bunghole, the dandy of Bath an'

Wells. Look at the far-famed Lord Dishralli, the well-known Prime Minister; look at Owing Nares, the highly respected acting gentleman. Besides—"

"Besides what?" asked The Miller, when he paused.

Evans coughed.

"My young lady likes it," he said, with an attempt at offhandedness.

The Miller's mouth opened.

"What, another?"

Evans smiled.

"This young lady's different," he said. "She's what you might call an 'eyebrow.' Very superior—don't know nothing about racing—mad on classicals— poetry, picture paintin', artistic stone masonry—"

"Sculpture," said The Miller helpfully.

"Everythin' like that. She don't even know I'm on the turf—can't bear racin'—everythin' like that's low. But poetry—! She's fair pot—mad about it. She likes mine."

"Yours!" said The Miller, aghast.

Evans went to his hanging jacket and took out a folded paper. He was flushed and his eyes were bright.

"I just dashed it off last night," he said carelessly. "Never knew I had the gift till I tried. It's funny how a person can have poetry inside him and never know it."

The Miller unfolded the sheet slowly and read the title.

"To a Lady of Manchester Square."

"After 'Errick, the celebrated poem maker," explained Evans. "She's very fond of 'Errick."

"Eric who?" The Miller was wilfully dense.

"I don't know his other name," confessed Mr. Evans. "It's probably a *Nong de Plume.*" The Miller read:

The world turns round in twenty-four hours,
Thus causing the night and the day,
Also the seasons, hence the flowers,
Or so the people say.

"That's not bad," said The Miller.

"It's education," said Evans gravely. "My young lady's like that—she wears glasses."

The Miller attacked the second *stanza.*

Thou are not like Lewdcreature Burgia,

341

The female Crippen of France,
Thou art like the Princess of Surgia,
Who gave every gentleman a chance.

"Who is the Princess and where is Surgia?" Mr. Evans rubbed his nose.

"I made that bit up," he admitted. "Poet's licence."

"Issued by the Jockey Club?"

"Post Office," said Evans. "I've never seen one but I've heard of 'em. I put in 'France' because 'Italy' wouldn't rhyme."

The Miller resumed.

I worship the pavement where your fairy feet
Pedestrianates so bright and neat.
You're like the wife of the well-known Julius Caesar
And if she'll have me I'll try to please her."

"That's wonderful," said The Miller, as he folded the paper. "All you want is something like:

"If your mind is at sixes and sevens,
Go to Educated Evans,
Merchant of street corner rumours,
Send five bob and get his stumers."

"Who wrote that?" asked Evans suspiciously.

"Kipling," replied The Miller.

Now Evans had only stated a vital fact in the mildest possible way when he said that Miss Hortense Curryfed was no lover of racing. She had been ruined by the turf. Her male parent had done in two egg and bacon shops by his rash and hazardous speculations in this department of human activity. Her first young man had put the money reserved for the purchase of a home upon St. Becan in the Derby, thereby paralysing all prospects of domestic happiness. Her second young man had been driven to financial embarrassment when Pons Asinorum failed to get his nose in front at the stick.

To add to her horror and detestation of the betting habits of mankind, she lived in the same house (and in the service) of a high-class Oxford Street bookmaker.

Mr. Evans had met her in favourable circumstances at a very high-class play in the Euston Road. He went to the Regent under the mistaken impression that "The Immortal Hour" was a new Chaplin film, and after he had survived the risk of being thrown out for laughing, he found himself in conversation with a sharp but not unpleasant-featured female who confided to him that she had seen the play twenty-five times. Luckily, he learnt of her antipathy to racing before he began to talk about himself—which means that she started telling him pretty soon after they were acquainted.

Miss Hortense was a governess (she also had taken out a poetic licence) and looked after the manners and morals of two violent children whom she described as "handfuls." She had, she hinted, a bit of money put aside for a rainy day. Her grandmamma had left her a small annuity and she was the owner of two houses in Peckham. Obviously a lady. She liked men older than herself—bits of boys she couldn't stand. They got on her nerves. Obviously a sensible lady.

"I'm in business for meself," Evans told her, and, when he referred to his clients, she was not sure whether he was a lawyer or a shingle specialist. She was too well brought up to inquire. She liked strong, silent men, she told him. Evans could be strong but he could not be silent.

At nights (three a week) they walked or took a cup of coffee together at the Corner House in the West End, or saw an improving picture. Evans saw all the improving pictures in London. All about Women's Souls and Fate and Railway Accidents and Little Children who said:

"Mama, you are not running away with that wicked man! Remember you owe a duty to your unfortunate progeny."

Mostly the plays were about heroic women who sacrificed their principles for the sake of the men they loved. This was Miss Curryfed's favourite theme.

So the courtship progressed and reached, as we have seen, the stage where poetry commenced.

And then the blow fell.

One night, Mr. Evans, returning from Lingfield somewhat short of temper and money, and with the knowledge that he had sent out to all clients old and new, them that had acted honourable and them that hadn't acted honourable, "Binge—fear nothing" (the same Binge having refused at the first fence like a sensible horse), ran into Miss Curryfed. His race glasses were slung over his shoulder as he strode across the broad meeting-ground of Victoria Station—there was no excuse.

Miss Curryfed confronted him.

"Mr. Evans—you are a common racing-man!"

"I just popped down—" began Evans.

"You've been horse-racing and betting—never speak to me again!"

Evans was not in his tenderest mood.

"Very well," he said haughtily, lifted his hat and strode on.

Now that his true character was revealed, Miss Curryfed had no difficulty in establishing the identity of the deceiver. Even her employer had heard his name, and spoke slightingly of him.

It needed but this to revivify the dormant romanticism in Miss Curryfed's bosom. Was she right, she asked herself. Was she doing her duty, she demanded? The memory of parallel cases oppressed her. She thought of the screen women married to rich husbands who had endured All for the sake of the child, or had endured All for the sake of their mothers. She thought of the pure young girls who had sacrificed their lives and futures, had given up All that they held Dear, and had married fat and bloated millionaires so that their sick sister should be attended by the great specialist whom they really loved. In her mind's eye she saw the young and beautiful girl, who, though she was loved by the rich, handsome and chivalrous leading man, stood by her poor and crotchety husband (quite a minor character) and endured All until he was providentially run over by a tramcar, when she married the rich and chivalrous suitor, and faded out on a long and lingering kiss.

Her mind was made up. The path of Duty was clear. That night for the first time she listened to the idle chatter of racing-men who gathered about her employer's table. She heard and shivered as they talked with coarse familiarity of strange animals to which they gave no name, referring rather to "that thing of Leader's" or "that so-and-so thing of Bennett's," but from the confusion of narrative emerged one golden thread. She recognised its importance by the low tones in which the information passed across the table.

"Poor Pup—keep it to yourself," said the informant, and her employer nodded. "And whatever you do, Joe, don't be a loser on it. They'll back it away, and you'll get your wires half an hour after the off."

Poor Pup! She bit her lip to suppress her emotion, and, going up to her room, she put on a dark coat and a shapeless hat and made her stealthy way from the house.

It was very dark; rain was falling in torrents, but she walked rapidly on. Could this be she? Miss Curryfed wondered bitterly, going forth in the night to this racing-man, to tell him of a horse that would win. But it was her duty.

She raised her chin proudly, drove back the tears, and reached Bayham Mews without any of the misadventures which usually overtake heroines when they are about to do something silly.

Presently she found Masked Marvel Mansions and, climbing the slippery wooden stairs, listened at the door. No sound came from within except an irregular groan that sounded like a vacuum cleaner that was working in fits and starts. Evans was sleeping. She knocked at the door gently, and, when no answer came, knocked louder.

"Hullo!" said Evans, struggling up. "Who's there?"

"Mr. Evans?" said a voice.

"Yes, that's me," said Evans.

"Poor Pup!" she said hollowly.

"Who is?" asked the indignant Evans.

"Poor Pup," she said again, and he recognised the voice.

"D'you call yourself a lady," he demanded wrathfully, "comin' here in the middle of the night an' callin' me names? Where's your education? Where's your dickyorum?"

"Poor Pup," she said again—"I do this for your sake."

He heard the sound of her feet on the stairs, and when he opened the door she was gone.

Two days later Mr. Evans opened his newspaper and read:

```
Poor Pup      - 1
Jellybag      - 2
Oh You!       - 3
100-9. 5-2. 6-1.
```

He clasped his forehead in despair, and there flashed upon him an understanding of that midnight scene.

All that day he paced in vain the pavement of Manchester Square, but she made no appearance. He remembered now that she was working for a bookmaker, and a happy sense of content and complacency came to him as he construed her action.

Two or three days later he was just dozing off to sleep when a tap came at his door.

"Joojah!" hissed a voice.

"Here, wait a minute, Miss Curryfed."

"Joojah—farewell."

She was gone when he walked out on to the rain-splattered landing. But this time he made no mistake. To all clients, ancient and modern, went forth the joyous news: "Joojah—Fear Nothing"; and Joojah accordingly obliged—at a modest price, it is true, but, as Evans said: "I can't help prices."

Night after night he waited on a chair behind the door for the coming of his mysterious informant. A week passed, but he neither saw nor heard her.

★★★★★★

Whilst it cannot be said that Mrs. Lube was without her own especial dreams, the type indeed that is very popular in certain cinema palaces where they are not so very particular, she had all a righteous wife's indignation at a philandering husband. Prosperity had come to her from an unexpected legacy, and Mr. Alf Lube had shared in that prosperity to the extent that he was able to go farther afield into bars where he was quite unknown, and where there was no necessity to wait patiently for a friend to enter and ask brightly, "What's yours, Alf?"

And in the course of his wandering Mr. Lube, who was of an inflammable nature, had met with one who embodied in her gracious person all the attractions of a siren, all the supple grace of a mermaid.

Every afternoon and every evening Mr. Lube lounged into the bar of the "Dog and Kettle," and fixed his languid eyes upon the beautiful manipulator of beer handles and deft turner-up of bottles. And they had private conversations not unconnected, on Mr. Lube's part, with the money that had come into his family. It is true that he gave the impression that he was the sole legatee, and he also hinted in his subtle way that he was unhappily married to a woman who did not understand him.

Miss Flossie, the barmaid, who was well acquainted with this type of husband, listened sympathetically; and when, one day, Alf laid a golden bangle on the counter, she took it with downcast eyes, which not only established in his mind the illusion of modesty, but enabled her to see that it was only nine carat. And from there on the friendship grew apace.

"I'm in the sporting line of business," said Alf. "I suppose you've heard of me?"

"You're not Educated Evans!" said Hebe, with interest.

"Him!" said Mr. Lube contemptuously. "I could lose him! No, I own Old Sam's Midnight Special."

"Go on!" she said.

He went on.

How far on he would have gone will never be known. Mrs. Lube had her suspicions aroused from the amazing fact that her husband had innovated a new domestic practice: he washed twice a day. That, and the purchase of clean collars and the discovery in his pocket of a tram-ticket, brought her like a bloodhound on his trail.

Miss Curryfed met the squat and stoutish lady on her way to Bayham Mews, and Mrs. Lube was not only very angry, but confided the cause of her wrath to the first acquaintance.

"Thank your lucky stars you're not married, young woman!" she said tremulously.

Miss Curryfed had never thanked her stars for anything so stupid.

"Me allowin' him money, with four mouths to feed, an' him carryin' on with a ginger-haired barmaid, an' I on'y heard about it tonight! I barmaided her!"

"You should forgive your husband," said Miss Curryfed gently. "Marriage calls for great sacrifice—"

"Two bob a day beer money—what's that?" snapped Mrs. Lube, who was returning from one of those occasional pilgrimages which the erratic affections of her husband made necessary.

"If you love him," murmured Miss Curryfed... "To know all is to forgive all."

"I'm not so sure that I do know all," said Mrs. Lube darkly.

"Now I," said Miss Curryfed, "am doing something I hate for the man of my choice."

And encouraged by the confidence that had been given to her, she told the story of those midnight visits.

"I shall never speak to him again, of course," said Miss Curryfed sadly, "but I must help him in his struggle."

"Is it Evans?" asked Mrs. Lube, all her wrath against her worser half disappearing.

"Yes, it is Evans—Hubert Evans," said the girl softly, and wiped her glasses.

Mrs. Lube almost stopped breathing.

"Don't take the risk, miss," she said earnestly. "You've no idea of the people that live down that mews. I quite sympathise an' understand, bein' one woman to another. I'll tell you what I'll do, young lady. I'll tell him! I don't mind dogs, an' I'm older than you. . . . You'll find me waitin' at the end of the mews every night at ten o'clock—either me or my husband. All you got to do is to tell him the horse. . . ."

★★★★★★

Week after week Evans listened in vain for the light footstep on the stairs. Week after week he bemoaned the surprising and startling success of Old Sam's Midnight Special, which was sending out three-star winners with disgusting frequency.

16.—The Particular Beauty

Educated Evans had many promising clients. They promised him odds to various sums, and a proportion of them kept their word and a proportion partly fulfilled their obligations and a large proportion deeply regretted that his information had come too late to be of any use to them, and finished up their letters of excuse with the pious hope that he would have "better luck next time."

"They're not actin' honourable," said Mr. Evans bitterly. "Here am I, goin' around happy as a king an' thinkin' of all the stuff that's comin', and here are they playin' robbers and thieves. They're worse than Amlet, the celebrated Danish gentleman—they say 'My kingdom for your guarantee special', an' when it clicks an' I ask for my dues they say '*Out dam spot!*' Is that fair?"

"It certainly is the limit," said The Miller. "Have you ever thought of suing them?"

"What's the good?" asked Evans. "I know as much about the lore as the next man—but what's the good? Take Marky Wirral. You couldn't get him to pay if you took Scotland Yard with you."

"Why don't you cut him off?"

"I do," said Evans gloomily, "and round he comes an' pitches a tale about his old mother—I 'm too soft-hearted."

"And headed," suggested The Miller.

There is honour amongst thieves—it is when you get down to the punting class that you touch the deeps of human depravity and artfulness.

"I'm weedin' 'em out," said Evans. "I wouldn't be surprised if I didn't chuck this low connection an' open up in a classy neighbourhood—Edgware Road or somewhere."

He tried employing a client who used to be in the fighting business, till his backers went broke. Tom got a bit out of every dollar he collected. The first night he came back with a shilling he'd got from Nosey Walker and a string of hard-luck tales that choked him as he related them. The second evening he came back with nothing more substantial than a skinful of beer, and he spent the night sitting on the bottom of the steps singing doleful songs about women. The next night he didn't come back at all.

Evans gave up all hope of collection. He had other matters of routine to bother him. And then Lew Emmings, the well-known fighting man, a fervent admirer and defender of Evans, came to him with a suggestion, offered in all deference and humility, but Evans shook his head.

"I'm very sorry, Lew. I'd like to oblige you, but I don't have no more women about this place. They're snakes in the grass, as hist'ry tells us. Take Mary Queen of Scotch——"

"Rebecca's Jewish," pleaded Lew.

"Well, take the well-known Queen of Sheba—her that done in the far-famed Solomon by gettin' him to go out and fight the Hi-tites while she was goin' round with another man."

"Rebecca's a respectable girl," urged Lew.

"So was Cleopatra, whose needle we all admire," said Evans rapidly. "So was Lewdcreature Burgia—up to a point. So was Bonny Mary, the well-known Duchess of Argyll. So was the celebrated an' highly respected Queen Elizabeth, commonly called the Verger Queen. No, Lew, I like an' respect you, but I can't give no jobs to no girl. Besides, I've got to think of your sister's reputation, workin' alone with me."

Lew argued in vain. But the deposed and dishonest secretary was not to be replaced.

And yet there was need of clerical assistance. He had recently renewed his association with the Midland Goods Yard, and there were forty £10 Specials to be struck off every morning between ten and twelve, after the runners came up.

Then again, he found his accounts were in bad order. He had written asking clients to act honourable who had acted honourable, and said so violently and offensively; and he had sent out his special messages to people who were on the back of his book—or would have been if he'd had a book.

"It's system an' order I want," he confided to The Miller. "I'm goin' to keep a file so they can't chisel me."

The Miller looked at him suspiciously, but the jest was an unconscious one.

"But wimmin!" Evans shook his head "I've been both stung an' bit, an' I'm rapidly turning into a mysograph—I am indeed, Mr. Challoner."

"That sounds like a writing machine to me," said the puzzled Miller. "You don't by any chance mean mysogynist?"

"Mysogynist or mysograph," said Evans carelessly. "One's Greek an' the other's Latin. Lew wants me to take his sister—"

"Why don't you?" said The Miller. "Little Rebecca is very pretty, very capable and very straight. If you take my advice, you'll give her fifty shillings a week and a commission on all the money she collects."

Evans thought the matter over and sent for Lew, and that faithful man came breathlessly.

"She's a good clurk an' a good collector, Mr. Evans," he said.

"She oughter be able to get a job anywhere, oughtn't she?" asked Evans suspiciously.

Lew hesitated.

"Well, I'll tell you the truth about Rebecca, Mr. Evans. She ought to get a job an' she could get a job, but she's very touchy about the way people look at her. She's so beautiful, Mr. Evans," he said earnestly, "that she can't allow nobody to get fresh with her, or cast aspersions on her. I've had more fights over Rebecca than I can remember. If a feller looks at her like this"—he leered—"home she comes to me and says 'Lew, I've been insulted,' an' out I go an' bash the bloke. A feller tried to hold her hand once in the City, an' she had hysterics for three hours an' twenty-seven minutes—by the clock. But you're a gentleman, Mr. Evans, an' as long as you're stern with her she won't mind that."

With some misgivings Mr. Evans awaited the arrival of the Particular Beauty.

She was all that The Miller had said and more, having one of those svelte figures that one associates with the bathing girls who appear on the covers of the summer magazines. She had fair hair and deep blue eyes, regular features and a complexion like milk and roses. Evans knew that it was going to be very difficult to be stern with her.

"Well, Miss—"he began.

"Call me Rebecca," she said with a dazzling smile.

Evans glanced at her brother to bear him witness that he had this permission.

She was immensely capable, too. Under her nimble fingers Mr. Order took a long farewell of Mrs. Chaos.

"She's a good girl," said Lew, as they walked down the High Street together, "an' I'd kill me best friend if he got fresh with her. I'd take him by the throat an' bash his head against the wall."

Evans avoided her all day, and when he did come into the office a set scowl was on his countenance and he kept at a respectful distance, lest by some mischance he touched that twinkling hand.

The next morning, armed with a list containing the names and addresses of defaulters and the amounts owing, she set forth. At three in the afternoon came Lew, with a respectable pile of money, which he put on the table.

"Rebecca can't come back today," he said gloomily. "She went to Harry Watson to collect the thirty bob he owes you, an' Harry looked at her funny. They've just took him to the hospital," he added.

On the next day Toby Lowe, a hired porter, met the request of Mr. Evans' new collector for immediate payment with a light-hearted suggestion that he'd pay twice over if she'd come and have a cup of tea with him. Ambulance bells rang loudly along Great College Street.

On the third day she came home in triumph with a bundle of Treasury notes, in various stages of cleanliness, and laid them before the frowning Evans.

"Only one man insulted me," she said brightly, "but Lew can't find him, I think he must have gone abroad."

Evans counted the money with a glow of joy. "You're one of the nicest little women I've ever—"

Then he remembered with a chill and looked up. A look of cold doubt was in her eyes.

"I'm talking alejorically or paridoxically," said Evans hastily. "Being educated, Miss Rebecca, you understand, I have to use all sorts of metaphorics an' poetry."

He composed his features to a scowl.

"I respect you as a lady an' as a woman of business," he went on rapidly. "You're a sort of machine, like a motor-bicycle or a beer engine. Her face cleared; the deadly suspicion passed from her eyes.

"I'm glad you told me that, Mr. Evans," she said seriously. "I shouldn't like to think you were Gay."

"Gay? Me?" Evans' face was contorted with stupefied wonder. "Why, Miss Rebecca, I'm no more gay than the Reverend Hinge— him that put the cracks in St. Paul's."

"I loathe people falling in love with me," said Rebecca.

"At the same time," said Evans, his natural gallantry overcoming his fear, "it's not to be wondered at. . . ."

And then, as the look of distrust reappeared: "It's not to be wondered at that you do, Miss Rebecca. Personally speakin', I hate people to fall in love with me. The wimmin that's tried to hold my hand! The girls that chase me around!"

She was interested, possibly sceptical. She had every right to be.

"I didn't know you were so fascinatin', Mr. Evans."

"In a way I am," admitted Evans modestly. "I suppose it's the education. But love don't mean any more to me than it meant to the celebrated and highly renowned Lewdcreature Burgia, the female Crippen of Rome, that done in her father with arsenic an' got pinched just as she was drawin' the insurance money. What a lady! Take B— Mary."

"What's 'B' mean?" She was alert for insults.

"Bolshevik," said Evans quickly. "There's a woman that never had no love for anybody. She had her head cut off an' never smiled again— see Hist'ry. Take Cleopatra, whose needle we all admire: she was stung to death by apses —a kind of needle that the Egyptians sewed their mummies up with. She found Moses in the bulrushes, and everybody used to say he had her nose! Which only goes to prove that the voice of scandal is the voice of the people—or in other words, *pro bono publico*—French."

He made his escape, feeling very moist under the collar. For the next two days he avoided his clurk and collector, insisting that her brother should accompany him whenever urgent necessity took him to his office.

To make doubly sure, he engaged old Mrs. Tomwit, whose son was doing seven, and had eighteen months to go to qualify for her old age pension, to come and sit in the office during Rebecca's working hours.

"She's all right," he admitted reluctantly to The Miller, "but she gets insulted. I wanted to send out Darling Mine for the three o'clock at Plumpton today, but I simply daren't say the words. But I got something for you on Friday—St. Cheese. He'll start at 10-1 an' he's money for nothin' I'm sendin' this horse out to all clients—"

"Old and new," murmured The Miller.

"To all clients," said Evans, "as my £10 Special. The Lubeses are sendin' out Ratrun, as I happen to know owin' to havin' a friend in the printing business. Ratrun don't."

"Don't what?" asked The Miller.

"Run," said Evans.

The days that followed were too busy for Mr. Evans to absent himself from the office. Lew came with him, and with the aged lady the room was rather crowded. Lew took his turn with the duplicator, and Rebecca worked like three women, too absorbed in her labours even to detect the least disrespectful glance.

Now the Lubes were also busy, for an unexpected piece of luck had come the way of the owners, proprietors and editors of Old Sam's Midnight Special. Mrs. Lube, to her fluttering joy, had become acquainted with a real jockey.

To tell the story of how this acquaintance was made is like examining the ancestry of the modern holder of an ancient peerage. Mrs. Lube's cousin, Arthur Stickleburn, the schoolmaster, coached in his spare time a staff-sergeant of the Army Service Corps who was working for his first-class certificate. This sergeant had a brother who was engaged to the sister of the young lady whom George Grob was walking out with. Now do you see?

To scrape acquaintance with George Grob was a fairly easy matter. He was a little man with a bullet head and a roving eye, who chewed gum, wrote his name with difficulty, and patronised a Sackville Street tailor. He was introduced to Mr. Stickleburn, who, having shared something of his cousin's prosperity, found an opportunity to pass on his capture to Mrs. Lube; and there was a great luncheon at an Oxford Street restaurant, which cost no less than £4 7s. 6d. including wine, at which Mrs. Lube met the great horseman (Old Sam and her husband were kept in the background); and the friendship was sealed when Mr. Grob informed his hostess that Ratrun was something to bet on.

"But the papers say it won't start," said Mrs. Lube.

Mr. Grob smiled a cryptic smile.

"If you believe everything you read in the papers," he said, in his most original manner, "you'll go off your chump! He runs and he'll win, and if any of your friends like to put me on a pony, I'll let 'em— that's a nice bit of fluff over there."

The bit of fluff, who was really a bit of fluff, gave him smile for smile, and thereafter Mr. Grob's interest in racing and tippery evaporated.

★★★★★★

"Them Lubeses," said Evans, "has gone off their nuts. They're sendin' out Ratrun, an' I happen to know from the boy who does him that he's bein' kept for Cheltenham. It's gaswork—absolutely gaswork."

"If Ratrun is in the field," said The Miller, "your St. Cheese will be beaten two fences."

"Fear Nothing," murmured Evans, and went on licking stamps.

The rivalry between the Evanses and the Lubeses was so keen and so widely canvassed in Camden Town that the knowledge that they were sending, with equal confidence, two horses for the same race, added a certain piquancy to the event. Once more Camden Town divided itself into the rival camps, and when the selections were known, the balance of opinion favoured the sanity of Old Sam's advisers.

Because Ratrun was a perfect fencer; it would be ridden by a crack jockey; and though the possibility was that 5-4 would be an outside offer, yet 5-4 in the hand is worth 1000-1 down the course. And it was also known, through some mysterious agency, that St. Cheese was not on the job. How these stories came into circulation has never been discovered, but it is generally believed that the big bookmakers in London employ a corps of fairy-tale-tellers to disseminate profitable news.

"He's on the job an' he's tryin'," said Evans when the story came to him. "I not only had it from the boy who does him, but I've had it from the barber who shaves the owner's uncle. An' if that's not good enough, what is?"

"I think I'll come along and see this animal perform," said The Miller, and Educated Evans showed every sign of relief.

"She's comin' down too"—he jerked his head towards Bayham Mews.—"She's never seen a race."

"You're not taking her, are you?" asked The Miller quickly.

"Not me I" said the fervent Evans. "Am I mad? Why, if I bought her an evenin' paper she'd scream for help. I never even take me hat off to her when I meet her in the street."

On a bright, wintry day Lingfield has its claims to loveliness, and Mr. Evans walked from the rattler with a light step and a light heart, confident that the sun would go down upon a great achievement and the roll of honour which included Braxted, what a beauty, and Eton Boy, Marked Marble (the danger) would be still further enriched.

The Miller had come down on his motor-bike. He came across the paddock to meet Mr. Evans. "Ratrun does," he said.

"What?" asked Evans, startled.

"Run," said The Miller laconically.

Evans frowned, opened his evening paper and scowled at the list of probables.

"It's not down here," he said.

"It's down here," said The Miller, pointing to the stables.

"You can't believe half these newspaper writers tell you," said Evans bitterly. "Half what they say's gaswork an' the other half ain't sense. They're like the well-known Volytare, the celebrated French officer, who wouldn't get out of bed till somebody told him how he got in it!"

In the depths of despair, he went in search of his party. The delighted Rebecca was standing by the ringside, watching the horses parade, and Lew was explaining to her the significance of the numbers on the boys' arms.

"Isn't it wonderful, Mr. Evans?" she said her eyes afire with excitement. "I've never been on a race-course in my life! And nobody looks at you—that's the wonderful thing. I could live here all my life. I heard somebody say just now 'Look at her beautiful legs,' and of course I got awfully upset, but they were talking about a horse—weren't they, Lew?"

"So he said," said Lew darkly. "If I thought he'd been talkin' about yours, Rebecca—"

"I'm sure he wasn't: he was a gentleman—he had an umbrella," she said.

Evans could take no part in their joy. His soul was harrowed with the knowledge that he had expended 600 pence, to say nothing of £1, 4s. in wires for extra special clients, in despatching to the world the glad tidings concerning St. Cheese. Undoubtedly Ratrun was on the job. He went and stared at him as he walked proudly round the paddock before the race. Compared with Ratrun, St. Cheese looked—well, just like St. Cheese.

The jockeys were coming out. Mr. Grob, the last to appear, strolled across the paddock, swinging his whip nonchalantly; and it so happened that Rebecca stood not only in his way but in his line of vision. He looked at her and winked! And, what's more, Lew saw him do it! In a second he had gripped the jockey's collar.

"Here, what d'you mean by insulting my sister?" he demanded hotly.

"He winked at me!" gasped Rebecca.

"Didn't I see him do it?" asked Lew wrathfully.

"Let go of me," said Mr. Grob, "or I'll give you a punch on the nose...."

The Miller was the first upon the spot, and his strong arms separated the contestants; not, however, before Mr. Grob's eye was slightly swollen and his nose ensanguined.

"I'll murder you when I come back!" he hissed, as he dodged under the rail. . .

A jockey with a black eye, a sore nose and a malignant desire for murder in his heart, is no fit pilot for a high-spirited thoroughbred. At the third fence from the back stretch Mr. Grob drove his mount savagely at a jump, took off too soon... and the race was over. St. Cheese, plugging away through the mud, held the lead he established when he came into the straight, out-jumped his opponent at the last fence, and scrambled home by a neck.

"They've sent the ambulance out for the jock," said Evans complacently.

Lew glowered.

"It'd have saved 'em a lot of trouble if he'd a-come back," he said. "They wouldn't have had so far to carry him!"

17.—THE LAST COOP OF ALL

"He's a rum-looking devil," said Lord Fanerly.

"He can go a bit, my lord," said the trainer.

The two-year-old under review was a leggy chestnut who had a poor neck, drooping quarters and bad hocks amongst other defects.

"He's the rummiest-looking devil I've ever seen—how is he bred, again?"

"By Short Cut out of Brief Survey, my lord." His lordship beamed round on his three pretty daughters.

"I'll give any of you a fiver who finds me a name for this atrocity!" he chuckled. "All right, Mr. Atkins; we'll let him run for the stakes."

Which was his lordship's favourite joke, for though he owned a stable of good horses, he only had one bet a year, and that was on the King's horse in the Derby.

And this is where the story of Mr. Evans' last and greatest coop begins. Perhaps it began in the latter part of last year, when he earned the hatred and loathing of Mr. Goolby. Mr. Goolby was a well-off man who owned a chain of public-houses and a string of comparatively bad horses.

But by some accident a good one came his way, and having fiddled with it for three months, running it down the course and out of its distance, he decided to have a go, and to this end he opened up new accounts all over the country. By ill-chance, Mr. Evans either heard or pricked with a pin the name of this gem, and sent it, amongst others, to one Issyheim, a shrewd bookmaker. Ordinarily, the fact that Evans sent out a horse made no more difference to its price than the printing of its name in the programme, but by a second mischance one of the wires despatched by Mr. Goolby and backing his horse each way, arrived at Issyheim's office in time for him to put through an inquiry to further bookmakers. They, too, had had wires—the 'phone to the course was set to work, and Goolby's horse started at 13-8.

Very unjustly, he blamed Evans, and after he had recovered from his six fits he set down to work his vengeance. He had in his stables a two-year-old by Newsboy out of Railway Tunnel. It was by far the worst two-year-old he had ever owned, but when his trainer suggested he should get rid of it, he shook his head.

"I've got a use for him," he said.

Mr. Goolby, as it happened, lived on the aristocratic fringe of Camden Town, so that Evans was something more than a vague personality. For three months this cunning man stalked his prey....

It was the habit of Detective-Inspector Arbuthnot Challoner to make a tri-weekly call upon the educated man. He made no excuse for his peculiar conduct, for "The Miller" was rather superior to public opinion.

"Goolby," he said, suspiciously, when Evans told him the good news. "Isn't he the fellow who said he'd murder you?"

Mr. Evans smiled.

"We all make our mistakes, Mr. Challoner," he said. "Take the well-known Napoleon Bonyparte, him that was drowned at the Battle of Trafalgar. Didn't he put his telescope to the wrong eye? Take the far-famed Mary Queen of Scotch; didn't she walk over Sir Francis Drake's cloak that he put down in the mud, an' didn't he stick a knife in her when she was saying her prayers in the highly-celebrated Tower of London? Take Lewdcreature Burgia—"

"I'm tired of taking that woman," said The Miller. "But what does Goolby want?"

"To do me a turn," replied Evans promptly. "He's got no children, being a bachelor; he's got millions of money. He took a fancy to me the minute we met."

"In the dark, I presume," said The Miller unpleasantly. "Take my tip, Evans—that man is going to do you dirt."

Evans smiled again.

That evening he went to dinner with Mr. Goolby, and the magnificence of Mr. Goolby's dining-room took his breath away. Never had Evans seen so much gold on so much purple wallpaper.

"The point is, Evans," said Mr. Goolby, over roast duck with green peas and sage stuffing, which latter was to cause Mr. Evans a certain amount of discomfiture and interrupt the smooth flow of his conversation, "the point is, I took a liking to you the first time I saw you."

"It is funny," said Mr. Evans. "The first time I see you, Mr. Goolby, I ses to myself: 'There's an educated man.' You remind me of the far-famed Volta, the well-known French cricket—excuse me!—'im that got Looey IX. and the far-famed Mary Auntynette executed in the well-known B. Tower. You remind me—excuse me!—of the far-famed Rishloo, who is well known to all the local inhabitants of France for his piousness and education."

"I'm going to make your fortune, Evans," said Mr. Goolby, as he poured out some of Gilbey's celebrated invalid port, "and I can do it if you'll keep your mouth shut."

Mr. Evans smiled.

"I've got the shuttest mouth in Camden Town, as all will admit," he said. "I've got stable secrets in me desk—excuse me—never could eat onions—that even the Jockey Club don't know anything about."

"I wonder if I *can* trust you," asked Mr. Goolby, surveying him gloomily.

Mr. Evans smiled again.

"I'm like the far-famed Michael Velli, the well-known Italian poet. What goes in me ears never comes out of me mouth—excuse me!"

Mr. Goolby went on to explain that he had in his stable a colt by Newsboy out of Railway Tunnel, and that this two-year-old could catch pigeons. He had tried this horse well enough to win any reasonable Derby, but unfortunately two-year-olds were not allowed to run for the Derby.

"If you send this out to your clients you are a mug. If I were in your place," said Mr. Goolby solemnly, "I should get together every penny I had in the world; I should sell my furniture, I should borrow money from my friends, I'd even use any money I had that didn't belong to me. Now, I'm telling you this as man to man, because I want to do you a turn."

"Naturally," murmured Mr. Evans.

"He's running at Sandown in a maiden race—"

"Are you backing him yourself?" asked Evans, anxiously.

Mr. Goolby shook his head:

"No, I've given up betting; I've taken a vow—or an oath, as the case may be—never to bet again. If I was betting, Evans, should I give you this information."

"I'd better write down the name," said Evans, producing a pencil and paper. "Railway Tunnel colt—"

"No, no!" corrected the other. "I'm calling him 'Press Cutting': in fact I am writing today to Wetherby's to name him. Come up and see me tomorrow, and I'll give you the latest about him. You ought to make enough money to sink a ship, and if you don't, then all I can say to you, if you don't mind my being offensive, is that you are a mug."

Evans walked back to Call Boy Castle on air. Who knew the secret his bosom held?

He would have passed Inspector Arbuthnot Challoner without noticing him, but The Miller called him back.

"You been drinking?" he asked suspiciously. "Or are you in possession of stolen property?"

"That's a game I never take on, Mr. Challoner," said Evans, good-humouredly. "No, I'm just going back to the Castle to have a bit of tea and a sluice. I got some work to do." He smiled mysteriously, and then, as a thought struck him:

"Suppose I was to ask you to lend me a tenner, Mr. Challoner?"

"I should pinch you, right away," said Mr. Challoner promptly. "But seriously, Evans, you don't want to borrow £10?"

Evans nodded.

"I got something I want to back," he said, mysteriously. "Something that I can't tell nobody about. Something that I can't even send to me £5 clients."

The Miller became suddenly interested.

"You're putting your own money on it and you are not sending it out?" he asked incredulously. "You're mad."

Evans was turning away with a shrug when The Miller called him back.

"I'll give you a tenner; in fact I'll send you two tenners, and you can put one of them on for me. I can see my life's savings going, but this is June, when even inspectors of police are entitled to go a little light-headed."

He was as good as his word. That very evening, he brought four crisp five-pound notes.

Mr. Evans put them into his pocket with an air of nonchalance which did not exactly tally with the state of his mind. For he had been very busy all that evening, and had been amazingly successful. Eighty-seven pounds of his own ill-gotten gains had been supplemented by no less a sum than £20 of borrowed money. To this must be added a sum of £30 that he had wangled—there is no other word for it—from the landlord of the White Hart, with whom he had been restored to friendship, and the prospect of what would happen when Press Cutting lost boggled his imagination.

He would dearly have loved to refuse The Miller's loan and investment. For if there was one person in the world on whom he did not wish to commit a petty larceny, it was an inspector of the C.I.D.

The next day added to his commitments by one of those extraordinary strokes of fate which may be recorded but cannot be explained. Mr. Highbrite, the well-known wholesale confectioner and sherbet manufacturer of Camden Town, came to Evans and asked him if he would purchase for the same Mr. Highbrite a small motor-van which had been placed in Evans' hands for sale. The negotiations had been going on for a month, and Evans was getting a fiver out of the transaction, for the owner of the motor-van was a very old friend of his.

Only for one moment, as he saw £75 placed on the table, in real money, did he falter—and then, in a spirit of restlessness, he clutched the money with a trembling hand.

"I sha'n't want this car for a couple of days, Mr. Evans," said Mr. Highbrite. "I am going down to Brighton for the week-end, and I know I can trust you."

"I am like the celebrated Caesar's wife," said Evans hollowly: "All things to all men!"

That night he saw Goolby, and told him in detail the manner in which he had accumulated £245, 10s. He did not exactly explain the motorcar incident: that sounded too much like robbery with violence.

Mr. Goolby listened and internally gloated. If there was one man in the world he desired to put it across, it was Educated Evans.

"Go down to Sandown yourself, my boy. Don't trust these S.P. bookmakers; it will only get about. Go up and down the rails and put on a tenner here and a tenner there, and you won't affect the price."

After Evans had gone, Mr. Goolby got on to the telephone to his Epsom trainer.

"Run that rag of mine on Saturday," he said.

"But he is shin sore," protested the voice at the other end, "and even if he wasn't, he hasn't got a ghost of a chance of winning the Maiden Plate."

"Run him," hissed Mr. Goolby.

Mr. Goolby had three cronies, men who were as wide as Broad Street, but had never been convicted, and it so happened that these three men had also suffered irreparable injury at the hands of Educated Evans, for they had been in Mr. Goolby's coup that had gone astray.

To them he confided the story of his fell deed.

That Friday was a very anxious day for Mr. Evans. He was torn between love and duty. He had acquired quite a number of good clients —men of substance who would act honourable in the event of a win. Should he leave them in the lurch, or put them in the cart, or leave them out? The thought was intolerable. His oath of secrecy was one lightly to be broken, for Mr. Evans was a God-fearing man who regarded all oaths concerning race-horses as *ultra vires* from the start.

He struggled with himself before he went to a wealthy poulterer, and then to an opulent furniture merchant, and thirdly to a plutocratic dealer in second-hand clothes, and told them the tale.

"You are on the odds to a fiver," said the second-hand gentleman, "and I'll put the wire in at the last minute."

The others promised almost as extravagant a reward.

Encouraged by this dream of easy wealth, Mr. Evans went further afield. He came back that night exhausted with his journeyings, but with the consciousness that he was on the odds to £60 with twenty-three reliable clients who had acted honourable before, and would no doubt act honourable again.

On. Waterloo platform next day he met The Miller, and to The Miller he confided his intelligence.

"Give me my tenner back," said The Miller. "I can get a better price myself."

He ran his eye down the programme.

"You mightn't see his name there," said Evans, anxiously. "He was only named a couple of days ago."

"He's here all right: where did you get him from?"

"From the owner," said Evans, and The Miller looked at him suspiciously.

"That sounds like a lie," he said, "and therefore it is a lie."

The race was the second on the card, and there was a horse in the race called Jujube, and apparently all the cognoscenti had been waiting for Jujube ever since the moment he was foaled. For no sooner did a reckless bookmaker—and you know how reckless bookmakers can be—open his mouth and shout "6-4 on the field," than he was almost trampled to death by the rush of gentlemen anxious to relieve him of his surplus wealth.

Evans waited till the market had settled before he sidled up to one of the loudest of the bookmakers, and then:

"... I'll lay a thousand to sixty Press Cutting."

Evans held up his hand like a small boy at school anxious to call his teacher's attention to his necessities.

"I'll take yer," he said, huskily.

The great bookmaker blinked at him, momentarily paralysed, but mechanically put out his hand to take the money, a gesture which no bookmaker ever forgets until he is dead.

From another adventurer Evans took 500-40. His last penny was invested when he turned a moist face to meet The Miller.

"What price did you get?" asked that energetic officer of the law.

"Sixteen's and twelve's," said Evans.

The Miller sneered.

"They saw you coming," he said. "I got 25-1 all right to my tenner. Now tell me the truth. Evans: do you really know Lord Fanerly?"

"Lord who?" asked the staggered Evans.

"Fanerly," said The Miller, impatiently. "You said you knew the owner of Press Cutting."

"He don't own him," said the agitated Evans. "He belongs to Goolby."

The Miller scowled from Evans to the card.

"Here's Goolby's horse," he said—"No. 4. Colt by Newsboy out of Railway Tunnel!... Here, hold up!"—for Mr. Evans had collapsed against him.

"I wanted to back Goolby's horse," he wailed. "Oh, my Gawd, I've backed the wrong 'un!"

The Miller shook him with an ungentle hand.

"You poor soused mackerel," he hissed. "Do you mean to tell me you've done in my tenner?"

At that moment the gate went up, and a crowd of silken jackets jumbled together. Halfway it was impossible to tell which of six horses was leading, but a furlong from home the puce-and-green jacket of Lord Fanerly forged to the front.

"We've won," gasped The Miller. "You lucky rat!"

In the unsaddling enclosure Lord Fanerly was talking to a friend.

"Yes, he's a rum-looking devil, and the queer thing is that when I named him, there was another feller applying for exactly the same name, but I got in five minutes ahead of him.

"Not badly named, is he?... By Short Cut out of Brief Survey...A rum-looking devil!"

A Present for Evans

(The Passing Show Christmas Number, 1924)

Even a Turf Tipster is entitled to enjoy a Merry Christmas, but our old friend Educated Evans, feasting sumptuously on bloaters and whisky, hardly expected a visit from Santa Claus.

Though it was a cold, raw day, with a grey sky and a chill wind sweeping down the length of Great College Street, Mr. Evans was standing at the windiest street corner, gazing pensively at the uninviting façade of the Veterinary College, when The Miller paused in his slow walk and passed, mechanically enough, the compliments of the season.

THE EDUCATED ONE

"And the same to you," said Educated Evans with a shiver. "If anybody wants to give me a Christmas present, he can send me the money instead. Havin' stood the winner of the November Handicap (what a beauty, what a beauty!) an' gen'rally speakin' gettin' my clients one and all their winter keep, it's up to them to act honourable. But have they acted honourable? I ask you!"

Detective-Sergeant Challoner chewed his straw and said nothing. His mind was too busily occupied over the presence of slush, which is the cant name for German-printed one-pound notes. They were kicking at headquarters, and the kick had reached the C.I.D. office in Albany Street.

"A nice Christmas for me!" said Evans bitterly. The church bells a-ringin' 'Peace an' Plenty' an' me with a bob—if I get coals with it I'll starve, an' if I buy food with it I'll freeze to death—why, it's worse than the Spanish Imposition what you read about in Foxe's Book of Martyrs; it was run by the celebrated Judge Jeffries (no relation to Bob, the highly respected bookmaker) an' was finally abolished in 1723 by the Spanish Armada bein' defeated by the well-known Christopher Columbus—him that was executed for givin' lip to B—— Mary."

"Where's Cochlan?" asked The Miller, and Educated Evans drew a long breath.

"He's no client of mine. I sent him Salmon Trout—unbeatable for the Ledger, an' he never asked me if I'd got a mouth. When clients don't act honourable—"

"Somebody was telling me he'd been abroad," suggested The Miller.

"So far as I'm concerned, he's a foreigner," replied Mr. Evans with decision. "We don't talk the same language. If him and other clients had behaved like true British sportsmen I wouldn't be lookin' forward to Christmas Day same as you might be lookin' forward to haven's your appendix bein' taken out by the famous doctor at St. Pancras Infirmary."

The Miller withdrew himself from his unpleasant thoughts and surveyed Mr. Evans with interest.

Educated Evans did not look anything like the world's champion turf prophet. His trousers were frayed, his frayed overcoat had a large rent near the pocket, and this had been unskilfully stitched.

"Why are you standing outside the Veterinary College?" asked The Miller. "Expecting to see that horse you gave me for the Newbury Hurdle come out of hospital?"

"He ought to have won." Said Evans indifferently. "If Frank Wootton had been riding him he'd have come home alone. Jockeyship."

The Miller, turning to go, put his hand in his pocket and produced a green note.

"Your tips have ruined me, Evans," he said. "Camden Town is strewn with the homes you have wrecked, but Christmas is Christmas."

Mr. Evans took the bill with dignity.

"Timmyhawk at Kempton Park on Bank Holiday—help yourself," he said tersely. "He's been tried two stone better than Stuff Gown. I've had it from the boy that does him."

He made his leisurely way back to Bayham Mews, and had not gone a hundred yards when a sharp-featured young man crossed the road and overtook him.

"What did that busy say?" asked Mr. Cochlan.

Evans favoured him with a gloomy frown.

"He said that people who owe money ought to act honourable," he said pointedly. "He said that when a man gives his clients Salmon Trout—fear nothing—"

"I know all about that," said Mr. Cochlan sourly, "but did he say anything about *me*?"

Educated Evans closed his eyes wearily.

"If he did, I gave him a civil answer," he said. "I'm no 'nose' to go givin' information. It's Christmas time, when everybody pays their debt. An' as good King Winklecuss says—"

"If you see him again, tell him you heard I was goin' abroad," said Mr. Cochlan earnestly. I'll settle with you, Evans—don't worry."

"I don't," said Evans.

He was in his happiest mood when he turned into his shabby rooms in Bayham Street. In the basket he carried were three fat bloaters, a loaf of bread, half a pound of "Likebut" (which truly looks like butter but isn't) and a pound of pieces—this being the technical name for those odds and ends of beef that butchers slice in their carving. These and two pounds of floury potatoes and a quarter bottle of whisky promised well for the morrow. In addition, Mr. Evans had purchased from a bookstall a slim volume entitled *The Christmas Carol* by a man called Dickens—who must not be confused with the gentleman young Tom Leader used to train for.

The bloaters were lovely; the Likebut was delicious. Mr. Evans drained a steaming glass of hot toddy, and felt happy as he turned again to the exciting adventures of Scrooge. . . .

Outside the wind was howling; rain pattered against the unwashed windows as the loud clang of a bell came down the chill mews. Educated Evans listened gravely. It was the clock of St. Pancras Church striking the midnight hour.

"A Merry Christmas!" Educated Evans raised his glass and murmured: "Happy days to everybody except Old Sam, the perishin' brain-sucker!"

Tap—tap—tap!

The stealthy knock on the door made Evans jump.

"Who's there?" he asked huskily.

Tap—tap—tap!

It was not the rain. Reluctantly, he rose and opened the door—and gasped.

On the wooden landing a slim figure stood revealed in an unearthly light. He wore a crimson jacket and a white cap—his legs were neatly breeched and booted.

"Good Gawd!" gasped Evans.

The curious thing was that the face might have been that of Fred Archer, and it might have been Carslake, or it might have been Donoghue.

"Come in, sir," said Evans trembling, and the apparition glided into the room.

"I am the ghost of Christmas to come," said the strange jockey. "What a beauty—what a beauty!"

"My very words," murmured the numb Evans. "Sit down, Mister—"

"I have come to tell you the winner of the Lincoln," said the spirit. Xnghroz will win."

"What name?" asked Evans agitatedly.

"Jzmnpl," said the apparition. (Evans could never remember the name, though it seemed familiar enough at the time). "An Vrxlgrq will win the National—farewell!"

"Here, hold hard!" squeaked Evans, but his hands caught the air.

He was standing, dazed and trembling, in the middle of the dark room. The fire was out—the door was open, and a sombre figure was silhouetted against the lesser dark outside.

"Evans!" it hissed.

"Hullo—I've been dreaming," said Evans sleepily.

"Here—stuff this in your bed—if you squeal on me I'll have your liver out of you!"

"Stuff this in your bed! If you squeal on me I'll have
your liver out of you!"

Evans grasped the bundle that was thrust into his hand.

"They're waitin' for me at the end of the mews," said Cochlan. "I'm goin' to get up on your roof and hop round into Bayham Street."

"What's this?" wailed Evans, holding out the package in his hand.

"A present from Father Christmas!" chuckled Cochlan.

"Bad money!" Evans almost howled.

"There ain't such a thing. Now hide it—if they find it here you'll be pinched."

In another second he was gone.

Evans stood grasping the money, perspiration streaming down his forehead. Creeping to the door, he looked down the mews. There was nobody in sight. There was only one thing to be done, and that was to burn the stuff. But a fire would attract attention at this hour. All night long he paced the room in an agony of apprehension, leaping at every sound. But no detectives came.

He looked at the bundle of money. They were beautifully forged—sixty one-pound notes, and all were artistically soiled and crumpled. His respect for the law made him hesitate about burning them. Suppose they were wanted for evidence? Putting on his hat, he went down to the station, and the first person he saw was The Miller.

"Merry Christmas!" said Sergeant Challoner. "What do *you* want?"

Evans tried to speak, but his throat was dry.

"About Cochlan," he croaked.

"Oh, we took him last night—and if he doesn't go down for life, I'm a Dutchman."

He chuckled as if at a good joke.

"Caught him twice," he said. "He had the forged notes on him, Evans, and the joke is that he thought they were good money. My theory is that he either gave them away or planted the real money by error and kept the 'duds.'"

Evans swallowed hard, his hand gripping the sixty perfectly good pounds that reposed in his trousers pocket.

"Well, what do you want, Evans?" asked the Miller again.

"Just come to—to wish you a Merry Christmas," said Educated Evans.

LEONAUR

ALSO FROM LEONAUR
AVAILABLE IN SOFTCOVER OR HARDCOVER WITH DUST JACKET

THE COLLECTED SCIENCE FICTION AND FANTASY OF STANLEY G. WEINBAUM 1—INTERPLANETARY ODYSSEYS *by Stanley G. Weinbaum*—Classic Tales of Interplanetary Adventure Including: A Martian Odyssey, its Sequel Valley of Dreams, the Complete 'Ham' Hammond Stories and Others.

THE COLLECTED SCIENCE FICTION AND FANTASY OF STANLEY G. WEINBAUM 2—OTHER EARTHS *by Stanley G. Weinbaum*—Classic Futuristic Tales Including: *Dawn of Flame* & its Sequel The Black Flame, plus The Revolution of 1960 & Others.

THE COLLECTED SCIENCE FICTION AND FANTASY OF STANLEY G. WEINBAUM 3—STRANGE GENIUS *by Stanley G. Weinbaum*—Classic Tales of the Human Mind at Work Including the Complete Novel The New Adam, the 'van Manderpootz' Stories and Others.

THE COLLECTED SCIENCE FICTION AND FANTASY OF STANLEY G. WEINBAUM 4—THE BLACK HEART *by Stanley G. Weinbaum*—Classic Strange Tales Including: the Complete Novel The Dark Other, Plus Proteus Island and Others.

THE COLLECTED SCIENCE FICTION & FANTASY OF JACK LONDON 1—BEFORE ADAM & OTHER STORIES *by Jack London*—included in this Volume Before Adam The Scarlet Plague A Relic of the Pliocene When the World Was Young The Red One Planchette A Thousand Deaths Goliah A Curious Fragment The Rejuvenation of Major Rathbone.

THE COLLECTED SCIENCE FICTION & FANTASY OF JACK LONDON 2—THE IRON HEEL & OTHER STORIES *by Jack London*—included in this Volume The Iron Heel The Enemy of All the World The Shadow and the Flash The Strength of the Strong The Unparalleled Invasion The Dream of Debs.

THE COLLECTED SCIENCE FICTION & FANTASY OF JACK LONDON 3—THE STAR ROVER & OTHER STORIES *by Jack London*—included in this Volume The Star Rover The Minions of Midas The Eternity of Forms The Man With the Gash.

THE CRETAN TEAT *by Brian Aldiss*—The Cretan Teat is a wry and comic novel that interweaves its own fiction with an inner fiction about the discovery of a Byzantine painting of the Mother of the Blessed Virgin Mary suckling the infant Jesus and a fake ikon that becomes an instrument of Nemesis.